STOE
JOLLY

PETER GEORGIADIS

**APS Books
Yorkshire**

APS Books,
The Stables Field Lane,
Aberford,
West Yorkshire,
LS25 3AE

APS Books is a subsidiary of the APS Publications imprint

www.andrewsparke.com

First published worldwide 2023 by APS Books

A catalogue record for this book is available from the British Library

STOKER JOLLY

1

James Jolly had finally turned forty. It had always seemed like an eternity, aging but without the actual years streaming by. Now he was finally there, forty years of age! Grey haired with a bald patch at the back of his head, which was growing wider by the month. Pot bellied from the beer, and greasy fatty food which was always being served up, round shouldered from the years of stooping, but proudly flashing at least half his own teeth, though only those at the front top were his own. Sadly, what were left, was cigarette stained, and showed serious signs of decay. As James viewed himself in the cracked misting up mirror he smiled, but it was more a smile of disdain.

Though he was immensely strong, he wheezed and coughed a great deal from the incredible amount of tobacco that he managed to smoke every day. It would seem to any onlooker, that James Jolly's hobby was spitting as far and as often as he could, that again was entirely due to the smoking of tobacco. This continuous spitting was something that had left him the with most appalling halitosis. So now, feeling even sorrier for himself than normal, he had the added bonus of realising everything he hated most in life was upon him, old age!

Though the beer with his docker friends was pleasant enough, he really wasn't a happy man. 'Forty, oh, Christ! More than the start of old age! Oh dear!' This was the persistent recurring thought that occupied his brain on this particular day. Our birthday boy was cursing the 28th May 1915. 'Well one thing though is good,' he thought quietly to himself as he slurped his seventh pint of mild and bitter, 'at least I am not at sea with that bucket of a cruiser. This so called spring weather is awful, will the wind and rain ever go away?' Then taking another large slurp of beer, James tried reflecting on what he had just thought. 'Though, I guess, it is an ill wind,' he chuckled inwardly to himself realising that he had almost thought of a merry jape, 'I am almost glad that it started to go awry. The engine was indeed sticky for a long time, but the hole in the keel was a fine excuse to have a some nice long shore leave.' What James didn't know was that the hole in the keel was a seriously rusting stretch, much worse than first expected, so much so that the Kings Navy's finest and noblest were now seriously wondering why such poor quality metal had been used to build HMS

Westfield in 1889 in the first place. By 1904 she was already seriously underpowered, not even having turbines.

For a ship of the line she was a poor excuse for a fighting vessel, and thought by many to be completely obsolete, except for one aspect which was the real reason which kept her afloat instead of being sent to the breakers yard, she had huge guns, sixteen inch. Plus the fact that there were eight of them in four turrets to boot. The cruiser was a conundrum in the eyes of the First Sea Lord. But those guns did make her formidable. Sadly though she was very slow, managing fifteen knots with an effort, and extremely cumbersome when trying to zigzag or do general manoeuvring. HMS Westfield was at least powerful enough to sink a Dreadnought, or so it was thought, though it was also taken for granted that it might prove unwise to fire an eight gun salvo as the recoil might turn the ship turtle.

So now in dry dock, the entire crew of the cruiser were given shore leave around Aberdeen while repairs were being undertaken. What should have been a few days was now turning into a few weeks as more and more faults were being found within the poor metal of the keel. How no one had noticed the state of play when she was in for a refit some months ago, was now turning into a possible government enquiry, which might result in dire consequences for anyone found to have been negligent. After all this was a time of war, and all weapons should be checked on a regular basis, and though maybe not the King's shiniest or finest, that's exactly what Westfield was, a weapon of war, so in a time of war, she was a necessary piece of naval equipment......

James Jolly was a rather dour Scotsman, brought up in the Gorbals one of the roughest toughest regions of Glasgow. His education had ended really before it started, having spent most of his childhood avoiding schooling and teachers, going absent whenever he thought he would get away with it. He spent his time wistfully watching ships entering and leaving the docks, or even sometimes just fishing with a bent pin and a worm. On one occasion he even caught some small dabs which he quickly cooked and ate over a fire.

As education seemed to have completely passed by James, by the time he was fourteen he could just barely read and write, and was scurrilously close to not even managing to do very basic sums. Jolly's idea of scholarly pursuits were simple, scratch your way through life as best you can. Reading, writing, sums, who needs all that rubbish. What he knew, he knew was enough for him, plus easily more than enough for his frustrated tutors, who were extremely glad to see the back of him when the wrought iron gates finally closed upon him for the last time.

No amount of punishment with the cane had ever persuaded the young James that school would or should be his bag of tricks, so with absolutely no qualifications he left Youngers Christian School and headed for the big wide world, a world that felt no pity and would swallow whole young foolish fellows such as our Glaswegian scallywag without any pity, then spit him out as just more human detritus along with millions of others, after all who is seriously going to give a damn!

His father Edward Jolly, a miner by profession, like his son was not blessed in the learning department, thus stated it was suggested by Edward that he should follow him down the mines, but a week before he was due to start there had been a pit fall and his father and ten others had been crushed to death. One thing about James, he quickly saw that just maybe mining was not a suitable job for a shifty know nothing such as himself and with his mother's blessing he thought twice about following his father's footsteps.

But now he became head of the Jolly household, he knew he must do something to alleviate the misery that his mother was suffering. All of a sudden being the so called bread winner of the family, he experienced an epiphany, which created a self awareness of his new set of responsibilities. He felt accountable for his mother and two younger brothers, something that he had never ever experienced before.

It was a terrible shock to his tender young system, but now he understood, and at least was wise enough to accept what was needed of him. If he was not going down the mines, what was he going to do? This was a moment in time when all of a sudden he wished he had some sort of education that just might take him somewhere, and thus allow him to fulfil his new found acceptance of accountability. This was the turning point in James Jolly's life, albeit a short and dramatic one.

It was a friend of his mother that suggested he might like to train to be a stoker in the Royal Navy. It was regular work and his pay could and would be sent home to help his dependents. Before getting a job with the Royal Navy he had to study a little more.

Strangely with this as a good enough reason he started to read books, lots of books, books on practically any subject. His reading skills quickly became proficient and the more he read the more he felt the need to read. What the schooling had failed to achieve, his own now new self control and resolve overcame the block that had stopped him from learning while under school tutelage.

Now with his own self discipline he leant anything and everything. His reading skills became more than proficient, they became very good. He even read a book on rudimentary mathematics, and with this particular volume he acquired an instant epiphany thus finally seeing the importance of numbers. This gave the young Jolly an insight into basic algebra and even decimals. He was now finally growing up fast. But still, his acceptance was, once a simple stoker, always a simple stoker, and that still seemed to be his epitaph in life.

After all, nobody knew that he had just about read everything on ship's engines, seamanship and anything to do with the Navy, including its progressive history throughout the ages. But why should they know? He never told anyone about his knowledge, and nobody ever saw the huge pile of reading matter that accumulated under his bunk. To be really fair to those of higher rank than James, hardly anybody even knew of his existence, let alone his educational skills. Had they taken the trouble to enquire after him, they would have seen an extremely scruffy, unkempt person with absolutely no social graces what-so-ever, so his career in the Kings Navy was one of obscurity and isolation.

As none of the other stokers could hardly read, those that knew of his ability and passion for the printed matter rather despised Stoker Jolly, thinking of him as a waste of time and space. To the other men he was just someone who never gambled or seriously drank, only the usual rum ration and roughly ten pints of Guinness and bitter at a sitting when on shore leave. He was never drunk, but his appearance showed a normal dirty, slovenly, unkempt, sweaty demeanour, which typified and accompanied all the lower deck workers.

He was not a fighting man, but often managed to get himself into serious scrapes. On several occasions he ended up in the brig because of his lack of self control, at least that was the official line taken by the sentencing officers. It was the fighting, or truth be known, defending himself that had put paid to most of his lower set of teeth, that and possibly gum disease.

But James Jolly did have friends, just not aboard the ship. He befriended dockers, and when away from Glasgow, he would always frequent the public houses that the dockers and stevedores used. Throughout Scotland he was known and respected by those said working people.

For some inexplicable reason those men seem to understand his longing for knowledge, and wherever he was, they wanted to listen to his philosophising and pontificating about anything and everything. To those working men he was a fountain of wonderful home spun truths.

He was known by those favoured working people as J.J., or old Stoker Jolly, but always with a certain reverence and respectful awe.

Anyway, he was always good for a drink or three, and he never begrudged his friends the time of day.

In some ways, James had through his reading developed a lust for home spun politics. The nearest he got to being really excited by a political party, was in the philosophy of the Home Rule For Scotland Party, mixed generously with Marxist philosophy. He was not a radical racist, nor a preacher of ideas. He didn't try to convert, just related what he, James Jolly thought about. What he knew were basic truths, at least within the framework of his own existence and experience, but he did understand that each individual had a perfect right to agree or disagree to anything he might be pontificating about, and because of this perfect idealistic acceptance he never judged peoples opposing views.

Having thought of himself as now someone who had been completely passed over by the hierarchy of naval life, knowing darn well that he was probably better read than even the Captain of his ship, one Captain Steiner. For sure he had better knowledge of all naval official history, technology, language and anything what-so-ever to do with the running of one of His Majesty's vessels, yet here he was still just the lowest of the low.

As James reflected on the total waste of his abilities, he took yet another pint of beer and mulled over the situation. He quickly forgot the pals that were sitting around patiently expecting wise words from this strange elderly stoker, one who might be better suited to being a foreman, or even running some sort of business, or maybe even owning a company. Most of his so called mates understood that they were in the presence of some sort of genius, but one that was good for a laugh and once again very good for the odd drink. How had it all come to this? How had all this wasted talent come about? How had it happened?

On the 28th May 1875, Mary Stuart Jolly went into labour. A local midwife who lived just nearly a street away from the tenement in which the Jolly's resided, one Agnes McBryant, but known as Fat Annie, was hurried around to help Mary in her time of great need, by a very agitated Edward Jolly, Mary's hard working coal mining husband. Edward had just come home after performing a night shift to find Mary Stuart lying on the floor in a pool of water. Contractions had already started and she was in an extremely distressed state. Being their first child, neither really knew what to do about giving birth, but because Mary's screams had woken the family next door, they told Edward where to find Agnes McBryant, the renowned Fat Annie.

Agnes was a very rotund lady of some fifty years of age, and on the promise of ten shillings she agreed to follow Edward back. By the time they arrived back, red faced and puffing wildly, Mary Stuart was getting ready to explode. The pain was terrible, and terror shone from every pore of her face. Her eyes virtually bulged out of her head, but totally unseeing. Her hair was wet and hung down her face making her appear like some sort of creature from bedlam. That look of almost a lunatic with those non seeing but strange starring eyes of disbelief and agony. She had carried this child for nine months, but no one had told her anything about giving birth. No tips on breathing, no understanding of pain control through panting. It was if she should just squat and everything would happen quickly. Somehow, that was what Mary Stuart had come to expect, but now she was in terrible pain, no one had explained about pain bordering on extreme agony.

Blood and water and excreta had spluttered everywhere. Poor Mary was not even able to sit up on her bottom. All she was only capable of lying in her own mess, clutching at the lump that now had somewhat slipped down a notch or two. Agnes told Edward to fetch some water, but instead of giving it to Mary, she drank it herself then wiped her profusely sweating face with her stiff dirty looking skirt.

"Come on Mary, get a grip. You cannot give birth lying in that mess."

Then she looked at Edward and frowning deeply, asked him,

"Give me a hand man. This is no place for her to be lying. Let's get her onto the bed. One, two, three, up she comes."

Mary screamed with the pain of being moved, but her strength had already failed her so it became an easier task for the Agnes and Edward to move her to the bed in the corner of their room.

Mary was a clean, tidy woman, with good housekeeping habits, at least in cleanliness. The bed was well made and spotless, with well worn sheets and blankets covering a hard wooden framed bed with a eiderdown mattress to soften the blow of lying on boards. The mattress had been part of her endowment given to her as a wedding gift from her own father and mother. It must have been fifty years old if it was a day, but it was worth its weight in gold to the Jolly family.

Now Mary Stuart was prone on the bed, bleeding badly, which worried Agnes. Though she would still take money for her toil. Though she was not a qualified midwife, she was someone who did midwifery when asked. To her it was an easy way to make some money, easy that is when the women giving birth already know what to do!

"Mary Stuart! You must help me to help you. Stop screaming, start pushing, and let go of your lump, allow it to come out naturally."

She looked at Edward and those eyes said it all, pity and fear. Edward looked at Mary, held her hand and managed to take her hands off the unborn child. Edward looked at his wife and the only thought that kept going through his mind was,

'Surely she is going to die! Who would look after my needs?'

It wasn't that Edward didn't love Mary, in his way he did, but he feared loneliness, and he feared having to possibly find another wife at his age.

"Listen to me woman, do as the midwife says or you will lose the bairn and possible die along with the infant. So, from now start pushing."

This time, death or the thought of it brought Mary to her senses. She stopped screaming and starting pushing. After what seemed like many hours, but was only just two, young James sprung out onto the world. Pink, bloody and bald as a badger, weighing a mere seven pounds, but to Mary and Edward who could only look and wonder at this little bundle of flesh and blood which was theirs, and was quite irrationally but highly usual already being showered with instant love and affection. Agnes picked him up by his feet and smacked him squarely and quite hard on his bottom. This had the immediate effect of bringing tears to both parents and yet more screams from both James and his mother Mary Stuart Jolly. The Jolly's first son was born.

Agnes took her ten shillings and left the newly formed family to fend for itself. Within an hour Mary was cleaning up herself, baby and the floor where she had been found. One week later, she was probably already pregnant again. Nearly ten months went by then an easier birth of their second son happened. They named him Charles.

Agnes once more brought him into the world, but was struggling with an excess of weight, being more than twenty-five stone. She sweated and struggled more than Mary, perspiration flowed like small fountains from every pore of her body. Both Mary and Edward reacted badly to the smell of obesity, and winced as the old woman passed by them. After Charles was born, Agnes took her ten shillings and struggled out of the tenement back to her own dwelling place. Ten months after Charles, came Dugan Jolly.

Agnes was now over thirty stone in weight, and after the birth of the third son she struggled to walk at all. Finally making it home, she lay down on her rickety sofa in her parlour and promptly died. She passed away having suffered a huge heart attack. She probably never felt a thing, just a simple feeling of relief leaving her enormous frame to be interred by others.

But as she had died in a strange manner, she was taken to the local mortuary where to the coroner's amazement, underneath all the layers of blubber, they discovered that she was still a virgin. She had in her years of life delivered many babies, but had never experienced the joy or pleasure of sex or men, which was probably why she was so cynical towards the male side of the species.

She was buried in a pauper's grave, and sadly mourned by no one. Even the vicar who stood at the graveside, as she was lowered into the abyss, he was seen to be yawning and looking at his fob watch out of boredom, just waiting to get out of the graveyard as soon as respectably possible, after all nobody wanted to stand in the rain and be smoked out by the pollution from the houses and factories, especially this middle aged rather disillusioned Presbyterian vicar.

James grew quickly and developed a liking for food and drink from a very early age. It wasn't just height that sprang forth, it was also weight. The young infant Jolly fast became rotund and obese, not to the excess of complete abnormality, but fat enough to become indolent and idle, shirking the chores that other children expected and managed to accomplish, during their formative growing years.

James always seemed to find a way out of work, even when being forced to labour in the first place. He quickly learned how to master excuses, and always had something or other in the way of a justifiable reason why he shouldn't be doing what was asked, or demanded of him, and always excuses came extremely quickly to hand. The young Jolly knew when to stay out of a parent's way, thus avoiding menial work that might have just kept his weight down and made him generally fitter.

On the corner of Dalmeny Road, where the tenements that housed the Jolly family and several hundred more Glaswegian folk were, there was a small sequence of dustbins that were put there for collecting all wasted food stuff. This was then taken to the local pig farm for help fatten the swine, which would later be slaughtered and sold to local people as pork loins, chops and bacon. This area was an ideal place for James to slide between. Those bins could hide him when his mother or father were looking with a job in mind for the young fellow to be doing. There was also the added bonus of free scraps to eat, albeit those very same scraps that were left for the pigs. These were often extremely bad and rotten to the taste, not that that would deter James. Somehow his digestive system never reacted badly to him eating this waste food stuff.

Edward was not a vicious man, though he was strict, hard and severe, but only when he thought it was the right thing to do. Generally he was considered by James and his brothers to be hard but fair. But he worked hard to earn his meagre pay, and often when coming home, wanted nothing more than to eat a hot meal then sleep, awaiting the next days hard toil. So if James needed chastising for whatever reason, Edward would often clout first then ask questions later. But this regular punishment had a detrimental effect. It just made James harden to the blows. If he cried he got absolutely no response from either parent, so why cry?

James was not a lonely child, insofar as he had his two brothers, and when permitted, the three would play happily together. It was in fact dwelling on this side of his past, these tender moments with his siblings, that kept James sane in later life, especially when far out to sea with no one ever really wanting to talk to him.

Thinking on this aspect of his past in hours of lonely contemplation between working shifts, kept James in a frame of mind that became resolute and hard-bitten to what else went on within the ships company. Whatever went on within those steel walls by-passed James, and whatever went on within the mind and soul of Jolly, by-passed the rest of the ship.

James would either read something, hopefully something new, but often a re-read of an earlier tome, or lie on his bunk and remember the old so called salad days, when he was the sole protector of his younger brothers.

There was one special occasion that he always remembered, but with some trepidation. At the tender age of five, playing with his two younger brothers in the roadway outside their abode, an older boy, roughly ten years of age, came up to the three of them demanding money with menaces. As money was something none of the three of them had ever experienced, hardly ever seen any and most certainly never as yet having any, they told the boy where to go and what to do when he got there. Much to the chagrin of young James, the older boy lashed out at Dugan the youngest, who on being hit, fell back and banged his head on the pavement. James immediately kicked the older boy in the shin, but in doing so broke his right metatarsal as he wore no protective shoes.

This though, did have the desired effect of hurting and stopping the lad from further torments on maybe Charles, but before departing he decided to then hit James full on the nose, breaking it squarely. Blood spouted everywhere, and with the sight of the blood and Dugan still lying prone on the pavement the boy took fright and ran away. James in serious pain from both his nose and his toe, managed to pick up Dugan and carry him up the stairs to his mother. Mary Stuart on seeing the two boys was immediately shocked and totally taken aback. Thinking that James was obviously to blame, she promptly thumped the luckless lad around the face with her clenched hand knocking him to the ground. Neither parent ever discovered the real story, thus James grew up with a wobbly toe, as the broken toe never ever got healed back in place. This gave him an ever so slightly strange awkward gait to his walking, with that and a nose that flattened as he grew older he was a picture of a sorry sight.

One would be forgiven in thinking that J.J's. troubles all stemmed back to those past so called salad days.

This was the time that James realised that he must look out for himself. He must toughen up, become strong and bold, but most of all be cunning and sly, after all he wasn't going to get much protection from his parents.

All three boys grew quickly, and as the years went by they all became exceptionally street wise. They could manage to look out for themselves to the extent they none of them got picked on, and were avoided by most of their contemporise and the police. It soon became the three Jolly boys against the world, well anyway maybe the neighbourhood!

James, Charles and the small, but strong as an oxen Dugan, soon became the scourge of the manor. If they needed something, they stole it. They all became adept in thievery. None of the trio saw what they did as being wrong, theirs was not a sin or a crime, just a touch of being naughty plus it was always fun.

Somehow in the collective minds of the trio, it was their right to take what was there for the taking. Strangely, everyone knew that they were extremely troublesome children, and guessed that they were the main perpetrators of the local crime wave that was seemingly always there.

But Glaswegians didn't tell tales, so they never came within the serious attention of the local constabulary. The police saw them as being a minor irritation as all young kids were to them. Scruffy, snotty, dirty and annoying, but just three more nuisances that they had to contend with in their daily labours as law enforcers.

2

Mr. Cluff was not a patient man; he was sick to the high teeth with the way that the boy Jolly played the fool in class. No matter what he the teacher did, he never seemed to get him to concentrate on doing any worthwhile work. Once again James was sat at the back of the class talking to Sydney Tackle when he should have been doing his sums. The wooden handled chalk cleaner zoomed through the air and hit James square on his head. Mr. Cluff rarely missed. After all, he had had plenty of practice in throwing the damned thing. James jumped and glared right back at his form teacher, then nursing the bruise that would very soon be appearing, he gently bent over the desk and retrieved the padded piece of beech wood block.

'Bastard, I 'ought to throw it back at him'.

But James knew that if he did that, more and sterner punishment would follow, and almost certainly from the headmaster, Mr. Woodward. Cluff may be strict, but Woodward just enjoyed half torturing the boys under his care. So for James, it wasn't worth the increased pain that would ensue.

James stood up and walked to the front, and while all the other class mates were giggling took the offending weapon to his form master, Mr. Cluff.

"Sorry sir, I was only asking Sydney for some help with the sums."

"Don't lie to me boy, I heard you both, you were gossiping about the forthcoming Rangers and Queens Park game this Saturday."

With that he took back his blackboard cleaner, and then banged his open palm against the side of Jolly's dirty greasy head, afterwards looking at his palm to see why it had such an oily feel to it, maybe there would be something nasty crawling over his hand coming from the Jolly boys hair which he expected to be alive with all sorts of unpleasant life forms. Fortunately there was nothing showing, much to the teachers thanks.

"Get back to your seat and do some work; if I have any more trouble from you today you will be sent to Mr. Woodward, and we both know he will quickly straighten you out, one way or another."

Mr. Cluff then turned and wiped the blackboard as if that would make everything right once again. And as he did so, James stuck two fingers up as a sign of defiance, much to the chagrin of the entire class who now showed their annoyance by hissing at young James Jolly.

Mr. Cluff knew exactly what gesture was being shown, but really couldn't be bothered to respond to this further disruption and just finished cleaning away the last lesson. He shook his head slowly, sighed and gave a last lingering thought to young Jolly.

'This boy will come to an awful end. There really is little hope for youngsters such as the Jolly family, so little hope…O dear, what a to do? It's as if the world will just pass them by, these kids never learn, they become tomorrow's petty villains and crooks. It always seems as if death, misery and mayhem await their fate!'

Mr. Cluff thought the prognosis was a bad one for the brothers and many more like them, but then chuckling inside his own head he knew he could be an awful pessimist.

He then promptly forgot all that had happened as the final bell went and the class was dismissed and Hugh Cluff could go home and enjoy a decent meal, and the company of his loving wife and family. All of today's stresses and stains will just evaporate out of the window, only to be re-awakened the next day back in the class, along with so many other failing humans like the Jolly boys.

In Cluff's eyes the lads like James, plus there were plenty of them within the walls of the old early Victorian school, they were the bane of his teaching life. Teaching would be fun and pleasurable if there were class sizes of maybe just ten or fifteen lads instead of the fifty three that were his charges in this particular year.

He knew that if class sizes could have been smaller, he the teacher could have had some hope of gaining the upper hand and actually getting the children to learn something.

The classroom that Cluff was master of was incredibly cold in the winter, the school heating was minimal with just two huge pipes going around the inside of the outside wall, though they often boiled, buzzed and sputtered in sound, the convection of the heat was poor to say the very least.

Cluff would allow the boys to wear all the clothing they could acquire in the wintery long dark days. It was a pitiful sight to see boys dressed in anything their mothers could spare, even girls clothing, but very few could afford to buy their lads shoes. Often, boys would suffer terribly from chilblains from the cold within their feet, something that did bring pity to Hugh Cluff's mind.

In the very worst weather he would bring in big bags of cough sweets, these he liberally handed around in the vain hope that it stopped some of the boys from getting colds and any possible worst disease. It was a decent gesture, one that most boys appreciated, but it only brought some comfort in a physiological way, but then the thought was that anything was better than nothing, which is what most of the other teaching staff did, absolutely nothing!

Though the room was on the ground floor it had a ceiling height of more than thirty feet, which once again made their lives hard as the height absorbed all the heat in cold weather. The length of the room was fifty feet by forty, barely enough space to accommodate fifty three young hopefuls.

Disease from colds or influenza was endemic, and would travel around a class in a matter of hours, then gradually around the entire school.

On one occasion just before the Jolly boys were made to attend classes, a bout of tuberculosis swept throughout the school actually closing it for some weeks; because of that disease eight young charges died. It would and could have been far worse except for the quick decision making of the headmaster, though possibly not seriously caring for the well being of the youngsters, more a chance of getting some time off to go fishing upon the delta regions of the river Clyde.

On another occasion, once again before the Jolly boys, the school had to be closed and fumigated as a serious bout of lice and fleas brought everyone to an itchy standstill. Such were the daily going's on at Youngers Christian School for boys.

Such schools became a haven for the cruel sadistic tendencies of some of the teaching staff, and as teaching was supposed to be a cushy existence, some of the poorly qualified teachers who saw themselves as dictatorial leading lights who could and would do anything to fulfil their own personal glutinous sadistic and often paedophilic tendencies upon the unhappy young charges.

The strangest thing about what went on within the walls of the building, everyone knew but no one ever talked about it. Whatever happened wouldn't do the boys any lasting harm, would it! Could it? Of course not!

The day would start with the gates being opened at eight o'clock in the morning sharp, this was so that any parent that had to go to work around that time could in theory leave they child in safe hands. There of course lay the problem, if anyone turned up at eight, they were made to stay out in the open until eight forty-five when school officially opened. No matter what the weather, clothed or partially clothed children would huddle awaiting school doors to be opened so they could get in out of rain, snow and cold.

At exactly nine o'clock assembly would be called with the ringing of a huge hand bell. Any child, who dared talk, either when going to assembly, or while in the assembly hall, would be guaranteed a severe thrashing from the headmaster; this had become an absolute certainty. If any child had an accident, either peeing or something worse, then that child was for the high jump, there was absolutely no excuses acceptable, they should have gone before school or after assembly. Even if a toddler was taken ill, and of course that happened a lot, but still prayers always came first.

That young person would have to suffer until assembly was over. As the school boasted being a Christian establishment, prayers were obligatory, hymns and prayers, prayers and hymns and always with the same monotonous regularity of performance; same old prayers, same old hymns.

It was an absolute certainty that God was as bored as everyone else.

Sometimes a child yawned while in the congregation, God got to know real quickly what the sound of screaming little boys sounded like, and it wasn't the sound of a sung "Requiem", though for the children in question it might well have been their own personal requiem.

After the children were finally sent back to their form rooms, lessons began. Usually two lessons of arithmetic, two lessons of English, then interspersed with history and geography. But always before leaving classes at the end of the day there were yet more prayers.

Academic standards were abysmally low, but to the local council Youngers Christian School was there doing its job of keeping potential future criminals off the streets, at least for the time being.

As there was always a small break in the morning then an hour for lunch, plus another small break in the afternoon, the day was broken up making it seem to be over reasonably quickly, at least for the teaching staff.

No matter how bad the weather was, the children were made to take their breaks outside, and that could be awful especially if the said child had few clothes and no shoes. Most kids devised a way of being naughty just before break, especially when winters extremely cold days came, they were often told to stay and do extra work inside the building. This was always more preferable to being outside in the shivering cold. It was a scary time in the late autumn and winter months, this was the time when many children caught colds and influenza, which could and often did kill them.

Suffering was endemic, a way of life, one thought was that being poor meant you should suffer the children, but not unto God, more likely suffer them unto paedophilic sadistic swine who had the audacity to call themselves members of the teaching fraternity.

The years passed quickly for James and before he knew it he was at senior school pretending to be interested in learning from the lessons, once again failing miserably on both counts. He was not at all interested in gaining knowledge, partly because he saw himself as being dumb, partly because he hated the school and every teacher within it; but most of all because he saw his future mapped out already for him, that being the mines. After all, you didn't need to be a genius to work as a coal miner.

Unfortunately for James, his actions within the classroom also made him rather despised by the rest of his class mates of whom some would have liked to have gained some little learning, but felt held back by the Jolly boy. Never-the-less James had a great influence on the classrooms collective disobedience. After all, now there was something that he managed to excel in.

To Mr. Hugh Cluff's miserable dismay when James was wilfully disobedient, it usually involved the rest of the class with laughter and their own form of skittishness. Laughter creates more laughter which creates more disobedience, thus a vicious circle. Once a child felt he could create laughter, he tried constantly to do so, even when it meant serious reprisal from the higher authority.

In some ways Mr. Cluff admired and also despised the Jolly boy, all at the same time. Even though he seemed to be a continuous form of annoyance, the boy seemed impervious to most forms of punishment. Though saying that, he was frightened of being sent to Mr. Woodward the headmaster, but then Cluff himself was loath to send too many boys to the head, he knew but didn't want to admit it, that Woodward was a complete sadist and possibly yet another paedophile as well.

Mr. Cluff was well aware that there were three or four masters who possibly prayed on the boy's vulnerability, thus using that fear for their own sexual gratification. Strangely all knew but no one ever admitted to that conceivable truth. After all, jobs depended on silence, one must never rock that boat.

Youngers Christian School had an extremely dismal appearance with its dirty red brick facing, red it might have been once, now just a grime covered edifice that had more the look of a workhouse than a place of learning. Since its opening in the mid nineteenth century its reputation had been one of a severe school of hard knocks, literally!

Over the last seventy years, there had been several murders, many cases of boys being buggered then badly beaten, and it was obvious to all that it didn't all happen from people outside of the establishment. Yet it was the only school in the area, and after all boys must supposedly attend school.

One notorious boy in the late eighteen eighties had been caught torturing a younger boy, interfering with him in a sexual manner then putting his head down the toilet drowning him. It turned out that after the event, which was heard by one of the masters, but on hearing the scuffling noises waited until it went quiet before investigating. The boy now caught by the teacher turned on him. Then proceeded to kick him until he too nearly died, but the screams brought more teachers to the toilets. The boy was caught and handed over to the police. After an extensive open trial, the lad whose name was John Tanner, was taken to a place just outside of Ayr where he was summarily executed by hanging. The lad was barely thirteen when the crime took place. His father had spent most of his adult life behind bars for various misdemeanours, which meant he had been raised by his mother and her many lovers.

His carved initials were still to be seen on the toilet wall, and to some boys they stood for a beacon of hope and defiance to authority.

Not in all the history of the school had any teacher been prosecuted for any wrong doings. Yet as stated before, everyone knew that many unpleasant things went on behind those enclosed walls.

Not all the staff were of poor quality and suffered in their charges in sexually perverted ways. A good example was Hugh Cluff, he was actually thought of as a very fair minded man, hard, vicious at times, but he would always support the poorer children, even often giving them his own food and warm drinks in winter time, he knew that some of them went for a whole day without anything more nourishing than the rather rusty tasting water that came directly from a well which dated back to Elizabethan times, this being located in the rear of the school. Hardly enough nourishment to sustain life and limb!

No one knew that he was a potential push over and philanthropist, no one ever got to hear how he saved several children from being sent to the headmaster, when he suspected that the man was in a severe poor vicious mood, a caprice that might generate the sort of nastiness to the young charges that he knew should not take place. Instead to Cluff, the nicest thing to do was that he would beat them himself, which was never, or at least rarely causing long lasting pain or discomfort.

He had even saved James Jolly on several occasions, though he did once use a punishment that he later regretted. James had once been his normal disruptive self and playing up to the class for laughs. Cluff finally lost patients with the lad, threw some chalk at him which missed, instead hitting the boy next to Jolly. This miscalculation of aim, so incensed Cluff who now in a rage ran over to James, his speed of movement was so fast it made his cheeks puff into bright red balloons. This was man who through the poor stupid annoyances of one boy, Jolly by name but not this time by nature, for once Cluff was raging and was immensely angry indeed. He dragged the luckless Jolly to the front of the class, banging him around the head all the time. He then, with a seriously raised voice asked him why he was being such a pain, and the only answer he got back was,

"Sorry sir, but I'm bloody cold."

This answer enraged the master even more, and with a snarling spitting voice he said,

"Well then, we had better warm you up hadn't we?"

He then dragged the luckless lad over to the outside wall and made him kneel on the hot water pipe which ran through each class as its only form of heat. The heat immediately burnt James knees badly, so much so that for the first time Mr. Cluff watched James Jolly burst into tears, then start screaming for some sort of reprieve of sentence. Hugh saw that the lad was in serious distress and relented immediately, but the damage was done. James had second degree burns on both knees, scars that he carried for the rest of his life. Hugh Cluff knew instantly that he had made a huge mistake, a poor serious breach of judgement. He took the boy to the toilets and managed to cool the skin down and place some bandage around the surface of his skin what was bubbling from the sudden shock of the intense heat. Cluff could see clearly that blood blisters were forming and once they were ready to burst, that might become infected, that would lead to trouble which might cost him his job.

But he should have known better, after school James went home, finding it hard to walk properly with the pain coming from his damaged knees, yet his mother on being told what had befallen him, just said in her normal tired voice in its normal monotone way,

"Well, you obviously deserved it. Just you wait until your father comes home, you will be for it then."

But by the time his father did come home, it was extremely late and he was very drunk and tired, and all three boys were in their beds sound asleep, so the incident was never again spoken of.

The problem now was that James had a broken toe which was always going to give him grief. A broken nose that was now flat and pushed slightly to the right side of his face, thus giving him an awkward expression which when seen for the first time could be very disconcerting to the onlooker. And now, to make matter worse, his gait was even more pronounced as both knees had permanent scarring.

James Jolly was very quickly starting to look a lot older than his twelve years of age.

The next two years passed much the same as the last, more trouble, less learning, always holding up the potential of the class as a whole.

But to Hugh Cluff's chagrin the years had passed without any real improvement in the Jolly boy, and now horror of horrors, he had the two younger brothers coming into the school which meant he would have to deal with them too, should they be assigned to his class.

But eventually came the day that James had been longing for since the very first day he entered the portals of the school, it was leaving day.

The bell had rung for the last time on the Jolly terms of schooling. Hugh Cluff was subdued and somewhat passive as he wished all the boys the best in the forthcoming careers, he then dismissed them, and carefully watched them leave the room, that was all except James who he held back.

"Jolly, I worry about you!"

"Sir!"

James was startled by this sudden show of warmth and emotion.

"What do you mean sir?"

"I mean, and I emphasize sadly, that I have failed dismally with you. You have spent all your time wasting and playing up, you have been an enormous problem to me and the class in general."

He paused, took a deep breath then concluded with,

"Can you actually see that? In fact have you ever seen that simple truth?"

"Sir, I really don't know what to say? In many ways you have been good to me, I know you have a kind streak within you, but I haven't been able to help myself. I sometimes feel as if there are more than two or even three people within my body."

He smiled and chuckled at what he was saying and then quickly added,

"Anyway I seem to eat for three."

This time he laughed out loud at his own joke, but it was met with silence from his teacher.

"I don't really know why I play up, I know I do. I guess the real truth is I really have never felt the need to learn things from this school. I know I shall follow my pop down the mine, and what difference will being able to read a book be to me there?"

Mr. Cluff shook his head slowly, and with a final sigh of sadness tried to answer the lad.

"James, learning is something we should never tire of doing. I am nearly sixty years of age, but I learn something new every single day. How the hell would the world progress if everyone thought as you do? Being human is not about instincts like animals, it's about progression."

He breathed in deeply as if he was going to dive deep into icy water.

"Even in your short life, your fourteen years, look at the changes that have gone on. Steam ships taking over from sail! Balloons that can take man high into the air, giving him the feeling of flying like a bird.

Cameras that can capture your image for ever! Travel, easier than ever before. One can circumnavigate the globe, and though expensive, we could all do it if we wanted to."

He took another deep breath and plunged in yet again.

"Boy, the world is your oyster, or at least it could and should be."

His brow now furrowed with deep lines he once again emphasized.

"It is to late for you within these walls, but take learning serious, try and read some books. James, I promise you it will open up a whole new life for you. I feel great sadness on the simple expedient that I have, in the years you have been in my charge, failed to excite your brain. All you lads have such great potential, we are coming soon to the end of this century, and exciting things are ahead, if only you apply yourself."

He now was in full flow and sweat was forming on his brow.

"Now you are going into the real world, and if you fail there it will just swallow you up. Your life will be over before you know it, and you will look back and wonder where the hell it all went wrong."

Hugh took a handkerchief from his waistcoat pocket then blew his nose hard, then wiped his brow, then placed the soiled hanky back into his fluff filled pocket.

"I don't know what will happen to you young Jolly, but I do wish you well for the future. Come and see me sometime and let me know how your life is progressing."

With this statement James Jolly was dismissed. This was the longest that Mr. Cluff had ever spoken to the young fellow, but for the first time James started to think.

"Thank you sir!"

He held out his hand to shake his teachers, which he did. He then turned and left the building for the last time. Once in the road, James leapt into the air and clicked his heals together. but he knew his life would never be quite the same again.

'Christ o'bloody Reilly, have I really blown my entire future? Surely not!'

He started for home, whistling as he went.

James arrived home nearly two hours after school had closed its rusting iron gates on him for the last time. His thoughts surprisingly immediately went to thinking that he would treat himself to an apple off the fruit vendors stall while he was distracted by a customer. It was all so easy, the hand was so much quicker than the eye. He took his prize down to the Clyde, just in time to see an old tea clipper being towed down river to the breakers yard. For an hour he watched as it disappeared from view.

3

Then there he was; his minds eye had made him James Jolly Captain of this piece of history taking it in high seas to far off India to pick up its precious cargo of Assam tea. He saw the Dolphins and Whales, all swimming close to his clipper. He looked up into the rigging to watch as a young Charles Jolly was pulling on one of the high ropes to adjust a sail. Young Dugan came across from the galley, struggling to bring him a mug of cocoa. This he accepted and drank quickly even though it was steaming hot. He gave the mug back and prepared another compass reading, when one of his crew asked permission to kill the Whale and cut it up for meat.

But being a very humane Captain he decided against it, thinking only of the enormous weight of beauty that this beast carried for everyone's pleasure. Just to watch this creature in all its majesty was infinitely better than having it roasted and served with two vegetables.

"No, leave the creature alone. If you want to eat fish, I will have you thrown into the sea where you can fight it out…."

At that moment of dreaming, a young policeman ambled up and spoke to him.

"Out of school then?"

"O, yes sir! I have just finished for good and glad of it."

"I remember well my own school days. I wish those days were able to come back, aging is no fun and neither is working for a living."

The policeman leant up against the bridge support, slightly leaning over the Clyde. He spat and watched it drop into the river and immediately be swept out seaward. He was in a very contemplative mood and it showed.

"So my boy! What are you going to do with the rest of your life?"

James now visibly relaxed as he realised that the officer wasn't after his neck. He finished the last morsel of his apple and dropped the small piece of core into the river after the policeman's spit. Turning his attention to the question he answered,

"I am expected to follow dad down the mine. I cannot really get enthusiastic about the prospect though, but I must earn a crust to help the family. Things are tough for our lot, so I really don't have much choice."

"Well now, mmm, ever thought of joining the force?"

What a question to ask a young man from the Gorbals. James shrunk visibly at the very thought of being a copper, but he was polite with his answer.

"The truth is, I didn't get my exams." James sighed for effect, then ever so politely but in a matter of fact way, "I wouldn't pass the entrance exam."

The young policeman rubbed his chin as if it was full of stubble.

"Well lad, I can't stand here all day gassing. Good luck to you in whatever you do. Keep out of trouble won't you? O, by the way, you will pay the vendor for that apple won't you?"

He then winked at James and strolled away and crossed the bridge chuckling to himself.

Jolly smiled and thought how nice that copper was. They are obviously not all potential killers and baby snatchers, as his family had brought him up to think.

James looked back at the flowing water, thought about the ship again, but then realised just how dirty the Clyde was as a bloated dead dog drifted by. He looked up at the dark blue sky, then felt the first drop of rain fall on his head.

'Better get on home, I am hungry and it will be time to eat soon.'

He turned away from the river and started on the half mile walk back to his home. The rain never materialised, just the odd drop or two, but that dark blue-black sky didn't change for an instant, as he looked it gave him a feeling of foreboding, of a warning from the Gods of terrible things to come. Was this the way that life was going to go? Down the mines, work, sleep, work? For the first time in his life he pitied his father for the miserable existence he seemed to have had.

'Can I do any better?'

"Hello dad, how are you?"

Edward looked at James as he walked through the door; he seemed surprised that James had even spoken to him, let alone in a friendly sort of way.

"Hello young James. So, have you now finished school?"

But before the lad could answer he carried on.

"Are you ready to come to work with me at Clergon Mine? I talked with Jack Bentory our foreman and he said there will be no problem you getting a job, as long as you are prepared to work hard."

He looked completely worn out, and quickly slumped into the only armchair that was in their apartment. He hadn't even changed into some other clothing. He just wanted his dinner as always, then he would take the trouble to wash once more and change into some clean clothes, he would then last a little less than one hour before going off to bed.

For some reason Mary had gone to a little trouble to produce a decent meal, she had managed to get hold of some lamb chops. Meat was expensive, usually out of their pocket range, but Mary had got these comparatively cheap. She had decided to make a real family meal. Though not said, it was probably because James had now finished with school and had officially become a man. Much to James's surprise neither Charles or Dugan had eaten anything when they too had arrived home from school, so they all sat around the small table and made the most of Mary's sort of hotpot of a stew. It tasted good and by the end of the eating session there was absolutely nothing left in the pot, which quietly upset Mary, hoping that the meal might stretch to the next day.

After having finished with the washing up James and his brothers went back into the room to see that their father was already asleep in the armchair and mother was sewing away at a blouse that she had rescued from a charity sale.

James looked closely at his father, maybe for the first time in his life.

He noticed that this man, who was barely forty years of age was lined, grey and worn out. Though he was immensely strong, his shoulders were sloping and his rib cage bent inwards as opposed to the opposite, he had the appearance of a man that was in fact emaciated, which he most certainly was not. His facial features had the demeanour of a map of the canal system of the British Isles. He was entirely lined with grooves that ran deep, in fact so deep that he never seemed to retrieve all the coal dust which had been accumulated at work, this gave him the appearance of someone that had a tattooed face. In fact it made him look not unlike Maoris from New Zealand.

This was a person that carried the troubles of the world on his shoulders, if only he knew and understood what those troubles were.

After half an hour more, Edward awoke and stated in a matter of fact voice,

"Well I'm off to bed. Night all!"

Fifteen minutes after their father had departed, the rest of them went too.

There were just three rooms to the entire apartment, which was two more than most, two bedrooms and one dinner come kitchen and everything room. The toilet was in the hall and shared by four other apartments. It always smelt bad, and was always dirty.

There was supposedly a rota for keeping the said toilet room clean. It was Mary who usually was the only one who was actually prepared to clean the place, often it was so disgusting that Mary would have to have a wet towel wrapped around her face covering her mouth and nose, just to stop her from being sick. Sometimes and actually quite often, the toilets up stairs would block up and cause a flooding into their own system. This was even more disgusting, and once again it was Mary who was looked upon to clean it all up. And the cheek of it was, when this problem occurred, a neighbour would knock on the Jolly's door asking Mary Stuart to do what was needed as if it was her duty and hers alone. Now each of the boys lined up to do their ablutions and wash and tidy up for bed. By the time James, being the last, was finished there were another eight neighbours lining up to use the facilities.

Just before sleep overtook James, Charles said to him,

"You are so lucky, finished with school, I wish it was me!"

"Mmm, well that's as maybe, but please don't be like me."

For once James was very sincere in his words and voice.

He now came across with a worried expression on his face, and it showed to the siblings that this time he was seriously concerned that they shouldn't go through their schooling life acting a complete moron like he had.

"Try and learn something in your last year. I'm already starting to regret not working harder." He then snorted and quickly added, "Harder! O Christ what a joke, I feel quite sick. For Gods sake please both of you listen to what I am saying, don't' be another me."

James repeated himself thinking of what Mr. Cluff had said to him.

"I don't want you two lads to get to be like I am! No, I want that you should both spend your last couple of years achieving something. Yes, work harder, achieve something. Oh my Lord, you two don't ever think of also going down the mine. There is a world out there, go and explore it. All you need is some knowledge to succeed."

But the words had already fallen on deaf ears, they were both asleep. James lay there looking at the shadows on the ceiling, wondering if he would ever amount to anything during his life, or was he destined to be just another nobody like the thousands of wasters around the Gorbals areas of Glasgow.

The next day was Saturday the twenty-ninth of July 1889. James Jolly now woke up at eight in the morning much to his own displeasure. He had become used to rising on what he called the crack of dawn, he got up and washed. His father had already gone to work, he started at seven in the morning, so he had to rise by five-thirty to make sure he made it there on time. Mary, was washing out clothes as she normally did. She made a small income from taking in the neighbours laundry, but it usually meant a few extra coppers, but even those few pennies might put a meal on the table.

"Morning mum, is there any chance of something to eat?"

"I could make you some bread with the drippings from last nights dinner if you like, that or make yourself some toast."

James didn't have to think long and hard about what to choose.

"Last nights dripping will do fine. Any tea or coffee?"

"What a stupid question, we haven't had coffee in several months. I can't go wasting our precious resources on luxuries such as coffee, use your loaf lad."

But she smiled warmly as she said it.

James sat by the window, looked out onto the road, mainly to see whom was coming and going. It was a warm sunny morning, but a cloud of brownie yellow thin smoke hung over the street and though the sun was there, it could barely penetrate that layer of smog that clung to everything. This particular cloud was generated from the potteries not more than a few hundred yards away from their road. The smell that came with the pollution was not at all pleasant, it smelt slightly of sulphurous bad eggs and burning wet wood. Not completely overpowering, but there in the air sent just to annoy one.

There were lots going on outside, people coming and going, two rather fat women were chatting while leaning on a rusting stair railing, some small wee children playing in the gutter, one little boy, no more than two years of age, playing happily with a snail or some other crustacean, he was dirty and completely naked in an unabashed manner. Almost certainly he had just got out of bed and wondered down into the road with the hope of finding other kids to play with.

A horse and cart were standing idle on the other side of the street, what he was there for was anyone's guess? A small dirty black dog was defecating in the middle of the road, then having completed its toiletry task it turned and smelt its own little heap before licking his own private parts, then promptly sat on its rear and scratched vigorously at its obviously flea ridden neck. This task hadn't gone unnoticed by the small boy, now interested in what the cur had been doing, decided that he too should leave a deposit of poo. His toiletry too just might suit the occasion as well as the dog, so he squatted in the gutter and added his share. Neither the dog nor the little boy gave a hoot as to the gathering of excrement within the road, as far as they were concerned their piles just added extra interest to a shabby run down area of the city.

In the distance James heard the sound of a goods train rumbling nearby, the clanging of the trucks immediately made some sort of sense to him, he had watched on many occasions trains shunting in the sidings and the noise and smell and pollution from the engines smoke stacks was overpowering to him in spirit and reality, to him those huge steam engines were like dinosaurs, relics of the past but though very dangerous, somehow magnificent as well. To James these huge rusting leviathans were breathing clanging hissing monsters that had somehow been very nearly tamed by humans.

Glasgow was all James had ever known, but the heavy industrial side fascinated him more than he realised at that moment in time. These were areas that he just loved to spend his waking times at, just to stand and watch was very special to him.

'Yes,' he thought, 'that's what I'll do today; I'll go to the yard and watch the men working on the engines. Who knows, maybe there could be some work there for me? I am sure that working with steam engines is better than mining.'

Another hour went by, the two brothers Charles and Dugan had arisen from their bed, washed, eaten the crust off each end of the loaf that Mary had made the previous night, and were waiting for James to take them on an adventure to the railway terminal and good yard.

'The three Gorbals boys, each with enough energy to create mayhem and devastation throughout the whole of Glasgow. Now they were going to the goods yard where danger awaited at ever point of the compass.' That was their collective thoughts about going off to the yard. James knew he must make hay while the sun shines as he would probably have to go to work on Monday morning with his father.

The three boys put on there newly acquired second hand shoes, and subsequently went on their way to the start of new exciting things. The noise of the trains was getting louder as every step they took, and each step took them closer to the yard.

Men were busy pushing and guiding trucks into various lanes of rails, and to their collective delight, one man who knew the Jolly boys waved a greeting to them, followed by,

"Be careful lads, there is a great deal of traffic today. I don't want to be the one to go and explain to your mum and dad that you won't be coming home, because your bodies lay squashed under some loaded truck. Watch out for everything."

The boys heeded his advice, though all three were extremely wise to the dangers of the railways anyway.

They headed for the main engine shed, this James knew was where the cleaning and repairing took place, most everything was done in the way of maintenance from within this particular building. Something was always going on twenty-four hours a day, seven days a week.

Woe betides anyone living within hearing distance of this shed, no sleep or quiet time was their only reward, plus the clouds of filth and dusty smoke as it billowed into the surrounding air only added extra to the chain of human misery.

Just before they reached the main opening to the shed, the sun finally broke through the smog and smut, a dazzling display of light reacted all over the rails which were kept shiny by the constant use of the engines and trucks riding over them.

Just for a brief moment the lads were startled and delighted by the demonstration of Gods wondrous firework showcase of light, then just as quickly, things became dull again as that freak of nature was beaten back by mans over exuberance with industrial chaos.

The shed was vast, holding seven lanes of train lines into it. Each rail had something that was either being steamed up, cleaned, repaired or just stored. There must have been at least one hundred men buzzing about in there, none of which took the slightest notice of three young scruffs that had just entered. Only a foreman noticed the boys, he approached and seeing that James was obviously the oldest spoke to him.

"I don't mind you watching what's going on lads. But please stay out of harms way, keep from under the feet of the workers, and don't steal anything! If you do, then I will have to inform the police, and that is not a threat, it is a promise. But stay around, look and learn who knows you might be working here one day yourselves."

Then as a passing quip he stated.

"That's how I got involved. Just like the three of you, engine sheds are fascinating places and that is why it captivated me."

He smirked with the clear memory, and then added in passing,

"And what's more they still do."

He turned away and laughed as if he had said something funny. But the foreman was right, the three of them were enthralled.

On the first rail on the left hand side of the building a large 0-4-0 open aired foot plated locomotive with tender, which had come especially for its makeover from Furness.

It was being thoroughly cleaned from the inside of the boiler. A young fellow was crawling around inside the boiler dusting and drawing all the waste ash and clinker, making one hell of a mess. He was throwing it out behind him and a plume of dust hung in the air all around the front of the engine. The lad was covered from head to foot in dust and smoke, much of which he breathed into his lungs. The boys name was John Crawley, he was only two years older than James who he knew well. James had recognised this person long before he himself was spotted and acknowledged.

"Hi-yo John, how's it all going?"

The lad stopped what he was doing and turned outwards to try and view who had spoken to him. It took a few seconds before the penny dropped, then he smiled showing some whitish teeth through all the rest of the grime. His voice was weak, as over the last year he had eaten and breathed nothing but smoke, dust and clinker from the cleaning of engines.

"What-ye Jimmy, how's it hanging?"

But James had a problem trying to interpret what had come from John's mouth.

John Crawley was only sixteen years of age, but working for the railway was already killing him. His knees were worn so badly from always being in a kneeling position, that his cartilage had been worn away, as well as bone from his knees. The skin was now completely hard and leathery, and though he had pain from both knees twenty-four hours a day, he had absolutely no feeling in the lower or upper reaches of his legs. He could hardly talk, and was almost inaudible as his voice was only just above a whisper, he could no longer bear to eat or drink anything that might be the slightest bit warm, let alone hot. His eyes were permanently red with conjunctivitis and the rubbing of them was ever so gradually making him go blind. He had already formed the start of cataracts in each of them. His future was assured, but probably for no more than another two years, then a painful death. At the rate of his deterioration he would be dead long before he was to going to be completely blind. But of course he or anyone else, had no idea how serious working in those conditions really were. And being sixteen meant that he earned just eight shilling, this wage packet was for a fifty hours a week.

"What are you doing here? Not looking for work I hope!"

He didn't wait for an answer.

"Anyway, the foreman is watching, catch you some other time."

He then turned his back on the three lads and went back into his own personal hell hole. Their attention was taken away from John, the three lads turned and watched another young lad crawling up onto the very high smoke stack that old "Coppernob" had, and he was attempting to clean and polish it.

This particular engine had been built in 1846 in Birmingham, not that James or his brothers knew that fact. She was yet another fascinating dinosaur that kept the highways of trade alive even after forty three years of permanent non stop service.

Someone else was cleaning the wheels and trying hard to find some colour in the framework. The entire machine was just a grimy greyish brown colour, but should have been shiny dark black. But like all the trains that were used in Glasgow, it worked well even if it didn't shine well anymore.

The boys had been standing watching for nearly twenty minutes when a huge crashing sound made them jump, but just only the three of them, no one else even blinked at this sudden crashing sound. It was the sound of several trucks crashing into some more then being joined up so that they could be pulled out of the shed. Once again, the dirt and grime was more pronounced than any colour that the trucks might have had. These particular trucks were off to be loaded with coal from the mines in Ayr.

Gradually another locomotive, a smaller version of a 0-4-0, this time a saddle tank workhorse came in the shed on the rails that housed the trucks. It banged quite hard into the last one, and the plate man ran over and coupled the engine up to the trucks, then very gradually the driver moved forward and started to haul them out. As the engine passed the lads, the driver called down to the lads and asked,

"You got any fags lads, I am right out and boy, am I gasping for a drag?"

But he only got a shake of the head from the three. None of them had ever smoked a cigarette, probably because none of them ever had any money. Strangely though, all three seemed impervious to the idea of putting paper and dried weed things in ones mouth then setting light to it. The two younger brothers would never smoke properly, though every other vice was fair game to them. James was the only one in the family that took to nicotine, but not until some years on.

As the engine finally passed by, but not completely out of the shed, it blew a huge column of dirty dark black smoke out of its funnel. The smoke hung in the air, some came down and made the boys splutter somewhat, but then as if not quite knowing what to do next the smoke drifted upwards, and then the open shutters within the roof draw most of it out into the outside air, but only to add yet more soot to the grime and pollution to that which was already hovering around. Dirt, grime, grime, dirt, that was Glasgow, plus just about every city within the boundaries of the sea that encased the island that is Britain.

In the far left hand corner of the shed, a foundry was being pumped up by a heavily set leather apron wearing man. This fellow was almost ready in age to retire, he stood easily six foot four inches in height thus next to the boys this made him an absolute giant.

In some ways he stood out amongst everything else because he had a huge mop of wavy silver white hair, which in this den of iniquity seemed strangely luminescent. That white mat of hair made James think of crashing surf on beaches with all those curls being the waves. How did they stay so clean looking? He looked and was, extremely strong, his face was lined and pitted from years of being spat on by hot fire, but his hard grim demeanour softened when the boys approached to see what he was up to. In fact he was making another spindle for some part of some engine somewhere. But to watch him work with red hot metal was a joy for the boys to behold.

There was a sort of magic being performed before their very eyes, as a craftsman manufactured whatever it was he was making.

'This was a craftsman,' thought James 'this is someone that can make anything and mend anything, and what's more he can put shoes on horse's hooves.'

"Er, Mister, what are yer making?"

The answer was quickly and enthusiastically replied,

"I am repairing the spindle that goes just behind the drive wheel on that loco."

He pointed to another dirty train that had people the size of ants, or so it seemed to the boys, crawling all over it.

"Its job is to drive a fan when needed, the fan will blow in more air to the fire, thus creating more heat, more steam, and more speed. Got the idea?"

James nodded but really hadn't understood any of this mans final sentence. But that didn't matter as this man was a craftsman. In the eyes of the three boys this man could do anything with engines.

Several hours passed with the blink of an eye. The boys had enjoyed themselves thoroughly and all three were getting hungry for some food. James suggested that they make their way back home, but they could have some fun on the way. But first, he wished to talk to the foreman. After a few abortive attempts he found him having a cup of tea with the foundry man. This was tea that you could stand a spoon up in, lots of tea, little milk, lots of sugar. They were both laughing and then were deep in conversation and neither of them noticed young James approaching, not until he was almost on top of them both.

"Hello, hello! And what do we owe the pleasure for this time?"

The foreman came across as a very friendly affable sort of person, the sort of man that enjoyed the company of others, and didn't mind the younger set. He smiled at James and waited for an answer to his own enquiry.

"I was wondering, well I was sort of hoping, are there any jobs for young lads like me? I would love to work as a foundry man. How do I get into a workshop like this? I would work hard, and I am always on time."

The as an after thought he added,

"I really don't want to go down the mines!"

The two men looked at one another, and then looked back at James and his two siblings.

"I would have to talk to my governor, but you could be in luck! We might offer a chance for the right person to become an apprentice, and maybe right here in the foundry. Old Bill 'ere will be coming up to retirement in a couple of years, so we will be thinking about his replacement. I suggest you talk to your parents then come back and talk to me. How's that sound?"

James didn't have to be told twice.

"Gee, thanks mister. I will talk to mum and dad, I expect to come back and see you next week if that's fine with you?"

"What's your name; I shall write it down and talk to my governor."

"It's James Jolly, I left school yesterday. I have to help support the family along with dad."

Without any hesitation James walked over to the two men, held out his hand and shook theirs. This impressed the foreman immensely; he already liked this young James Jolly, yes, he knew if the boy returned he would make sure there was a place there for him.

On the way home, unperturbed by the thick dirty air and the intense heat generating from the sun that struggled hard to break through the clouds of filth, the three brothers played kicking a stone as a football, that was until it disappeared down a drain, then as a jape they decided to try and see how many houses they could play knockdown ginger on before being seen. It meant a huge effort to run down the terraced road towards Dalmeny road knocking on all the doors as they ran, and to make it harder they didn't want to be recognised if they were seen. They only managed ten houses before one of the first doors was opened by a very irate man. He screamed after the three of them, the abusive language coming up from the pit of his stomach was electrifying the air.

"I know who you are, I'll be coming to see your fucking parents, you'll be for the high jump that I promise you. You young bastards, I'll rip your balls off, I'll smash your nasty faces into pulp then make you eat your own shit. I am on nights and this is the only sleep time I get. I'll be coming just you wait and…"

But his voice became inaudible as they reached the end of the road and turned the corner into their own residential area. But James was almost beside himself with laughter. he bent over double, almost touching his knees with his nose, his breathing was light but laboured, but despite being somewhat over weight he could hold his own in a run, especially when it was fleeing from someone or something.

James looked at his two sibling brother and smiled inwardly. He loved the two little buggers, something he didn't do concerning his parents. He knew that he would walk over burning coals for Charles and Dugan and woe betides anyone trying to hurt them! That was the reason he was prepared to stay here in Glasgow, that was just until they both left school and the three of them could make the world their oyster.

James was going to take them away and start a new life somewhere far away from the misery, poverty, dirt and danger from the inevitable crime of the Gorbals and Glasgow. That was why he was prepared to start a job, get some money saved, prepare for the day when they were ready for when their own personal adventure was really going to begin. James knew that everything up until the day, freedom day, moving away day, escaping day, and many more adjectives that he conjured into his mind. He was just marking time before the three of them would escape the torture of life in Clyde's riverside city.

"Listen you two. When you both leave school, let's move down south together? We can go and live in England. Maybe we can have a fine life without this stinking hole of a place always looming over our heads."

Charles and Dugan were not really listening as Dugan kicked at a dead rotting dog which stunk and fouled up the gutter. A million maggots fell from its open belly, its eye sockets and from its gaping mouth, but as fast as they appeared, they struggled to try and make their way back into that prone unmoving larder. It was such a fascinating sight for the youngest, so interesting that he felt the need to kick it again. Unfortunately this produced the worst smell that either of the lads had ever really experienced, so they backed away from the luckless creature.

James tried once more to interest his siblings in a collective future.

"I shall get work and make sure that I save money, enough for us to leave when you both finish your schooling. What do you think of that idea?"

Poor James, his words were in fact completely falling on deaf ears.

None of them noticed that the same horse and cart was still opposite on the other side of the road, it hadn't moved since they had started off that morning, just standing there attached to the cart, looking terribly forlorn and crest fallen, with a bag of seeds and chaff lying on the cobblestones beneath its head.

The young baby was nowhere to be seen, probably scooped up by its mother many hours before and taken inside.

Now there were four dogs where just one had been before, and they were scratching and scurrying around the area, they had all spent a very pleasant time defecating and peeing just about everywhere. Every lamp post had been christened, and almost every paving slab had a special gift from them, laid especially for any unsuspecting traveller, human or not, to step into, these packets of joy had been deposited by them and the many others that roamed the streets before them.

One of the lead dogs climbed onto the back of one of the others, it was most definitely in the mood for some romance, but as it pushed hard from its rear the other dog turned sharply and bit him firmly and squarely on the mounted animal, who then squealed and jumped off, it was only then that it realised that it had clambered onto yet another male.

None of these little distractions were noticed by the lads, but they did hear the roar of a trains whistle and the expulsion of its surplus steam as it went on its merry way to somewhere, and to James at least, anywhere was better than being there in Glasgow, actually especially anywhere.

They approached their own tenement building, and just as they were about to enter a suited man was coming out. He passed them walked down the ten steps onto the pavement, stopped, turned, looked hard at the three of them, and then asked,

"Are you the Jolly boys?"

James was the first to turn and look. As the man hadn't asked in a threatening way, but in a gentle soft voice, so he answered in the affirmative.

"Yes, can I help you?"

"Best get in quickly boys, your mother is going to need your support. There is no easy way to say this. Your father was killed first thing this morning when a tunnel he was in collapsed. I have just been to see your mother, she is in a terrible state. Best get up there quickly. Sorry boys, so sorry! The company will be in touch real soon. Good luck to you all."

Though he was polite in his approach to all this sad news, but he was somewhat abrupt, he now departed as if going on a date with a rather lovely young woman. As he went down the roadway, James thought he could hear the man whistling a catchy tune.

James turned back to Charles and Dugan, both lads were looking at James for some sort of guidance. Just as suddenly Dugan burst out.

"Dad, dead! James what are we going to do?"

"Christ lads, lets get upstairs and talk to mum. Maybe he was lying or mistaken."

He added that statement pointing towards the man that was now turning the corner into the next road.

The boys crept quietly into their apartment, there was Mary lying on her bed with the door wide open. She was sobbing quite uncontrollably, but as soon as she saw the lads, she lost control completely. Her wailing was so sudden and unexpected that all three boys sank back in a fright. None of them knew what to do, how do you console your mother, a bereaved wife, who had just received the news of her husband dying, how do you help and especially when you are fourteen years of age and younger?

James took the first step forward, realising for the first time that commitment meant having values for all the family, not just your two younger brothers.

"Mum, I am so, so sorry. I shall start working and become the bread winner within our family. I know I have responsibilities to all of us now, me being the oldest. You just rest and I shall make some tea for all of us."

He paused as he noticed that she was in fact listening to him. She had now stopped her wailing and sobbing. Mary looked at all three sons, tears were still streaming down her cheeks, but no sound came from her lips. She extended her arms and all three of them went to her, for an embrace. After a short time, James broke free and asked a very grown up question.

"Mum, what are the mine owners going to do for dad and us?"

Mary now became very alert, thought for a good twenty seconds before answering.

"They brought me a week's wages, that is all. I don't think I will get any sort of pension from them, but they did say they would bury your father locally, and that should save quite a bit of money. They will also pay for a wake and a meal for the mourners."

She took a deep breath and carried on.

"Yes James, you will have to go to work now, but not down that awful hole in the ground. Have you any concept of what you might like to do?"

This was James's moment of truth.

"Mum, I do know what I want. You may not be aware but I love steam engines, all steam engines, so I am going to start and apprenticeship as a foundry worker and learn everything about engines. I talked it over with the foreman at the engine shed. He told me to come back in a day or two after talking to you. I know I have been useless at school, and now that it is to late to do anything about my schooling, I can see where I went wrong and I will step up and become a man. Old Mr. Cluff was right when he told me that learning is everything, and as from today I shall put my best efforts into learning to read and write properly. I shall ask him next time I see him to recommend books for me to read."

He was sad about his father, but this was a moment to savour, this had been an epiphany, his life was changing and almost certainly for the better.

"You see mum, I will be a good provider, honest!"

4

James got to his feet and made the tea for all four of them, then many more meals afterwards. He became that model son and worked diligently to replace his father.

Mary was managing, but only just, there was no money to spare, and every penny went on the three boys, either in clothing or food. She did receive a small pension from the mine, plus they had paid for all the funeral expenses. Nearly one hundred and thirty people turned up for the funeral, most of which were just hangers on hoping for a free drink and some food. But there were also plenty of Edwards mining friends there as well as representatives of the mine, it somehow turned into a fine social occasion, much to the chagrin of Mary Stuart Jolly who would have preferred a more sombre ceremony, but the day was much talked about in the ensuing months to come.

James had landed the job as an apprentice foundry-man. Working alongside Bill McGregor was an enlightening experience, one they both enjoyed.

The old man, though happily married had never had any children, and what's more never had an apprentice before, so getting to know young Jolly was a pleasure for him.

Bill would often bring lunch for both of them, he understood the difficult time that the Jolly family were experiencing. James's earnings were only three shillings and four pence a week, for which he worked a hard fifty hour week, though his face most definitely fitted within the engine workshops, he was informed that the salary would only rise as he progressed in his studies.

Of course, as an extremely low earner he didn't pay any taxes, so the money was net, which went to his mother Mary Stuart. She would allow him two shillings and sixpence back from his wages, this was for him to spend on whatever he wanted, but the only things James wanted was books, then more books.

The first book that James was given was "A tale of two cities," it took him two months to struggle all the way through, but once he got to the end he wanted more. It wasn't long before his reading abilities were as good as anyone else. He had progressed to reading a book every week, then two a week. Sometimes he would read and absorb three or even four books in a seven day period.

But to James's credit, he didn't just read the classics, he would read text books, first on the steam engine, then on ships steam engines, then gradually on ship and shipping and all things naval, including naval history.

He had read just about every aspect of the navy, so much so that he could have become an officer, or even a Captain, that is except for his social background and his lack of finesse. But he certainly could have run a ship of any size or speed. He could and often did hold chapter and verse on ships and naval things to absolutely anyone that was there to listen to him. James became intrigued by the British war ships, the cruisers, battleships, frigates, from the very earliest men-of-war in Roman times to Queen Victoria's incredible navy that was the envy of the rest of the world.

James understood about politics, and not just of Britain but of most European countries, plus Russia and America. From his readings his leaning were most definitely to the left. He quickly decided that he seriously admired the writings of Karl Marx, having read 'Das Kapital' and 'The Communist Manifesto', not once but three times. He even made sure that he visited his grave in Highgate cemetery and laid flowers on his tombstone as a sign of his respect for his hero.

The three year apprenticeship went by so quickly that it seemed as a blink of an eye to both Bill and James. The day had come when young James would get his letters, proving that he was a fit and able foundry man, and at the same time as his indentures were completed he was able to wish Bill McGregor a happy retirement. James was now perfectly able to take Bill's place.

His wages had now gone up to one pound and ten shillings and three pence, which meant he had to pay a small amount in tax every week, something that seemed abhorrent to him.

Charles had left school and joined the Highland Rifle Brigade, much to the worry of his mother, and they had been dispatched to South Africa, as some of the natives had grown restless.

Dugan had also now left school, and was one of the very few from the Youngers Christian School that ever made it to University. He was studying law, specialising in naval law. Fortunately he had acquired a nice scholarship to attend Birmingham University, where he boarded at the expense of the University. His studies kept him so busy, thus he was not able to attend the small ceremony that was being played out within the old engine shed.

Dugan had managed to achieve this incredible feat by the tender age of just sixteen, making him one of the youngest scholars ever to attend that place of learning.

Both boys knew they owed an enormous debt of gratitude to their older brother, as he had spent all his time aiding and abetting their futures.

James felt quite proud of himself as he received his indentures from the engine house manager, a man he had never seen before, and probably wouldn't ever see again as management were housed in the centre of Glasgow within Central Station.

James had now finally become a fully qualified foundry worker, and in the three years that he had worked for the Glasgow and Southern Railways, there was hardly anything that he didn't know about engines, and that circumscribed him for all types of steam engines large and small, old or new.

Bill had taught him well, much to McGregor's personal satisfaction. James was quite capable to taking any part from anywhere within the engine and either replicating it or mending the said item. And being still so young gave him unreserved praise and friendship from all the workers who knew him. Young Jolly had been extremely lucky to have had such a good and loyal friend as Bill McGregor, and between them they squeezed five years of apprenticeship into three very hard working and industrious years. No one before had ever managed to get their indentures in such a short space of time.

James was proud, his family was proud, Bill was proud and the Glasgow and Southern Railway were proud. They even managed to get an article published in the local paper, not that James or his family ever got to know about that as they never took the said paper.

Now all three of the boys had left the senior school, and only James was still living with Mary, things had become easier financially for them.

Mary Stuart now started to put her feet up and take life easier. It was in this period that she met Ivan Kolinsky, a fifty-two year old ex-soldier of the Polish army, who ten years ago had fallen on tough times, then out of the blue he up and left his family of a wife and six children, who still lived in Warsaw in Poland.

He had decided to desert the army after he was caught with his fingers in the officers mess money box, as he denied stealing and swore that he had been told to take the money by a superior officer, and as no one had as yet managed to prove his story one way or another, they didn't lock him up, instead swore him to a parole, which he immediately broke and ran away.

He absconded before any proof was brought to bare against him, so then at a whim he dumped his uniform and stole someone else's clothes, he literally walked into a farmers house while the man was labouring in the fields and helped himself to some civvies. He then walked into Germany which seemed the obvious way to go. After walking and stealing food to keep body and soul alive he arrived not far from the Dutch border, he knew he was a hunted man and in all probabilities would now also be being chased by the German police, it was time to move into yet another country, somewhere he could keep his nose clean and out of the hands of the Polish army, so he swam across the river Ems one dark moonless night, thus avoiding German and Dutch border patrols. Once safely across and in Dutch territory, he walked hard and made an inroad well into the Nederland's. The next morning having finally managed to get dry, Ivan secured a lift in a horse and cart which took him some miles, eventually, worn out, dirty and dishevelled, he found his way to Hook van Holland.

Having studies the situation there over a period of several weeks, he finally plucked up the courage to enquire about a job with a small shipping company.

He was a good cook, and after an extensive interview he managed to secure a job working for a paddle steamer which went back and forth to Dover in England. Life quickly became good once more, the hours were long but the pay was reasonable. He quickly learnt how to get by in the Dutch language, so his life became one of comparative safety. In his free time he managed to meet many people, that included women, and it was most definitely the ladies that he liked.

He spent six months chugging backwards and forwards on that new paddle steamer, the tedium could sometimes overpower his senses, as on board ship the routine drifted into, work, eating, and if the weather permitted some walking around the deck area, then sleeping, and back to square one again.

He did manage a few onboard romances, but nothing that could be construed as being able to fill the loneliness he felt for a woman that could fill that gap within his existence.

Ivan started to feel that age old itch once more.

He was now trusted onboard and excepted by all his fellow workers, that was because his food was so good, the Captain asked him to cook for him especially, this gave Ivan a lot of leeway, once docked in Dover he was sometimes allowed time ashore. The more times he went ashore and returned without causing delays or problems, the more trusted he became. Often while in Dover he would buy some extra provisions, sometimes something typically English, just to vary the menu.

Even the customs and border officials in Dover got to know him well, and there was always a cheery smile and a wave as he passed through the dockyard gates.

The problem occurred after eight months on board the steamer, the Captain had a new number one working for him, and First Officer van Grievel turned out to be a bully. On one occasion when Ivan was delivering the Captains meal, he tripped him up in front of the other officers. The food went everywhere, then the new number one accused Ivan of trying to throw the food over him, much to the laughter of all around as it had been plain to see who was really at fault. Ivan went red with rage, but thought better of it. He stood erect and glared at the man.

"Better clean up your mess before the Captain sees what a fool he has employed as a chef. Come on move your arse man, get this mess away from my bridge."

Ivan started to twitch with annoyance, but still he held his cool. He knew he could get his own back in other ways.

The bridge area was cleaned up, and Ivan made a new meal for the Captain, which was duly delivered. But Ivan seethed and plotted his own form of revenge.

The next morning the first officer came down to the mess to inquire what was going to be for lunch. One of the other cooks explained what was going to be on the menu, he told the officer it was roasted chicken pieces wrapped in vine leaves and rosemary, with roasted bananas wrapped in bacon strips. This would be accompanied with wild brown rice. The man asked if when the Captains food was being taken to him, they could also deliver his.

James saw his moment was about to come to fruition, he said that he would take care of the two meals, but he asked that someone else take them to their prospective recipients.

Ivan prepared the meals himself, but with the first officer, he managed to place some human excrement underneath the chicken.

'This will show that bastard! The ignorant slob will get his just deserts.'

He laughed out loud at his own witticism.

Having handed over the two plates of food, making doubly sure that the waiter knew what was for the Captain and what was for the first officer. Grinning to himself and feeling rather smug with himself he decided that he would go outside to where the starboard paddle splashed merrily away to have a cigarette, after all it was a calm sunny day, he worked hard, he deserved a cigarette break.

He was enjoying his first Players Please for the day, when he noticed a very irate officer almost running towards him, he was purple with rage and was screaming abuse, not that Ivan could hear it as the sound of the paddle drowned out everything else around. But Ivan was not a stupid man, he knew that this man was intent on causing him some serious grief. He braised himself for a fight as he soon noticed that the officer's fists were clenched and his right arm brought back ready to throw the first blow. Ivan automatIcelandandly straightened himself and prepared for the fight that was obviously going to happen. Then he could finally hear the abusive language that was exuding from his adversary's mouth,

"You fucking bastard, I know what was wrapped in that chicken, you are going to pay for that."

He swung his fist to hit Ivan in the face, but he wasn't quick enough and anyway, Ivan was in fact a trained soldier, quite able to look after himself. The chef ducked and moved sharply to his right, the fist passed harmlessly across the top of his head. Ivan retaliated by bringing his own fist hard up into the officers stomach. He caught him absolutely full on, this brought the luckless man to a sudden halt and he was then struggling badly to catch his breath. Now Ivan was moving around to the back side of the man who was still trying hard to get air into his lungs. As he moved around he once again brought his fist up hard to hit the man, this time straight into his kidneys. The first officer choked with the pain, with his eyes watering badly and not really able to utter a sound the first officer choking leant hard up against the ships rail, then without saying another word his hand fell off the railing and the luckless officer fell forwards right over the rail and into the path of the paddle, as he fell his eyes followed Ivan until he hit the water.

Ivan was shocked at just how quickly all this had happened, he hadn't wanted to seriously injure the man, just to keep him away and not be bullied by him in any way any more, he just wanted to teach the bastard a lesson.

The officer was immediately dragged up through the paddle and was spun around twice before disappearing from view. It was for sure that he was dead, his body would have been broken in many placed by the force of those paddles.

Ivan now in a total state of shock though,

'Christ, what the hell am I to do?'

But before he could even think of some sort of answer, one of the stewards came through the door and walked casually up to him.

"Have you got a spare cigarette Ivan, er, please?"

Ivan quickly knew he must get to grips with the situation, he fumbled into his pocket and took out a packet of his English cigarettes. His hand was shaking not that the steward noticed as he took one. Ivan took one as well and then tried to strike a match, but now was shaking too much.

The steward didn't really notice the Polish cook's new infirmity, but he instinctively took hold of the box of Lucifer's and lit both cigarettes. He then thanked Ivan, handed back his matches then moved away so as to not allow the spray to spoil his hard drawing on the said cigarette.

Ivan knew that before long the officer would be missed, he must retrieve the offending plate of food, wash it completely clean, and then make sure that he is not associated with the disappearance, after all, he was well aware that several other officers saw the incident that occurred with the Captains plate of food, it wouldn't take a genius long to put two and two together and make four.

Many hours went by, Ivan had become more and more agitated, so much so that he felt sure that his working associates would notice and wonder why he was in such a nervous state.

It was at this point that he made up his mind what he would do, he would leave the ship at Dover, walk into the town, then catch a train north, anywhere north, in fact the further north the better. It was just as well that he had made up his mind about leaving the ship once and for all, as a hew-and-cry had developed around the vessel as the Captain had now missed his first officer for many hours. Then just before they reached land the Captain called Ivan to the bridge.

"As you know, there has been a large group of officers and men searching the ship for Mr. van Grievel, our first officer. He seems to have gone missing some time after you brought up our food at lunch. I am also aware that you and he had some sort of confrontation a day or two ago!"

The Captain was looking directly into Ivan's eyes, which unnerved the Polish refugee hugely.

"Having now searched the ship thoroughly and finding no one, I have to ask a couple of searching questions."

His stare penetrated deep into Ivan's psyche. Ivan could feel that the Captain suspected he was involved with the officer's disappearance. Kolinsky was shaking slightly, hoping it wouldn't notice, but his shallow almost panting breath was a sure give away. Sweat was pouring from every pore of his body, and he knew that his number was almost certainly up. No one would ever believe that he hadn't pushed the blasted scum of a man overboard.

"I have always liked you Ivan and I know what a mean bastard van Grievel could be. He liked a joke especially when it was at someone else's expense. So, having said that, do you know what happened to the man? Where you involved with him in some way? Did you two fight? You must realise I shall have to turn the ship around and go and look for a body, you could help!"

At that precise moment the Captain sneezed heavily, this had the desired effect of destroying the moment. The Captain blow his nose, then smiled with a certain amount of embarrassment.

"Sorry about that! So where were we? Ah, yes, do you have any information that would help me in finding out what has happened?"

Ivan had in that last sentence managed to pull himself together. He had stopped the shakes and managed not to sweat quite so badly.

"Captain, it is true that the man was a pig to me. I brought your lunch up to you, and in a classic stupid clownish moment made me drop the plate spilling your lunch all over the floor, then in front of the other officers made me feel a total fool. Of course I was extremely angry at that precise moment, but I managed to laugh it off. After all, I have often experienced such men as your first officer, you get them in every organisation. To me the man was a childish fool and a typical bully. I always think it is sad that so many men such as van Grievel get positions of power such as they do. I never cease to be amazed by that simple expedient."

Ivan was now feeling quite relaxed, the moment of panic was passing with every second.

"But to answer your question, I have absolutely no idea of where he is, are you sure that every part of the ship has been searched? He wouldn't just disappear, would he? I cannot believe that he would have fallen over the side. Did he drink at all?"

The Captain now was entirely at ease with Ivan. The Polish chef seemed to have won the moment all be it by the skin of his teeth.

The Captain did order another search of the vessel, but as no officer was found the few passengers that the ship carried were informed that the ship would be turning around whilst looking for a possible victim to the sea.

The SS Brede, turned back trying hard to retrace the route that she had come. Three hours were allotted to the task of searching, but of course nothing was found. Captain Jenson finally turned the paddle steamer back to Dover, and it was just logged that the officer had been lost at sea.

To Ivan this was more or less the end of the story, he then decided against deserting the ship as he was now out of danger from being accused of killing someone whom he felt had brought his own destruction upon himself. He was now relaxed and was once again breathing normally.

Some weeks later when practically everyone had forgotten First Officer Harold van Grievel, on a return journey to Hook van Holland, and Ivan met a widow who had been in England for several months and was now returning to her native Holland. Her name was Elsa Jorgen, late of Elsa Petersen, she had reverted back to her maiden name after the death of her husband.

Elsa was now a wealthy lady in her late thirties, barely in the prime of her life. This Dutch heiress had married to an extremely rich Icelandic ship owner, who nearly twice her age had come to live in Hilversum Holland, and even though it was practically as far away from his fishing fleet as one could get in small flat Nederland's.

Olav Petersen, had gradually over thirty years acquired thirty fishing boats, all big enough to catch just about anything that swam in the oceans. His main fleet concentrated on whaling, because in the north of the Atlantic many types of whales could be found, and the prize for landing whales was enormous, not just for the meat, but also the oils and bones, everything about the whale had a rich market value, so the money just kept swimming in, making Olav and Iceland worth something that could hold its own in world commerce. He personally was fast becoming mega-rich.

Olav had been married to an Icelandic woman, but she had drunk herself into an early grave, which seemed to be the fashion within that tiny volcanic island. Strange as it may seem, Icelandanders being a very religious people they followed a very tight form of Lutherism, that meant no beer, beer was the ruin of all human beings, but no one said anything perverse about strong spirits, so more or less everyone drank home made alcohol usually made by fermenting then distilling potatoes, something they eventually called Brenavin.

But this home made alcohol was a deadly concoction which often sent the drinker mad, but not before firstly sending them blind. Everyone knew the lethal status of the drink, but that didn't stop the populace from consuming gallons of the stuff.

Olav drank just like his wife, but the man had a stronger constitution, he never got drunk and it never affected his judgement, he was impervious to the deadly nature of spirits. Strangely for an Icelander he actually got bored with his own drinking culture and more or less gave up all alcoholic drinks, thus no one could accuse him of being a drunken alcoholic.

Olav had tired of Icelandic ways of life, those dreadful long winters, with its cold, snow, freezing rain, winds and darkness.

It was that darkness that seemed to be the reason why people drank so much, so there came a time when Olav had had enough of seeing men, women and children lying comatose on the clinker streets in a state of drunken stupor.

The problem came to a head when his wife died, vomiting blood and just about everything that she had consumed that day, plus parts of destroyed stomach lining that the alcohol had brought to a head. She keeled over looked at him in a terrified state and the then just stopped breathing.

To Olav it seemed as if though terrified of what was to come after death, she had quickly given in to the inevitability of her situation. The man was saddened, but not mortified. In many ways he had bored of his wife, though he hadn't wanted to admit to it to anyone or himself, so when she passed over to the other side he took a long hard look at everything around him, then he wondered why he stayed in this awful squalid place. Having travelled considerably in earlier years, he knew that Reykjavik and Icelandand were just a backwater in Europe and the world. After all with his money, the world was his for the taking.

After his wife was put to rest and a few weeks had passed, showing a more or less respectable time for mourning, he took a map of the world from the bookcase, spun it around on the table, then stuck a finger down upon it.

Hilversum, Holland, and which was where he was now going to move his entire operation too. 'Good bye to Iceland forever'.

The fleet would still operate from Reykjavik, he knew he owed the country that, but the monies that he earned would after taxes be dispatched to a designated bank in Holland. So all he had to do was promote his good young honest manager, to a status of general manager, then everything could and would go ahead. This he duly did. Life was already beginning to change and excite the Icelandic millionaire.

Hilversum was all that he expected, clean, bright and only dark when the sun went down in the west, and then only for some hours, no more twenty-four hour dark periods. He liked the flatness of the countryside, always green in colour. He loved the idea of cattle instead of sheep, plus something entirely new to him, pigs. But the best thing was something that Iceland didn't have, trees, beautiful, tall erect sentinel trees.

There was another aspect as to why he had chosen wisely, albeit without much thought, he liked and respected the people, which he considered being somewhat on the simple side. The Dutch with their clogged footwear, pointed shaped felt hats and stiff colourful woollen clothes were a delight to him. They were polite and courteous, always bowing and doffing their hats at him whenever he was out walking or riding his horse.

The men seemed to wear a great deal of leather and woollen clothing, but all of them seemed to smoke long clay pipes, which they puffed at furiously. The women mainly wore colourful heavily petticoated dresses, which showed off their white stocking netted legs much to Olav's pleasure, as he did appreciate the nice shape of women's legs. But much to his chagrin, they too smokes pipes, but somewhat shorter, but they all puffed just as frantIcally as their male counterpoint.

It took quite a long time for Olav not to smile too broadly when passing the peasants of Hilversum, he realised his observations concerning the local people could be interpreted badly had they suspected his way of thinking, it might have been thought of as insulting, though really his thoughts weren't meant to be. After all, he didn't want to offend anyone just to live in peaceful coexistence with them.

It had quickly got around the town that an eccentric millionaire had come amongst them and so everyone was out to please him, mainly because if it was true and there may be work for some of the populace.

Olav, soon learned how to speak the language and very quickly became a leading pillar within Hilversum society.

He was elected to the chamber of commerce and quickly became its chairman. This gave him some small powers in what went on with the confines of the community, specially re-business. It was while at one of their meetings that he met a young woman who had become their new secretary, her new job was in taking the minutes.

This woman was in her early thirties, typically Dutch, rather square headed, with blond pigtailed hair. Her skin was almost silky white with a shimmering slight shade of pink, though she did rouge her cheeks so as to emphasise her looks. When she smiled it was a delight for all to see. Unlike most women of her age in the area, her teeth were perfect in shape and cleanliness, being ivory white, they virtually sparkled. To Olav, she epitomised the local indigenous peoples, but to a greater degree. In his eyes she was just beautiful.

But Elsa was perfectly aware of this foreign gentleman's intensions, and surprisingly that seemed to be absolutely agreeable to her. She enjoyed all his smiles, winks, then his obvious sexual advances, after all she was still single, though hardly virginal, and most of all she desired to be wealthy and married. The important factor was, she was well aware that time was passing her by all too quickly.

After his second encounter the secretary Elsa, Olav invited her out to dine at the local inn, She accepted quickly with some excitement in her voice. There was a dearth of men within the Hilversum area and what men were there, were in Elsa's mind were not adequate thus being totally unacceptable as marriage material, so this strange foreigner from that cold northern country, though much older, he did offer the sort of respectability and wealth that appealed to this Dutch maiden.

Olav took her to an inn that had a fine reputation for good food.

Since coming to the Nederland's he had gained quite an amount of excess weight, it had been many long years since he experienced such abundance of choice, that is where food was concerned. So many different cuts of meat, so many varieties of vegetables, all always fresh and large, unlike Iceland where the few varieties of vegetables that could be obtained were usually small and discoloured by the lava dust that constituted the growing soil of the country. In Iceland the potatoes were good to eat if you dug them up from the fields at the right time, but they were always purple in colour. Apart from potatoes, turnips and swedes were just about all that could be grown, again always discoloured and surprisingly small compared to what could be got in the Netherlands's.

The repast was a great success and this impressed Elsa who then took to Olav immediately. She was nicely surprised that he talked about artistic things with such depth of knowledge. He knew about classical music, about famous painters, he seemed to be born with an insight to politics and all things intellectual. She was impressed and getting more interested as each minute ticked by.

Their meal consisted of some finely cooked beef, cooked in a French style, this came with an especially delicious sauce; the meat was accompanied by vegetables, even peas and broccoli, which neither had ever eaten before.

Then a cheese board was brought to their table. This they managed just a smattering of as both were already full from the main course.

After some time a beautiful desert was presented, almost as if offering up a crown at a coronation of some royal personage. It was some exotic fruit, something called peaches. This exotic delicacy came piping hot, they had been poached and were drowning in a bowl of egg custard. It was fantastically entertaining and good on the palate. With the food came wine, all good French wines, all of which Elsa adored, but Olav would have preferred good Dutch beer, but as the company was so delightful he was happy to go along with anything this young beauty wanted.

While there was a quiet moment, Olav asked the question that was hanging on every fibre of his being,

"Sweet Elsa, can I take you home after we have finished eating?"

At first Elsa looked shocked by the question, then after a few seconds having thought about, she replied.

"I can't take you home to my house; I still live with my parents, both of which would be horrified if I took a man home with me. But, I could come back to your house as long as you promise to get me home before morning."

Olav was pleased with the answer, plus satisfied with the meal. He wasn't a young man any more, plus the fact that it had been some time before he had experienced any sex with a woman. He hoped he could perform well enough, in fact he now felt very nervous at what was to come.

The Icelander left a large tip along with the payment, he hoped that this would be the last transaction he would have to pay out on that night as he knew nothing about this young lady.

When they returned to Olav's detached house with its huge dinning room and its six bedrooms, Elsa was very impressed. Maybe, if all went well tonight he would propose and they could marry, thus she would get all she dreamed about.

Being a wealthy man meant Olav could afford to have servants looking after him, so it wasn't a big surprise when a tired looking valet opened the front door for them both. He was thanked then dismissed so he could go back to his bed, this left Olav and Elsa free and alone in the most important part of the house.

"Would you like a glass of port? It has been brought all the way from Portugal, one thing I can assure you of that it is a very fine vintage, at least that's what I have been told."

He shrugged his shoulders and winked slightly, then they both smirked at the understanding that Olav actually didn't really know anything about vintages, or wines in general. He was completely dependent on advise from more experienced vintners.

"Yes please, I would love to try some port. I have never had any before, so the experience might be a pleasant one! At least I hope so?"

Again they both smiled, drank a little then both reddened knowing what was to come.

One hour later they both were laying on Olav's huge bed, in his own bedroom, both naked as the day they had been born. Sweat was still pouring from a now tired but contented Icelander, he felt that he had performed admirably considering, and he just hoped that Elsa's sighs and groans were real and that she was not just faking for his benefit.

In fact Elsa had enjoyed the frolic very much, it had been some time ago since she too had experienced the delights of a man inside her, indeed she had felt satisfaction as she too was lying in her own sweat, feeling complete and somewhat exhausted. She smiled to herself and at that precise moment she had an epiphany, this was definitely going to be her man, this was the man she would marry. It didn't matter about the age difference, many young women prefer older more experienced men. Anyway, he didn't look or act his age, he was like a young bull, once having tasted the fruits she and he wanted more. He was kind generous, rich and sexy. But most of all he was rich! What better reason for taking on a man as a husband, and even though he might not ask for her hand! But that thought didn't faze Elsa, she knew he would thus again she smiled as she lay there and wiped the sweat from her eyes.

Six months to the day the couple were married. As they were both protestant in religion there was no objections from the church, and as Olav had bought Elsa's parents a nice new house, there were no objections from them either.

Elsa took to married life very quickly. She oversaw the day to day running of their home which was not too strenuous as there were now eight servants to do everything that needed doing. The house came with roughly four acres of reasonable arable land, and it had cattle grazing on it when Olav took over the property, but Elsa liked the idea that they should grow their own vegetables, so the land was ploughed under. A small area was set aside so that the new lady of the house could grow herbs, something very new to Olav Petersen. The rest of the field was taken up by a local gardener, who with agreement could use the field more or less as he wished but in return would give twenty percent of the produce to the household, to use at any time they wished. This system worked well, much to everyone's satisfaction, and fresh good vegetables were being served with most meals.

Olav's life was now idyllic, he spent most evening with his young attractive bride, of which she was prepared to sacrifice Monday, Wednesday and Saturday sharing the marital bed, after all that was her duty. Of course now they were a married couple, sex for Elsa was of secondary thoughts, her own personal status and standing within the community became paramount, and that had leapt up in leaps and bounds. Everyone she passed now doffed their caps, offering respect to her, and did Elsa play the queen to the full, you bet she did!

Before marrying Olav, Elsa was a nobody albeit a good looking nobody, now a married wealthy lady, that was all that was needed and in the eyes of her kinfolk she had become, a respected and respectable lady one that was worthy of an odd scrape and bow.

Olav's days were spent very productively, either working on accounts of his business back in Reykjavik, or doing civic duties there in Hilversum where he was thought of as next to royalty. In fact the couple were so highly prized within the town that Olav was selected to meet the king when he visited. To Elsa this was the ultimate prize, all her Christmas's had arrived in one little visit.

No babies appeared even though Olav tried desperately hard to achieve what was now his goal in life, an heir to his kingdom. Elsa too, was disappointed with the fact that she hadn't produced, and soon became increasingly frustrated with this annoying turn of events. It got to a stage that Elsa thought of nothing else, her household duties were being neglected as her prevailing thoughts were about babies. They had just celebrated their second wedding anniversary, and still no offspring had come forth, so Elsa now insisted that he perform his marital duty every night, though immediately afterwards she would disappear to what had quickly become her own bedroom three doors down the corridor. This had become a very unpleasant routine, one they both would sooner have done without, but they both wanted children, and what other way was there to achieve this, only through intercourse.

Part of the problem was that Olav was now very obese, his great love in life had become the various bountiful repasts that he ate every single day, and the selection was enormous, so Olav had gotten to like just about everything that could be consumed through his mouth. Not just eating, his drinking habits had become more pronounced as well, and subsequently always managed to drink a bottle or two of good French red wine, plus after each meal some port and brandy as this would help the food lay in his ever expanding stomach.

His nightly performance soon became more and more laboured, but to give Olav his due he always gave it his best shot even though it cost him a flushed complexion and a pounding heart.

One Saturday night, in fact it was the twenty-first of July, an extraordinarily hot night, extremely close with a very high humidity, once again Olav was asked to perform his duty. He struggled to even get out of his clothing let alone leap onto the bed and perform feats of wondrous delights upon his bride. She lay on the bed completely naked, bored at the thought of what was to come, she opened her legs and was watching a spider cross the ceiling and wondered if she should in fact get up and kill this intruder.

Olav finally got onto the bed, he was panting hard, sweat was pouring from all over his body, and the smell of his perspiration was quite unpleasant to the delicate nose of Elsa, this made her wince and try hard to only breath through her mouth. Olav was fumbling frantically with his member, he just couldn't raise an erection.

"Else, for gods sake help me to get a hard on. Stop looking at whatever it is up there on the ceiling, or shall we just forget tonight's actions?"

"O, give it here."

She grabbed at his penis quite hard, and yanked it so much that he cried out in pain. Realising that she had gone to far, she tried another tact. Elsa bent down to where he was laying on the bed, then she touched him gently around his genitalia, caressing his gonads, and then surprising herself she bent further forward and pushed his penis into her mouth. This was a shock and delight to Olav, but quite repulsed poor Elsa, but it did the trick and before a few seconds had passed he was as erect as he would ever be.

She lay back still with the horrible thought of what she had just done, and the taste of rather cheesy things lay in her mind as he now having acquired a second wind decided that this was going to be the performance that would top everything.

Olav pumped and pumped at his wife, he thrust as far in as he could possibly go, moving like a young man, one a third of his age. Sweat was now streaming from him, which made Elsa wet too, his face was a dark crimson in colour and still he thrust in and out, then after less than five minutes, Olav was fit to burst. Now his colour had gone from crimson to almost black. In out, in out, all the time pumping hard. Then it happened, he started to ejaculate. There came an awful UGGGG sound from his mouth along with an incredible amount of spittle. He was ejecting the biggest amount of semen that he had ever done before. His whole body was jerking on top of her, then he collapsed in a heap with a huge sigh. They both lay there in a state of complete exhaustion, anyway, Elsa did.

After what seemed an eternity Elsa now recovering said,

"Olav, get off me, I cannot breath. Olav get off. Olav!"

But Olav couldn't move, he was dead.

And as the local coroner said later at the inquest.

"I pronounce that this man died of a massive heart attack brought on by his excess of weight brought on by an over indulgence in food and drink. He over luxuriated in his eating habits, always a bad thing to do. But as we have heard from Mrs. Petersen, there was this final excessive strenuous sexual activity. It is fair to say that Olav Petersen came and went at the same time!"

I didn't make Elsa laugh, she just turned a deep shade of red, but to the onlookers, this statement might have been thought up as a joke to end all jokes. Sadly this had been the intention of the coroner as he actually didn't like this intruding Icelander who had bought his way into the hearts of the community, or so he wished to believe.

5

Elsa was now a widow, and only thirty six tender years of age. Too young to take permanently to black, but old enough to know that she now had serious responsibilities, one's she was not entirely sure she was capable of handling.

Her father very quickly became her adviser.

"Darling girl, we are all sad about Olav, he seemed a decent man and he treated you well. But, several weeks have passed and we must get all your affairs in order. There are taxes to pay, and we know darned well that the government won't wait long for their money. Firstly we must contact Iceland and the manager that has been put in charge of the fleet. Do you even know his name?"

Elsa went to the bureau that held all of the papers, shuffled through them and came up with a name.

"His name is Jon Johnson. Here is the address to contact him. I don't suppose he even knows that poor Olav is dead. What say we take a trip to this land of ice and lava?"

She looked at her father for some sort of guidance, but he was deep in thought. Elsa too was deep in thought, thinking that once again she wasn't pregnant, sadly she felt her period coming on. She excused herself and went to the bathroom.

When she returned her father was still in thought, then as if a light bulb had been turned on above his head, a eureka moment happened.

"We will have to take a trip to this, err...Reykjavik place. Maybe we can take your mother too and make some sort of holiday out of it. What do you think? It could be fun going to a new country, one that none of us know anything about, and then apart from getting the business sorted out we can spend time seeing the countryside, if it's worth seeing?"

He sat down in the captain's chair with its plush leather arms and swivelled it around so as to face his daughter.

"Have you checked with the bank yet? Is your money still arriving from this strange land? One thing about Olav, he should have left you well catered for."

Two weeks passed like a beat of the heart. Elsa was now taking to her role as the Captain of the ship with great strength of willpower. The bank which received the monies from Iceland had been less than helpful, and it was suspected that the manager was colluding with others to siphon off some of Peterson's money for his own uses.

He had totally underestimated Elsa's resolve and tenacity, she saw through him immediately and forced with the help of a lawyer from Amsterdam to have an immediate audit done on the bank, and the withdrawal of monies by various members of the bank. The audit showed that there had been several dips into the Peterson's funds and that they stemmed back to the manager and his number one.

After threatening them with possible prison, all the money plus interest and expenses were forthcoming from both the perpetrators. Once the money was safely secured back into the account, the lawyer being a very shrewd and wise judge of character, immediately informed both the main bank in Rotterdam, then the police in Hilversum. Both men were sacked by the bank then arrested by the police. Elsa was beginning to enjoy her new found powers.

The passage to Iceland by ship was not going to be easy, being a Danish colony meant that they had to take a ferry to Hamburg in Germany from Hook van Holland, and then another one to Esbjerg in Denmark, then change and get a boat to, first the Faroe Islands, then Reykjavik in Iceland.

The journey just to Hamburg took two whole days, and though the ship was comfortable and new, it rocked badly during rough seas. Then the journey onward was with a Danish ferry direct to Esbjerg. Again a modern screw and sail vessel, but oh so painfully slow. Though, it now only late September, storms seemed to be the norm in the seas, and the small trip which should have taken less than twenty-six hours took nearly three and a half days, all of which consisted of rough stormy seas that confined all the passengers to their respective cabins.

When they finally got to Esbjerg, tired and somewhat emaciated from lack of food, they realised that they had missed their connection onwards to their goal. They would now have to wait another four days before the next ferry departed, and that would happen only if the weather conditions were right. But to Elsa and her mother, this was a blessing in disguise. They quickly found a nice hotel to, rest, eat and drink, but mainly to recover from the seasickness that they all had suffered from. But resting soon build them up for the next part of their, what was now turning into an epic adventure.

By the next day they had once again found their balance for walking on the land. They had slept, eaten well, drank loads of water, wine and anything else that was available, so as to re-hydrate themselves after their ordeal by confinement. Life now started to seem reasonably good once more, and just maybe possibly still worth living.

Esbjerg was a smallish fishing town with a population of roughly sixteen thousand souls. But its saving grace was that it did have a deep water harbour plus a mole that stretched out into the sea making a barrier from the North Seas inclement weather. It was a safe haven for ferries, cargo vessels and fishing boats to dock, thus it became an important exit and entry point for travellers who wished to visit Danish colonies in the North Sea.

There was also a fine example of a bog standard Napoleonic fort. It was better than most of the same because it was so heavily armed with cannon, far stronger than anywhere else in Scandinavia. But now it lay in ruins, un-manned and un-wanted, except for stay animals and birds that had discovered their perfect home, made by man, abandoned by man, but used gratefully by creatures.

The houses were well built with fine neat brickwork, often with patterned designs in various colours, but the roofing tiles were always of red, giving a very neat and tidy colourful experience to any strangers to the town. It had a daily farmers market in the town square, this brought in a great deal of trade and money for the local council to improve things as they saw fit, and they did see fit. Though not a large place, it was vibrant, yet somehow sleepy too. It exuded peace and tranquillity, yet trade came and went making Esbjerg a jolly place to be stuck in for a few days.

Elsa and her father and mother enjoyed their stay, they spent money buying new clothes and bits and pieces to take back to their native Holland when they came back on their return journey.

Eventually the day came that they would have to brave the North Sea once more, all three of them were reticent about getting on board yet again, even though the weather forecast was reasonable. In fact the sun was shining when they alighted up the boarding ramp. The sea was calm and all looked well with the world. The ferry was an early wooden steam powered side paddle, with just one very tall smoke stack smack in the middle of the ship. The capacity for passengers was only one hundred, with most sharing rooms, or canvas bunks below. She was built primarily to tote freight, so now she spent most of the day disgorging, then reloading new items of cargo for the stations that they would be visiting.

All the first class cabins were on the outside of the upper deck, and woe betide anyone who didn't watch the weather carefully, as getting out of ones cabin and walking along the gangway even with its safety rails placed at various height so people could hang on, was decidedly dangerous. There were always accidents where passengers were swept overboard dressed in all their finery, as they were going to dine or enjoy the entertainment that might be on offer, but in many cases never made that last journey having been swept over the side of the vessel, thus to become yet more food for hungry fish. There had been several litigations against the ferry company for incompetence concerning the loss of passengers, but nothing much had been done to change the situation, there was still that dangerous outside gangway.

But the cabins were spacious and extraordinarily comfortable, giving luxury where it was not expected.

As the sun started to set in the west behind the ship on the landward side, Elsa looked over the safety rail and sighed.

'How beautiful all this is, if the weather stays clement I shall endeavour to enjoy this stretch of our journey.'

A little while later the dinner gong sounded, and all passengers were called to take in a fine repast. This was in a small room, but capable of dining all the first class passengers with consummate ease and comfort. Below, on a lower deck were all other passengers, they dined in a smaller room that only comprised of long benches and bench seats to match.

As Elsa and her family dined, the food turned out to be ample and excellent, the sun was setting fast leaving a red tint shimmering on the ripples of waves that stretched for ever. Gulls were circling overhead, probably thinking that this was yet another fishing vessel. The engines gave a throbbing which was so consistent in tempo it almost lulled all on board into a dreamlike state. So the ship departed Esbjerg for the Faroe Islands and yet another new country to explore.

Next morning Elsa was woken by a shudder which knocked her from one side of the bunk to another. Startled and confused she got into her dressing gown and went to the door, on opening it she realised that though the wind had picked up a little it was still comparatively calm in North Sea standards. It was sunny and extremely fresh, the wind that touched her face was not cold, but she knew that autumn would quickly be turning into winter. On the swell of the sea, the ship rocked very gently, but there were white horses on some of the waves albeit small foals, but their dances was a fascination to any onlookers.

With imagination an observer could have thought that they were watching a performance of Swan Lake, because those small waves with their small white horses had a delicate beauty all of their own, yes it even reminded Elsa of a scene from the ballet of Swan Lake. Tchaikovsky would have been pleased by seeing this scene, hearing the rhythm of the engines tapping out the tempo of his wonderful music to the ballet.

She smiled to herself, shivered slightly, then went back into her cabin and looked at her fob watch. Seven-eighteen, still time to have some more sleep before having breakfast which would be rung just after eight-thirty. She lay on her bunk bed and looked up at the ceiling, there unnoticed before was a mural of ships out at sea. It took up about a metre square, and was obviously done by an artist of some little renown, this particular artist forgot to put in some perspective to the painting, and sadly some of the colours had faded quite badly. But so much was crammed into this small but interesting piece of folk art, many ships, masses of vessels were scurrying here there and everywhere, small boats, fishing boats, large warships and speeding passenger vessels all doing their thing within a very small existence.

'Do all the cabins have these sorts of paintings above the sleeping quarters? I will have to find out about this. This is quite crazy, why didn't I notice this before, after all I slept right underneath this mural. God, I must have been extremely tired last night.'

When see looked very closely at the work of art, she noticed a small signature in the bottom right had side of the scene. It was sighed Edvard Munch with a pencil date of 1882 printed below the signature. Elsa liked the offering but thought that the said artist needed some clear understanding of perspective if he was to get anywhere.

She couldn't get back to her slumbering dreamlike state, so instead she used the cupboard toilet, then washed herself thoroughly, dressed and went down to await her parents and breakfast. When she asked a steward about the painting in her cabin, he denied any knowledge of it, plus assured her that none of the other cabins would have such a thing.

The ship was ponderously slow and it took another twenty-eight hours before they sighted the huge rock outcrop that went to make up part of the Faroe Islands. As they closed in on the islands, the first thing that one noticed was the smell. Fish, the aroma of fish oil hung in the air far out to sea. Whaling and fishing for cod, herring and red snappers was the basic reason why these small set of islands were occupied by the past Viking Danes.

The language the Faroese spoke was a dialect of the old Viking language, and when you saw the square jawed inhabitants, one felt you had stepped back one thousand year in time, no stranger would have been surprised to see men wearing animals cloths and carrying spears, swords and shields, they were Vikings albeit a bit more affable. As they entered the small busy harbour, full of fishing vessels big and small. It was a difficult job for the paddle steamer to manoeuvre and come to rest at the dockside. Within seconds of landing people were starting to unload the cargo that had been brought, some passengers alighted, but that was just a handful of the ordinary steerage customers, not a single first class even went near the gangplank.

Elsa was fascinated by what she was witnessing, the hustle and bustle was excessive to the extreme, and it was as if one's life depended on a quick getaway the way people rushed hither and dither, all fleeing some unacknowledged terror lurking there to startle one. Elsa shook her head which brought her back into reality from her fantasy thoughts. She smiled a knowing smile, one that said dreams are there to trick the mind.

She looked up at the cliffs which gently sloped up on all sides. Most had wooden frames, a sort of 'A' frame that stretched as far as the eye could see, on these frames hung fish, hundreds of thousands of fish all drying.

'That accounts for the awful smell.'

But what Elsa couldn't see was the bay that housed the whaling fleet. It was the smell of whale meat and guts that Elsa and the other passengers smelt and this odour stung the back of their collective throats.

Torshavn, which was what the capital was called, housed roughly ninety-five percent of the forty thousand inhabitants. The squalor was clear to see all around, dirty muddy streets running hickle-dee-pickle-dee, with no sense of order about the layout of the road system what-so-ever, no thought had ever been made to this hamlet being a capital city. There were some brick and stone buildings, but one would assume that they were made for the Danish colonials, and that included a huge building in granite that was almost certainly the administrative centre of the islands.

The houses that seemed to be for the indigenous peoples were themselves mainly made from mud and wattle, with very little design or finesse. What Elsa and the other passengers that stayed on the ship didn't see was the finely carved wooden churches, many dating back to their Viking past. In fact had the passengers taken the trouble, they could have seem many fine dwelling places, many fine brick and stone buildings, often built with great care, with fine wooden carvings and sculptured stonework. And had they really taken the trouble with time to do a tour of this main island, and they would have seen the finest views that any of them were ever likely to see.

Striking to Elsa was that firstly the native people where square headed large people, strong through hard toil, but most looked like they had never washed since being born. The men all seemed to wear waterproofs made from some animal hide, probably walrus or whale or even shark skin. Elsa didn't know and really didn't care either, she had already made up her mind that this was obviously the nearest place to hell. The women all seemed to be large very fat ladies, most of which smoke through the normal clay pipes. Again, like their men folk, they could do with some serious cleansing, and then maybe sport a good hairdressing salon, though of course there wasn't anything like that outside of Denmark.

After what seemed an eternity to Elsa, but was roughly six hours, the vessel was once again ready to continue its journey, this last leg to Reykjavik. Elsa hoped dearly that the Icelandic capital was going to be an improvement on Torshavn.

The weather was still quite buoyant considering it was now coming on to winter, the nights were drawing in fast, darkness now fell at six o'clock, and next week it would be less, till early December it would be dark more or less twenty-four hours in a day. All you could expect was just a gloomy sort of light around midday for about an hour. Not the best time to be travelling northward, this was now the time for storms, something Elsa and her family hadn't taken into consideration, but so far they had been lucky. The sea was calm, it typified that awful feeling that this was the calm before the storm, but being calm the paddle steamer made better time than normal. The captain was a shrewd judge, better to burn more coal and get there early than be caught in a frightful North Sea storm and maybe not get there at all.

That night Elsa dined well on a variety of fish, locally caught, not that that information would have made any difference to the way most of the passengers having now completely prejudiced themselves against the last stop at Torshavn.

After the meal an Icelandic gentleman produced a concertina which he had recently acquired in Liverpool. As he was a fine pianist, playing this contraption came easy to him. At first he started playing some Icelandic songs which he also sang to, but they were somewhat dour in wording and melody and as nobody really cared for them, he was persuaded to play some modern songs from around Europe which he had leant. The evening went well, everyone was enjoying themselves immensely, that was until the vessel shuddered badly making everyone either fall out of the chairs, drop their drinks or go flying across the floor. This was the third time that this had happened since leaving Esbjerg, but this one was the worst yet.

Elsa's father Koos decided to find out what was going on? Was there some sort of problem with the ship, or was this some natural occurrence, a freak event of nature, but something that was explainable to everyone? The only way to find out what was going on was to invite the captain to explain.

The man was summoned and duly came.

"Captain, I know you are a busy man, but on at least three different occasions this ship has been lifted almost as high as itself and then thrown back down again with a crash. But as far as I am aware it was on just the one crash on each occasion. Can you explain to us what is happening please? Is there something wrong with your ship, or is it a natural event, something that happens on a regular basis, but something we don't know about?"

Koos sat down and waited for a chance to answer. The captain was smiling in a gentle way, there were no worried frowns that could be seen on his brow.

"It is all perfectly natural sir!"

He was actually enjoying the occasion, a chance to inform people something about the sea in this part of the ocean.

"We have experienced several movements of landmass under the sea. These are small earthquakes and they are happening all the time within this sector of the ocean. Iceland and the surrounding sea is a vast volcanic area, so quite often another quake is triggered, and the movement causes big waves that seem to travel for ever, but they are usually just the one wave that is until the next quake. There is nothing to fear here, it is not like travelling in the Pacific regions were huge earthquakes can cause waves that tear into ships and land alike killing many. No sir, there is absolutely nothing to fret about. The size of the waves in this region might cause sea sickness, but not death, well not very often."

He smiled broadly leaving the listening passengers wondering whether he was jesting or what?

"This ship is quite capable of handling what the North Sea has to throw at it."

He smiled again, a warm reassuring smile that left everyone feeling relaxed.

"Now if you will excuse me, I must get back to my bridge, I have a steaming hot mug of cocoa awaiting my pleasure."

At the thought of the captain being held back from his hot beverage caused a ripple of laughter amongst the assembled passengers.

After another hour of supposed merriment, Elsa retired to her cabin. She lay on her bunk and contemplated the painting above her head, she was beginning to appreciate it much better.

'This Munch fellow might have something after all, though the work is crammed full almost to the point of bursting, it never the less is very thought provoking. Yes, I think I like it.'

As the vessel had managed to pick up speed from the calmness of the sea, it was late the next night that it berthed at the dockside in Reykjavik. No one was expected to leave the ship, but to sleep peacefully through the night and alight in the morning, after all the ship was many hours early.

But Elsa couldn't sleep, she was somewhat excited about the land of her dead husband. She now wanted and needed to experience what he had once loved.

Her marriage hadn't been a raging romantic success, but since Olav's demise, it had seemed to have developed into a more satisfactory arrangement than the truth and reality would have dictated. As the time progressed so did Elsa's imagination concerning her departed. She now tended to see him as something much more special than before he had died, not that she had been unhappy with him, well not really unhappy. The truth is, if she really had cared to find it, was that the age gap had actually made a difference, but that was something for others to speculate about, she closed her eyes and mind to such thoughts.

Now as each day passed, Olav's image was that of a devoted husband and a wonderful provider, both being quite true. What was not exactly correct were the feelings that were returned to the Icelander from this Dutch lady, she hadn't been a bad wife, she had never had affairs with other men, she hadn't been unfaithful in deed or thought, she had just not been able to give what they both wanted and needed. After all, she was someone that had supposedly everything, but yet again not the real thing that she wanted, so just like Olav, Elsa went without. Had Elsa managed to be honest with herself she would have realised what had been missing from their union, that would have been passion. Neither had really experienced this with the other, they had both just marked time in their marriage, albeit a pleasant marking of time.

She stood on the gangway aisle just outside of her cabin, she looked onto the flickering gas and oil lights of the town, and of course that smell once again. This was the first thing to impact on her senses. Rotting fish, drying fish, every sort of fish smell under the stars. At first she retched slightly, but still managed to hold back from actually being sick.

After some minutes another smell was prevalent almost above the aroma of fish, it was the smell of bad eggs, or as it was, sulphur from the water that permeated up through the ground rocks by the thermal working of the molten lava that was the basis of what Iceland laid upon. Not that Elsa knew any of these things.

The occasional worker could be seen scurrying around doing whatever workers do. Fishing vessels were coming and going, which caused a great deal of noise in the distance.

'Strange' thought Elsa, 'It is late into the evening and pitch black with no moon to give light, but there are so many people milling around. Wow, it's as if nobody sleeps in this town, so much hustle and bustle.'

Elsa turned her attention to several fishing boats leaving from further down the quayside, they were much nearer to the town centre.

'I wonder if they belong to me.'

And with that thought mulling through her brain, she went back to bed.

A few hours later, as the gloom of the new day decided to shine down upon the ship, the captain blew his whistle so as to make sure all passengers had their breakfast and for the last time alighted the vessel.

Elsa and her parents had finished packing their trunks and were wondering if the companies agent would actually be there at the dockside to meet them. They needn't have worried, he was in fact eating breakfast along with the ships master whom he knew very well.

As soon as the trio walked into the dining area, Jon Johnson stood up to acknowledge his actual employer. He was a tall blond haired man of early forties, slim in build but extremely muscular. He had a certain rugged handsomeness that showed through a very deep lined face.

Jon bowed graciously to Elsa then her mother and then held out his hand to her father. Then speaking in very good English he said,

"Welcome to Iceland Mrs. Peterson, you have brought fine weather with you."

He smiled and offered seats to them all. Then without waiting to be asked sat down again himself and continued to finish his breakfast of smoked cod pieces, which he took and dipped in a sort of yogurt, which was locally known as skyre.

Elsa looked at him eating away merrily and wondered just what sort of man has the manners to stand when a lady approaches, but then immediately sit back down and eat like a pig within a trough? The noise coming from him as he munched his way through dried fish was quite disgusting to her senses, but it hadn't gone unnoticed that the man did have a certain charm as well.

"Mr. Johnson! Please, can you refrain from gnarling your way through that poor dead fish just long enough for us to speak to one another?"

Jon was shaken by this sudden attack on him, but not as surprised as Elsa who had just said it.

"I am sorry Mrs. Peterson,"

Jon retorted in a manner that sounded like a bewildered child.

"But to tell you the truth I have been working all night long on company business matters, and my friend the captain here invited me to join him in partaking of breakfast, and it seemed a perfect chance to catch up on my eating as I was very hungry. We didn't expect you for some time. Please except my apologies."

He then carried on eating.

Elsa had not expected such an interesting fellow to be part of the work force, and she was also very surprised to hear how well he spoke English, much better than she or her parents did.

She finally smiled at him trying to release all the tensions that had so quickly built up.

"Tell me where did you learn to speak such good English?"

"It's obvious that Olav never told you anything about me. I am a second or third cousin to your late husband, and he put me through university, and while at that place of learning I went into a course of modern European languages, specialising in English. I owed Olav a great debt of gratitude, and now I am your servant."

He smiled deeply showing a set of broken teeth. This finally put Elsa off any romantic thoughts even though she wasn't aware that she had had any.

"So, have you made provision for us in a reasonable hotel?"

"Yes indeed I have,"

He said as if this was a wonderful achievement.

"You will all be staying at a new stone built hotel called Hotel Gotherfoss. It is not far away, just about in the centre of Reykjavik, close to a vast lake called Tchurnin. It has twenty rooms, and I have reserved two of the best for you and your parents. I am sure it will meet with your approval."

Now Jon had abandoned any further attempts at finishing his repast, he was once again resigned to work. Now his mindset was once again entirely focussed on his duty to his employer.

"Would you like to go there straight away?"

"Yes Mr. Johnson, I think that would be best. Then I suggest that you go and get some sleep, then come for us, say three this afternoon and take us to the offices where I would like to meet the staff. Is that meeting with your approval?"

"Of course Mrs. Peterson, anything you wish is what I am here for."

Jon quickly stumbled in his sentence as another thought crossed his mind.

"I have a request to ask, could you call me Jon and I you Elsa?"

"No Mr. Johnson, I think not. I am Mrs. Peterson and you are Mr. Johnson, I will not tolerate informality, is that perfectly understood?"

"Er. Yes madam, er, Mrs. Peterson. I will arrange for your bags to be brought be a porter."

He was now completely red faced and physically shocked by Elsa's response to him. But now at least he knew where things stood.

"Shall we go?"

He then turned to shake his friend the captain's hand.

"See you around Michael, have a safe journey back, and thanks for the bottles of beer."

The captain smiled broadly, and then answered,

"You are more than welcome Jon, take care of yourself."

He then turned to Elsa.

"I hope you found everything in order, and I hope the journey hasn't been too arduous for you?"

Then before anyone could answer, he continued,

"I expect to see you all on your return trip. Goodbye."

Then without waiting for any response he turned on his heels and walked away leaving them open mouthed and somewhat flabbergasted.

He had understood that Jon had only tried to be friendly, yet somehow these rather stupid people, and in particular Elsa, had rebuffed a man who was incredibly honest and fair, he hadn't liked Elsa for her abruptness and he made sure it showed.

'Oh dear,' thought Elsa, 'this hasn't been a good start!'

6

They all clambered down the gangplank, of which one side was open to the sea. This worried Elsa very much as she couldn't swim. She looked down into the cold dirty looking water, she then wished she had not looked, it was full of dead bits of fish, giving a very smelly brownish oily sheen to the surface. This brine was most definitely something one didn't want to fall into.

Elsa hesitated at the top even though it was at least four feet wide and she could have just held onto the rails on the left hand side. She watched as Angnita and Koos, her parents walked down it in a very casual way, unafraid and aware that falling into the brine would be at very least, extremely unpleasant. Jon Johnson saw immediately that Elsa was unsure of her footing, so he hurried to her assistance, taking her arm before she could protest he led her down the gangway to safety, depositing her on terra firma. Being extremely polite he was quick to smile warmly at her, in the most disarming manner that he could conjure up.

On the muddy cinder track that constituted as a road, was a tired looking pony with long mangy brownish hair and looking somewhat emaciated from lack of decent nourishment. It was tethered to a trap just big enough for the four of them plus the driver, the luggage would follow just behind them, placed in a rickety old handcart and an even rickety old Icelandic man who struggled to push it. The aged old Viking was Gunna Jackobssen a fifty-five year old retainer who was always there to assist in any way that would make him a few Icelandic Kroner. He was bent almost double giving him the look more like an eighty year old person that his meagre fifty-five, this bent posture was only exacerbated by the simple fact that he stood no more than five feet tall, and that was when he managed to stand erect. He had little hair, what he did have was silver in colour and threadbare showing huge bald areas that to the onlooker shone like a mirror. His face had so many wrinkles it had the appearance of a world map of roadways, and what's more it glistened as the morning light reflected upon his countenance, only then could one see that underneath all that aging, there was still a twinkle in his eye that showed kindness and a willing to be helpful, even though he was prematurely old and wizened. His clothing seemed to all who observed Gunna that it had never ever left his body, and this confused the guests as they couldn't recognise the material that it was originally made from, like his face it glistened in the sunlight. Strangely though, everyone wanted to assist him, possibly even take the load upon themselves, which might well have been Gunna Jackobssen's idea in the first place. Sadly for Gunna on this occasion no one came to his aid, he just had to achieve the awkward walk all by himself.

It really wasn't far to the hotel, just about two thirds of a mile, but it was pretty well up hill all the way, and the Icelandic pony agonised under the effort that its small frame had to contend with. The baggage would have an even tougher journey, with old man Gunna puffing and panting, stopping and starting every couple of minutes.

Elsa and her parents spoke about what they were witnessing concerning the town of Reykjavik. They noticed that there were very few houses or buildings that were built of stone, brick houses seemed to be unheard of, most dwelling places were made of wood, with wooden slatted roofs. Again this seemed somewhat weird to Elsa as she had already understood that there were very few trees on the island, and which meant everything had to be imported to Iceland. All were painted red in colour, and when Elsa asked Jon why they were all red, he laughed and jokingly said,

"That is because that was the only paint colour that came to this country, importers wanted various colours, but whom ever they asked obviously only wanted to sell them red. The supplier probably had too much."

Elsa wasn't at all sure if it was the truth or not, but didn't try to pursue the matter any further.

The people were quite drab in their manner of dress, very much in the same ilk as the Faroe Islanders. The men seemed destined to wear baggy untidy, dirty looking oilskin clothes, somewhat like the Faroe men. Strange though every now and again a suited gentleman was seen scurrying around showing that there were indeed white collar workers. In contrast the women looked beautiful. Their long blond flowing hair, with bright white faces, some dressed in black national costume but some also sporting a more colourful display of fashion. The family also noticed that there were many cats around, but no dogs. When Elsa inquired as to why that was so, the answer came readily from John.

"The cats are tolerated because we are plagued with rats and mice, all coming from foreign vessels that dock here in Iceland. Dogs are only allowed in the far off hinterland, here in our towns and this particular metropolis we found that they got underfoot and also terrorised the sheep. Of course the other factor that went against dogs, was they are always defecating, usually where most people walk. Most just got eaten, and very good they tasted too."

Elsa cringed at the very thought of eating dog meat, but again said nothing.

Eventually they reached what appeared to be a newish building, and as stated by Jon, built from imported granite stone. It was a four storey building which against all the wooden dwelling places looked incredibly impressive. Inside the foyer, Elsa was pleased to see a comfortable looking establishment, one that didn't disappoint. The rooms were clean, bright and airy. Someone had gone to the trouble of spraying rosewater around so as to lessen the smell of sulphur in the very water that was drunk or used to wash in.

Each room had its own water closet with a flushing cistern that took the effluence somewhere away from the room, this impressed Elsa immensely. She now saw that the story of the paint was in fact not true, as her room had a clean brown colour painted on the woodwork, this made her smile. But the most impressive fact was that there was new highly patterned wallpaper hanging beautifully on the four walls, making the entire room seem so warm and cosy. Yes, she liked this place.

Elsa didn't have a clue as to how long they would be staying in this cold unforgiving country. What with its earthquakes, volcanoes, snow, wind, rain and darkness, the very things that made her wonder how anyone could live in such an environment.

All she knew was that she must find out about the business, make sure that the death duties were paid, and that she wasn't being swindled in any way. It might take days, or it might take weeks, but it would all be complete before they left for the home comforts of Hilversum again.

While standing at the window looking out towards Lake Tchurnin, there was a sharp rap at the door, but before she could say a word, it was opened and the old man Gu8nna bustled in mumbling under his breath with her trunks. Elsa watched with utter amazement that this aged gentleman should have just barged in, but she said nothing, instead gave him some coins of Dutch origin, not knowing whether they were going to be any use here in Iceland. The old man, bright red in the face and panting with exhaustion, looked at them, turned them over, bit one of them and put them in his waistcoat pocket, and then walked out without actually saying anything to her, just that general mumbling under his breath.

Elsa, smiled as he departed closing the door after himself, then she burst out laughing, after which fatigue overtook her and she decided that she would have a slight nap, then find some lunch.

She lay on top of what turned out to be a very comfortable eider duck feather down bed, and immediately fell into a dreamless sleep. She was awoken a couple of hours later by Koos her father knocking gently on the door.

"Sweetheart, your mother and I are extremely hungry having had no breakfast. Please can we all go down and find somewhere and something to eat?"

"Oh, mmm, hello dad!"

Elsa yawned deeply; she was still half asleep but hardly half awake.

"Yes dad! Just give me a minute to get myself together and we will go down together."

The three of them soon found themselves in the restaurant area of the hotel, there was no one else being served or even in the place at all, but unperturbed they sat themselves down. Within a minute, after coughing loudly to attract some sort of attention, out came from what was obviously the kitchen a waiter with a white tea towel wrapped around his middle. He pointed to a large wall clock trying to indicate that they were either too late or too early for any food. But Elsa was insistent, telling him to get the manager who at least spoke English.

"What seems to be the trouble madam?"

The manager was smiling broadly trying hard to defuse a possible situation.

"Please inform your chef that we desire some food, we haven't eaten since late last night, and strangely enough that tends to make us hungry. I don't wish to complain, but this is a hotel for guests, we are said guests, and please tell me if I'm wrong, but aren't the guests supposed always to be right?"

The smile left the managers countenance. He thought for a moment, then looked pointedly at the unfortunate waiter, then babbled something in Icelandic to him. Immediately the luckless waiter ran as fast as his long lanky legs could carry him to the kitchen area. He returned a couple of minutes later, this time with a grin on his face. He spoke once more to the manager, who in turn translated the account to his guests.

"It seems madam that the kitchen in fact had actually closed. But having said that the chef is there and prepared to rustle up some lunch for you all. It will take roughly twenty minutes, but I am sure you will enjoy it. The dish is boiled smoked lamb, it comes with potatoes which are grown here just outside of Reykjavik. Yes madam, I am very sure you will all enjoy the meal."

There was a pause, then quietly the manager concluded by adding,

"Can I be of any further service to you?"

"No, and thank you for your cooperation, I am sure we will love your food."

But the reply had been said with any great conviction.

In due course the meal arrived, the trio looked long and hard at the food. A whole leg of lamb came on a platter, along with what can only be described as purple potatoes. Elsa's father carved the lamb, but looked very hard once again at it. It looked as if it was going mouldy, there were streaks of discolouration running all the way through the meat, and the aroma of the smoked then boiled leg had a very off smell.

Elsa was the first to speak.

"I could get the manager back if you wanted father, or we could just try it and see? What do you think?"

"Mmm. I really don't fancy disturbing the manager once again. One never knows how we will be treated in the future if we keep going on complaining."

He picked up a small piece of the meat, smelt it again, then smiled and said,

"I dare you both, let's give it a whirl, who knows we might just like it."

He then put the piece into his open mouth.

"My goodness! You know what! I do like it, though I have never tasted lamb like this before. Come on get stuck in."

All three of them liked the lamb even though it looked and smelt like it was going bad, but the potatoes were another thing, they hardly looked like any potato they had ever seen before. They were small and pretty well completely purple in colour, and they tasted just like they looked, rather drab and definitely off colour. Overall though, the meal was a success and sated their appetites. All three smiled and felt somewhat foolish for even giving the meal a second glance, always try before you judge!

They finished when Jon came to pick up Elsa to start the tour of inspection. This was her time now, now she would be in a position to see just how prosperous she was, though she seriously hoped that things were only going to improve. Elsa knew that she had been too abrupt and rather unfriendly to Jon, but she hoped that would soon be in the past. Jon greeted her and the family with cordial wariness, he had had time to think about this young lady, and his first impression had become one of slight suspicion and apprehension.

'Had she come all this way just to sell to some foreigner, or had she come just to interfere?'

These were his underlying thoughts, he was now cautious as to how he should approach his employer. His approach in the first instance was of a friendly close friend, but his smiles and warmth had been seriously rebuffed, he now wasn't at all sure how to play it. So he had picked the line of least resistance and plumped for wary alertness. Somehow he must over the next few days assess the state of play concerning the business, after all he had helped build up the business with Olav Peterson, and yet with all his hard work and efforts, he actually had no stake in it at all, just a reasonable salary. Now that did worry him!

"I am going to take you down to the fish market first, which is where we have our office. You will meet the five office staff working there. It is their job just to run the actual North Sea fishing side of the business."

He shuffled from one foot to the other as he noticed that her attention was completely focussed on him, in his mind she had the eyes of a hawk, completely alert.

"Then Mrs. Peterson, I shall take you down to the whaling bay, which is about one and a half miles north-east on this side of the docks. It is purposely kept away from the centre of town as the smell can be somewhat overpowering. If you would like to get into the buggy I shall have the driver take us to the office."

Jon ordered the driver to get yet another sad looking pony to move down the hill towards the dockyard and the fish market. Elsa had been careful to take a posy nosegay, saturated in not too expensive perfume, this she now held close to her nose.

As the horse trundled down the cinder muddy roadway, it kicked up mud which some came back on the three passengers. There was no disguising the aroma of filth as it had mastered the art of permeating through all clothing, no matter what one wore. There was no escaping the fact that one was going to smell of fish oil, it was everywhere and on everything. By now though Elsa had resolved herself to that smell, and also being covered in slimy oily mud, making her look as scruffy and unkempt as everyone else. In fact as she surveyed the scene around her, she smiled at the very prospect of being taken for just another dirty looking local, albeit she was the only one carrying a scented posy up to her nose.

The road was busy, and it didn't go unnoticed to Elsa that people were extremely interested in watching her carriage go by. Iceland is a small island in terms of population, only four hundred thousand souls. Originally their descendents had come from Norway, thus they were of Viking stock.

It was taught through the writings of ancient Sagas, which were preserved throughout the distance of time, that Eric the Red, who's real name was Erik Thorvaldsen, found the new land and settled a new colony there. He named it Iceland so as to put off any further invasion of peoples from Norway or Sweden, Finland and Denmark. It is said that he also discovered Greenland, and named that new land thus, to tempt potential explorers or refugees with the idea of a lush garden of Eden instead of a rocky snow bound continent, frozen in time and reality.

Somehow the guise had worked, there hadn't been any invasion of peoples, and the new indigenous peoples had a chance to breed within themselves creating Icelandanders as apposed to Norwegian Vikings.

Over the last thousand years the population had become somewhat interbred, thus this made everyone more or less cousins, albeit a long way back.

Having said that, all the people were in some way related, but strangely there was no inbreeding, no degeneration of the line, no apparent genetic mutations from such close interbreeding. People were still compos mentis, no deformities other than perfectly natural ones through some problem within the birth itself. All in all, Icelandanders seemed to be a very stable well balanced nation of folk, peace loving and at ease with themselves.

Though having stated that sentence, things change in the dark winter nights, this is when drinking takes the place of common sense. There is, and always has been a high percentage of alcoholism, everyone knows it is down primarily to the constant darkness in winter time, it becomes very, very depressing, a sort of primeval latitude that created a complete indifference to life itself. When the darkness comes, so comes the suicides. It seemed that all northern countries around the globe have the same problems, to much drink, heavy depression often leading to a complete physical and mental breakdown, thus then suicide.

In those dark, cold winters, with the gales and snow and biting wet winds, drink often takes the place of everything else, it was quite normal to see town folk lying in the gutters all the worse for alcohol. It was a rather sad common occurrence to see a man or women dead in the road, having passed out through over indulgence and died from exposure.

Everyone knew who Elsa was, and many had been closely related to Olav, and equally as many owe their very livelihood to the continued existence of Peterson's Fishing and Whaling Company.

They reached the fish market within fifteen minutes, passing through the very centre of Reykjavik, Elsa was now quite excited about how many interesting buildings she now saw, many down in the very centre were of stone, many stone and wood, but all were in perfectly painted well preserved order, though to Elsa's astonishment everything was in the same old red colour.

She smiled and thought to herself.

'Maybe that story of the paint is true after all!'

The actual fish market was about one hundred yards long by fifty yards wide, it was in fact the longest and widest building in the whole of Iceland. Inside there were masses of fish sorting, gutting and drying areas, then at the back part of the building were ten small offices, of which one was the Peterson Fishing Cooperative. Why it was called a cooperative, no one really knew, except that in the early days, no catch from any fisherman was turned away, all were bought. But the business itself was entirely owed by Olav Peterson, and thus now his widow Elsa Peterson.

The five white collar workers all stood up as Elsa entered. They were dressed in white shirts and dark trousers, but the shirts had no collars, and were open at the front. All five men stood erect as if to attention, making Elsa realise that they had been primed carefully by Jon.

The manager introduced each one of the workers to their new employer, each bowed graciously, making Elsa smile inwardly to herself. As they passed from one to another Jon told his new master what each one did within the business. One was for buying, one for selling, one for dealing with the drying of the cod and the last two just for auditing and invoicing.

Elsa was impressed by the efficiency of the entire operation, but she still didn't have any facts or figures.

"So, Jon, how many fishing boats do we own?"

"You own!"

He was careful to make sure that he imparted the right tone of voice and correct procedure.

"Thirty-eight vessels, twenty of which are three man fishing boats with sails, ten much bigger vessels with sails, and they were carrying ten men each. Lastly, eight largish, you could call them ships, they have been converted to steam and sail and they are used for whaling. In many ways these ships are like floating factories, we catch the whale, gradually drag in on board, cut it up, extract the oils and either store the meat or render it down in large vats which can be boiled. But this fleet is getting smaller all the time, the animals are getting more and more scarce, hard to find and extremely hard to catch."

Once again he shuffled from foot to foot, which once again didn't go unnoticed to Elsa.

"The whaling fleet is old, in fact very old. Many of the ships are in a great deal of disrepair. I feel with some of them, they are so bad that we could expect a tragedy one of these days. I was always telling Olav that we should scrap many of them and get some iron ships made which would be better suited to the environmental problems of the sea. What we need Mrs. Peterson are proper screw driven ships, with the ability to do everything that is needed before heading back to port, in fact two ships would be enough as they would be approximately double the size of the old wooden fleet. It would take capital, lots of money, and unfortunately they couldn't be made here in Iceland, and probably the best place would be Scotland."

He paused and noticed that she was looking around as if not listening.

"I am sorry Mrs. Peterson, I am going on about a pet project of mine, and I realise that I shouldn't."

Her attention was at once again drawn back to what he was saying.

"Jon, I know absolutely nothing about the business. You are an expert, you know what is what, so help me to help the business. One thing I already know, we are going to keep Peterson Fishing Cooperative at the forefront of the industry. I am already very excited about what it is doing, and I hope with you we can see and maybe do, is to carry it forward to bigger and better things."

With that she smiled broadly at her manager. His thoughts were now of elation, and that was how he described what had been said to the other five workers who were there wondering about their own personal futures.

Now all of them were smiling and talking, Elsa and Jon in English, the others in Icelandic, all the Icelandanders now looked infinitely relieved.

It took another hour for Jon Johnson to show her all the workings of the market, and while they were there, as if planned, on cue came one of her smallest fishing smacks, three laughing Icelandic men, all with dirty features and three days of stubble on their faces landed a huge haul of cod and red snapper. Elsa watched fascinated as the boat was unloaded and the catch weighed and taken into the market for sorting. The three fishermen were quickly given some money and told to go home and have a two day break, then they could go out once more.

By now it was getting dark, and Elsa asked if they could postpone the trip to the whaling factory until the next day. She was very tired, dirty, covered in local mud, oil and fish parts, she looked and stunk just like the local women that were gutting the catches.

"Jon, I need a bath as I am as filthy as everyone else with the mud and bits and pieces of fish lying everywhere. Take me back to the hotel, and then ask the manager if we can eat about eight o'clock, and I want you to come and join us for dinner. I have never asked you, do you have a wife?"

"Well, not really, but I live with a school teacher and we have three children of our own. Marriages tend to fall apart in this country, so don't get married."

Elsa was shocked but didn't show it.

"Would you and your wi.., partner, like to join us too?"

"That's kind of you, but no, she looks after the children, I earn the real money that keeps our bodies and souls together."

Again he shuffled from foot to foot, Elsa realised that she must put him at ease.

"Look Jon, I know we didn't get off to the right sort of start, but I have already realised that you are an honest, upright figure in the community, and thus I guess I am lucky to have you in the business. So, I suggest while no one in our employ is around, you can call me by my Christian name, which is Elsa. Does that make you feel more comfortable?"

"Yes Mrs. Peterson, I mean Elsa! It does make me feel more at ease, I thank you for that indulgence."

Jon stood erect and concluded his little speech with,

"Elsa, I have always done my best for Olav, after all I knew him all my life."

He stood tall and erect as a post. Then with his right hand held over his heart he stated in a very matter of fact tone of voice,

"You have my word that I shall also do my best for you."

Elsa smiled at that last comment. There was a small pause then.

"Now let me take you back to the hotel, and we shall meet again over dinner."

The meal turned out to be a very disappointing affair as far as Elsa, mother and father were concerned. Jon thought that the Canada goose was delicious, but to Elsa it was far too greasy, almost inedible. Once again purple potatoes, and once again rather bland in taste, the only other vegetable was a roasted turnip, which again was bland and hardly edible. After the main course came some dried fish, this was going to give the vitamins and protein that the main course lacked. Surprisingly, Elsa and her father liked the dried cod fish. It reminded them of layers of dried brittle paper, but with an interesting taste. Then came coffee with Brenavin and a sort of cake made from wheat flower mixed with potato, yet again Elsa was totally unimpressed by what she considered to be a nothing flavour.

But over the drinks Elsa surprised Jon by asking him to inform her father what she had been told concerning the whaling fleet, and the idea for new ships and possible expansion.

The now quite excited manager didn't need to be told twice, so he chatted away ten to a dozen about where the whaling fleet should go, including the idea of two iron screw driven factory ships, they would replace all the whaling ships that they have now.

It was almost midnight when Jon and Elsa had finished with the coffee, drinks and talk. It was now time to send Jon home and arrange to be picked up at a sensible time in the morning.

The Icelandic manager left feeling quite excited, he thought he was finally on to something with Elsa, he was sure now that the business could expand in the right direction, with more efficiency, also newer, bigger, fewer but safer vessels, not just for the well being of Peterson Fishing Cooperative, but also for the sake of his peoples well being, prosperity and safety.

In turn, Elsa decided to have just ten more minutes talking everything over with her father.

"So, firstly tell me what you think of Jon Johnson?"

There was a pause while he lit up his wooden pipe, this was now crammed full of English Old Shag Pipe Tobacco. He puffed away at it until the red glow had turned into a proper smoking funnel, giving him the satisfaction that he craved on a regular basis. He leaned back on his chair quite precariously, almost to the point of going over backwards. This had given him the time to think out the right response to his daughter's question.

"Mmm. On reflection I must say I like him. I would never interfere, but as you ask me about him, I must say in your mother's and my opinion, you treated him very badly when we first were met on board the ferry. There is an age old adage that when in someone else's country, which is good to observe, that is – when in Rome, do as the Romans do. I think he is genuinely dedicated to your business and to expansion, and so far from what I have heard, it is time to give that man his head."

He leaned back again, and the chair groaned under the strain of being pushed back on the two back legs. Another huge puff on his pipe, smoke drifted ceiling ward, he then got his little pipe cleaner and pushed down hard on the already lit tobacco, then drew heavily again. He was now completely in his own right element, so he now leaned forward and poured himself some more Brenavin and added some water.

"If you think I can be of some use, let me come to the whaling station tomorrow?"

"I would like that dad, thank you."

They both sat there in silence, the only sound being the contented breathing of Koos and the occasional groan of the chair. Then when the pipe was finished, it was decided that it might be a good idea to retire as it was already nearly one o'clock in the morning.

The next morning after a sleepy breakfast, Elsa and her Koos waited for Jon to come and pick them up. While they waited both indulged in more and more coffee, which they both enjoyed immensely, though to Elsa it did have a slight tang of acorns about it.

The weather outside was awful, a grey windy day, with the temperature being no higher than five centigrade, with a wind chill factor that brought frost with it. There was cold rain in the air, and the day threatened to deteriorate into something far worst than what was happening now. This was typical Icelandic weather for this time of year, plus it could get worse by turning into a ferocious storm, or it could peter-out and become mild again, who was to know about the Icelandic weather, the aged old crones were all still asleep recovering from their hangovers.

Jon appeared at ten o'clock sharp, this time with a covered coach and two ponies. He rushed both his passengers out and into the coach, battened down the window areas with water proofs, then got the ponies on their way.

The wind did start to pick up as they approached the dockside, but once by the seaward side the wind had nothing to block its way. It was coming down hard from the north, swirling round the coast and up through the fjords and rivers. The gusts were at times so strong that the carriage seemed certain to be turned over, taking them and the ponies straight into the icy sea. Strangely the sea was not particularly rough, the wind was in fact just blowing the tops off the waves making a further spray of salty water. But out to sea would be another matter, and Elsa and her father were extremely grateful that they weren't back on the ferry, which would by now catching the full force. The two ponies had seen it all hundreds of times before and just trudged along as they normally would, all with an air of haughty indifference.

After less than one hour, they reached the pier and quayside to the whaling factory. Elsa knew they were there by the awful smell that had been systematically growing worse as they approached. It was an aroma that one just couldn't over look. The smell, like the rain got everywhere and clung on as if its very existence depended on it. Once the fragrance got on clothing, it stayed, that is until it was washed away in hot water and soap.

Elsa looked out through a gap in the water proofing, and the sight that greeted her was like a scene from Dante's Inferno. There in the distance was this vast building with a very large slipway going directly down into the sea. Upon that slipway were the carcasses of three huge humpback whales. Two of them had been nearly stripped completely to the bone; the third was lying there still awaiting the surgeons long cutting tools.

There within the vast wooden building was the glow of big demonic furnace fires, this was where the bones were boiled up, either to produce the oil that was so much in demand, and or to be in a position to soften the bones so they could be reduced and then ground down to create fertiliser for the fields, plus of course some of those bones would also be used to make glue, this was the substance that gave off the worst smell.

Some of the meat was being cooked in vast vats and then dried and packed for shipment mainly to Japan and the Far East, lots of the meat was being kept for local consumption, because Icelandic folk loved whale meat too, and the company gladly took the loss of export money to keep the local indigenous natives happy.

As the weather worsened and the light grew even dimmer, the scene really had a horrific sense of unreality about it. Of course Jon was used to this factory, though he rather felt a certain amount of nausea when visiting, he knew he would never ever really get used to the conditions, he just didn't like it.

The truth is that he had never really overcame the awful smell, he had never got used to it, but when something makes you a living, you adjust to except the situation so much quicker than if you didn't have anything to do with it all.

Apart from the smell there was also a terrible noise exuding from the establishment. It had the sound of general pandemonium and chaos about it, but the closer they approached the more varied were the sounds. There was a terrible racket coming from two huge driven steam saws, they were cutting up huge bones extremely quickly, but to unknowing ears it had the familiar sound of large animals screaming in their death throws.

With the glow of furnaces giving off its luminescent red glow which shone right to the outside of the building, plus the general sounds that were being bombarded into outside air, so taking these elements into consideration, plus the fact that the weather was now reaching gale force with screaming wind and rain, not forgetting that it was now bitterly cold and somewhat icy. This was all culminating into giving the impression of the entrance to hell, or in the case of the Viking folk of Iceland this was indeed the portals to Hades.

If demons with pointed tails, breathing fire and brimstone had appeared at the doors of the factory beckoning, neither Elsa nor her father would have been at all surprised. All in all, this was becoming a very harrowing experience for both Elsa and Koos.

Before the two ponies finally came to a stop, Elsa's mind was running away with its own picturesque and colourful imagination. This, in Elsa's healthy creative visions, had now become a painting of hell by the fifteenth century German artist, Albrecht Durer, though in her mind the horror was just imagination not reality, so she could smile at her own stupidity.

Jon turned to look at both Elsa and her father, his face turned from a smile to a frown.

"Are you two all right?"

He had good cause to fret as Elsa started to choke badly and looked distinctly like she was about to lose her breakfast.

"Is it the weather or this factory?"

Her father answered.

"It is a bit of both, but neither of us expected such an awful place as this, especially after the orderly way that the fish market appeared to be yesterday."

Jon tried to smile again, trying hard to lighten the situation.

"Elsa, this is the biggest money earner that the business has, we generate vast sums of overseas currencies through our whaling activities. One could say that this, and I completely agree, disgusting establishment is probably the real reason that our little country can hold its head high, foreign currency, giving us the ability to trade with other nations and buy the things that modern day consumers want, which we cannot make."

Jon had a rather smug knowing frown growing ever larger on his face, he knew he was going to have to sell the idea of the whaling factory, but after all – money speaks all tongues!

"Whales are huge creatures that are not easy to render down to their separate components. I agree, it is not nice, but then killing and using the corpse for our own purposes is what we are about, a simple fact of life. After all, what's the difference from killing a huge creature like a whale, or killing a small fish like a cod? They all wanted to live out their lives, and how do they do that, by killing smaller things than themselves. It is a greedy cruel world that we live in, so what can I say?"

Jon shrugged his shoulders, and for a moment looked helpless, then in a quieter tone he added,

"Would you prefer that we didn't go in, should I just turn this carriage around and take you back to the hotel?"

There was a long pause from Elsa, after all it was her decision to make. At least thirty seconds passed before she came up with an answer,

"No…! We are here to see what must be done now, and for the future. We will visit this awful place, but I won't hold you responsible if I am sick in there."

She attempted a weak smile, showing that she was jesting, but Jon frowned anyway.

Elsa and father were soaked to their very marrow, with the cold icy wind and rain that blew hard into their bodies as they ran to the main entrance. Their clothing was totally inadequate for the job in hand, but then when they packed they had absolutely no idea of what to expect.

Inside the entrance was the factory manager who was there awaiting their pleasure. He ushered them into his office where another three white collar workers were heads down writing away at ledgers and invoices on high desks. Once again Elsa realised that the workforce had been primed as to how to behave. Elsa and her father Koos, very nearly exploded with laughter, as the three were writing so fast, with their collective heads almost touching their ledgers, that one would have thought that their speed of scribing might just have ignited the paper.

"Please relax you scribes, we are not executioners."

This remark immediately calmed the atmosphere within the room.

Strangely Elsa liked the interior of the office, it was made from pine and had on many occasions been washed so clean that it had become white, thus the room had an airy clean warm feel about it. Actually the more she looked the more she realised that everywhere was clean, which meant they cleaned thoroughly on a very regular basis. This made her wonder if the entire factory was scrubbed so precisely? But on this cold blustery wet day the idea did warm her somewhat.

All three stood to attention as the party walked over to formally meet them, but after introductions were made, they discretely went back to their labours. Once again Elsa noticed that the men wore suit trousers and white shirts, but with no collars. The manager who's name was Gustav Sveinson, made a pot of piping hot and very welcome tea, it was the very stuff that would put life back into tired aching, extremely wet and cold people.

He didn't speak a word of English, so everything had to go through Jon, not that it worried him. Gustav was a very self assured person, one that knew he was doing a good job and thus making the business lots of foreign money, all of which went into the Icelandic National Banking Society.

Interestingly, huge amounts of Japanese yen, American dollars and English pounds were collected through the sale of fish and whale products, these went straight into the banks foreign banking department, this much needed foreign currencies was so that the country as a whole could trade abroad themselves. Foreign currencies were needed desperately to trade with, especially for buying extra food stocks that couldn't be grown in the country of Iceland.

They were taken everywhere within the factory area, nothing was missed out, and Elsa had to admit that everything she had seem in the last two days had been absolutely on top form. Everyone they met was polite, and considering the conditions that the men and women had to work in, they all seemed very cheerful and appreciative of the work that they had to do. Elsa told her father when they had a moment alone,

"You know, once we have inspected the books and know exactly what the business is taking on a monthly basis, I think I would like to offer a bonus incentive. What say, the more they work, the more they earn? I am somewhat surprised that Olav hadn't formed a proper working relationship with his employers, after all the business is called Peterson Fishing Cooperative, maybe it's time we really made it one?"

Hours later, after some food consisting of strange earthy tasting bread, along with dried cod, which the manager dunked into his tea, Jon took them back to the hotel. All in all it had been a very enlightening experience for Elsa and Koos.

The first thing they noticed as they left the whaling factory was that the weather had become more clement once more. The rain and wind had eased, but it was cold, but not yet freezing, and it was perfectly obvious that darkness was now coming earlier on a daily basis.

As things stood in Iceland, and they were completely dependent on their connections with Denmark, their main form of currency came from fish and their by products, some money was transferred directly to Denmark in the form of a national debt, while the rest was used for buying equipment and so called luxuries from foreign countries.

There biggest exports were to Scandinavia, then Britain. Then there were exports going to the Far East, but that was a small proportion of their returning earnings. And as the Japanese Yen was not really a hard currency, it was often traded off against goods instead.

But this small island with its small population somehow managed to keep its head above water. There were no natural mineral resources, other than lava that could be mined, though their energy could come from the thermal springs that were everywhere. It is a welcome fact that no one went cold in Iceland as houses were all connected with piping hot thermal water, the same stuff that gave off the terrible smell of bad eggs.

Their coal came from either Norway or Britain, specialist foods came from just about anywhere. Machinery tended to be imported from the United States of America, and as Iceland had a strategic place within the Atlantic, they did tend to get preferential treatment from countries that had aspirations to dominate the seas, so a base at Reykjavik or the far north in Akureyri, where coal could be bought and loaded made a lot of sense, but that was for the future.

So, coal was bought cheaply within the British Isles, only to be sold on with a huge mark up, either back to the British Navy or other countries fleets of ships, when they too appeared within Icelandic waters.

Coaling ships were always coming to the various ports around Iceland, and unloading their cargo, then going back for more, it was a never ending circle of trade. It made sense to the locals that they should make money against any and all other nation, and it made extra sense to the British and other sea fairing nations to be allowed to use Icelandic ports, even at the cost of having to buy back the very coal that they had sold to the Icelandic people in the first place.

But ships, especially foreign war ships, needed coal to keep their engines turning the propellers. The naval vessels from the various countries that felt strongly about their place within the Atlantic and North Sea would often need the ports for refuge in extreme weather conditions, and sometimes even small repairs, for those things Iceland was perfectly situated.

As trading was the name of the game, any money that came into the hands of the Icelandic banks was extremely welcome. So anchorage rights, portside docking fees, sailors shore leave all created more wealth for that little volcanic lump high in the North Atlantic Ocean.

The next day was Sunday, and Elsa was collected by Jon and taken to the local church. Though she didn't understand any of the preacher's sermonising, and as the preacher seemed to be looking directly at her most of their time there, she quickly started to wonder if the words spoken were steered towards her, fortunately she did recognise the hymns, which she joined in and managed to sing them in Dutch, much to the delighted amusement of the entire congregation.

The church was quite small, capable of holding roughly sixty believers, but on that Sunday, it was full to overflowing, there must have been over one hundred and fifty people crammed into that small space. The air became very stale and smelt of a cocktail of sweat and alcohol, not a pleasant combination, and this permeated around the building extremely quickly, much to the chagrin of Elsa' tender nose.

For the first time Elsa witnessed both men and women wearing decent clothes, some men wore suits, the women wearing woollen dresses and very colourful woollen tops. These garments were all made from Icelandic sheep whose wool is some of the thickest in the ovine world, very much sort after by northern countries women folk.

The little church's structure was entirely made from wood, with wooden slates to match the wooden walls, it even sported a small slightly lopsided wooden steeple. Once again the predominant colour was red, but newly painted red, and what's more it even smelt of new paint, this too permeated with the other smells. Smelling various smells around her had already become a serious distraction for the Dutch lady, and she seriously wished she had brought her scented nosegay with her.

The pews were extremely hard, made from imported oak. Though hard and plain on the seat, no cushions allowed, the ends were carefully carved with beautiful scenes from the bible, done in relief. One end was Adam and Eve, under an apple tree, with the serpent curling around the trunk. Another was Noah's Ark, and the animals were marching in two by two, the only trouble was that the animals were penguins, seals, wolves, and only animals that the indigenous people of Iceland would really know about, and that turned out to be an extremely limited issue. The preacher's pulpit was part of an old fishing boat, as was the altar table. The whole church had a Heath Robinson approach and feel to its design and making, yet to Elsa it was positively delightful.

Though she understood very little she was entranced by the service and wanted to meet the minister afterwards. The man was only about five feet six tall, rather small in Icelandic terms for men, yet there was something very powerful about this man. He had jet black hair, swept back and combed down tightly, and a ruddy red face that was lined and aged far beyond his forty-two years. His garment was a black smock, which came down almost touching the ground, around his neck was a white ruff, that possibly was the only embellishment that there was upon him. He was not a handsome man, yet not ugly either, but his premature aging didn't help his looks. He was introduced being yet another Jon Johnson, one of hundreds if not thousands that lived with that common name in Iceland, and he looked like a stern man and was not given to laughter or frivolity, so Elsa's approach at being nice went down rather badly. It was conspicuous that his approach to God was one of damnation and hellfire, which was where Elsa was probably going to end up, as she was only here in Reykjavik to cause trouble for his congregation, people he thought of as pure simple folk.

He couldn't speak any English, but Elsa knew that her John was getting an awful earful obviously concerning her and her parents. One thing one learnt quickly when arriving in Iceland, and no business was private to Icelanders.

Elsa knew that she was being frowned upon, she even guessed what his fears might be, Jon was being bombarded with questions. There was some obvious venom in the preachers tone, but Jon handled it well giving back as much as he got but to absolutely no avail. But then to Elsa, it really didn't matter a hoot, she had already long decided that she liked the preacher and his biased feelings, even his resentment towards her.

She understood without speaking the language that he was preaching fire and brimstone to Jon, and it all would be about her selling the business and taking the money from this land of Ice and Fire back to heathen lands such as Nederland's.

She also very quickly understood that his intentions were basically good, he was seriously concerned about the welfare of his flock, what he didn't understand was, so was she.

As he got closer to her and his speech got more venomous, he was almost spitting the words in her face, that was when she smelt the obvious signs of alcohol on his breath. This now was a huge disappointment to her, she thought, no hoped he would be different, but no, he too was a hard drinker.

The rest of that day was spent nicely, either wondering around muddy wet Reykjavik or resting in the hotel. Jon showed Elsa some of the delights of the town, mainly around the harbour area, where the hustle and bustle never stopped. This area with the ongoing traffic really fascinated Elsa Peterson, who now was hooked on the business and all things Icelandic. After an extensive tour, it was agreed that hot tea or coffee might be a nice thing, but not before Jon took them both on a walk around Lake Tchurnin.

Elsa was amazed to see just how many different forms of bird life seem to reside there, so many different types, none of them at all bothered by the fact that humans milled around them all day, they just weren't at all bothered, which to Elsa and dad was so pleasant to observe. But the predominant species was perfectly obvious to see, it was the Canada Geese. Two and two made four very quickly. This was the town's main form of eatable birdlife, a very rich form of protein and fats that the body needed. But as long as the birds resided in Lake Tchurnin, they were safe. And the very same birds feed on the very rich form of moss that grows everywhere, plus seaweed that lay in abundance around the shoreline. But even the peoples of Reykjavik weren't going to decimate this species in a hurry. In Lake Tchurnin alone there were several thousands of the squawking, flapping, feathery creatures, but there was an estimated ten thousand landing, eating, breading and being shot and eaten by the local inhabitants, within the local area of South Iceland.

Jon spent the entire day with Elsa and her family, it was very agreeable day for them all. So over many cups of tea and coffee Elsa gradually allowed Jon to once again air his views, she completely gave him his head to talk about expansion within the framework of the business, in fact anything and everything concerning Peterson Fishing Cooperative.

But there was one cloud that hung over everything, and that would have to be addressed the very next day. They must go to the records office and declare Olav's death, showing the death certificate and anything else they might insist on, and then to work out some sort of deal concerning death duties that would surely have to be paid.

The Monday morning arrived, Elsa told her father that she wished to go to the government office alone with Jon, this was something she was quite worried about, and so could he possibly keep mother company while they were away?

Jon appeared promptly just as Elsa was finishing her breakfast of the strange tasting bread and eggs, so small they looked more like pigeon eggs, but in fact they were stolen from the Puffins, brought over on a regular basis from the Faroe Islands. She liked the taste but thought they were possibly too gamy for chickens.

The office was down the slope towards the harbour and was one of the few stone built constructions. It was three stories high, which made it one of the tallest in Iceland. The rooms were small and crammed with ledger shelving, all chocker block with paperwork. To Elsa, this was just about the most untidy office she had ever experienced. They were beckoned to a row of seats and told to sit and wait until someone came to see them. So they sat and sat and sat.

After two hours of waiting Jon's patience was at braking point, and for the first time Elsa saw that he really did have some fight in him.

"For goodness sake, is anyone ever going to come and see us?"

Elsa could only guess what was being said, but it certainly didn't take a genius to see and hear that he was becoming furious. She smiled to herself and thought,

'Good, he doesn't just let things happen, he really is a go getter.'

An elderly man who should have retired years ago came shuffling into the anti-room where they sat, puffing and panting as if he just ran a mile. He wore a dark suit of serge material, it had long since seen better days now being rather threadbare. Strange to see for Elsa was that the man was straight out of a Dickens book. He was a good seventy odd years out of his time, his jacket was buttoned up only by the top button, thus allowing the jacket to flare out over his hips. Underneath he wore a whitish collarless shirt, which still had signs of his previous meal splattered over the front of it. His shoes were highly polished but extremely aged in appearance, and though his trousers were narrow, he still wore spats over his shoes, this really gave him a comical look, as it showed off his rather bandy legs. He, unlike all the other office workers wasn't wearing wooden clogs over their otherwise bare feet only those black large aging leather shoes. Despite the appearance of being an old untidy man, when he spoke he had a very matter of fact way, this exuded an air of authority about it.

The fellow then turned to Elsa, and in almost perfect English said,

"Mrs. Peterson, please allow me to give my sincere condolences for your loss. I suspect that you long realised that everyone in this capital city of ours knew and loved your husband, and sadly now he is gone."

This sentence he spoke in a passive sad tone of voice, but it did heighten when he stated the next sentence,

"But I can assure you he will not be forgotten. Now let's sit down at my desk and we can work out roughly what taxes you will have to pay."

He smiled showing a very poor set of rotting teeth.

"Please remember, we want to make sure that Peterson Fishing Cooperative will carry on and grow giving yet more employment to our people, we are not here to rob you and destroy the company."

He smiled once again, it was in a certain knowing way. Elsa knew she was now up against quite an adversary.

The inspector of taxes went through everything, there was not a fish fin or scale ignored. Eventually a compromise was settled on, and a sum of money was agreed, also it could be paid over the next year in regular intervals. Jon had worked tirelessly to keep on top of what the tax man wanted, but at the end of a very long Monday, Elsa and Jon went away feeling somewhat smug knowing that it could have been a darn sight worse with much more money being paid in death duties.

It was agreed that two sets of lawyers would formulate a binding contract, and that would be that, and Jon knew exactly who he would approach to do their bidding.

He escorted Elsa back to the hotel, agreed to come back for dinner after he had changed into something that didn't contain body sweat from that hard days haggling.

Elsa now knew what she was going to do with the business.

That night over a sumptuous meal of Goose, this time not at all greasy, which completely surprised Elsa, Koos and Angnita as goose is by far greasier than duck. They understood that it had probably come direct from outside the lake area, thus shot with impunity, not that anyone would have complained. This was their first really fine feast of a meal.

Elsa thought for a moment then decided this was now the right time to tell Jon what she intended doing concerning the business.

"Jon, we are going to go back on the next ferry, so I am going to leave you with some changes."

She smiled a knowing smile at her parents who both sat there with self centred smug expressions on their knowing faces.

"I am going to make you a full partner in all of Peterson Fishing Cooperative, but I do also want to incorporate a few changes, as long as you agree to them?"

Jon was now grinning from one side of his face to the other.

"Firstly, I want you to form a board of directors, they are there to help you organise the new whaling fleet that you want. By all means take them and yourself and visit the shipping yards in Scotland work out some pricing and order the first of your two new vessels, I have every confidence that you can handle a good deal for us, and I am quite sure we can actually afford the costing of such a vessel. You will appoint who you think is worthy enough to sit on the board with you, but at least one manual worker from the whaling factory and the fish market would be good idea. It will be entirely up to you and the board to work out salary structures for all our employees. In theory, I will at this time stay on as chairman, or in my case chairwoman, but you will represent me in everything. All board meetings should be properly addressed with minutes, and then those minutes sent to me to peruse. I intend at present to be an absentee chairperson, that is unless anything drastic goes awry, but you won't have any interference from me at all on any of the day to day running of our business."

She stopped talking and took a drink from a glass of water, she was quick to note that even cold water smelt slightly of sulphur. After a couple of seconds she continued in a very emphatic manner,

"Jon, you will get your fleet of iron whaling ships, though I rather think it might take a few years to get them both. The other aspect of the business that I would want you to incorporate is - we call the business a cooperative, but it isn't, but it should be. Get some form of bonus scheme working for all the employees, the harder they work, the more they earn. Surely we make enough money to be fairer with what we pay?"

Another intake of cool Icelandic air, then she concluded.

"My monies should be sent to my bank in Hilversum as you have done in the past, but a small percentage, say ten percent should be kept in Iceland in your bank but in my name. Does all of this meet with your approval?"

Jon was in a state of wonderment, his life had now just experienced a serious upturn in wealth and status. He had always wanted that his uncle should make him a partner, but it had never been forthcoming, but now, an equal partner, he was ecstatic.

"I, er, really don't know what to say. I guess thank you would be a good starting point. I shall work hard for the good of all of us that you can be assured of. The idea of bonuses scheme to the workers is fantastic and generous, I suspect they will want to erect a statue of you in the main square."

They all laughed at this idea, but Elsa rather liked that interesting thought.

"Elsa, may I be as bold as to ask you when you are thinking of going, when is the next ferry?"

He shuffled on his chair in slight embarrassment.

"The reason I ask is because now the business is done, why not let me take you all around some of the beauty spots of this island, anyway at least down south here?"

Elsa looked towards her parents, in the mean time Jon was in full flow.

"I would be honoured to take you all to Thingvelir, which you may know was the meeting place for the old Vikings. It is reputed to be the oldest parliament in the world. Then we can visit Gullfoss, this is a staggeringly beautiful waterfall, this place has magical connotations about it. Captured enemies of the old original settlers were thrown into the boiling caldron of water, only to be dashed going over the falls on the rocks below. We still get people throwing themselves into it in darkest winter months, when the human spirit is at its lowest. We could stay at our cabin which is set in the lava fields, but is very beautiful and peaceful, a couple of days would do us all good. What do you think?"

It was Elsa's father who interjected first.

"I think it would be a wonderful idea, you can't come to another country without seeing what it has to offer in the way of beauty. How will we travel? And where will we stay?"

"We will take three ponies, use two and keep one for spare, the business has its own almost new covered landau, this will hold the four of us in complete comfort, plus it has ample space to fit food and luggage. This will be adequate for our use. The third pony we can tie to the back and pull him along. We will stay in an old sheep herder's cottage which I bought some years ago and modernised. You will hopefully be pleasantly surprised as it has three bedrooms, a kitchen and an outside toilet which sadly is a little primitive, but is functional. We could leave first thing tomorrow morning, after I have sorted out the business for this week, and purchased lots of food and drink. Shall I get this organised?"

He had an excited expectant look across his countenance, his eyes were wide open and almost sparkling, it made Elsa think of him as a little boy waiting on an expected toy which was to appear at any moment, after all, it's true to say Jon's Christmas's had come early. She smiled to herself, and then shivered as she heard the wind pick up outside the hotel.

"Jon, what about the weather, what if it's snowing or rainy and windy. Won't it be dangerous in the hinterland, and what if we have an accident?"

Now it was Jon's turn to smile.

"Elsa, surely that's part of the charm! Yes, it could be lousy weather, here in Iceland you never really know what the next day brings, but we don't worry about it too much. As to having accidents, again that's possible, but we will have three ponies, all of which would be able to take the three of you back home in an emergency, and if heavens forbid, that a wheel came of the landau, then I am quite capable of fixing it. But there is always a risk element, and surely that's just part of the fun?"

The next day, being Tuesday, they had an early breakfast and waited for the expected Jon and transport to appear. The weather was windy and quite cool, not cold, but it was obvious to anyone with half a brain that the temperature was on its way down as apposed to up. The wind kept blowing cinder dust into their faces which stung the eyes and became a nuisance to the humans and animals alike. But it was journeying weather, wind and cold wouldn't hold the four of them back from their new adventure.

Once they got outside of Reykjavik, the going became easier, partly because there was very little other traffic, but mainly because surprisingly to the Dutch contingent, the roads were smooth quite wide cinder tracks, big enough to accommodate their passage without even bumps. Before two hours were up, they had entirely lost sight and sound of the capital town, and now journeying between two huge hills, this gave a certain amount of freedom from the wind, all it did was to help push them along through the valley. They were heading in a slightly north-easterly direction and had to travel roughly thirty miles until they reached Jon Johnson's cabin. They passed several settlements all of which seemed to be occupied, but surprisingly no one ever appeared to be interested in the travellers that passed by, strange to think these might well be the only visitors to actually pass by in an entire month.

Elsa realised quickly just how hard an existence life must be for the people outside of the towns. These country folk all seemed to have small allotments, but these latches of cultivated strips of land could only possibly have grown purple potatoes and swedes and turnips. But that wasn't their only dietary intake. Everyone raised sheep, very rugged, woolly creatures that gave wonderful wool and fine eating meat. It wasn't hard to imagine that the surplus would be driven into Reykjavik and sold in the markets, then the money used for buying all the other things they would need for the year ahead.

It did disturb Elsa that wherever she looked, she saw absolutely no trees. There were clumps of woody shrubbery occasionally, but no trees! This she started to feel sad about, she knew she couldn't live in a country that didn't have trees. The further they travelled the narrower the track way became, but they did stay even. Elsa was deeply impressed that this roadway was so level, it made her wonder how it was maintained, she would have to ask Jon?

The journey to the cabin took five hours and it was late afternoon when they had unloaded the provisions and suitcases. Jon fed and watered the ponies and secured their night in the small windy rather dilapidated barn that was not more than fifty feet from the main cabin. The wood that made up their temporary accommodation was made from old ships timbers, and just by the front door was a rather rotting figurehead of a mermaid that had once graced the bow of a fine wooden sailing ship, but like everything else it had seen better times, the years and weather had taken its toll, all the paint had gone, and the actual wood was now rotting and saturated, unless someone was to do something drastic to improve its lot, that poor mermaid was going to disappear into the ether.

The family were pleasantly surprised at just how roomy the building was, the wind was making it creak, but somehow that gave a warming feeling even though the temperature was still as cold inside as it was outside. Jon quickly lit a fire with very dry wood, and then he produced some coal, which must have taken some effort to bring all the way from their coaling depot in Reykjavik, the one near the whaling station.

Before thirty minutes was up the cabin was alive and warm. Elsa and her mother Angnita were making food and the two men were sitting back by the fire drinking some fine concocted hooch. A warm cosy evening was spent in the wooden building which lay so isolated in the middle of lava fields several miles from the main roadway. It was so isolated that it was perfectly obvious that absolutely no one would be in the vicinity, and again no one would pass by from one month to another, the three visitors did feel somewhat exposed and vulnerable, being no trees to shade them from winds and weather in general, there it stood exposed and bleak, yet somehow a haven of warmth and tranquillity exuded from those dated timbers.

As for washing and cleaning, there was constant piping hot water coming gushing into a outdoor bath, this came straight up from the ground, from the interior of that very lava. The water was hot enough almost to be impossible to get into, only after carefully lowing oneself gently into the extremely hot sulphurous water, gasping to get ones breath as you did so, did one manage to complete that job. Once in, it was wonderful, as you cleansed the grime and worries of the day away, the very filth that you might have lost in the bath was soon replaced by more hot clean water, it just never ended. It was Elsa who was the first to experience this wonderful sensation, she had abandoned all her clothes and gently lowered herself into the bath, which was just a normal household porcelain tub that gave roughly four feet of water to sit in, and there she sat with the water up to her neck wondering why this wasn't done everywhere in Iceland.

Her mind gradually drifted off to less stressful times when Olav and she were first married. She knew that she had been a reasonably good wife, but she had never really grown to love him, and she was now convinced that it was all down to the age difference.

"Elsa, Elsa! Are you alright?"

It was Jon, and he had come out to make sure that she was indeed still alive. He knew that on many occasions people fell asleep and slipped under the water and drowned.

She jumped when the realisation of being called awakened her. There in front of her looking directly at her and her now very red skinned breasts was Jon, he had the look of someone quite concerned, but relieved to find that his concern was in fact unfounded.

"Please Jon, I have nothing on!"

She had place both hand over her two tight but smallish breasts, and now was going red for another reason other than just hot water.

"Sorry Elsa, but I had to make sure you were still in the land of the living! People are known to have just slipped under the hot water and drowned, and you have been in there for a long time now. There is enough room for all of us, what say I ask your mother and father to come and enjoy the hot water. It is perfectly normal for friends and family to share a common bath such as this one. Do you not think it would be a pleasant thing to do?"

Jon was perfectly serious, but Elsa was horrified at the thought of her privacy being invaded, especially by her parents who probably hadn't seen in the nude since she had been a small child.

"No Jon, I don't wish any of you to be here while I am in this tub, please leave me to get dressed."

Elsa was now beginning to get somewhat annoyed at being put in this compromising situation.

"I mean right now!"

When Elsa had dressed and returned into the cabin she was surprised to see how cosy the other three had become. Her father looked casually in her direction, but her mother avoided any eye contact, being on the edge of laughter.

"I think your mother and I will try out this bath together, then after us, Jon can. Is it as good as Jon says?"

"Well before he burst out there..."

At this statement, Elsa's mother Angnita finally cracked and burst out laughing. But Elsa continued with her flow,

"As I was saying, until Jon surprised me I was having a wonderful time, the tub is the most relaxing thing I have ever experience. But as for Jon, well I suppose he is Icelandic after all, but Jon we don't tend to see one another naked in Holland."

But then she thought to herself,

'Maybe, just maybe, mores the pity?'

That was that in Elsa's eyes, but not in her father Koos, who then turned to his wife and said,

"Last one in is a sissy."

He was then gone, shedding his jacket as he went. Elsa had never seen her father so animated before, it was if all his prohibitions had suddenly flown out of the window leaving him naked within his very soul, and soon naked on the outside of his soul, and what's more Angnita, his wife was just about to show the same degree of social freedom. Once again Elsa was aghast with the wonderment of this moment, liberated parents, what ever next?

Jon came and sat next to Elsa, he looked her straight in the eyes.

"I am terribly sorry to have embarrassed you so out there. Here in Iceland men and women often bathe together, and without clothing of any sort, so please believe me, no insult was meant."

"You are forgiven!"

Elsa said that with a broad grin showing, she had only felt the shame of showing her body. Like most foreigners, she had a special loathing for her own body, and was somewhat ashamed of her appearance, even though most people thought of her as being an attractive woman, not pretty, but pleasant.

A loud screech of delight came from the outside, and both John and Elsa knew that Koos and Angnita were enjoying their moment of freedom. Lots of laughing ensued, then some silence, which to Jon and Elsa was much more embarrassing. Then ten minutes later, with Jon and Elsa sitting quietly getting more and more embarrassed, a serious scream came, not of delight but of fear.

Jon was the first to rush out into the lava field, there in all their glory were Koos and Angnita, absolutely stark naked standing looking up at the night sky.

They had discovered the aurora borealis, the light from this phenomenon was changing colours all the time, it was swirling around the night sky, hanging like a cobweb curtain but taking up what seemed to be miles and miles of space. It was turning into a wonderful free aerobatic display. These northern lights were one of the great mysterious wonders of northern countries.

This time the display was just for the four of them. The colour varied from moment to moment, all the time swirling this way and that, changing shape and spreading all over the night sky. Koos, Angnita and Elsa stood there completely absorbed by this display of nature. It was only when Jon coughed out very loud that Koos realised that he was still as naked as the day he was born, but now extremely cold and wet. Then Elsa looked down from the sky to her mother, her mouth dropped open and a small but distinct gasp came from her lips. Angnita then realised that she too was wet and starting to freeze, but completely unabashed, gathered her clothes and walked into the warm cabin. All the time, Jon was trying very hard to suppress a laugh.

But Elsa even after her parents lack of modesty appeared to stand once again watching the night sky. Now completely absorbed by this strange silent phenomenon, with all its incredible beauty, she completely forgot that her mother and father had been standing there in the cold, completely naked watching up at something they had never even heard of before, let alone seen. All four had been in a state of trance, admiring with admiration what nature could do as it showed itself in all its wonderment.

Elsa finally said,

"Jon what is this display called…?"

The next morning they all rose comparatively early, around nine o'clock, they had eaten some breakfast and were now ready for the next part of their adventure.

Jon, who had risen earlier, had now coupled the ponies to the landau and was in the process of coaxing his guests to depart from the table and come and proceed on the journey to Thingvelir, the Old Icelandic Parliament.

It only took one and a half hours to get there, and all three of the Dutch visitors were impressed to see this strange landscape with its deep fissures into the ground.

"I was half expecting to see some sort of structure, something like a stone circle or whatever."

Bewilderment showed itself.

"So the people used to gather here and make legal decisions concerning new laws and such like?"

Elsa was amazed and slightly disappointed all at the same time.

"Yes that is right. This is Thingvelir the oldest know parliamentary gathering area in the world! Many ideas have been banded around here, many new laws have been enforced. They even had a court assembly here where people were tried for various offences, and justice was done. The guilty would often by thrown over the Gulfoss falls."

He pondered that idea, and then followed it up with,

"I could think of one or two people that might benefit by a swim over the falls."

Sighed then looked around for any response, there was no reaction.

After wondering around the area, it was pointed out to Elsa the one and only forest. Blink and one would have missed it. There were many small hedge type beech trees growing in one of the fissures, they stood roughly five feet in height, looked healthy but windswept with their upper branches bending the way of the predominant wind flow, from north to south. Whether these small trees would ever reach lofty heights was not known by anyone, people just hoped they would, and were prepared to just wait and see.

The wonderful greenness of the moss was incredibly impressive, the green was so lush and had a luminescence that seemed to glow night or day. All the sheep grazed on the thick carpet of nourishment, the same could be said for the cattle too, though they would also eat dried seaweed and any fish remains that were being dumped in their pens. But to feed them the entrails of the fish did often effect the taste of the milk , and not always favourably.

Angnita had made some food that they could eat while out in the open air, open air was the greatest understatement that could have been made. Here they were in the hinterland, miles from any civilisation, and the smell of good honest clean air was intoxicating to all of them. Elsa and her parents had never experienced such a momentous feeling of exuberance just by breathing in this cold health giving high oxygenated air. Holland may be a back water, or at least Hilversum might be, but it still stunk of human waste, along with the animal excrement that was spread liberally over the fields at all times of the year. Then there was the smell of factories, most might be as much as thirty miles away from where they resided, but pollution found its way everywhere. But not there in Iceland, and at least not in the hinterland.

All four of them stood close to the actual meeting place, slightly higher than most areas around, faced into the wind which was hitting them at about fifteen miles per hour and just breathed in this wondrous clean air. To Elsa and her father and mother, this was a way of breathing in life giving cleansing oxygen and it was wonderful.

Their exuberance for seeing Gullfoss showed absolutely no abatement, without question they wanted to see more of this country. On the way to the waterfall they passed by the famous geyser, once again Elsa was completely blown away with wonderment. The water jet spurted skyward reaching the dizzy heights of sometimes one hundred feet. Jon made them stand well back, as the water was in fact boiling hot, so when it burst forth, the steam from the water could still burn anyone unlucky enough to have boiling steamy water dropping over them.

Whoosh, up it went, so regular that you could have set your pocket watch by it. Every twenty-five seconds day and night, jets of water hit the air. Though here the predominant aroma was once again of sulphur, still the air was good to breathe in. A little way down the track the released water was cool enough to collect and drink. The taste was not particularly nice, tasting slightly rusty, but it was good to quickly wash ones hands and face in. The two ponies stood, refusing to move until they had taken their fill of water, then having sated their appetites, they immediately gave some back.

After watching this for an hour they carried on to the waterfall.

Gullfoss is one of the great wonders of the Icelandic world, the beauty of it is quite staggering to behold. Even though they can hear the roar from several miles away, when they came within seeing distance the vapour that drifted up from that boiling caldron almost obscured everything around.

The ponies were not happy going so close to this thunderous noisy place, so Jon got off the landau and actually led them from the reins. They got right up to where the water fell over the top and quickly realised that to speak to one another meant shouting at the top of their voices. The level of the river was very high almost flooding over onto the viewing area. Elsa and her father went close to the edge to look at the cascading, bubbling inferno as it crashed down several hundred feet to the next level of the river. Just by standing there, they got very wet from the spray, and after some time, thoroughly soaked, they decided enough was enough.

That night back at the cabin while eating their evening meal, they discussed the events of the day. It had been wonderful, but tomorrow they would return to Reykjavik, and the day after, all being well, they would catch the ferry and do the return trip back to Holland.

That night before retiring, the four of them went outside to watch the silent seemingly regular light display. The Aurora Borealis left them speechless with excitement. Eventually Elsa was left standing outside on her own, that was until she heard in the not to distance a screech, it made her jump. She didn't know it, but it was probably a silver fox calling to its mate. To Elsa it might well have been a Troll at the very least, anyway she was now icy cold.

The journey back to the capital was uneventful, the weather had improved and the sun was most definitely showing some interest, it amazed the three of them that Iceland was totally about extremes, and the weather was the culmination of all those extremes.

When they got to the hotel, Elsa asked Jon if it was not too late to see a lawyer.

One hour and a half later, the lawyer had drafted a rough contract that both Jon and Elsa signed, it gave all the authority that had been discussed earlier to Jon. Better contracts would be made and signed over the next few months, but at least this gave the authority for Jon to get on and do things that he and Elsa wanted done.

"Elsa you have made me a very proud man, you have my word that I will always do my best for the business, you can rely on me, and as any lawyer would say, my word is my bond."

Elsa went over to him smiling, she leant forward and kissed him very lightly on both his cheeks.

"I know you will always do your best, I trust you implicitly. But, tomorrow we once again head for our homeland."

Jon was sad to see his partner talk about leaving, but his mind was racing ahead to the future and making Peterson Fishing Cooperative, bigger, better and ready for the twentieth century.

"When you go to Scotland, and or wherever you decide that you want the first ship made, if I am free, I might come and visit you there, mostly for the journey, but be assured not to interfere."

The journey back to Holland went without a hitch; the weather was clement enough for them to arrive back in the Hook, nearly a day earlier than they thought. They now all need some small break from travelling, and both mum and dad had decided that they might go and visit Koos brother in Rotterdam. Elsa just wanted her house and some peace to think everything out. Elsa thanked Koos and Angnita for agreeing to come with her, it had been a pleasant and fruitful trip, but all good things come of an end and soon they were parted.

7

Eighteen ninety-nine was a fine year for James Jolly, now twenty-four years of age, finally having found a woman who could put up with his excessive reading habits, his slovenly manners, lack of cleanliness, and the most appalling eating habits, not to forget his incredible ability to preach on subjects that generally no one would be interested in, but to be fair, his preaching would only last for hours at a time, the boy had no end of talents.

Lucy Charles, was the daughter of a Gordon Charles an engine driver, one who knew and rather admired the young James Jolly, and it had been Gordon that instigated their first meeting, then made sure that they complied to a satisfactory understanding that it was expected that they actually should appeal to one another, thus he brought about a successful union between the two young people.

James was now earning quite good money in the foundry, so he could think of acquiring a wife. His career had blossomed with his incredible adeptness for engineering. There was virtually nothing that he couldn't replicate from a trains engine, he had learned his trade extremely well.

There was a somewhat embarrassing hassle with one of the sheds company managers, who had long realised that James knew much more than he did, about trains and engineering in general. This had led to small conflicting disagreements concerning ways of doing things. James had little tact and would stand his ground and argue his points of reference for very long periods of time.

One particular occasion was when they needed a newly made coupling which should have been easy if James had only been left alone to do what he did so well. But the manager decided, as often managers do, that he wanted the coupling made in a certain way, contrary to what James thought. After an hour of wrangling, the manager told Jolly that either he did it his way, or bugger off home. James did the latter.

The next day when James returned to work there was an inquiry concerning young Jolly's behaviour. He was marched unceremoniously up to the office to be quizzed by the managing director, one Mr. Stephen Shakeshaft. The managing director was a fair man, but easily swayed by his underlings, especially one floor manager Brian Waters.

"So Jolly, what have you got to say for yourself?"

Shakeshaft sat at his desk, a pipe lay by the side having very recently gone out. A cold cup of tea was still waiting to be drunk and piles of papers lay in neat bundles on the top of his desk. The trouble with those papers was the simple expedient that there just wasn't enough hours in the day for Stephen to clear up the backlog, so life was beginning to get him down.

He was fatigued, wasn't sleeping well worrying, always about work related matters, it was causing him to become obese with over eating, his hair had gone white over just six month period, plus going bald as well, making him extremely unhappy, truth was he no longer enjoyed his job, or come to that work in general. To make matters worse his wife of thirty years was caught having an affair with a young man half his and her ages. No, he most definitely wasn't a happy man.

"Why did you leave your post yesterday?"

"Mr. Shakeshaft, you have known me long enough to know that I didn't just leave but was told to go."

He looked at Waters in an accusing way.

"Your floor manager, Mr. Waters, thinks he knows about engineering, but he doesn't! I know, and you know, I know much more than him. Yesterday he ordered me to make a new coupling, but then decided the way I wanted to do it wasn't right. But, if I did it his way, the coupling wouldn't last but a couple of months, whereas mine would last a lifetime. I find him annoyingly arrogant, and like I have already said, he doesn't know the right way to do things."

By this time, Brian Waters was now fuming with rage, and now prepared to lie through his teeth. It no longer mattered about the bloody coupling, he just wanted this young whippersnapper out of his life once and for all.

"None of what he is saying is true, I came to look for him and he had just downed tools and gone home. I do believe sir, that that is a sackable offence. I must insist vehemently, that James Jolly be dismissed immediately…"

He didn't finish the sentence as James in a rare showing of anger, swung his fist round and caught the manager squarely on his cheek. It didn't damage his appearance, but it did dent his pride. At the same time as Waters was reeling from the blow, Shakeshaft saw no other way than to comply with the request, even though he guessed that Waters was in fact lying.

"Oh dear! Why on earth did you do that? You now leave me no choice than to let you go with immediate effect."

He then turned to Brian Waters, and in a rather gruff tone said,

"You may leave us. I have some things to say to James here. Get your face washed and cleaned up, you certainly don't want the other men to know what happened here do you!"

Brian left still wiping his face vigorously, with the hope that he wouldn't develop a black eye.

Mr. Shakeshaft then turned back to young Jolly, shaking his head and looking extremely downcast, he carried on saying,

"Why did you have to go and let that extremely stupid man goad you into hitting him? I didn't believe him for a moment, but you striking a blow at him, gave me absolutely no choice other than to sack you. I am really sorry James, but it will be from immediate effect, but I will pay you for the entire week, and if needed, I will give you a fine reference, with no mention of this act of stupidity. I want you to leave knowing that many of us here knew you were a fine well read young man who's prospects could have taken you to the top. Now you will have to get there in someone else's service. I am so sorry, come back tomorrow for your money."

Mr. Shakeshaft then stood up and shook Jolly's hand vigorously. Then in a saddened tone of voice said,

"Good bye and good luck!"

Still shaking his head, he withdrew a handkerchief and blew his nose with so much strength, that it made James look up from watching his feet. Mr. Shakeshaft, then started to look at a pile of papers, but with a tut, looked out towards the window instead, not that he could see anything as it was filthy with engine smoke and pollution, it obviously hadn't been cleaned since the day the pane of glass had been put into the window frame.

There were tears in James's eyes, he had never worked anywhere else other than here in the engine sheds, and the responsibility had been wonderful for him. His days had been spent diligently giving off of his best, and his best was better than all the others put together, he had been an incredibly good engineer and foundry worker, what is more, generally liked and trusted by his fellow workers. Had he learned to smarten up his personal appearance and managed to speak something that was somewhat better than eternal Glaswegian slang, his prospects would have been a lot better than they were before being sacked. But then maybe, he wouldn't have been so popular with the other workers? But none of that mattered now, he had to go down stairs back into the shed, collect his gear, say goodbye to his chums after he had told his side of the story, then leave with as much dignity as he could muster.

When James reached home, he was still in a state of shock, Lucy was feeding their son Herbert Jolly a baby of one year, bonnie and bouncing, but showing all the signs of his fathers scruffiness. His face was dirty and food was splattered all down his front. Yes no question about it, he was very much his father's son.

Lucy put young Herbert back in his cot, then looked back at James and asked in an accusing manner,

"That bugger hasn't sent you home again, has he?"

At that, the emotions of the day settled down once and for all on James's shoulders, he did something he hadn't done since childhood, he burst into tears.

"I've been sacked, me fired, and all because of that bastard yesterday. Old Shakeshaft was nice about it all, but as I had hit that shit faced Waters, I was summarily dismissed."

"You hit him! Why did you hit him?"

"I caught him a beauty around his left cheek, he should have a cracking shiner by now, and hopefully all the fellows at the shed will give him stick over it. He lied to Shakeshaft, the bastard lied about me, that's why I hit him. Now, I wish I hadn't, but it's too late."

James wiped his eyes and his nose on his sleeve. He now felt rather embarrassed at showing such emotion, but now at least it was in the open, Lucy would understand and forgive him for losing such a well paid job. He would just have to get another one now, surely, that shouldn't be too hard, should it? After all his knowledge should see him through any interview!

"Christ Lucy, I don't know what to do, I'll have to look around and try and get another job quickly, with mother lying ill, and our baby I can't afford to be idle. I'll get something real quick, you see if I don't."

James slumped directly into the only armchair that sat prominently in their dining come bedroom. It was completely threadbare, right through to the springs, yet it meant something to both of them as it was the first stick of furniture that they had bought together, albeit that it came from a rag and bone man and cost just one shilling. But to James and Lucy, this was Chippendale, it must be, as it cost twelve copper pennies and it was indeed, all theirs.

He felt as if the world had once again folded in on him, he had responsibilities that most definitely exceeded his still tender years.

'What can I do? I could join the army and go and fight the Boer's, or maybe go to sea. They must be looking for engineers in the navy? I'll read some books on the subject.'

The next day, not only did young Jolly get a job, but it was a job making spare parts for the new fangled automobiles, and he was expected to be ably to make axles and brake drums for a local firm which made these components for three Glaswegian car manufacturers.

One of the cars that were being produced ran on steam power, something that James was very interested in and knew a great deal about, steam engines was most definitely his forte, and now he was off the railways, he wanted to find an inroad to other forms of steam locomotion. He hoped that working at Bryers Precision Engineers would give him an introduction to the steam car producer McLaren & sons.

Lucy was so relieved when he returned to their small tenement with the news. Their tenure in the flat would last one week if the rent wasn't paid on time, the landlord was notorious about just throwing people out onto the streets, no matter what their circumstances may have been or were likely to be, he would have someone else established in the flat within the hour.

The money that James would earn wasn't quite as good as the engine sheds, but work is work and money is money, as long as they had enough to get by, that was fine.

James Jolly went back and picked up his money from the engine shed, and while there went to see Mr. Shakeshaft who he respected and liked.

"I wanted you to be the first to know, I have found a job with Bryers engineering. I want to thank you for giving me the chance to make something of myself, and I don't blame you in any way for the stupid thing that I did yesterday. I should never have hit Mr. Waters, he may be a liar and a cheat, but he didn't deserve a black eye from me. I shall always think kindly about my time here, I have leant a great deal, so once again thank you for everything."

Shakeshaft was struck dumb, but had the good grace to once again hold out his hand in friendship and wish young Jolly all the best in the future.

On the way out James saw out the corner of his eye Brian Waters hiding behind one of the locomotives, this made James smile wryly to himself, but he said nothing and just walked on.

8

Six months had passed since Elsa and her parents had returned to Hilversum from Iceland. Life was now easy for them, they had money coming in on a regular basis, and once again wealth led to esteem within the community.

Elsa was no longer looked upon as if she was a lowly servant, as now she had a position in life. Everyone knew about her business acumen in Iceland, and everyone knew that she had a regular small fortune coming into the local bank. The strangest aspect of this wealth was just how quickly Elsa adjusted to it. She didn't lord it over people, but she did take full advantage of not having to now carry money, her credit was accepted everywhere.

When Elsa walked down into the town, men would doff their hats and bow ever so slightly and it was done out of genuine respect, women wanted to befriend her, thus she was invited to everything, the doors were now open to her and for the first time. In Hilversum, Elsa had become royalty and she loved it with a passion.

She was now receiving regular minutes from the board meetings within the business, and everything seemed to be progressing extremely well. Jon Johnson had managed to find some prominent business men in the town, who were only to happy to buy into the business, even under the restrictions that Elsa had imposed, he had even managed to recruit two of his best and most loyal fishermen to sit on the board, and that now seemed to be working well, though there was embarrassment at first as both men had always thought of themselves as just the lowest workers with Peterson Fishing Cooperative, and now they had been lifted to bizarre phenomenal heights that scared and bewildered them initially.

But like most things in life, they soon learned to appreciate their new role within the business, and they quickly started to contribute sensible ideas, in fact their input became crucial to the business. It was a momentous idea to bring workers on to the board. A Eureka moment when thought out, it actually made so much sense. These two men had a lifetime of experience and knowledge, they knew what was needed and what should be thrown out. To Jon this innovation was the best thing that Elsa had thought up, and by giving these two men a position, it had been seen within the work force that anyone could have a chance to maybe work their way to higher positions in life.

What is more, these two men were now as they were growing older, able to get a decent salary, without risking life and limb, yet there thoughts, dreams, hopes and aspirations for the business would always be listened too, other board members soon quickly realised their particular worth. But best of all, business was booming, which meant now all the workers were doing better, with more money in their back pockets. This also had a good effect on the economy within Reykjavik as a whole, the more money that the ordinary workers received, the more they spent in shops. Very much a win, win situation for all.

Elsa and Jon were getting rich on the cod and red snappers, which was still in abundance, the whaling side was slightly slower, and it was a truism that those poor unfortunate creatures were obviously in decline. But having said that, one could still say that the money still came rolling in off the backs of dead whales.

The bank was doing well as much more needed foreign currencies were coming into the bank, and Iceland as a country was progressing along nicely, though the government had finally made one momentous resolution, they had unanimously decided to put a tax on all alcohol. The idea being that, make it too expensive for the common folk to buy, that might mean less alcoholics, less drunken forays into the nights, and hopefully fewer suicides.

The reality became, make your own hooch, cheap, strong, and probably full of wood alcohol, which possibly sends the drinker quickly into blindness and madness.

January, eighteen ninety eight came around like a bolt out of the blue, but it was a good bolt for the business as now Jon felt the company was in a position to invest in at least one new whaling ship. He knew exactly what he wanted, it would be made of good iron plates, it would consist of two engines, one always as a spare, and one turning a screw.

It would be roughly one hundred and fifty feet long and fifty feet wide, it must be able to catch, kill, lift on board, and then do most of the work of gutting, cleaning and cooking the meat of the animals thus doing away with the use of two or more smaller wooden ships. Now they had the funds, it was time to spend some of that money.

He sent his normal report to Elsa explaining that he intended to go to visit a shipyard in Glasgow, would she like to meet him there, and then they could check out plans and pricing together?

It was decided that they would meet on the 30th of June at Kleinbeck Shipyard, just between Glasgow and Greenock on the river Clyde, this company was renowned for its big fishing vessels, with the most up to-date equipment. It seemed like the perfect solution to their whaling fleet problems. Elsa was once again animated at the prospect of taking an exciting trip abroad. This time she was going alone, she knew she was up to it, she would make the right decisions without her father backing her up. She now felt strong enough to negotiate anything with anyone, that being in Iceland or Scotland, and she didn't need a nod of approval from anyone, which included her father Koos.

As the weeks past, Elsa got everything ready including making sure that banking arrangements were in order. She had decided to travel to Hook van Holland, and catch the overnight ferry to Harwich in England, and then get a train to London and then after a couple of days of rest and recovery time, maybe a little shopping to while away the time, then a Pullman Class express to Glasgow, another couple of days to recover then down to the shipyard and business.

Elsa had decided this was going to be a sort of holiday, and she wanted pleasure and luxury, all wrapped up in one package. Though she took the buying of a new vessel very serious, it was going to take second place to her having a fling with life.

June the 20th came around like a ball off a tennis racket, with a spin and at such a speed, so fast as to not remember where all the other days went. She said her goodbyes and boarded the train to the Hook, and then she entered her first ever state room on the ferry. The room was an outside cabin with aisle way walks into the restaurant and any entertainment that might be happening on board. It was a cabin that consisted of three rooms, a small but beautifully equipped bedroom, a bathroom and toilet, and a state room big enough to have a board meeting. Fruit, wine and chocolates were there for her to use as she wished. All the days papers were ready for her perusal, plus even yesterdays English Times.

This was quite a large ship that had built especially for just such work. It was geared up to take masses of freight and several hundred passengers as well. Though for the company to exist, it carried much of the mail to England that was destined for the entire British Isles.

Elsa went to explore what delights this vessel had to offer, she had boarded at six o'clock in the evening, but the ship was not due to sail until after midnight, as one of the holds would be loading live pigs, destined for slaughter in Britain and then onto some of London's best west-end restaurants.

Elsa found her way down and into the restaurant, looking around she was somewhat disappointed with the décor, she had expected a much higher standard in this particular place of eating, instead of the luxurious finery that being on this ferry was supposed to promise, it resembled more a workers rest room. There were paintings on the walls, but all of them looked cheap and rather bourgeois, no finesse, rather middle class, except it was meant to be first class.

'Pictures should depict pleasure or create feelings of excitement or pain, not just bland scenes of nothing in particular.'

Elsa was sorely disappointed with what she was staring at and her face reflected her feelings. The furniture was all old English oak, far better suited to a church, courtroom; somewhere were austerity should mean something. For a restaurant on an expensive first class ferry, this was all totally out of place. She wondered how customers would manage in extremely rough weather. Would this cumbersome furniture turn into lethal weapons being tossed around in big waves? Elsa pictured people and chairs being thrown from one end of the room to the other. Then she smiled to herself, thinking of who would be eating in a restaurant in rough weather.

One thing that did catch her eye was a wonderful table of fresh food, prominently out on display. She went over to look more closely, eyeing lobsters with their claws strapped, but still alive, cuts of meat, such as beef, lamb and pork. Whole turkey and duck, and of course chickens, several really beautifully cooked pullets, all looking good enough to eat. Fresh vegetables, tempting the onlooker into salivation, to any discerning onlooker, raw they may be, but in the form of presentation that was showing, it just had to make ones mouth water.

Then amidst a rock pile of ice was the fish display, wonderfully fresh looking cod and conger eels. There were smaller fish, though Elsa didn't know what they were she thought that they were probably extremely large sardines, but then Elsa's eyes were dazzled almost to distraction by the masses of shrimp and shell fish.

This was without doubt the best showing of good food that she had ever encountered. Elsa was then stopped in her tracks by the deserts, lots and lots of different types of puddings and then to top it all there was fresh fruit. At the end of this vast display came the cheeses. Of course most were Dutch, but she did notice some that must have come from other countries.

"Can I be of assistance madam?"

There standing at the beginning of the table stood a chef dressed all in white with a soft white cap upon his head. In the brief moment that she had looked at him, she had already noticed that under that cap was a mop of wavy shiny black hair. His skin was soft and pale greyish white, clean shaven and immaculate in appearance, even down to his shoes, which were dark brown and shining so brightly that you could almost see your own face reflecting back at you.

This was a man that knew how to present himself.

"Well, I would like to eat something, but I would also like a drink, maybe some Chablis would be nice!"

She looked again at this man, he stood maybe an inch or two taller than she did, he looked trim and fit, as if he knew how to look after himself. But what most intrigued her was his accent.

She stood her ground and asked,

"Where did you learn to speak Dutch? Are you German?"

"No madam, I am Polish, I was a chef in the Polish army. When I was discharged I choose to come to live in Holland, and so of course I had to learn the language. Which I hasten to add has been extremely hard, and so testing on the brain."

He was smiling broadly and was so relaxed and confident, that it almost made Elsa feel uncomfortable. He carried on as if they had been friends for years,

"When I landed the job of chief chef in this company, I was so out of my depth trying hard to make myself understood, but after a couple of years reading and studying, I think I have done just fine!"

He was so relaxed that he almost stood on one leg and slightly leaned against the table. His smile was so bright his shining teeth lit up the room, or so Elsa thought. He was standing tall and now sounded just ever so slightly smug, and then quickly checked himself as he realised that a frown had appeared on Elsa's countenance.

"Madam, I shall quickly get you a fine bottle of chilled Chablis."

He bowed deeply, then carried on speaking but in a softer more pleasant tone of voice,

"Please excuse my rudeness for continuous chattering. I rarely get to meet our customers so when I do, I find it a real sincere pleasure to be able to talk to someone like your good self."

"There is nothing to forgive, anyway, you sound as if you have had an extremely interesting life, you should tell me more."

Elsa looked around the room, being empty of customers made it all seem quite surreal. She selected a table near to the food, sat down and waited for the bottle to appear.

Eventually the chef came back bearing a bottle in a silver cooler, he then placed it before her, took a crystal glass, wiped it clean, even though it already was spotless, then poured a glass of pure golden yellow French Chablis. The smell that hit her was of elderflowers and foxgloves, it was almost overpowering in its intoxication. Lifting the glass to her nose she breathed in deeply, and then very carefully she put it to her lips and sipped that first drop. It made a tingle go up her spine, it was unbelievably fine, just enough age to give body and take away that acidity that came with new wines.

"This is beautiful. Well done, why don't you join me in a glass?"

The chef almost jumped back.

"No madam, I couldn't possibly accept a glass of wine from you, it is more than my job is worth."

"Oh, sorry, I should have thought. So, what delights are you going to prepare for me?"

Now coming down from his fear of retribution, he leaned forward onto the table and answered,

"Would you allow me to make you something really special?"

"That would be absolutely wonderful. I haven't eaten for hours, so three courses would be good. I will gladly leave it entirely in your, I am sure, perfectly capable hands. By the way, what is your name?"

"Madam, my name is Ivan Kolinsky, and I am at your service."

He clicked his heals sharply, for a moment he was back in the army.

"Ivan, are you related to Ivan the Terrible?"

As she said this sentence, Elsa caught herself from almost laughing out loud, but she did give a small snigger, teasing this Ivan was an enjoyable pastime.

No other passengers came to the first class restaurant while Elsa was awaiting her food, she drank heavily of the wine and ordered another bottle. She was now almost completely intoxicated and enjoying every moment of it. The ship itself was a disappointment, but the food and wine were wonderful.

Ivan excelled himself, he made three beautiful dishes for Elsa. Sadly for the shipping company not one other person came into the first class restaurant, so Ivan's services were not needed elsewhere, he was there exclusively for Elsa. He came out after she had finally finished her desert, and offered her an English cigarette and a glass of French Brandy, which she gladly accepted both, even though she didn't actually smoke. But having now drunk two full bottles of Chablis and about to drink a tot of brandy, she no longer cared if she had ever smoked before or not. She put the cigarette into her mouth and sucked in the smoke. After a couple of puffs she coughed and spluttered, and then suddenly started to turn green. Ivan quickly retrieved the burning cigarette from her and put it out in an ashtray, then realising that she might be sick he quickly went for some help. He found the bursar, a chap who quickly recognised Ivan's value as he loved his food intake. He was a stout fellow in his late thirties with a name that didn't match his appearance.

Kevin Thin looked at Ivan and asked,

"What has happened you look worried?"

"Kevin my friend, please come and help me, a lady in the restaurant has over done the wine and brandy, I need to get her back to her cabin. Firstly, which is her cabin, then what is her name, and will you please help me get her back there before any officers sees her in this state and starts blaming me for her sorry state?"

At the moment the ship started to pull away from the quayside, there was a great deal of noise and crashing as engines turned and ropes and men were kept busy doing whatever they needed to clear the harbour.

"Her name is Peterson, Mrs. Elsa Peterson. She comes from Hilversum and is going to Harwich. She is in an outside stateroom, 2-A. You want me to help you take her there?"

"Please Kevin! I really don't want any trouble because of this rich lady. I will cook you a special if you help me."

"You're on my boy!"

The bursars face lit up at the thought of a special Ivan Kolinsky meal.

"But we had better move her now, everyone is busy and I can spare a couple of minutes. Here, take the master key."

They both entered the restaurant, and fortunately there still weren't any customers other than Elsa in there. Elsa now had her head firmly planted on the table with her arms dangling down by her side.

'O my God, she's out for the count.'

"Kevin, you take one arm and I will take the other, let's walk her to her cabin."

They both managed to pick her up and gently guided her through the corridor and out onto the side aisle where the first class cabins were situated. Ivan opened the door and they both carried her in and laid her on her bunk bed.

They both discreetly left without touching anything. Kevin thanked his friend and said that he would cook him a meal immediately he was free from his bursar obligations, which would be agreeable to both. Thus Kevin Thin went back to his desk, smirking and licking his lips anticipating a fine culinary treat. Ivan went back and signed a chit relating to the cost that Elsa would have to pay for the drinks and the meal. It was then that he realised he still had the master key.

It played on Ivan's mind while he was cooking up a sumptuous meal for his partner in crime, he just hoped that Elsa would not blame him for her state of being and complain to an officer. He liked his job, no not true, he loved his job, especially now he had transferred to the more lucrative Harwich run instead of the Dover one, which tended to get a lower class of passengers, he feared for his future and he just didn't want to lose this job.

It was nearly one in the morning when he had cleaned away all the food, throwing most of it overboard, and then he washed up all the bits and pieces, not leaving it to the cleaners and waiters, he was still worried and needed to be busy.

No one was around and he was still thinking of Elsa. Should he dare to approach her tonight or wait until the morning? He decided that it might be better to strike while the iron is hot. He went to her cabin and knocked very carefully on the door, there was no reply, not a sound could be heard coming from the inside. He placed the master key in the lock and turned it to open the door. It was then that he heard the sound of Elsa turning.

"Er, excuse me Mrs. Peterson, it is me Ivan, the chef. I was worried about you, can I come in?"

Just a small groan came back as a reply. There was silence for a moment while Ivan entered and re-closed the door. The silence was deafening, and then all of a sudden a voice came back with an alarming tone to it,

"Who's there? I'll call for help, who are you?"

"Please Mrs. Peterson, calm yourself, I was truly worried about you and wondered if you were all right, you were very drunk when we brought you back to your cabin, I only…"

He didn't get a chance to finish the sentence.

"Ivan, Ivan the chef, is that you? How did you get in? Just a moment I will come out of this bedroom, just wait there for a minute."

There was silence again for a couple of minutes, then a diminutive rather worse for wear lady appeared at the door.

"Can you please put on the light, I feel stupid enough as it is, without standing here in the darkness."

Ivan put on the new electric lighting. She looked vulnerable but beautiful, and he realised for the first time that they were both about the same age, being in their thirties, albeit late thirties. Her hair was somewhat ruffled and her makeup had seen better days, but that didn't matter. His heart leapt somewhat as he noticed that her breasts were slightly showing through her dressing gown. He noticed that she not only had a very interesting face but her body was slight and curvaceous. At these thoughts he couldn't stop the erection that was starting to expand in his trousers.

Elsa looked at him and now noticed a man that stood roughly five feet eight to ten inches tall, had a fine figure not showing the slightest flab or obesity, which was strange considering his job working with food all day long. His flush of shiny black hair shone in the glow of the electric light and she then noticed his fine rugged features, he was indeed all man. And for the first time since the death of her husband, and Elsa felt herself becoming wet.

"What was it you wanted?"

"I am sorry, I shouldn't have come here. The truth is I was worried about you. You looked terrible, and I felt responsible for your state. Are you all right now?"

Elsa relaxed and laughed not loudly but enough for him to hear.

"Ivan, sit down and relax. I think it is very nice of you to fret on my behalf. Please do sit down, I'm just fine. I know, let's have that drink together now, there is lots of bottles here, I guess they are for my use, so let's have one."

"Are you sure? You were pretty drunk."

"Ivan, I was drunk, but I am not now. I think what really got to me, was you offering me that blasted cigarette. I have never smoked before, and I shall not do it again, how anybody can enjoy such a disgusting habit is far beyond me. It made me feel really sick. But, as you can see, I have recovered."

Her charming smile lifted both their spirits, Ivan sat down and watched as Elsa bent over to pick a bottle, open it and pour a couple of glasses. He watched as the outline of her bottom showed clearly through the loose fitting fabric of her gown. Now he was almost beyond help, he felt like grabbing her, throwing her onto the bed and ravaging her thoroughly. But of course he didn't, he didn't need to.

Within five minutes Elsa was in his arms, not even quite knowing how, she was kissing him passionately and feeling all over his body, a real mans body. Then she felt the bulge in his trousers and squealed with delight. She rose, grabbed at his arm and without saying a word took him into the bedroom took off his clothes, caressed his body with kisses, pulled off her own garment and urged him to make love to her.

That part wasn't difficult, in fact he managed to make love three times before dawn started to show through the window, both had reached a state of exhaustion, but the tiredness was a delight to both.

"Elsa, I have to go and prepare breakfast. It is my job to feed the crew before six o'clock in the morning, on the return journey I can sleep in, but the outward journey is always a tough one. Forgive me, but I must leave."

He kissed her private parts and noticed that she once again squealed.

'Oh well! The crew can just wait a few minutes more.'

Once again passion took over from their reasoning.

A couple of hours later, Elsa went down to partake in some food. She saw Ivan and smiled meekly at him. They pretended that they didn't know one another as a few other passengers were gathering to acquire some nourishment.

"Madam, can I be of assistance?"

"Why thank you. Yes, I would like some scrambled eggs on rye bread, and some French coffee please. I shall sit over there, will you bring it to me?"

"Yes madam, it will be my pleasure."

Even though there were waiters to do the tasks for the passengers, Ivan made the scrambled eggs, boiled up the water and made the coffee himself, then he placed it all on a tray, placed a flower in a small vase and took it to her table. Elsa said quietly,

"Ivan, I have to go to Glasgow, I might be a couple of weeks, though am not sure about the timing. But when I return I shall be using this ferry, will you be on it still?"

"Yes Elsa, I will be here, waiting and ready for you. Last night was paradise, at least for me."

"For me too."

She assured him.

"You are the first since the death of my husband. I absolutely loved every second of it."

She smiled a special smile, which was meant just for him, then she brushed her hand gently against his, light enough to give him a tingle, but in a way that no one else would be aware of.

They docked in Harwich later that day, and Elsa disembarked wondering if she would ever see Ivan again?

'Ivan, what a fine lover to have had. I needed last night, but ships in the night, nice but not serious.'

Then her thoughts parted from Ivan and descended on the reason as to why she was going to Glasgow, work!

Once in London, Elsa booked herself into the Strand Hotel, and she decided to stay three nights and days. Now here was luxury, not just the word but the real thing. Her room was large and sumptuous. It oozed affluence and prosperity, everything was of top quality, the service was excellent, everything about the hotel just shone out as high society, it virtually oozed money.

'Here is where the elite of Britain mingle. I wonder just how many Lords and Ladies are here now?'

Three whole days of eating, sightseeing and shopping, this was heaven to Elsa, but she knew that she must soon concentrate on work. The last night in London was going to be spent going to a concert, seeing and listening to one of the many orchestras that seemed to be doing their thing around the capital at this time. She noted that a young English composer was conducting some of his music in the Queens Hall. His name was Edward Elgar, but Elsa had never heard of him, it should be at least interesting, and there was always the chance that the Queen might attend.

It was rumoured that she was now being seen around attending things again, and the very thought made Elsa's heart flutter with excitement.

The concert was interesting, and Elgar was as English as anyone could be. She realised that had she met him in the Gobi Desert she would surely have asked him if he was from Great Britain that is how much his Englishness stood out, at least in her eyes.

The next morning came with the famous world renown London smog, there was warm smoky air making everything feel like a choking steam bath, except that breathing in meant taking into your lungs air that was so contaminated with soot, smoke and industrial waste, more than bad enough so that the person breathing it always felt asthmatic at best. The smell of the river Thames was not to pleasant either, but Elsa only noticed these things now that she was leaving. A handsome cab driver took her luggage, placed it carefully on his luggage rack and then escorted Elsa into a seat. The horse had his nose covered in a wet rag, but it trotted off managing to take them to Euston Railway station, and the train to Glasgow.

Once again, having pre-booked her first class seat, it was going to be an interesting journey for her. A porter showed her to her carriage, then explained where the dining car was, loaded her luggage into the luggage van, then stood there with his hand out waiting for his tip.

The journey up to Glasgow was uneventful, but somewhat boring as it was a long hard trek. The service in the dining car was excellent, but the meal took a long time to arrive, leaving Elsa rather frustrated as she was growing used to first class service.

She had acquired a couple of newspapers, and took her time to read in English. Queen Victoria had been at the Chelsea Barracks inspecting the troops, many had just come back from fighting the Boers in South Africa, and reading about her distant country folk as if they were the warmongers of the world rather upset Elsa.

The countryside right up until they reached beyond Crewe was uninteresting, with more pollution and firing factories burst their guts to out produce the next factory, and to hell with the health of the people around. But after Crewe, the country became hillier, more colourful and very much more rural. The sites attracted Elsa's eyes, Holland was so flat, and here were small mountains, vast amounts of sheep grazed the fields, cattle seemed to be roaming freely, and as the sun had finally broken through the smog, the cattle looked like paintings as they shimmered under the glare of the gleaming suns rays. Greenery overtook the grey filth of cities, and the pollution was soon forgotten.

It was dusk as the train entered the main station in Glasgow, again they were back to bad dirty air, but this was not like London. Elsa got a porter to help with the luggage, and it was carried the few yards to the entrance of the Station Hotel, a fine edifies of a building that showed all the grandeur of wealthy Victorian Britain, luxury was once again the key word.

Glasgow turned out to be a delight, luxurious shopping, fine restaurants and good things to see. There was a ferry that cruised up and down the Clyde, though not first class in stylisation, it did offer a fine chance to see what the outside of Glasgow was about, what better way than from the major river. The SS Invaglory was an old paddle steamer that was still running, but more for the pleasure of its passengers than the to-ing and fro-ing of goods. Fortunately the second day in Glasgow was a beautifully sunny day, giving ideal conditions for a trip on the Clyde.

The journey started at nine o'clock in the morning and would return not later than six at night. Elsa laid out on a deck chair, and very gradually watched as the city turned into suburbs, then into rural countryside. And as the journey progressed the river got wider and wider, and started to look more like sea than a river, islands came in to view, not that she was told that they were indeed islands, to Elsa they looked like extended spits of land gutting into an ever increasing sizable river, but never-the-less she was enjoying the beauty of it all.

It was interesting for Elsa to pass by the very ship building yard that she was to meet Jon Johnson in two days time. Kleinbeck Shipyard, was not particularly imposing, in fact had not one of the crew came up and told her that they were just about to pass the yard, she would never had guessed. It had a very large slipway, made from concrete, but the cranes and rigging, didn't impose itself on anyone.

'So what makes this yard so special?'

The more she looked, the more she had her doubts. There were two vessels being built, both rather small iron fishing boats, nothing outstanding about that. Elsa was perplexed, but still kept an open mind.

'Jon will have done his homework I am sure of that!'

Though she wasn't that naïve to really expect an Icelandic fishing partner to have all the answers to all possible questions concerning the production of whaling ships. But she lived in hope that her judgement wasn't misplaced!

The Invaglory stopped to unload some post and parcels at the port in Greenock, but Elsa knew there wasn't enough time to visit this small grey depressing little port. Very few building were using brick, all seemed to be built with either granite or sandstone, and often grey sandstone at that. Smoke seemed to be drifting everywhere, and the entire town seemed to be rather destitute of people, probably because they all were at work in the many mills and factories that abounded within the area.

Soon the paddle steamer was underway again, some more passengers had joined, as some had left. Next stop would be Gourock, then onto Dunoon. As they sailed, Elsa realised that firstly the sun was probably to hot for her overly white complexion, she didn't want to get burnt, that would hardly be fitting for a lady of her means. That decided, it might be time to go below and find something to eat. There was a form of a restaurant, but the cuisine was hardly gourmet. All that was on offer were cod fillets with boiled potatoes and a hunk of brown rather hard bread. She actually was hoping for some meat, maybe some Angus steaks that she had heard so much about, that would have been nice, but fish what was on offer, and when hunger takes over, your stomach doesn't argue with what is on or off the menu. Strangely, it was all quite tasty and filling, but again, hardly gourmet.

Once again, both the next two ports were very disappointing from the point of view of beauty or come to that any real interesting industrial facets, both were rather dirty, grimy grey towns with dirty grey harbours to sidle up against.

The colour of the water around each of the ports reminded her of Reykjavik, with oily water, full of filth and flotsam and jetsam, plus not to forget human effluence that seemed to be swimming around everywhere. The very air was alive with smells that would really not be wanted on board, and surprisingly considering it was now sea, brine didn't usually attract such an incredibly large amount of flies and mosquitoes, they seemed to be a perpetual menace to all the passengers on board. These insects only left you alone when out in the middle of the river, other than that, they were part of your very being, you just couldn't keep brushing them away all the time as there were just too many.

This area of Scotland was a total intimidation to Elsa's thinking of Britain in general and the people that lived there. This part of her journey had now coloured her mind against this country called Great Britain, there was absolutely nothing great about the filth and pollution, and the poverty was rampant and endemic.

She returned to the hotel now a little shaken, though Holland, and of course Hilversum, were backward compared to Britain, but there wasn't the sort of poverty that showed itself like Scotland or England.

Everyone in Holland could afford to wear clogs, even if they couldn't afford leather shoes. Everyone had a change of clothes when what they were wearing became too dirty to be seen in. But not here in Britain. Everyone in the Nederland's could get a decent amount of food to eat on a daily basis, but not necessarily in the British Isles.

Elsa was cutely aware that people in Britain could quite easily starve, have no place to live, not have enough shoes and clothing. In fact the majority of working class people were extremely poor.

Elsa saw Britain as a country of extremes, on the one hand she saw the most beautiful rugged terrain, with nature being allowed to show off all its beauty. Mountains, waterfalls, lakes, rivers, and the wonderful greenery as shown through the different trees that grew practically everywhere. Then you have the horrors of the industrial areas, with all its poverty, pollution and filth, its run down buildings, housing run down people. As the British as a nation brag about their countries wealth, it doesn't come across as a prosperous nation when you see the degradation. The sun may never set on the British Empire, but in Elsa's eyes it never rises to shine on the cities and industrial towns.

It was agreed by Jon and Elsa that they would meet at Kleinbeck Shipyard on the 30th at eleven o'clock in the morning, the appointment was with a designer and manager at twelve, which meant that they had one hour to talk about the entire project.

Elsa reached the gate at ten forty-five to find Jon already waiting dressed in a very smart suit, with his blond locks of hair slicked back. He looked every bit the business man and looked extremely smart in what was obviously a new suit..

"Wow, you look just the ticket. It is nice to see you dressed up and city slick, you will represent Peterson Fishing Cooperative with a certain amount of decorum, exactly right for the occasion. We don't want these damned Scottish peasants to think they are dealing with yokels."

Elsa winked as she said this. Jon didn't understand the analogy and just shrugged it off as some sort of Dutch phrasing of sentences.

There was a small café across the road from the shipyard gate, so it was decided that they should partake in a coffee, then arrive exactly on time. The coffee tasted of burnt acorns, stewed up to make a sort of coffee brew, which as it happens was exactly what it was. A very cheap and easy substitute for coffee beans.

When they went back across the road to the gatehouse, there was the designer and floor manager already waiting for them to come back.

"Madam, sir, may I be the first at Kleinbeck to say how glad we are to receive you both. I do hope that your visit to our wonderful country has been an interesting one. I was told by the gatekeeper that you had gone across to the café, I hope it wasn't a too unpleasant experience for you."

This was the manager, his name was Joseph Kettle, a slim built smartly dressed man, with dark straight hair, he didn't look British, maybe eastern European origins. His English had a very broad accent about it, obviously stemming from Glasgow or Greenock, but spoken in a soft warm way, that immediately put the two guests at ease. He didn't for one second question the fact that Elsa seemed to be in charge, he was diplomacy itself.

"We will give you some real coffee, and something maybe a bit stronger to wash away the taste that that awful place leaves on pallets of discerning people."

Again a broad grin on his countenance, plus a twinkle in his eye, these expressions of confidence and friendliness would have disarmed a warring Mongol.

Both Jon and Elsa felt comfortable, but somewhat gullible. They hadn't realised, probably forgotten, just how good these salesman could be, and what they might well be up against in the war of commerce, maybe this was going to be a learning curve for them both, but somehow with the friendly atmosphere it didn't matter at this particular time.

They were shown into an extremely opulent board room, and there seated were members of the management team like spiders on a web, waiting for the arrival of the prey. Elsa and Jon were completely taken aback, not expecting this formidable array of people to be there greeting them. They were sat down in very comfortable leather seated chairs. A waiter immediately came with cups of coffee for everyone there, and after the polite conversation was said, expressing good wishes and safe journeys etc.....

They got down to business.

"Have you brought drawing of the sort of vessel that you are looking to build?"

The manager who had actually greeted them at the gate seemed to be in charge.

"Obviously, we are limited to sizing on this particular yard, but if this yard couldn't accommodate your needs we have a much bigger yard in Prestwick just north of Ayr. But then you would know that wouldn't you."

Elsa smiled to Jon, who just looked somewhat blank.

"We of course know of your capacity, what you can and cannot do. And Jon, my partner has sketches of what we are looking for, and I rather suspect that you can accommodate all our needs in this yard."

She smiled sweetly at the complete management team, then towards Jon,

"Show them your drawings please Jon."

Jon brought up his new leather briefcase and plunged inside to retrieve a collection of sketches and plans that he and some other board members had drawn up.

Jon then took centre stage.

"As you can see from these drawings, we are looking for a vessel that will handle well in extreme northern weather conditions, it must have a rear control tower which combines the crew sleeping quarters and mess areas. There, if you look at this particular drawing will be a factory area for cutting up and processing whales. We want good steam engines capable of at least ten knots, and one extra standby engine in case of emergencies. The cranes and rigging should be as shown, they should be strong enough to lift up to twenty tons and be housed around this sort of area. In fact these drawings cover most things. As for weight and length, we were not sure just how to calculate these necessities. But then I don't need to do everything for you, do I."

Jon Johnson took another a small shallow breath and then added,

"After all this is what we are going to be paying for, your expertise."

This created a small ripple of laughter. But Jon had started well and now the management team were all ears and full of attention.

The meeting went on for several hours which surprised Elsa who had expected everything to be settled within just one hour, this made her smile and realise just how naïve she could be concerning business matters. But she was content with knowing that she was indeed holding her head aloft and not looking a complete and utter fool.

Eventually it was time for a break, and a very welcome lunch took place within the board room, and a fine friendly repast was enjoyed by all that attended. Eventually in the late afternoon, the chairman came into the board room, introduced himself and then asked if all the time they had been there, had they actually been shown around? Jon was to busy explaining and arguing points of this or that, but Elsa had spent the last hour feeling very uncomfortable hardly daring to breath let alone speak. She was now completely out of her depth, and she knew it, as did everyone else there. So she accepted the invitation of a tour of inspection with grateful thanks, anything to break the monotone droning of men with missions.

Frank Kleinbeck was a third generation Kleinbeck since the founding of the shipbuilding yard in seventeen ninety. He was an upright tall elegant man in his late sixties, he was immensely proud of the family's achievement in boat and ship building. He wore an immaculately cut three piece suit which was quite obviously tailored in London. He came across as being dapper and with his beautifully groomed handlebar moustache, he looked all of what she thought of as the English Victorian gentleman, not Scottish but most definitely English, though for sure Frank was a true blue Scotsman through and through, plus in many ways totally anti English. In fact he was an active member of the home rule party, though he would have been quite keen if England became associated and come under Scottish rule, with Parliament being placed in Edinburgh

This was in fact the original yard, and though somewhat rundown and looking as if it had seen better days, it showed itself as efficiency personified. The metalwork walling, in places had rusted through, but on the whole the weather was kept out of the main building shed and slipway. The river lapped up against the jetty that followed the slipway down into the water, and Elsa couldn't help but notice that there were several small craft tied up awaiting delivery, she hadn't noticed these when sailing past on the paddle steamer, only the two vessels that were on the other bigger slipway. The jetty was made from concrete posts and wooden slats for walking on, but she wouldn't be walking across any of those, her fear of slipping into the filthy water saw to that.

"Allow me to show the two tug boats that are being constructed on the other slipway. Here take my arm. I don't want you slipping on the slope here."

Elsa was amused at the gentlemanly way old Frank Kleinbeck conducted himself. He would be the one to allow her to walk through the door first, would always stand when a woman entered the room and would only sit down again when she was sitting, he walked on the outside of a pavement, and would always take a ladies arm to support her, even though she was younger and probably stronger than he was. But manners maketh the man, and Frank was without doubt that man. His manners were from a lifetime of thinking of woman as the helpless gender, but that only heightened Elsa's delight in being pampered but such a man.

Frank showed her every part of the constructions that were in progress, even taking her through the bigger factory complex that now made the steam engines. Though generally the company would bring in standard outside made engines, but he always made sure that the company made all the boilers, as they would have to be bespoke to the special size of each ship. But there in this building, they had the capability to build from scratch their own design in engines, and that now included a very high performance steam engine.

The talks went well with Jon and the designer and management team, it was decided that they would stay in Glasgow for some days, and the team would come up with a special design that would suit the whaler's needs. Anyway, it would take two or three days to work out some sort of price structure. That was acceptable to all parties, once agreed Jon and Elsa decided it was time to return to her hotel.

Frank Kleinbeck, still the gentleman insisted that his chauffeur should drive them both back in his new automobile, in fact he was going to accompany them too, then after they had settled in he wanted, in fact insisted, that he take them both to dinner at his club within the city centre.

This was the first time that Jon had been driven in an automobile, and by the time they reached the outskirts of Glasgow, he had decided that he wanted one, and that he would have it taken by ship to Reykjavik, even though Iceland didn't have any petrol stations facilities as such.

The Station Hotel had plenty of room to accommodate Jon, in fact his stateroom was even more luxurious than Elsa's, not that she got to see the inside of it. Frank settled down in the bar area and acquired a large glass of single malt whisky while he waited for his two guests to get changed for the journey to his club. Old Kleinbeck was looking like a proper gentleman, his suit and tie were still showing as if they had just been put on, not actually spending a working day in them.

He had the barman make him a Scotch on the rocks, as he didn't want to just sit there looking rather serious and like a lost penny, at the same time he bought his chauffeur a large glass of whisky and had a waiter take it out to where he was still sitting in the drivers seat in the car.

Eventually Jon came down and joined Frank, but declined the offer of a drink. Being what he thought of as canny, he didn't want to be at a disadvantage by consuming intoxicating liquor. But that didn't stop the old man from acquiring yet another double for himself, after all it still might be some time before the lady appeared. Ten minutes and yet another drink later, Elsa appeared dressed in the most appealing plus alluring dress. She was dressed in a dark purple gown, that being full length dragged a large amount of cloth behind her, her top was matching, yet underneath and showing itself to all, she wore a pure white silken blouse, though pure and virginal in colour, it gave an outline of her curvaceous figure, a figure that neither she or anyone else knew she had before this evening. Her footwear were brown buttoned up boots with a small one inch heal lifting her gently into new heights. Her hair was lifted and curled around the top of her head, and she had on several head hair pins that gave the look of being extremely expensive accessories being diamonds, she also sported a diamond brooch, that was pinned just above her left breast. Both men were open mouthed as she approached them, she looked wonderful.

"My dear lady, you look ravishing."

"Elsa, may I second that, you look a million dollars."

Elsa gave a small curtsy.

"Why thank you kind sirs."

Three days later a proposal for the vessel had been laid out for the duo to see in full. Though obviously not all specifications were there to see, the outline of SS Saga King, as it was going to be called were there to be viewed. It was all that Jon Johnson wanted in his new steam powered whaling ship. This was going to be the first of many, if he got his way! The only thing that the management team had not come up with was an accurate pricing, that would take several months with also leeway to be allowed on either side of the ballpoint figure.

But as a specific sum had been agreed by both parties in principal, it seemed as if it would be all systems go. Both Jon and Elsa were told that once started, and that wouldn't be for at least another two months, it would possibly take seven more months to complete, run off the slipway, fit out and do the trials in.

That was acceptable in the eyes of the two partners, and the primary go ahead was given. But of course nothing was cast in stone until an agreed down payment was received and contracts had been signed.

Four more days went by, Jon had gone back to Musselburgh, where he had contracted one of the companies fishing boats to take him to Esbjerg in Denmark, then either wait for one of the many Icelandic fishing boats to come by and sell their stock, or catch the ferry outward to Reykjavik, whatever was quicker in coming.

It turned out to be the ferry.

By the time Jon was on his way to Denmark, Elsa was boarding the SS Breakspeare, the self same ferry that brought her to England was now going to take her back to Holland. She acquired the same cabin as before, went to it and had her luggage placed carefully against the far wall away from the drinks cabinet and the door to the toilet and washroom. She had forgotten all about her experience with the Polish chef, she couldn't even remember his name. But the porter remembered her and he had heard the tales of an exciting night spent by his friend, so the next thing he did was to go direct to his chum and inform him of who was now once again on board. It was now just a matter of time before Ivan would see her in the restaurant, thus he waited patiently.

The ship left Harwich an hour later, having spent the entire morning loading cargo for the Nederland's. And now only ten minutes after boarding had finally finished the ropes were cast off, engines kicked the ship forward and the ferry moved in a somewhat throbbing lethargic motion out towards the North Sea.

As the ship passed by the last spit of land Elsa was leaning over the railings watching other ships large and small manoeuvring around the various ports, quays and harbours either coming or going.

What a busy waterway Harwich was, and yet the town was nothing, a very uninteresting place with a small Napoleonic fort, and a modern lighthouse that was built almost a couple of hundred yards inland, which made one wonder if the builder was expecting the sea to start reclaiming the land.

The sea was grey in colour and very choppy, rough enough to make the ship wobble from side to side. This tempestuous roughness of the water was not from the existing wind within the weather, because there was no such wind, but from the very serious tidal flow that came into the river Stour and Orwell, which connected at the same estuary, when the tides were flowing, the force of water from the North Sea was tremendous, and it surged into those two rivers twice a day with incredibly ferocity. Elsa could imagine how dangerous it would be to actually fall into the water at this point, unless one was an exceptional swimmer, one would be swept to ones death in seconds.

The vessel passed by the currents quickly and out into calmer seas. Here fishing vessels were busy dragging nets and catching herring, mackerel, even cod and haddock, because of those cold Northern waters, the seas were alive and thriving with the fish that the British wanted, and as much as they could get to compliment their chips.

It wasn't long before England was just a line in the distance, growing ever smaller as each minute passed. Once passed the dangerous currents the vessel slowed down somewhat, so that they would arrive back at Hook van Holland in the early hours of the morning.

Elsa realised that it was now getting colder, and she was getting hungry. It was at this thought that she remembered Ivan Kolinsky the Polish chef.

'O dear, do I really want to bump into him again?'

She pondered that thought for several minutes, and then hunger dictated her decision for her. She changed her clothes to something a little more formal. As now the ship was busy, she hoped that the first class restaurant would have more people in it than on the outward journey, thus giving her a way of avoiding Ivan.

The décor was exactly the same as she remembered it to be, opulent and rather bourgeois, but poorly done, rather trashy poor taste giving it a look of being cheap and somewhat tatty. It almost made her squirm as she realised that this poor standard was endemic of all Dutch things to do with style. The people of the Netherlands never seemed to have grasped the ideas of, say England, with its royal traditions, customs and ceremonies that made everything that was meant to be first class just that.

In many ways Elsa understood the differences between the two countries, Britain had its wealth from its many colonies, the Dutch on the other hand, had not really exploited their overseas territories to the same extent. The other factor was slightly more obvious, there were less peoples residing in Holland as there were in Great Britain, also Britain had such diverse standards of wealth. In England, and Wales, Scotland and Ireland, and people of the lower classes were really kept low, they worked hard for their meagre rations, they couldn't afford better clothing, and children rarely managed to obtain shoes, were as in Holland, though there was poverty, people didn't starve and they could pretty well always afford clothing and shoes.

The peasants working the land often had it extremely hard, but a certain fairness in wages showed that the workers always managed to obtain the very basics for a satisfactory standard of living. England had incredible beauty within its boundaries, Holland was flat and somewhat boring. The pollution in Britain, though entirely due to the march of the industrial revolutionary progress, was appalling, and to any passing anthropologist this cocktail was very dangerous, giving the people that lived within the industrial zones a fallout of the lethal fumes that caused many diseases, many incurable, and so many that hardly existed before the industrial revolution. Holland really didn't have those problems as of yet. But like most of the western worlds countries, they too chased the sort of prosperity that industrial filth seemed to give, so pollution and extremes in wealth was what the hierarchy of Holland wanted and thus looked enviously at Britain, yearning for those same problems.

Human waste was a great problem with the millions of people living in Britain, and the rivers and seas were terribly polluted, in fact most of the rivers connecting to towns were dead and dangerous. But, once again in Holland, and this problem didn't seriously occur. One of the reasons why this wasn't as yet a serious problem was because human waste along with the animals, was used for fertilising the fields.

While Elsa stood in the entrance to the restaurant agonising on these ponderous thoughts, a small but intimate voice spoke to her,

"Hello Elsa, I have kept a table aside for you."

Elsa jumped not expecting anyone to call her by name. She looked up and saw the handsome features of Ivan. She once again noticed how impressive he looked in his immaculate whites and his dark wavy hair shining and gleaming through his chef's cap, his dark brown eyes staring directly into hers, she immediately melted.

Like a lamb to the slaughter, she followed him to the table that he had put aside especially for her. There was already an opened bottle of Chablis standing in a cooler, plus a glass with crushed ice flowing from it awaiting her pleasure. She sat down unable to say a word, she didn't need to.

"I have missed you, and have been waiting with longing for your return. Can I prepare you something special?"

"You have been waiting for me? Yes, er, what, make something special, please, can you?"

Somehow she didn't make any sense, and she noticed that a broad grin had crossed his face. Elsa went bright red, and then on looking around noticed that the actual restaurant was almost full, not like last time.

Ivan poured her a glass of sparkling golden yellow Chablis, which she took gladly and drank it down as if it was a glass of water. Then realising what she had done, once again went bright red. Another glass was filled but this time she resisted the temptation to down it in one. Ivan left her to start his pleasurable duty of catering for her.

Elsa sat there still in a state of shock wondering why her stomach was churning so badly. To overcome the feeling of dampness between her legs she started to study the people around her.

That night when she had retired to her cabin, she got herself cleaned and into her night attire. She made the experience of washing and undressing last almost an hour, she knew he would eventually come to her door. It was just striking midnight when there was a light tap on her door, Elsa knew that whatever she had good intentions about, once he entered, all those good intensions went straight out the self same door to be washed away by the North Sea.

There he stood looking for the entire world like an Eastern Prince in her eyes, and to her astonishment in his hand he was carrying a small posy of flowers, he entered the room as if he owned it. He didn't wait for any small talk, he just dropped the posy on a seat, moved over to where she was, swept her off her feet and carried her into the bedroom. There they spent the night in love making. The journey out had been a fine experience, but this time, it was the greatest experience that Elsa had ever known. She had orgasm after orgasm, something completely alien to her, and completely unknown in her marriage. Throughout the entire night she lay in ecstasy having totally lost control of every fibre of her being, her muscles no longer did as requested, her nerves ends had total control of themselves, Elsa twitched, turned, rolled this way and that, but the excitement was such that anyway she no longer cared. In that night of pure unadulterated sex, they had both explored every inch of one another's bodies, playing with this or that, either with fingers, hands or tongues. Sleep was a thing that only others did, this was their night of passion.

It was nearly nine o'clock when the door was being knocked on again. Elsa had been asleep.

There was no Ivan, he had excused himself some time earlier so as to start on the breakfasts. This time it was the maid.

135

"Sorry to wake you madam, but we have actually docked and you should now leave the ship. I will come back in say, ten minutes, that should give you time to rise and wash."

With that she left, closing the door noisily, so that Elsa knew it really was time to rise and go.

It was only when she started to pack her night attire in her suitcase that she noticed the letter from Ivan, this she put in her purse and then promptly forgot about it. The porter and the maid appeared a few minutes later, then Elsa and her baggage where unceremoniously dumped on the quayside. She hadn't seen Ivan to say goodbye and now it was just too late. This was only the second serious man in her life, she didn't feel any love for Ivan, but he did stir her loins into a frenzy. She had experienced feelings on these occasions that she didn't know existed within her, they were at the very least exciting and breathtaking, and she would miss such experiences and feeling, but miss them she must. She wasn't going to throw herself at a Polish vagabond, no fear about that. And once again she quickly forgot all about her soldier lover, she had much more important things to think about.

Five weeks later, the contracts had been signed and money for the large deposit had been forwarded to the shipyards bank in Glasgow. She heard that the start date for the laying down of the keel would be within the next four weeks, then anything up to seven months until completion of the vessel. From time to time, Jon would travel all the way to the shipyard in Scotland to keep an eye on the progress, and when the time came, Elsa would come over for the launching.

The very next day that this was all agreed Elsa got sick. She didn't understand what was wrong with herself, but the thought of eating bread or cheese made her throw up.

Her mother was the first to ask the question,

"Elsa, are you pregnant?"

Elsa looked stunned, but her mother continued the cross examination,

"Have you been with some other man since your poor husband died?"

Now Elsa was glowing bright crimson, she didn't need to answer any of the questions, her face showed the answers.

It was at this moment that Elsa remembered the letter that she had put in her purse, one that she rarely used. She retrieved the letter and read it....

My dearest Elsa,

I have to leave you early because I have to get the breakfasts ready for our remaining customers. But, I couldn't let you go without telling you how much your two visits have meant to me. I am quite sure I am deeply in love with you, even knowing that you hardly know anything about me, or visa versa. But please will you try and understand, and I am first a Pole, then a soldier, then a chef. I didn't engineer to be in Holland, and but I guess it was a certain amount of fate and luck that brought me here, but now I am here I would be very happy to spend the rest of my life here and with you.

Would you come back again, let us get to know one another, then God willing, let us get married and raise a family together.

I have to go now; but be assured I will love you forever.

Your

Ivan Kolinsky

Elsa was shocked by this very naïve expression of passion, but now what should she do, she was expecting Ivan's baby, but she knew she wouldn't want to be stuck with a foreign loser such as a Polish soldier. And reading between the lines, surely he was just hunting for an heiress, someone with money and power. He could possibly be in love after just two encounters, whether he was or wasn't, the fact remained that she couldn't possibly feel the same.

As to having someone else's baby, didn't really frighten her, she had always wanted to give birth and raise a family, and it hadn't happened under Olav, but now she was pregnant, she wouldn't waste this golden opportunity, after all, she was getting old and that famous biological clock was racing round. She tore up the paper that had been written by Ivan, she knew she would be going back to England in the not to distant future, if he was still serving on the ferry she would confront him with the news that he was once again going to be a father, albeit with a Dutch lady. He wouldn't owe her anything, she was independently secure, anyway his small wage wouldn't keep a fly alive let alone the sort of style she had gotten used too. No, he would be allowed to see his child if he acted in accordance of her rules. But he didn't have any rights what-so-ever over the child or herself. Once that had been made clear, everything would be all right again. To make doubly sure that he didn't cause any trouble, she would take a tough looking lawyer she knew with her, that way a legal contract could be drawn up with Ivan.

As the weeks passed, Elsa began to show her bump. At first her mother and father had been shocked, ashamed and alarmed, plus saddened by the simple expedient that the child would be born out of wedlock, thus being a bastard. But as time went by and the local population too became aware of Elsa's state of being, she lost her status as part of the hierarchy of the town, she became just another cheap woman who got herself stuck in the family way, though having lots of money helped the social situation somewhat, people, especially poor people were always going to give respect to their supposed betters, that being people that can afford to buy social status.

The day came in early September when Elsa had yet again agreed to meet Jon in Scotland, and this was to view how far advanced the ship had got, plus to pay the second instalment as per agreement. To say Elsa was not looking forward to this trip was just about the understatement of the nineteenth century, it was like asking Queen Victoria if she was happy that Prince Albert was dead. The horror of the question would be too much.

So that was how Elsa felt, first she would have to face Ivan with the news that though there was absolutely no future for the two of them as a couple, but she never-the-less was indeed going to be having his child.

Then she would have to face Jon Johnson, he had no idea of Elsa's state of being. As far as he was concerned she had locked herself away from men, she might have joined a convent for all he knew.

Then she was going to have to face the men that were building her ship, that dear old Victorian gentleman Frank Kleinbeck, someone like that would never understand how a rich youngish woman was even single let alone single and with child.

No, Elsa was not looking forward to this trip. The only consolation in this was she was going to be accompanied by Gregory van Husson, her trusted lawyer from the early days when she first married Olav

Peterson. Gregory now owned his own law practice, he specialised in divorce and contractual marriages, which was what happened when she first decided to marry Olav. She had insisted that he buy her mother and father a house, as well as one for her which they lived in as a couple. Gregory had been the one to draw up all the legal documents, and as he liked both Elsa and Olav he soon became a close friend. When asked by Elsa if he would accompany her on this journey, it took him all of two seconds to agree to it. Of course Elsa was going to pay for his services anyway, so in Gregory's eyes, what's the difference from earning his daily bread in an office, or on a journey to a far foreign land.

The day came when they left for Scotland, and it was a bright Indian summer's day, dry, warm and slightly humid with a low pressure zone coming in to affect the stillness of that balmy day. Once of board the SS Breakspeare, they both settled into their prospective cabins which happened to be adjoining. Gregory suggested that they suspend their restaurant trip until they discovered whether Ivan Kolinsky was in fact on board or not, in the mean time Gregory would do some snooping and see what he could dig up on the Polish chef, just in case there was any possible trouble that Ivan might cause. And as it turned out, Gregory knew the Captain, so a word to him might find some hidden secrets that Ivan might not like used against himself.

The ship set off dead on time, the weather was still as quiet as the grave. Gregory asked the bursar if he could quickly meet Captain Sorenson, his old friend who he had been in university with. The answer was immediate and he was shown to the bridge.

"Good lord, Gregory van Husson. How long has it been? Crikey, it must be twenty years at least. So how are you and what are you doing these days?"

"Well, I don't know! It's really good to see you too. I am on my way to Scotland with a woman who owns a fishing empire in Iceland though she herself is Dutch."

Gregory explained everything and then told about his own life, married with four children, three girls and a son. He told about Elsa and her problem concerning the Polish chef Ivan Kolinsky. That immediately brought a frown to the captain's brow. He actually enjoyed the food that Ivan produced especially for him, so he was at first reluctant to say too much. But on being assured that in the end Ivan would come out of this affair smelling of roses, he did impart one piece of information.

"There was a problem between him and my first officer on the old paddle steamer, prior to this vessel. There must have been some sort of fight, and the first officer, who was a well known bully just disappeared. I personally suspected that in a scuffle between the two of them, the officer went overboard. But when questioned Ivan denied any knowledge what-so-ever, so as there were no witnesses or proof of anything untoward, end of story.

Since then Ivan has been a wonderful chef, a decent fellow to have around and loved by all the crew members, so I really don't care what happened to that idiot officer, he was probably just so much waste of space. I have told you this in confidence, don't use it against him, it is just for your ears only."

Then his tone of voice changed completely, much, much friendlier.

"What about Mrs. Peterson and you dining with me, say in one hours time? Let's say, once we are in open water."

That night, knowing that Ivan was now aware of Elsa presence aboard the ship, plus also perfectly aware that she was expecting a child, probably guessing that it was indeed his. All Elsa and Gregory had to do was wait until after midnight, then expect a knock on her cabin door and for sure it would be the Polish chef.

They didn't have to wait that long, just after eleven thirty, when most passengers were nicely tucked up in their bunks, that knock came. Elsa went over and opened it just a fraction, there was an extremely handsome Ivan, looking for the entire world like a much younger man. It amazed Elsa that being the age he was, maybe a year or two older than herself, he actually looked no more than thirty years of age.

"Elsa, my darling you have come back to me, I was so happy to hear that you we..! Who is this man?"

"This man is my lawyer, his name is Gregory van Husson. Don't stand there in the frame of the door, do come in, we wish to talk to you."

Elsa stood aside, and though she felt safe and strong, she was trembling slightly.

"Come in Mr. Kolinsky, do come in. Nothing to really worry about, we just want to have a calm word or two about the future, mainly your future."

After saying that Gregory stood up to make sure that Ivan saw that he was no small budding pushover, if necessary, he could and would, match the Pole ounce for ounce.

It was now Ivan's turn to look a little worried.

"What is all this Elsa, why is this man here? I thought, or rather I hoped, that you had come back for me, but I now think I was mistaken."

Gregory now took the floor as Ivan had seated himself very close to the doorway, he looked just a tad worried, a large frown had descended right down the side of his face, now making him look ten years older.

"As you can see, Mrs. Peterson is pregnant with your child. Now, I have come on this voyage to make sure that fair play is reached concerning both parties, that means Mrs. Peterson and your good self. As you have obviously realised, the baby that Mrs. Peterson is carrying is as I have already stated yours. She actually intends to keep it, but I want a written assurance from you that there will never be any trouble, no demands for money and no demands for the child, whatever sex it is. It has been agreed that you can have some visiting rights, but only to the child, and only under agreed supervision. If you agree to these clauses in the contract that I have here in my briefcase, no further action will be taken. If you refuse, then we will sue you for maintenance, which with a certain word here and there will finish your days in this shipping company and in Holland as well. Before you protest or say something you will later regret, let me tell you, we know about first officer van Grievel. Even the captain of this vessel thinks you were involved with his disappearance. Personally I don't care either way, but one word from me and you will be arrested on suspicion of at least the manslaughter of that self same first officer, but a good jury, one well versed by family and friends, just might find you guilty of murder. Now at the very least, the authorities will inform the Polish government, and if you left Poland under a cloud, then they will ship you right back there. Do we understand one another?"

Ivan was shocked and instead of saying anything cohesive he just grunted and started to dribble as his mouth was wide agape. He started to mumble something, but no words of any meaning came forth. He just sat there his eyes starring into nothingness as he watched his future drift past his own conscientiousness and out into the cold North Sea.

He was a lamb being led to the slaughter, he was given the contract, he didn't even bother to read it, he just signed on the dotted line, then he was dismissed like a naughty boy.

After he had departed, Gregory turned to Elsa, noticed that she still shaking rather badly. He patted her shoulder and then caressed her left cheek.

Strangely he too was slightly shaken, it had gone easier than he had hoped for, but it was still an ordeal to perform.

Turning once again to Elsa he told her what the captain had told him.

"Before joining this ferry to Harwich he was on the Dover run in a paddle steamer. It was there that the rumour ran rampant about the disappearance of the first officer. As you could see from his expression, there was more to it than he had ever stated in the records. I really do suspect that he was involved with the killing and disposing of that man, van Grievel. Seriously Elsa, I do believe you have had a lucky escape there. Now let's forget him and enjoy ourselves, what about opening a bottle of champagne?"

"What about my baby?"

"Elsa, Elsa, a drink or two can't do any harm, after all I am a lawyer you can trust me."

The next day they arrived in Harwich, and then gained access to the train to London, then directly on to Glasgow.

What neither Elsa nor Gregory saw was one Polish chef, leaving the ship before they did. He got on a train to Birmingham, then change to go also to Glasgow. Ivan had panicked, he thought that he was surely going to be arrested and charged with the murder of the first officer van Grievel, and he believed the lawyer when he said that they would probably have him sent back to Poland. It was now time to start a new life, and the reason that Glasgow was chosen was simply because he had heard of it somehow, somewhere, probably from Elsa herself, but none of that mattered, what did matter was that it was far away from where people might expect him to go.

Elsa introduced Gregory to Jon, then to the management team at the shipyard. It was true to say that both her partner and the entire board of the shipyard looked at Elsa with more than a little sadness, everyone knew she had been made a widow long before pregnancy could possibly have occurred.

More payments were made, agreement for extra money was signed for and everything was going exceedingly well. The keel had been laid down, and the superstructure which included the crew's quarters was being assembled and craned onto the ship. It was for all the world now looking like a ship, maybe even a whaling vessel.

Elsa was excited and happy, Jon was thrilled and elated that his ideas were coming to fruition, Gregory was delighted, he was having a holiday, yet still being paid for it. Now all Elsa had to do was make sure she was at the launch, hopefully after giving birth. Maybe even by making sure she would stall the launch until she was carrying her baby with her and not inside her.

9

Ivan hadn't slept for one minute the night he was tricked into signing the contract with Elsa's lawyer. He knew that it was now time to start yet another chapter of his life. If he stayed in the Netherlands he might at least be imprisoned for manslaughter, at worst he could be indicted for murder, and if found guilty, he might even be hanged. Also, there was the possibility that the authorities might check him out with the Polish army. If he was deported back to Poland, he would spend the next twenty years doing double time hard labour in a military prison. And he knew that very few people ever survived that ordeal.

No there was only one thing to do, jump ship at Harwich, make his way to the railway station and get as far north as possible. That was when he remembered Glasgow being mentioned somewhere. Glasgow, it sort of had a magic ring about the name. One thing for sure it is a huge city and it would carry the lives of millions, especially foreigners that didn't want to be found. One could get lost easily in such a city.

Once in Glasgow central station, Ivan realised that he had better change what money he had in Gilders into Pounds. He found a small branch of Scottish Swallow Bank, entered just in time to find that it was being robbed by three masked men.

"Get down on the ground, you piece of dogs turd. Get down now, or I'll shoot this girl, and it will be all your fault. Last chance, get down."

Bang...

The gun which was pointing at the young bank teller went off, the noise was deafening, and the sight of brains and blood flying all over the place was just too much for most of the people within the building. The screaming started, hysterically, wildly out of control deep from the stomach screaming.

At this point one of the robbers, who now was looking at his gun firing colleague, had his mouth dropping almost to the ground said,

"Joe boy, what have you done?"

His voice was almost out of control, his hand was trembling, all he wanted to do was drop the gun and run like hell.

He then started to back away from the sight of blood and brains and the dead body of what once was a pretty girl no older than twenty years of age.

"It was an accident! I didn't mean to pull the bloody trigger. Take another hostage and let's get the hell out of here."

The other robber looked towards Ivan, and raised his hand holding his pistol.

"This is your fault, you should have dropped to the ground when ordered too. The blood of this lady is on your head. Now you can come with us, you are going to be our hostage."

Waving his gun wildly, almost to the point of panic, he approached Ivan with the intent of grabbing him and then dragging him out of the building. Another bang went off, this time into the ceiling, but it made the man who was going to grab Ivan jump. This was Ivan's chance, he grabbed at the man, forcing him to swing his gun hand back towards Joe, the robber who had shot the girl. Bang, again the noise was deafening, but this time Joe fell to the ground clutching his throat. Blood was gushing from his main artery, which the bullet had pierced. Gradually, choking and loosing the will to live, Joe now on his knees, looked towards his friend, who now in a total state of shock had dropped his gun, and was in the throws of losing his bow movement.

Joe pointed his hand, and opened his mouth trying to say something, but all that came out was blood and gurgling sounds. A second later he fell forward straight onto his nose. A large cracking sound was heard as his nose, hit hard into the wooden floor. He kicked twice than lay still, quite dead.

All the time this was going on Ivan had hit the other man with a tremendous rabbit punch, quite literally snapping his neck, he too dropped to the ground dead. The last robber, who now was a quivering mess of excrement and sweat, lay on the floor sobbing, then two of the men who were there just trying to do their banking, started to kick him ferociously, and then all hell breaks loose. What with the screaming, blood, smell of cordite and the noise of the last robber actually being kicked to death, that particular bank was just one vast assembly of mayhem.

The alarm was ringing wildly, people were running to and fro, the bodies of two robbers and one bank teller are leaving their impression all over the floor of the bank. Even the manager, a middle aged man, working out his remaining year before retirement, had a serious heart murmur, but even in his pain still had the common sense to try and get out of the building and onto the pathway to call for help. All this time, Ivan is wondering what the hell he had landed himself into.

'I mustn't be caught here by the police. I must get away. Jesus Christos', I have now killed another man. Get away, get away. Oh shit, let me out of here. Lord, please protect me from what is going on I beg of you!'

Everyone in the building was screaming and crying. Ivan had a moment of lucidity, he dropped his arms, casually stepped over the body of the man whose neck he had just broken and walked out of the building into the sunlight and the crowds of people that are starting to gather. He walked past a theatre, stopped and looked to see what is playing. It was a French Farce by someone called Georges Feydeau, called La Dame De Chez Maxim. He looks up to see what the theatre is called, The Citizens Theatre.

He smiles to himself thinking how socialistic the name sounds.

He looks back towards the bank, notices that the police are swarming around the building, and people are pointing this way and that.

'They may be looking for me. Er, what day is this, yes, Thursday, afternoon, a matinee performance is showing right now? I had better get off the road. Well Feydeau, you had better be funny.'

Ivan Kolinsky walks directly into the foyer, looks at the very bored looking ticket seller who is filing her finger nails.

"A ticket please. Has it started yet?"

"No sir."

She said in a very sarcastic fashion, and then added in an almost sneering reproachful way,

"They are waiting for you to arrive before the performance gets underway!"

He entered the auditorium to see that there were probably less than thirty people seated wherever they so desired. True to her word, no sooner had Ivan entered than the lights were dimmed and the curtains opened. Ivan had absolutely no idea as to what to expect, but a farce in any language is running from bedroom to sitting room, back to bedroom.

The few patrons that were there, were laughing almost hysterically, and it was everyone else's laughter that made Ivan laugh too, not really the play which though in English was presented in such a broad Scottish accent as to be almost unintelligible to the Pole, but laughter is contagious, like some disease, it will sweep through everyone, just like a pandemic.

But when the interval came, Ivan was already sound asleep, snoring gently to himself. It had been a stressful couple of days for him, now things had to be resolved quickly for him, it was important for his sanity that he kicked his life into something more normal once more.

On leaving the theatre after the performance had ended, he was glad to see that it was still light, though just about getting dark. His first priority was to change those Gilders into Pounds, which on thinking made him look towards the bank. Police were still there and the entire area had been sectioned off. He probably had enough money in sterling to get through the night, so maybe the first thing to do was find some lodgings for the night.

Which way should he go, this indeed was the burning question. He took a coin out of his pocket and spun it, heads he turned left, tails right and go passed the bank that had been in the process of being robbed. The coin came down tails, so he walked with his rucksack over his shoulder to the right, he tried to be nonchalant about the way he looked as he went passed on the opposite side of the street. No one gave him a second glance, even though police and doctors seemed to be coming and going all the time within the bank, not one looked in his direction, he was just another traveller passing a building. But Ivan felt more fear passing through that obstacle than on any other single occasion in his past life.

He walked for about a mile, slightly into the suburbs, and he had already noticed that the area was getting dirtier, rougher and more polluted. He came across a road called Dalmeny Road, it was full from one end to the other with high tenement blocks, all housing dozens of families.

'This is the sort of place that I might find something temporary until I think things have calmed.'

He walked along until he came across a man fixing a cycle.

"Excuse me friend, would you happen to know if anyone takes in lodgers?"

The man, put down his spanner, laid the bike on the pavement and thought hard about it. And then, in a ponderous monotone voice, answered the question,

"Well now, let me think. There is Mrs. Jolly, a widow now, and her boys have more or less left home. I have heard before that she is inclined to take in people, though of course I could be wrong. She lives across the road in that block there, top floor. Nice lady, whose husband died in a mining accident."

Ivan thanked the man, looked up at the dirty sooty building. He noticed that very few windows were clean, most looked as if they had never been cleaned since the day they were installed. The red sandstone which was what the edifice was constructed out of looked pitted from the acid in the pollution, and in some case seriously eaten into. He noticed that the gutters on the roof had collapsed in many areas and huge damp patches showed themselves down the walls, they actually seemed to be the only clean areas. All in all, these were very run down properties, and that made this place ideal for Mr. Kolinsky, he could disappear into the woodwork without becoming a seemingly suspicious person, just another immigrant.

He found his way up the stairwell to the flat that had been indicated, knocked on the door and waited. A second or two later a greying lady obviously nearer to fifty years of age than forty, came to the door. Though aged through hard work, somehow she had some dignity about herself. She stood there in front of Ivan, looked him straight in the eyes.

"Yes, and what can I do for you?"

"I am sorry to trouble you, my name is Ivan Kolinsky and I have just arrived here in Glasgow and need a place to stay, I was informed by a gentleman down in the road that you might be interested in taking in a lodger. I should add, I have money and can pay my way."

Mary Stuart didn't blink an eye, she just stood there weighing up the pros and cons. Ivan was starting to feel uncomfortable as she looked as if she was in a trance. Just when Ivan felt he should start again, Mary answered his question.

"Come in Mr. Kolinsky, I'll make us both a cup of tea, then we can talk it over."

The flat was clean, but sparsely furnished, he was shown to the only seat, and then five minutes later a piping hot cup of reviving tea was being drunk by them both.

"So tell me, what made you come to Glasgow?"

"I am, as you probably guessed, from Poland. I want to work, and I was led to believe that my skills might be in demand here in Scotland. I am by profession a chef."

"Aye, that they might be at that. There are more and more hotels being built and they all need good cooks. And how long would you be staying here?"

"I am hoping to settle here, but time will tell. First I must get work, if I like the area, I will stay, if not I will try elsewhere, maybe higher up your country."

"No, I meant how long would you want to stay here in my flat? If I decide you can have the room."

"O, I see, well I would hope for a long time, but that would depend on you. I am really hoping that Glasgow is going to suit, I need to settle down, maybe find a woman, have kids, you know, become normal!"

"Right then, yes, you can have the room, it was my sons, but they have all gone they own ways. The rent will be four shilling a week. But for that money you will get breakfast and a meal in the day, should you want it. And for an extra one shilling, I shall do all your laundry. But, no women in the room, I won't have any of that goings on in my apartment, and I will want a weeks rent in advance."

Now she stood there just in front of him with her hand out ready to receive the first payment.

That night Ivan slept the best he had for many a long time, Mary Stuart insisted that they should both retire at ten o'clock, under normal circumstances much too early for Ivan, but he knew he had to comply with her wishes. As soon as he put his head upon the pillow, he fell in to a deep dreamless sleep, one he didn't wake from until almost eight o'clock the very next morning. He only woke then, as the smell of bloaters being cooked roused him. That was their breakfast.

That morning was spent pleasantly enough, he liked his new landlady, Mrs. Mary Stuart Jolly was a fine upright lady, who once must have been quite good looking. She still had that air of better days about her. She smiled a lot, and talked incessantly about her oldest son James, who lived near by, was married and had his own child. She was obviously proud of him, and it was nice for Ivan to hear these sort of things, things that create a form of normality.

Ivan now felt that need to settle down, keep his nose to the grind stone, make a little money and start to live a life that doesn't exactly consist of crass-ridden women, babies and lawyers.

"Mary, I am going to go in to town, change my Gilders into pounds and try and find some work. Don't expect me for some time. If things go well I shall bring some food back and make you a meal, but let's see how the day goes!"

Ivan had nothing really to hide, so he unpacked the few clothes that he had managed to bring and went out to start his new life.

This part of Glasgow was extremely dirty, full of poverty and sickness. The alcohol problem was endemic, and no matter what time of day or night you would witness drunken behaviour, even sometimes appalling violence. Thievery was in abundance, but those that got caught would and did feel the entire weight of the law come down heavily upon them. Even small petty crimes could be followed up with long custodial sentences with extreme hard labour thrown in. Young children could also be sent to prisons full of hardened criminals, and there they would learn their future trade from the older hardened professional prisoners. Prostitution was also rife, which made venereal disease being on the increase. Gorbals was not the best area within the city, but it might possibly have been the worst.

By contrast the further out of town one went the more affluent property became, proving that Glasgow was not short of its very wealthy patrons as well.

It wasn't a long walk to the city centre, and so once again Ivan passed by the bank that he had been involved with yesterday. The police had gone, and it was business as usual. But, he wasn't going to push his luck, he went further into the centre and found another bank. There he changed all his Gilders and received a tidy sum of fifty-two pounds three shillings and four pence halfpenny. If he was prudent that sum should keep him going for upwards of a year at the very least.

Across the road was the Queen Anne Hotel, it had all the appearances of being a fine establishment, just the right place to see whether he could find his sort of employment. Ivan went to the rear, he had learned that one should never present oneself for a job at front of house, management never ever liked that. He asked for the floor manager and waited patiently for someone to come.

"Yes, can I help you?"

This came from a very demure toned voice. Ivan had been lost in his own thoughts, and was shaken to find a middle-aged women standing before him. He stood there for a second or two, and then nearly asked once again to see the manager, but caught himself as he realised this was the manager.

"I am sorry to trouble you madam, but I am a chef late of a Dutch ferry company, and before that I was head chef in a section of the Polish armed forces. I have just arrived here in Glasgow and am going to be married to a Scottish lady, so I need to get a job and as quickly as possible."

"Well, maybe you are in luck, but we would need some references from your last employers, we don't take anyone you know. How good a chef are you? If I was to give you some ingredients, what could you produce right now?"

"Madam, I would be only to happy to get you the references you require, but that might take a couple of weeks to obtain. As for cooking, lead me to those ingredients and I shall be very happy to show you just what I am quite capable of."

"What is your name, and I shall of course need those addresses, plus your own now. But first, let's see what you can do."

Joyce Barton was a fine manager, and highly respected throughout the hotel fraternity in Scotland. She was fair, but quite severe, always expected top quality from her employees, never accepted second rate. She was paid reasonably well for Glasgow, and it would be true to say she earned every penny. But what her employees liked most of all was the simple expedient that she always gave good honest advice when asked, or when she thought it was needed. But most of all she never suffered fools gladly, any nonsense and out they went. She was forty three years of age, never been married, and sadly rather put off by a disastrously bad affair with a married man many years before.

Her preferences now tended to be younger women, though she was discretion itself when it came to her frequent casual romantic trysts. She looked her age, but managed to look quite decently turned out. Obviously for her job and her own satisfaction her appearance meant a lot to her, as of course it did to the hotel as well. She kept herself trim, never overeating, and because she was for ever running around within the hotel, this kept her reasonably fit and healthy. Her clothes always tended to be long tightly made black dresses accompanied by a frilly white blouses, she often sported a necklace, but never wore make up, even though it might have made her look younger. In fact one could never accuse Joyce of being vain.

She escorted Ivan to the kitchen area, it was still quiet, and only one chef was getting ready for the lunch time trade. She went to the cupboard and came back with many unusual item of food. She handed them to Ivan, and said,

"Right Mr. What is your name?"

"Ivan Kolinsky madam."

"Right Mr. Kolinsky, you have forty-five minutes and not a second more. I expect a good tasting meal to be presented to me in that time. I shall come back then, if you need any help, call Michael there, but only if you need something. I do expect you to produce the meal off your own head. Understood?"

Ivan looked at the ingredients: Artichoke, lamb cutlet, potato, various herbs and spices, plus one or two things he hadn't got a clue about.

Ivan went to work. He boiled very lightly the artichoke, and then covered it with brandy, and then just let it soak. The potato, he mashed and pressed into a small mound, then coated with cheddar cheese and made ready to lightly fry the little hillock of potato and cheese. The lamb cutlet he seared quickly on both sides then gently cooked it in some boiling herbs and some of the spices that he recognised. He made a sauce out of various things that he scrounged from the other chef, and then waited for Joyce to come back before finishing. Five minutes later she turned up expecting everything to be awaiting her pleasure.

"Well where is it all?"

"Please madam, a little patience, I have been ready to serve for at least five minutes, but I want to finish it off while you are here so that it's nicely hot and tasty."

He moved back to his marinating lamb chop, very quickly fried then flamed it, and then placed it with the fried the fluffy potato mound, just enough to make the cheese soft and gooey. He then quickly placed his special sauce on a small delicate saucer, and flamed the artichoke to rid it of alcohol but leave the taste. Now everything was ready for her to try.

Michael too had now become interested in what this well spoken foreigner was doing. Joyce picked off several leaves and dipped them into the sauce, scraped them on her lower set of teeth, and made a huge exclamation of, "Mmm!"

She then got her knife and cut into the lamb chop, noticed that it was slightly pink inside but thoroughly cooked, took a mouthful with the potato, and once again went,

"Mmm!"

Joyce Barton was sold. She even liked the man she saw in front of her. He talked well, looked good, and was incredibly fit, she immediately thought that Ivan had obviously worked out in a gym and that must have come from his soldiering days.

"Well, well Mr. Kolinsky. You might well have landed on your feet. As luck would have it for you, we do need a chef, one that is capable of stirring the imagination of our clientele, is that you? I am prepared to give you a two week trial, if then you pass that we will talk about your future. You will earn one pound and three shilling a week, but if you stay with us we will talk a further rise in money. Is that acceptable to you?"

"Madam, I am extremely happy with that arrangement, and I am quite sure I will meet your excellent standards."

All the time this talk between Joyce Barton and Ivan Kolinsky was going on, Michael Peters, the other chef was standing there with a large smile on his countenance, the pressure was now off of his shoulders.

When Ivan returned to Dalmeny Road, he was carrying a parcel full of different foods. Tonight he was going to celebrate by cooking the meal for his new landlady, and he even managed to buy a bottle of wine to go with the meal. He was feeling on top of the world, a new beginning a reasonable start to work and he knew that if he didn't like the position he would soon find another job, he would be in demand.

When he got back he was very excited, but not so much that he didn't noticed that Mary Stuart had bought some new curtains and put them up in his room. The bed had been made, and everything looked clean and somewhat cosy. Ivan smiled, less than twenty-four hours had passed, but somehow he felt at home.

"Mary, sit down put your feet up. I am cooking tonight, I managed to get a job as a chef in the Queen Anne Hotel, starting Monday. What do you say to that then?"

"I am of course happy for you, but I couldn't possibly let you cook the meal, what would people say if they got to hear?"

"Who cares what people will say? Anyway, how would they ever get to know? No excuses, I am cooking and that is that! I have bought some fine prime steak, which I will sear and then grill. Er, you do have a grill, don't you?"

"Grill!"

She said with a startled but excited voice.

"I don't think anyone around here would even know what a grill is. There are two rings which are fired by coal gas and a small oven should you ever need it. I personally rarely use the oven, it's too much trouble."

Mary laughed out loud.

"That's all there is, this is backward Scotland, and not sophisticated London or Poland."

But Mary was now having a wonderful time with her Polish gentleman.

"Right then, a rethink! I shall fry the steaks, create a creamy mash of potatoes, with fried onions and lots of tender bean shoots and broccoli."

"What is broccoli?"

"Mine Godt!"

He joked,

"Where have you been hiding woman?"

Mary was now almost crying with joy. It had been so, so long before she had enjoyed the company of a man.

"Also, here in my bag, I have a bottle of fine Burgundy wine. To tell the truth I have no idea if it will suit the meal, but it will be fun and anyway, I bought it, we both drink it! Agreed?"

"Agreed."

"Then my dear landlady, allow me to take control of the kitchen, and I shall rustle up something that might please you. Who knows, maybe you will have to go out to work and I stay at home and do the cooking."

Ivan spun a meal that Mary Stuart could only have ever dreamed about. She had never drunk wine before. No one in her family could ever afford a bottle of French wine, the nearest she had ever got to wine was drinking some home made fermented Perry.

She loved every drop of red Burgundy, though to Ivan it was probably a little too new and slightly too acidic. But that didn't matter as the overall effect for that evening was one of pleasure and mutual friendliness. Mary was slightly tipsy when the meal was finished, and she sat in the armchair and started to believe that her life was at last beginning to change for the better.

Here perhaps was her saviour? Maybe, just maybe her saviour would be this Polish man, someone who might well stay for some time and alter her personality and mannerisms? She now quickly realised that she Mary Stuart Jolly once again needed to live, she really had just been passing through life without being aware of the outside world, and after just twenty-four hours, she realised that there was an outside world. Three sons, a dead husband, and work, more work and always the serious threat of poverty. That was Mary Stuart's sum total, not much to go on and Mary knew it. She felt grateful but how could she repay that feeling of gratitude?

Later, just before going to bed, Mary got out the old bathtub and started heating water. She had decided that she wanted a thorough cleaning of her body. She managed about three inches of water and climbed in. Ten minutes later, having dried herself and thrown the water out into the yard, she looked at herself in the broken piece of mirror that stood in the kitchen area. 'Not so bad for an oldie'. She combed her hair, put on the night attire, and went back into the living quarters. Ivan was asleep in the chair, she went over to him and shook his shoulder gently.

"Ivan, time for bed. You were asleep in the chair, you might have fallen and hurt yourself."

"O, right. Yes, time for bed."

"Ivan before you go, can I ask you something personal?"

"Why, yes of course, what is the problem?"

"Not a problem, just a request. Ivan could I sleep with you tonight? It has been so long since a man made love to me. I promise I won't make any demands. It can be a once only if you want. But tonight has been so wonderful love making would just top it off nicely. Neither of us has to be up early tomorrow. What do you say?"

She was bright red almost with shame, but somehow she just didn't care. Mary Stuart knew that chances must be grabbed quickly when they came along.

Ivan was taken aback, not expecting such a request. But it didn't faze him enough for him to be offended. He took her in his arms and kissed her gently on the lips, then led her to the bedroom.

Ivan liked Mary Stuart Jolly, not in a passionate want for nothing way, but in a deepening friendship that would hopefully bring a satisfactory reward to them both, after all, while here in Mary's flat, he could hardly bring another woman home, that was most definitely out of the question, so sex with Mary was obviously on tap any time he felt the urge. He felt more than a little smug, but he also most certainly felt the urge.

They performed the act of lovemaking three times that night, Mary loved every second of it, and Ivan was exhausted after the first time, but demands on his body made him perform twice more. In the morning he got up and made some scrambled eggs for them both and took it along with a pot of piping hot tea back to the bed.

After the breakfast, Mary insisted that he perform once more. Afterwards Ivan reminded Mary that no demands were to be made on him, and that meant any more sex that day. He needed more sleep. Again he felt smug, but then also entirely dead to the world.

Poland had lost a good chef, Scotland achieved something that they were not used to, they had gained a good chef, one that had a fine true imagination. People were now coming from far and wide to experience the fine cuisine at the Queen Anne Hotel.

Ivan's earnings had passed from just fine to extraordinarily good. Within the three months that he had become the top chef, his salary had gone from the one pound three shillings to one pound eight shilling a week. The idea that he must produce references were long forgotten, and here he was at the top of his profession with accolades pouring in on a daily basis. The hotel was expanding and doing well, their reputation had sailed through the roof, booking for lunches and dinners were now only available by writing in up to two weeks in advance, and even then one might be disappointed.

But what made Ivan happiest, was that he was now given the position of showing other chefs working under him what they could do with a lot of knowledge of ingredients and some classic imagination. These were heady times for Ivan, ones to savour, and he did savour each moment. He even banked in the Scottish Swallow Bank where he witnessed the robbery.

The killings and the robbery had now passed into legend. All three of the perpetrators had died at the scene, sadly the girl that died was in fact expecting her first baby, but that was only discovered at her inquest.

There was absolutely no compensation for her new husband from the bank. In fact other than a short note of sympathy from head office, plus her wages up to the end of the week, that was it as far as the bank and the police were concerned, that was the end of the matter. As for the mysterious man that killed one of the robbers, that was left to folklore, he would be there to be turned into a Robin Hood, or Robert the Bruce figure.

Ivan's relationship with Mary was sometimes fraught though. Mary was in love, Ivan wasn't. Anyway Mary was some years older than Ivan and looked it, so Ivan started to look elsewhere for his pleasures, and he was also saving to buy his own property, one that wouldn't include Mary Stuart.

To be fair to Mary and to Ivan, she looked after him extremely well, and in return he was at least kind and generous to her, she didn't want for anything. He even gave her money to go to the new beauty salons that were springing up all over the better parts of the city. She had her hair cut and coloured, she would have her fingers and toes manicured. She started to buy new clothes, and not things that other people had discarded. Mary cut a fine figure down Dalmeny Road, in fact she now brought attention to herself. Mary Stuart Jolly now knew she finally stood out from the crowd. Her past friends either pestered her to borrow money, or just ignored her when they saw her. Some people thought she was whoring, because how come she had so much money to buy things for the apartment and herself.

10

James now had been working for yet another engineering company, one that supplied equipment to the shipping trade. He was doing well, but never felt that he was being pressed with all his acquired knowledge. Once again, he would go to the management team with drawings that could improve the various items that he was asked to produce. Always, someone else would take the plaudits, and somehow James always allowed it to happen. He was never allowed near the directors with his ideas, the managers made sure that he was kept far away from the offices. Often a ten shilling piece would be given to him as some sort of reward, but never the sort of money he should have been getting.

James felt wasted and useless, he needed something special in his life, and he knew working for Potters Brothers was not it. He had often spoken to his wife about leaving, but she was happy to get a regular amount of money to pay the bills and keep body and soul alive, especially now her first born was almost school age and she was once again expecting another child.

James knew that he somehow liked Ivan Kolinsky, though it never entered his brain that he respected and liked him because of the simple expedient that the man made his mother happy. His brain might well contain the knowledge of a simple genius, but that was the truth, a simple genius, that summed up this now responsible aging James Jolly. Responsible James decided that he would visit his mother when Ivan would be there, and talk to the Pole about giving him some advice for his own future. James knew how far Ivan had climbed in his work in such a short time, and if a Polish ex-soldier can do it, so could a well read Scotsman.

The date was the twenty-second of January nineteen hundred and one. James was on his way round to Dalmeny Road to visit his mother and hopefully Ivan. People were on the streets everywhere, flags were flying at half mast, windows had black curtains hanging, and the tone was one of subdued pessimism.

The news was that finally the old Queen had died, evidently on the Isle of Wight, within the confines of Osborne House, Victoria's favourite residence. It always seemed strange to James that people in Scotland could give a damn about an English Queen, especially when she had been married to a German Prince. But somehow, Queen Victoria caught the imagination of the entire British Islands, not just England. Scottish folk were equally upset about her demise, as were the Welsh and Irish, all of whom would love to break up the union. But the thing that really worried people was the Edward the seventh was now going to be King. Edward had an appalling reputation for being a huge waster of public money and a frightful philanderer, always having affairs with young women. People could only speculate as to how many bastards he had sired. Now, within a short space of time, he would rule over the biggest Empire the world had ever known. Not surprising that it even worried the folk of the Gorbals in Glasgow.

James entered the tenement and pushed his way through the people of the stairwell, until he got to his mothers apartment. He knocked and waited, a few seconds later his mother opened the door and was surprised to see him.

"Hello James, what do we owe the pleasure of this visit?"

Jolly entered the flat now completely oblivious to the fact that it had changed out of recognition since he lived there. Firstly it had been decorated throughout, and glossy brown paint covered all the woodwork, and there was more to come, there was wallpaper on the walls. There was a three piece leather suite in the main living room. Though new, it had an antique look about it. There were new tables and chairs, but the soft furnishings were a little too garish for James's taste, but somehow the entire flat had a cosy lived in look to it.

In the kitchen, there was a major transformation, with a new gas cooker complete with a big enough oven to accommodate any large bird or joint of meat. And all the pots and pans that hung neatly on the wall, the sink had been changed and the plumbing bettered. All in all a much cleaner, brighter, cosier apartment to live in. And nobody mistook the fact that it was all down to the Polish man, who was either Mary Stuart's pimp, or her keeper in some way or another. Not one person in the building knew about his job, and even if they had known, they wouldn't have understood the concept of a chef and creativity in cooking.

No, he was younger than Mary, he was handsome, very fit and extremely attractive to women in general, he had to be a drug dealing pimp at the very least.

Mary Stuart went immediately to make a pot of tea, and while in the kitchen she asked once more,

"Why are you here James?"

"I want to speak to Ivan, is he here? I need some advice."

"He will be back very soon, he has gone down to buy a newspaper. You must have heard about the Queen dying."

"One couldn't miss it, the entire country has come to a stop, and it seems that everyone in the entire world is on the pavements talking about the event. For Christ's sake, what's all the fuss? She was eighty-one years old, not a bad age by any standards. Then what the bloody hell do royalty do, nothing seriously strenuous, all they have to worry about is getting old."

And then he smiled and added as a laugh,

"Oh, and not getting caught by sniping anarchists. Sodding easy existence if you ask me."

At that moment the door opened and in walked Ivan Kolinsky, he was dressed in a smart suit of a chequered greenish yellow design, though somewhat brassy, it did suit the Pole very well. His shoes were patent leather, brown in colour and he sported white spats to keep the dirt off of them. His shirt was two tone, brown coloured with white stripes, plus a rounded white collar. Everything had been handmade especially for him. His tie was almost a broad cravat, but tied in the fashion of the time, with a gold pearl tipped tie pin holding the creation in place. On his head, but not hiding his shiny black wavy hair was a trilby hat in the self same colour as the suit. He knew he looked a million dollars.

"Ah, young Jolly, how the heck are you?"

He held out his hand in friendship and was readily accepted by James.

"Well, I'm fine I guess, but I want your advice, can we sit down and talk, maybe over a cup of mum's tea?"

"Of course, of course. What's on your mind?"

"Ivan, I don't know, how do I start? To tell you the truth, I am extremely unhappy in my job. I give all my good ideas to some manager or other, they incorporate the idea, I get nothing, the directors think the sun shines out of their arses and in return they pat me on the head, pop a lump of sugar into my mouth and smile. It's all so bloody unfair. I believe it's time I left, but I want to use my knowledge, but I never get a chance. What do you think I should do?"

"A good question! The trouble is you never got your exams at school. You have no paperwork to show what you achieved when you were very young. Strangely enough, our future lives are governed by that scrap of paper which we earn when leaving school at a tender age. It's quite a crazy stupid system really. After all one only starts to learn and live, when life is happening around you. That should be allowed to be taken into account, life itself. You and others like you should be allowed to shine just through your knowledge and work ability, which in your case is engineering, and I know you are really good at what you do."

Ivan stopped, took a long sip on his tea, smiled at Mary Stuart who was sitting quietly listening to supposed wise words of wisdom coming from her man.

He then continued,

"There is more trouble brewing in South Africa, and now the Queen is dead and Edward is going to be crowned King, I bet those bloody Boers will take advantage of the situation and create trouble. Now you might wonder why I am talking about South Africa, well there is a connection in my thinking. This country has the biggest and best navy in the world, and like Lord Nelson, it was Lord Nelson at Trafalgar wasn't it? Like Nelson, the navy gives go ahead young men an opportunity to shine. You could start as a midshipman and rise to Captain in no time at all, no paperwork needed, just abilities. Why not join the navy and work your way up? One thing about being in the British navy is that no country will ever go up against you, there will never be sea battles again. So, you could be sent to Africa, but on board ship you would always be safe."

"Join the navy! Mmm, that really is something to think about. An engineer in the Royal Navy would mean I would get seen and maybe work my way up the ladder and achieve some real satisfaction. The only time I ever felt I was contributing something was when I worked in the train depot, everything else has been marking time. Navy, mmm, you really have given me some good ideas."

He thanked Ivan for his thoughts, said goodbye to his mother and decided to walk down to the Clyde and watch the ships.

Three days later, James having spoken to his wife, went into town and found the recruiting office for the navy and signed on there and then. He was told that he would be requested to attend Portsmouth in England where he would undergo vigorous training, and there they would assess what his role would be in the new Kings Royal Navy. He was assured that his engineering skills would stand him in good stead, they were always looking for engineers. All he had to do now was to resign from Potters Brothers, work out his time and then wait until he was called to go down to Portsmouth. A railway warrant would be issued in due course.

James had been caught up in the heat of the moment, the old Queen dies, the new King enters the fray, patriotism takes hold. Now his mind is curled up into thinking that joining the navy would be the answer to his prayers.

Fifteen days later, James is standing outside the gates of Portsmouth Academy for Naval recruits, in Gosport. His new life was just about to begin.

"Name? Quickly man, when a petty officer asks you a question you jump to it with a quick answer. Once again, name?"

"James Jolly sir."

"Well Mr. Jolly, you don't seem very jolly to me, a bit of a misery guts I would say, and the way you talk, Scottish are you not?"

"Yes sir, from Glasgow. I am an engineer and I wish…"

He was stopped dead in his tracks.

"Did I ask you what you did? I think not! Only speak when spoken too. That my boy is the first thing you learn, got it?"

"Sir, yes sir."

"Right boy, now we have cleared that little matter up, follow me and the other recruits standing over yonder, and no talking while we march."

The petty officer, sticking his exaggerated chest right out, barked the orders that they had to obey.

"Right you bunch of dead beat scum bags. With your left foot forward first, we will march to the barracks at HMS Genghis. Left, right, left, right. Boy, don't you yet know your left from your right?"

He pounced upon a small luckless boy who was certainly not older than sixteen, probably somewhat younger. The poor lad was an East End Londoner, who was already ruing the day he put pen to paper. There were tears in his eyes and having been aware of the young fellows streaming eyes it made James wonder just how long the lad would last.

After less than one week the twenty new recruits were stronger quicker, cleaner, healthier and better fed than they had ever been before joining up. To a man they hated what they had let themselves in for. This wasn't the glory that they thought that they had signed up for, this was just continuous bullying by petty officers and drill sergeants. James had in one week lost seven pounds in weight, his biceps were now bulging and he could actually run, and what is more he could now run without stopping for nearly half a mile. For that achievement he was grateful to the navy, but so far, only that.

The weeks passed quickly. James learned a great deal more about the navy than what he had read from books, though that didn't stop him from obtaining yet more books about shipping, war ships throughout the ages, plus the secrets of naval warfare, all of which he read within four days. The trouble with taking so much time in reading meant that his bull tended to be left somewhat undone. He was still not the smartest person on the parade ground, always tending to be slightly dirty looking, often not completely clean shaven, with hair all over the place and probably too long for the drill sergeants comfort. His shoes most definitely needed a bit more spit and polish and his trousers could always do with pressing. He was getting more and more trouble from his superiors for his slovenly ways, now once again on parade he was ticked off by a passing commodore for looking like something the cat dragged through a hedge. For this insult, he was caged for twenty-four hours, given extra chores to do and docked one weeks pay. James Jolly just didn't understand what all the fuss was about.

The following Monday, the recruits along with many more recruits were to sail on a tall ship. That meant climbing rigging, tying knots, scrubbing decks, and trying very hard not to fall overboard, or be seasick.

James loathed every second of it, and because his group came last in all the practical tests, this was because James was generally to slow they started to bully him. This started a trend that was to go on for many years.

Eventually, James Jolly and the rest of the recruits were to pass out. They had all passed their individual testing, many by copying the answers from James, who actually got one hundred percent of the questions right. This truly amazed the hierarchy, who had long ago put Jolly down as a wasteful idler, or was that idling waster. The real sadness was that no one understood him, no one really liked him or even had any time for him.

So the day had come when each recruit would be assigned to a ship. As they all looked down the list Jolly's eyes fell on his own situation.

Seaman James Jolly – HMS Westfield – Stoker second class.

James couldn't believe what he was looking at. He went to see petty officer Cramer, he was seething with indignation.

"Why am I made into a stoker, I am a fully qualified engineer. I know more about seamanship than anyone in this bloody training centre. Sure, I know I am not the fittest person here, but my intellect is unquestioned surely?"

Cramer was stunned and almost stupefied, he stood there erect, almost at attention. In all his years in the Royal Navy, no one had ever spoken to him like that. He regained his composure very gradually his face went from red to scarlet, his blood pressure was almost certainly now at a dangerous high point, he was fuming with righteous indignation.

"Why you snivelling little turd, do you really think you know more than anyone else? How dare you compare yourself to your betters?"

James once now had started, he wasn't about to be put off his stride.

"Yes, I know much more than anyone here, much more. I have read about every aspect of ships, the Royal Navy, plus naval warfare. I suspect not even the commanding commodore could compete in a written exam against me. Go on set up a test, let me prove my point."

"You really are the nastiest little piece of doggy doo that I have ever had the misfortune to meet. You were supposed to get one week leave starting today. Forget it, you are going to the brig for insubordination. Right turn, quick march."

James never got home, he never saw his wife or second child, this wasn't going to be the last time that he would miss leave.

The week passed quickly as everything that James did in the brig was done at the double, so when finally light were put out, Jolly was asleep snoring before the bulb had lost its glow.

Finally, James was given his orders, and by no less than the commanding commodore. James entered the office looking reasonably smart, at least smart for him. As he entered, he marvelled at the wondrous pictures of past ship painting of various sea battles. One huge painting of the battle of Trafalgar, another of Lord Nelson lying dying in the arms of Hardy. There were paintings of past commodores, past admirals, past first sea Lords. Fine oak panels festooned the walls giving a feeling of warmth that really wasn't there. The furniture all stemmed from the finest makers, this gave an air of fashion and elegance, also adding to the feeling of warmth.

"On the double lad, halt. Salute the officer. Sir, Seaman James Jolly."

"Right Jolly, I have been hearing a lot about you. You are scruffy, unkempt, you look dirty, do you even clean your teeth. Why, you even smell somewhat unpleasant. Your conduct has been at best, sort of belligerent, at worst down right bellicose. Petty Officer Cramer tells me that your written exam scored one hundred percent, which leaves us all to think that you must have cheated along the way."

"Sir, I must protest, I have…"

Quicker than a blink of the eye, Cramer jumped forward and screamed into Jolly's right ear,

"Shut up Jolly, no one asked for you to speak. You only speak when asked, and no one asked. Stand to attention."

"Don't you see Jolly! It's just this sort of action that brings you so much trouble. Now you will leave here today, get a train to Plymouth and be on the Westfield not later than three o'clock tomorrow afternoon. If for any reason you were to go AWL, then I promise you that you will get at least one years hard labour. Now, if you really believe that you know it all, get on the Westfield and prove your point by hard work. Dismiss."

"Salute the officer. About turn, quick march, left, right, left, right."

Outside in the bright sunshine, Cramer let his hair down with Jolly, after all this was going to be their last encounter.

"Jolly, why do you go on so much? Can't you see the damage it is causing your career in his Majesties Navy? Like the officer said, work hard and prove your point through work. Labour is the best way to quieten the senses, and heaven knows your senses are somewhere completely alien to the rest of you. Pull yourself together lad, who knows, you might make captain yet."

Now Cramer was laughing inside.

"Right get your railway ticket, get down the station and find your way to Plymouth. And lad, good luck to you."

James Jolly got to the dockyard in Plymouth easily and found his ship. He was shown the route down into the engines. His new life was about to start.

11

HMS Westfield was a cruiser, over big, underpowered. Built in 1889, it sported eight huge guns, four aft four forward. It was thought that had the ship ever fired a broadside in anger, it might have turned the ship over. But those four guns were extremely powerful being sixteen inch, they had a range of up to twelve miles, and if hitting anything would most certainly create a rather large hole in whatever it hit.

The Westfield was a heavy cruiser, come battle cruiser, and weighed over fourteen thousand tons. She lay low in the water, mainly because of the weight of her four big gun turrets. She also sported ten six inch guns, but in rough weather they would get swamped so they were more or less permanently kept shut from view. Her length was five hundred and fifty feet long with a breadth of eight feet. Her four prominent funnels showed her above the waves while the bulk was almost always below the waves.

She was hard pressed to manage fifteen knots, when most other cruisers could manage twenty-five knots. She struggled in the sea, and to manoeuvre, say into a zigzagging arrangement, this was a dangerous procedure at best of times. In places she would leak like a sieve, then for no apparent reason the area that was in danger would close up and be watertight once more. It wasn't that Westfield was jinxed, after all, nothing bad had happened to her, but she was untrustworthy, no crew member including the captain felt secure. The thoughts were that she might break in half at any unsuspecting minute, at least that was the general feeling.

But she was a major part of the Kings front line ships which now sported one seaman James Jolly on board as stoker second class.

There was no question about it, once on board James settled down to the mundane job of shovelling coal into the furnaces along with twelve other stokers. Before sailing Jolly made sure that he had stocked up with plenty of reading matter. Having now read practically all the classics, he was now once again onto anything to do with ships or shipping. But he had especially acquired an interest in maritime law and again brushing up his knowledge by reading books on the subject. He always carried dictionaries, three, just in cases he didn't understand what had been written. James Jolly made sure that every page was thoroughly absorbed into his grey matter.

Sadly for him, no one liked him, thinking that he was always talking above his station in life. After arguing with various crew members about some point or another, he would often completely lose his temper, but never had the skill to back up his bravado, so he would always be the one to come off worse. He seemed to permanently carry black eyes around, not that they showed up with the blackened skin after an eight hour stint of coal movement. After his eyes, he started to be attracting attention towards his teeth, and in the ensuing melees would either get one broken, of lose it altogether. He was starting to look a caricature of his former self. Black eyes, broken teeth, bruising on every part of his anatomy, this had become James's norm. Strangely though he never ever complained to any higher authority, but kept himself very much to himself.

All he actually desired was the time to just read and absorb the written word.

There was one serious occasion which very nearly ended his career and possibly his life. One of the other stokers, a burly smelly, unpleasant bully of a man, who seriously disliked James, decided to take it upon himself to teach this Glaswegian bag of snot, this appalling upstart, a lesson he wouldn't forget. He grabbed two of James's books, poems by Keats, and then making sure that Jolly followed him back into the engine room, once safely ensconced there with James looking on, he then started to tear the pages out of each book and throw them unto the fire.

No one had ever seen James anger turn to fury in such a quick manner, he leapt forward, picked up a wide flat spade and then brought it down hard on the back of Eric Cruttenden's head. Any other man would have died on the spot, but not Eric Cruttenden. He fell sharply to his knees, clutched at the back of his head, and then promptly threw up his breakfast. Then in front of a stunned audience, promptly burst into tears while rubbing the back of his head furiously. Two of the other stokers rushed over, grabbed the spade out of James's hand in case he was going to finish the job he started.

"You bloody fool, you might have killed him. You would have been hung for that. Get out of here, quickly, no one will say a word. Go back to your books! Smutty Crutty can't hurt you now. Go on, get out of here."

With that they led him out of the engine room. Cruttenden was badly shaken and was taken to the infirmary for a doctor to look at him. He was babbling like a baby, his eyes were almost spinning within their sockets, his mouth was uncontrollably salivating and the dribble was collecting all the way down his front. He couldn't talk, so he couldn't say anything.

"What the hell has happened to this man?"

"Sir, we really don't know, but he may have hit his head upon something hard. We found him lying on the floor in a terrible state. But he's always been a clumsy bastard."

The other stoker chipped in further.

"He babbles wildly about people all the time, blaming everyone except himself for all the ills of the world. I wouldn't listen to a word he says if I wuz you."

By the end of that sentence the doctor knew that Cruttenden had actually been beaten up, but he wasn't about to interfere in stokers squabbling.

Poor old Cruttenden never did recover completely, his memory had been wiped from his brain, and now he would only react like a small child. He cried a lot, and dribbled incessantly, he was a shadow of his former nasty self.

Only a mother could ever have loved him before the incident, now only a mother would be able to love him, he was going to need twenty-four hour a day care. There was no way that the man could ever be sent back to duty, he was finished in the navy. What would happen to him in the future was anyone's guess.

None of these aspects of Cruttenden's problems found there way back to the engine room, he quickly became yesterday's man. He was sent home as the ship docked at its next port of call. He would be returned to his mother in Knotty Ash, that poor woman would have to spend the rest of her life looking after a forty-odd, three year old man, this wasn't how she in her declining years saw her future.

It was March nineteen hundred and two, HMS Westfield was being sent to South Africa to stop raiders from destroying British supply ships from reaching the various ports.

The Boers had been creating appalling trouble up and down the coast of Africa, and the British government decided that a very hard lesson would be the order of the day.

The ship had coaled up at Plymouth prior to departure, it had taken several extremely hard working hours to barrow the coal from the jetty onto the ship and drop it down the shoot into the coal bunkers opposite the furnaces. The stoker's job was to gather the dropped coal and shovel it into a neater pile than when it just hit the ironclad bottom of the bunker.

Shovelling tons of coal was back breaking work and disgustingly unsavoury to the mouth, as every inhaled breath one would take in the dust from the coal. The eyes were always getting gritted, and usually the stoker would get conjunctivitis from this procedure and have three or four days of abject misery from the effects.

To James this was the worst aspect of being a stoker, because if he acquired through bad luck the eye infection, then his reading had to be curtailed until the problem got better. This one coaling would take them to Malta, and then they would dock and re-coal there. As time was now most important they only called into Valletta for the briefest moment then continued onwards.

It was interesting to the seamen aboard the cruiser that as soon as they set sail, they were being tailed by some foreign ship or another. Once moving away from Malta, an Italian battleship was just on the horizon. As they made their way towards the Suez Canal, a Greek destroyer signalled them, then shadowed for many miles, then a Turkish cruiser was spotted, and many fishing boats that didn't seem to be fishing. Once in the canal, along the banks on either side would be trains speeding alongside, cars, lorries and trains of camels going this way or that, but everyone got the distinct feeling that every foreign eye was spying on them, but for whom?

The weather in the canal was incredibly hot, and that heat permeated all the way deep in to the bows of the vessel, causing huge problems to over heated men doing incredibly backbreaking toil. The extreme heat of the sun against the cooler water started to make some of the steel plates buckle slightly, a common, but unnerving occurrence in ships, but nevertheless it was extremely disconcerting to hear those cracking sounds occur. To people that didn't know, it sounded like the vessel was tearing itself apart.

Once through the canal, the ship had to negotiate all the way along the Red Sea, with its pirates and despots all thinking of ways to create mayhem to foreign governments, plus capturing small vessels and extorting money from them before they were allowed to leave again.

But being a large over gunned ship of King Edward the seventh's Royal Navy, they got through just fine and dandy, but only because they had their smaller six inch guns ready for any trouble. Their destination this time was Aden, there they would coal up once more, this time with enough coal to last all the time that they would be in and around South Africa.

To keep the guns and their crews fit for action, when a big white shark was spotted, all hell would be let loose to give the gunners some practice. The amount of floating corpses of sharks was appalling. It was a discredit to the captain that this gun practice was more a sport, than anything serious. Not many big white's managed to escape as the ship passed on by.

Aden was a port that sailors loved to be visiting. Simple, it housed the most whore houses anywhere in the Middle East, the young girls were shipped in from Pakistan, India, Ceylon, and North Africa, and even European women could be bought extremely cheaply there. Of course the whore houses housed another problem, Syphilis. Venereal disease was endemic, and unless a sailor used a new rubber condom, he ran a very serious risk of taking home something he wished he hadn't. That still left Gonorrhoea, not quite so deadly, but still nasty, one was almost certain to be infected by it if again one didn't wear a condom.

But, just by laying next to one of these women was taking a risk, and a sailor would take on the problem of crabs almost as a sport. After all, if you didn't catch crabs in Aden, you obviously hadn't been there.

The shore police along with the various forms of military police tried desperately hard to keep the sailors away from the red-light areas, but those areas changed nightly if a restriction was placed on a house of ill repute. The police were fighting a losing battle. The only way, was to restrict the men from actually going ashore, quick visit, coal up and then get underway, that was the ideal situation. But if men insisted on shore leave, another way was to form a group, led by an officer, then he could be responsible for his group of men. That worked fine, until a certain un-named officer decided he too wanted to visit a particular woman, then all hell would yet again be let loose.

This wasn't a problem though for HMS Westfield, she docked and started coaling within fifteen minutes of the gangplank being landed.

It was all hands to the pumps, and even officers were supposed to get involved one way or another. Though truth be known most skived off, and those that didn't managed to just oversee and keep an account, thus not quite actually getting their hands dirty.

Aden was a port that had a certain magic about it, but in a squalid sort of way. If you liked low buildings, primarily made from mud and horse and camel dung, this was your place to be. If you didn't mind open sewers, with human waste floating past open cafes, where the clientele might be sitting outside drinking their very sugary tea and watching the world go by, along with the worlds excreta. If you didn't mind flies, billions of the annoying swine, all carrying pestilence that often created terrible sores on ones skin, if you didn't mind being cheated at every turn, and sold the worst of shoddy goods that any trader could possibly land you with. Then it was obvious that Aden was the place for you.

Of course another aspect of its delights was that it was in fact extremely dangerous. A man might be killed for the shoes he stood up in, robbed of every penny, and then he might well be dumped in the cesspit. But a sailor could disappear if he wanted, all it took was the right amount money. He might even get to where he wanted to flee to, which could be anywhere in the world, though generally not. The very reason the great white sharks were in the Red Sea, was because pirates often dumped their unwanted cargo over the sides of their vessels, straight in the sea, that cargo being human beings went a long way to help keep the Great White Sharks trim and perky. After all, there wasn't a code of conduct to be adhered too, take the money and swindle the payee, that was he norm, then let the sharks do the work of disposing of the remains. Yes, once again its true to say that in Aden life was extremely cheap.

Westfield was coaled within three hours, at the same time supplies had been loaded on, plus orders from the First Sea Lord to Captain Derry. His orders were to stake out the most southern part of Madagascar, there were small raiders owned by Boer settlements that were firing on cargo vessels trying to deliver goods to beleaguered soldiers in South Africa. One of these fast torpedo type boats had even managed to sink a four master clipper, with the entire crew being drowned. No one would have known except for the fact that two of the Boer raiders were overheard bragging about their exploits to some Boer farmers, then somehow it got back to the British. Revenge was now expected of HMS Westfield and quickly.

Once again the lumbering cruiser set sail, but now with vengeance in her throbbing pulsating heart. As they made their way into the Indian Ocean, a huge tropical storm could be seen in the distance. It was an eerie sight seeing streaks of lightning yet not have it near you, or actually hear the thunder. You knew that fifty miles away a storm of maybe terrible proportions was going on, yet all you knew of it was the silent lightening strikes that seemed to light up that distant maelstrom. The sea was boiling with rage ten miles off to the portside, yet be riding over milky silk smooth seas yourself had a weird unnerving feeling to it. It was as if you were witnessing in the distance the gateway to hell, but would you actually be called to enter it? The very air was alive with electricity, and with the heat it became hard for men even on the open decks to breath, for those below decks it was the stuff of nightmares. When James Jolly, now off duty, couldn't stand the closeness any more he too came up to take a constitutional around the wooden decking, he did something that he had never done before; he went to the side of the vessel and leaned over the rail to look at the sea. It was so calm that he noticed the gas bubbles appearing on the surface having travelled up from the floor of the ocean. It puzzled him, even though he knew what it was having read about the phenomenon in many books. Watching this as the ship glided by actually made him feel queasy. So he remembered that he was enjoying an American book on child psychology, and went below again to finish it. Soon the ship had passed by the storm, this one wasn't going to be trouble for them, but there would be many more that certainly would be a hazard to the fabric of the vessel.

Two days later, Westfield was positioned off the southern tip of Madagascar. It was late evening when she slipped her anchor. It was a moonless night, slightly windy with a damp feeling that threatened rain but never would really manage to produce it. The temperature was still eighty-two degrees and thus the metalwork on the outside of the vessel was hot to the touch. The Captain ordered a blackout, though they weren't expecting any problems as no Boers would know that they would be there. Even so, a guard was posted at various points around the ship, but other than driftwood hitting the side, nobody really thought about anything other than trying to get a good long night sleep.

It was approximately two fifteen in the morning. A loud crash of a shell hitting the side of the ship awakened everybody. As the ship had been sound asleep and extremely quiet, the shell had an echo effect, resounding all over the cruiser. A hole had been punched into the starboard side and ended up wrecking part of the main galley. No one was hurt, except pride. Whistles pierced the air, men scrambled from bunks to guns. A searchlight caught the reflection of a window in a small vessel when another shell hit the Westfield, this time barely above the waterline causing a hole roughly ten inches across. This shell exploded in a main larder, a lethal savage explosion was once again ringing through the aging cruiser, this time killing hundreds of tins of bully beef, which had been destined for the troops in South Africa.

For those troops fighting and starving, such as besieged garrisons, and there were many, these soldiers might have given their right arms for the food. But those that were eating well, were probably grateful for the death of those tins, because bully beef was definitely not the favourite meal for the cook to produce.

Now the six inch guns were opening up all along the starboard side. The shells were bursting everywhere, killing many enemy fish. Marines had now scrambled to the decks with their 303 Enfield rifles, and they were chattering away in the direction that they thought the enemy might be. Then another shell came towards the cruiser, but this time ricocheting over the calm sea, only to go towards the aft of the vessel and disappear beneath the waves. But that was the fatal shell for the Boer craft, the flash of there cannon was spotted. Now all five of the six inch guns opened up where the bright flare had been. There was a huge bang, then a fireball, followed by a roar and flames shooting skyward lifting bits of ship right up high into the sky, with several more smaller bangs going off for some seconds. Then it went dark with just a few pieces of wood that were still on fire floating around giving an illusion of more fires than there really were.

A few seconds later the area was engulfed in complete blackness, not a flicker of light to be seen. It took some more seconds before human eyes were once again adjusted to that lack of light. Then suddenly as eyes got once again accustomed the stars in the sky were once again visible, but then the silence had become almost deafening, nobody was even allowing themselves to breath.

The Captain ordered the searchlight to scour the area and see whether there were any Boer survivors. Of course it was a futile gesture, there were none to be seen, just a few pieces of what might have constituted as human remains. From then on, it was all hands to repair the two holes in the metal as best they could with the resources available, and then to clear up the galley and larder. Everyone else was to stand watch, with the searchlight doing sweeps every few minutes. It became a very nervy time and though everyone could now hear their own hearts beating, many cracks were heard as nervous Marines fired at what they thought were approaching craft. No more enemy boats appeared that night. As dawn thundered up from the east, what was left of the Boer craft could be seen floating around them. They were also aware of the dozens of sharks that were scouring the surface of the sea, all after a free breakfast.

Then as dawn grew into morning, ropes and planks were lowered over the side, and sailor engineers were lowered down to seal the holes with cut metal plates, these being the two holes that had pierced the side of the cruiser. They were rather Heath Robinson repairs, but they did the job. The vessel wouldn't sink because of those two small holes. But this event had been a very large wakeup call to the Captain and officers. It had become a fact of life to the Westfield and its crew, there would be no easy rides while they were south of the equator.

Captain Derry knew that when they got home there would be an enquiry into last night's events. How could a small fast craft creep up in the middle of the night and surprise one of his Majesties ships of the line? How could that have happened? There were sentries posted, lights were blackened, so why didn't someone hear the incoming craft.

After all it is a fact that In the quiet moments of a calm night sound travels for miles, yet not one person remembers hearing so much as a Lucifer being struck. The craft had managed to fire three shells, two of which did small damage, the third was, luckily for the British, a dud, which only managed to bounce its way towards the cruiser. But what if it hadn't been a bouncing bomb, what then? The Captain was old and wise enough to now realise that his story would have to stand up to scrutiny from clever legal Naval lawyers, or his standing as a Captain would be in Jeopardy.

Derry twitched uncontrollably at the very thought of what might have been, sweat seeped down his heavily lined worried face. He would have to sit down quietly and think up some good lines to put into his log. Something that just might make the Westfield into being a bit of a hero, instead of a stupid fool, caught with its proverbial pants down.

Now everyone on board was tired, weary and more than a little jumpy and concerned. But at least this heightened awareness would keep them safer than they had been. From now on, Captain Derry knew that he must never underestimate his enemy. They weren't just a bunch of rebellious farm labourers, these men were dedicated to the destruction and dismissal of the British out of Africa. Even though the signs had always been there, people like Derry thought of the Boers as nothing but lowland jokes, nothing to fret about, just ignore them and they will fall into line. So many senior commanders of the army, navy and eventually the flying corp., fell into the self same trap, that of underestimating the enemy.

Part of his remit was to exact some serious punishment upon those Dutch exiles. He knew that they would be heavily entrenched in townships all along the Natal regions. Though the Boers had been forced out of these areas some time before, they were now back, and they had settled in small enclaves and fortified villages all along the coastal areas, this way they could be re-enforced with supplies or evacuated easily if it became really necessary.

This was where the cruiser was going to strike, and it would be hard and fast. For the first time she was going to bring her big guns into action. It was decided that one, three, four, two, would be the safest way of firing them, but only after ten second intervals. If the ship was to keel over to much, then they would just stop firing and turn the ship to face the other way, then start again. It was going to be an interesting testing time for HMS Westfield, also the Captain and the crew.

It was going to be a whole days sailing to reach the coast of Natal, and the engine speed was governed in such a way as they would reach off shore and their first target just before dawn. In the mean time, all hands had to prepare and make sure that everything was in order, so that the next surprise would be on the Boers. The ship hoisted anchor and started to make for their first port of call, the border with Mozambique. This was the most northerly point that the Boer settlements were, literally by the border. The Portuguese were still the masters of Mozambique, and though it was the Lisbon government policy to stay Britain's oldest ally, in Mozambique the local feeling was tending to lie in favour of the distressed unhappy Boers, who under the dominating yolk of the British were being classed as second rate people. So, quietly the Portuguese colonists tended to help and support the Dutch immigrants.

The Boers had been badly treated by the British, and when gold and diamonds were being discovered by those Dutch immigrants, the British went in and took control of all the areas that were being mined, and then exacting serious consequences on those Boers that felt those lands should have been their own personal territories. But the self same people that were being pushed around by the British, were in fact very tenacious folk, and when gold and diamonds are involved, people back home in the old country of Netherlands tended to side with their kin folk, especially when it might possibly create more wealth back home.

So very covertly, the people of Holland would financially support their brethren who spoke Afrikaans, a sort of cross between Dutch and Flemish.

The cruiser was now well underway, her speed regulated by the distance, so a smooth uninterrupted crossing was hoped for, one that would hopefully take the Boer people completely by surprise. But Derry was taking no chances, and a vigilant watch was maintained throughout the entire journey.

As the speed was being kept to a minimum, only two stokers were required to keep the engines turning. Also by travelling at a slower speed, this kept the smoke down and the stacks were only blowing white smoke, which easily dispersed into a sort of cloud formation, at least that what the Captain hoped for. Should other shipping notice the smoke, hopefully it wouldn't be associated with a British ship of war, maybe just a tramp steamer plying its trade all along the Indian Ocean. Actually, Derry hadn't needed to worry, the sea was almost completely empty of ships, all the fishing smacks were far inshore, not so far out into the ocean. And the sort of tramp steamer that would have been plying its trade would almost certainly have been British, or some colony such as Australia or New Zealand. But there was nothing.

To keep the entire crew on its toes, Captain Derry had all idle hands doing something constructive, even if it was only washing down the decks or cleaning the superstructure, anything to stop men thinking about what was going too come.

In the late afternoon, they lowered their speed even more, just to seven knots, as in the very far distance a streak of what was land appeared through telescopes. Now men were allowed to take turns in resting, for in the morning before the break of a new day, hell was going to be let loose.

Darkness came down along with rain, at first light spluttering of wet penetrating rain, but soon the clouds broke down and the heavens opened. Once it started in earnest it was as if God was trying to tell the Captain not to do what he intended. There was very little wind which made the rain even denser. Soon no one could see anything, if you stuck your arm out you lost sight of your hand. Then the force of the rain was such that it actually hurt when moving through it. But this wasn't going to stop the bombardment. It was four in the morning, dawn should have been just around the corner, but the rain made the darkness linger.

The ship was now positioned roughly eight miles off the coast, they thought they knew exactly where they were. One and three guns were loaded, aimed towards the distant shore, and then a huge flash went, next the bang that brought tears to everyone's eyes, a few seconds later, number three broke her long silence with another flash, then another bang. There came an echo, which was reported to be the first shell landing on the shore, hopefully amongst the small hamlet that should have been there. Then another report, as the second shell found some sort of mark. It was now time, for number two gun, then number four. All the time the guns kept firing the ship swayed and veered. It really wasn't happy about these huge weapons being let loose on such a fragile vessel, but her creeks and complaints went unheeded.

Ever so gradually the ship moved along the coast line, all the time firing off these huge shells trying hard to seriously upset the Boer inhabitants. While this firing was happening, the rain got heavier and heavier. Steam was being created from the barrels of the guns as the rain tried in vain to cool those huge chunks of metal down, but without having much success.

After roughly twenty minutes of firing, the ship turned around and the guns turned the other way so now firing over the starboard side. This theory was that now they would work their way down the coast away from the Mozambique border area.

Once again the firing continued, this time the ship really did jolt from the recoil. Captain Derry turned to his first officer.

"What do you think is the reason that the ship is taking a bigger jolt on this side, as opposed to the other?"

The first officer shrugged his shoulders, and like his Captain was somewhat baffled. But by the time a set of four reports had burst forth, the vessel was indeed wobbling very badly.

"Tell the guns to change to, four, one, two, and three, see if this pattern makes any difference?"

There was silence for a few minutes while the gunners worked out their coordinates, and then started their pattern of firing once again. This time the ship was even made to veer somewhat, as for the wobble it became markedly worse, making things start to fall off shelves.

"Stop firing! Stop firing!"

Derry looked quite shaken, what was happening to his craft, this was something only a scientist could explain.

"Right! Let me get my hearing back. Fire just one shell every minute, that should give time for the ship to find its own level. Same sequence as before, but a gap of one minute between each shot."

The firing went on for another hour, by which time the ship had probably travelled no more than five miles down the country. In that time they had fired more than seventy five huge shell, any one of which was capable of sinking a large ship. Captain Derry could only imagine the appalling devastation that his shelling had caused along the coast of Natal.

The Boer men, women and children would most definitely learn an important lesson from his experience. And the entire time that this bombardment went on, the rain crashed to earth.

All hell was indeed let loose, but strangely not effecting the Boers, who were completely unaware of the cruisers attempts at routing them from the area. The bombardment had unfortunately landed in Mozambique, destroying a Portuguese farmstead, killing several hundred cows, three horses, an elephant and hundreds of birds and smaller animals. As the ship turned to go south, the final shots completely destroyed the border station and killed a Portuguese policeman and four native policemen.

Not one shell landed in Natal. Captain Derry would not become aware of this error of navigation until HMS Westfield returned back to Plymouth.

There he was to be severed from his command, and then arrested on behalf of Britain's oldest ally, then stripped of all naval ranking and cashiered out of the navy altogether with no pension. Three days later he was found hanging from a tree not far from the Portuguese embassy. It was convenient for the Admiralty to say that it was suicide, but many people who knew Derry, said that he would never throw his life away. He was probably murdered, but as it was not going to be pursued, no one would ever get to know the real truth.

12

Gradually the years rolled by and the troubled cruiser just went from bad to worse.

The next Captain was Abraham Steiner, the only Jewish Captain in the Royal Navy. A man of fifty years of age, very heavy built from eating just too much stodgy food, plus using the Captains prerogative of drinking copious quantities of alcohol, mainly ships rum. This all went to make him look a rather amusing caricature figure, more of a cartoon than a real live person.

But no one ever dared to smile, let alone laugh in the direction of Steiner, he was a tough ruthless individual who not only didn't suffer fools gladly, but would go out of his way to give the said person the worst drubbing of his life. Any mistakes from anyone, no matter how high the rank that person might be, would not be tolerated, he would and did severely punish one and all for the slightest misdemeanour and usually publicly to as to create an even bigger embarrassment to the offender.

Some people thought he was cruel because of his faith. The fact that Jews were often persecuted really seemed to suggest to the unenlightened that they in turn had been hard task masters with ruthless outcomes to their unfortunate victims, but truth be known this was a theory that was entirely unsupported by factual evidence. Nothing doing with Steiner though, he was just plain cruel just because he could be, thus showing all the ranks quite obviously that he rather enjoyed being so. He had been married, but the rumour that penetrated right down to the engine rooms, was that he had driven his wife to drink, then killed her by persuasion.

It was true that the luckless woman had died some years ago, but she passed away because she had contracted a virulent form of Malaria. But, Steiner was well aware of the back talk and to be perfectly honest, firstly it amused him to think that other people thought he was a potential murderer, secondly, having the crew wonder about his ruthlessness kept them all on their toes, yes, he was happy to accept being the so called wife killer.

It was finally June of nineteen hundred and eight, the winter had been hard and the spring practically non existent, but the first of June seemed to bring a renewed hope of calmer slightly warmer weather.

HMS Westfield had spent the entire winter and so called spring, sailing around the British Isles, searching out pirates and villainous scoundrels who were cashing in on the poor of the world by offering them passage and wealth in Britain, but always at a very high price, and that meant not just their fare. Many foreign ships had been seized while trying to deliver thousand of Chinese immigrants all looking to find economic success within the British Islands. On one occasion, in January, in extremely rough cold weather, they came across a reasonable large barge being towed off the southern coast of Ireland, and it was being pulled towards a bay in the most southern part of the emerald isles and an out of the way area called Mizen Head. There it would beach, then disgorging its human cargo, which would then be entirely on their own, the ship would then leave the poor half starved devils to their individual fates and make good its escape with the Captain and crew being that much richer.

There had been a tip off from a source not known to anyone on board the cruiser that this landing was going to occur, so once given the knowledge Captain Steiner was quickly in the area looking for the ship that was doing the pulling. They came across a Romanian vessel that seemed to be dragging a huge barge, big enough to hold several hundred people.

No-one had ever come across such a way to transport refugees before, and the thought of those people being towed in the then appalling sort of weather, that was to say the least extremely dangerous, was a very sick thought to the crew of the Westfield. This was trouble the like of which no one had seen before. When ordered to stand too, the small ship cast off her burden, then opened fire with a small cannon which immediately pierced the side of the barge, making sure that it was going to sink in deep water. Captain Steiner saw what was happening, the top of the barge was covered in steel netting, and as the vessel started to capsize, he noticed hundreds of hands clawing at the netting, all scrambling to try and escape. As the ship was still in international waters, Steiner was somewhat restricted, but instead of letting the immigrant people die with no retribution, he promptly ordered the Romanian ships Captain to follow him into British waters.

Then, once within the sight of land he got his gunners to try some target practice. Westfield sunk the small coastal vessel, and then went over the area making sure that there were no survivors, there was little wreckage to be seen. He knew that he couldn't suppress the news from reaching the media. He knew that some members of his crew would sell the story to anyone that offered them a drink, and he knew there would be an enquiry, but, just by saying that the ship looked ready to open fire on him, caused him to open up first, this was really enough so called provocation to take the action that he did take.

Captain Steiner knew a thing or two about repressed people being a Jew, and he most certainly wasn't about to allow the Captain and crew of that Romanian vessel to get away with their deeds. Had they been arrested the Romanian government would almost certainly have ordered their release and nobody would want that to happen, least of all the Romanian Government themselves.

There were other occasions that they intercepted ships on the high seas, gun running vessels from Russia and other countries seemed to be becoming a regular ongoing problem. Hard up Captains would often try to make a living by selling modern guns to the Irish. To Great Britain as a whole it was gradually becoming a very serious problem, as the Irish Republican Army was trying hard to recruit more and more men to their cause, and getting more recruits meant they then needed more and more arms and ammunition.

There was nothing new about wanting to kill British soldiers. It was a pastime that was being practises very efficiently all around the world, and had been for several centuries.

On every occasion the vessels carrying arms would be stopped and their cargo would be impounded. The guns, if any good, were given to the British army, if not worthy, then they were just destroyed by melting down. The ships were seized and dry docked until a very heavy fine was forthcoming, even then the ship might be sold off to British shipping lines, depending on how serious the Judge and jury thought the crime was. The crew would be held for some time and then deported back to their own countries, but only after a long and hard re-education had been authorised and administered.

There was one other occasion when roughly one hundred miles off the Scilly Islands, a small speeding craft being very low in the water looked like it was in trouble, when hailed to stop. It opened fire with an old Gatling machine gun. Though no one was hurt, the bullets did pepper the metalwork all over the now aging cruiser, plus they even broke a window. As the speeding craft was much faster than the Westfield, Steiner once again ordered the marines to practice their firing skills.

The first salvo of speeding bullets entered the back of the craft hitting one man who was steering, he fell backwards, this made the small speeding torpedo like craft start to jump from wave to wave out of control. The engineer down in the lower regions of the craft stopped both the engines before they capsized. They surrendered and the crew were taken on board and locked in the brig. When searching the craft, many boxes of jewels were found, along with really fine brandy.

But later more efficient searching revealed several large oil drums stuffed full of Opium. The four man crew were given over to the police. The man who had been shot was paralysed from the neck down, but did survive to spend the rest of his days in a prison hospital.

For this arrest a bounty was paid to the cruiser via its Captain, who according to their rank distributed the reward amongst the entire crew. One stoker James Jolly received fourteen shillings and four pence three farthings.

Now finally June had sprung forth, and the vessel was going in for a refit in Portsmouth, and that meant that most of the crew would get two weeks leave.

Stoker James Jolly was one of the first to receive his ticket to go on leave. Two weeks, what was he to do in the time off? He had long abandoned the idea of revisiting his family, his wife and children had long gone from his mind.

But he could go home and visit his mother, but did he really want to do that? It was a long train ride to Glasgow, and as no one ever wrote to him and hadn't done for more than four years now, so why bother to make the effort?

All James wanted to do to buy more books, then settle down and read them. It could even be on board the ship, though the noise of workmen might be a bit of a disturbance. No, he had now made up his mind what to do. He would find a nice boarding house close to the harbour area, so if he wanted to walk he could go around familiar territory. He would then find a good bookshop and invest in yet more reading matter, he was now well into psychology, psychiatry, the works of Jung and other great thinkers were fascinating to James, so maybe more of the same.

Maybe in the evening he would look for a debating society and go and listen to local thinkers, maybe even give his two pennies worth if the debate was about something that he read of.

James was so adept to philosophy thinking that he was seriously dwelling on the idea of writing his own book. It would not be for publication, just the fun of writing it.

When asked what he was going to do when he was ashore by the second mate. James answered with the following,

"Well, I intend to find a pleasant quiet boarding house for the next couple of weeks, then I might write a paper on God in the real world, is he there for us, or for himself? But first I want to read another work of Carl Gustav Jung, the Swiss psychiatrist and philosopher."

The officer thought that Jolly was taking the proverbial Mickey so ordered him to run around the deck ten times before leaving the vessel.

"You really are an unpleasant cocksure bastard Jolly, get the fuck off this ship, and no more stupid lip from you. You're lucky I don't cancel your leave."

James was completely puzzled, he had been asked a question and answered it honestly, but had been punished for telling the truth, also threatened with more possible punishment.

'Is there a God? If there is I think he is taking the piss!'

James walked around the harbour area, looking for the right sort of accommodation, nothing to expensive, but somewhere there would be peace and tranquillity. He was serious, he had been thinking of writing his own tome for months now, if he actually managed to finish it, he might well send it to his old school teacher, Mr. Cluff. He smiled at the prospect of Cluff reading his book, but never in a thousand years believing that that cretin James Jolly actually could ever write his name, let alone a book on psychology and philosophy. But first the digs, then Jung, then, if time, start the book.

James found the perfect digs, a quiet little cul-de-sac just off the main entrance to the harbour and dock area. Though the crashing and banging went on, more or less non stop twenty-four hours a day. That didn't really bother him, it was the sort of noise that Jolly was used to. It was the human voice that made him cringe, that is what he wanted to avoid at all costs.

The lady of the house rented out on a full board basis to gentlemen, and as she was actually a buxom fifty year old widow, those self same gentlemen often got extras that they didn't have to pay for.

Her clientele were generally semi-professional people, who would need accommodation for several months while they were there concluding some business or other. But Mrs. O'Rourke, liked the idea of a sailor even though it would be just two weeks. And as she showed James Jolly up the stairs she was already admiring his tight bottom and imagining what sort of action he would like if in the bed with her?

It was a back bedroom, with gas lighting and net curtains, the bed was covered in an eider down mattress, which sank deep when one lay upon it. In this bed it would be impossible not to sleep soundly and long, that is unless invaded by some oversexed landlady.

The digs came with a full breakfast and an evening meal. But, woe betides anyone not rising on time, all rooms had to be vacated not later than nine o'clock in the morning and her gentlemen had to be at home not later than ten o'clock at night, or doors were firmly locked.

James packed his few possessions in the draws provided, took out some money, then left the building looking for the better book shops and stationers. He had already explained to Mrs. O'Rourke what he wanted the room for, and was prepared to pay an extra shilling a day, so that he could actually stay within his room and work, if and when he wanted to.

He found an interesting antiquarian book shop, full to the gunnels with several hundred thousand books. James was now in heaven. He went directly to the clerk who seemed to know what he was doing.

"Excuse me, excuse me, er, can I have your attention please!"

The man, who was reading a letter as James spoke, casually looked up, looked Jolly up and down in a condescending sort of way then asked,

"Excuse you sir, could you not see I was busy. I take objection to being hailed like a common ruffian. This is my shop, I will serve and talk to you as and when I like. Anyway, we don't sell penny thrillers."

At that last remark, James grabbed at the man by his jacket collars and dragged him almost across his desk. There was terror showing in the mans eyes, he was wondering if his answer to this scruffy Scottish man had gone a touch to far?

"How dare you talk to me in that fashion, who the hell do you think you are. I came in here to buy some of your books written by Carl Gustav Jung, my money is as good as anyone's, and I absolutely object to the idea that I would only read penny thrillers. Why I ought to knock some sense into you right now."

With that he raised his right hand with a tightly clenched fist ready to bring it hard down on this petty little mans face.

"Don't, don't, I am most terribly sorry to have misjudged you. If you knew the morning I have had you would understand why I get so edgy and unpleasant with people. Please don't hit me. Jung, yes I have some books by that Swiss Psychologist, please, please let me show you."

James let the man slip back onto his stool. The bookshop owner, still frightened, gulped and tried hard to dignify himself. He took a couple of deep breaths and tried hard to stem the shaking that had been induced in his hands, arms and legs. He then straightened his jacket, stood and offered James a more polite gesture to follow him to a further section of the shop.

Upon many dusty shelves were thousand of books, all seemed to be in good condition, offering the reader a wealth of exciting possibilities with those leather bindings.

"Ah! Here we are Jung. This is his latest tome, written just last year, as you can see it is titled, On the Psychology and Pathology of So-Called Occult Phenomena."

The shop owner withdrew it from the shelf, blew the dust off and then handed it to young James Jolly.

"Is this the sort of work that you are interested in?"

James smiled broadly, no more feelings of aggression towards the man came to his mind, as he was now in his own particular element.

"Oh yes, this is exactly what I want. How much is it?"

"I have to tell you it's not cheap. It will cost you one pound and two shilling and six pence."

"I'll take it!"

Stoker Jolly paid the money gladly, much to the complete amazement of the shopkeeper. He would have accepted half that price if James had haggled. This was probably going to be a much better day than he thought possible, he had sold a book that he thought he might never be able to get rid of. 'Yes sir, this is going to be a very fine day.'

Which was more or less the same thought as James!

He was now the proud owner of a Jung tome, all he needed now was an exercise book and many pens and ink to start his own writings on, he looked for a stationers.

That evening James had already read two thirds of the Jung book, he was so absorbed that he forgot to go and retrieve his dinner. Mrs. O'Rourke, was not so much angry as somewhat disappointed, she had hoped to get to know this Glaswegian sailor better, though he lacked the social graces, she thought that he was indeed very attractive in other ways, being fit, well built and obviously very agile and probably full of stamina. Gladys O'Rourke was very, very oversexed. Almost certainly because her long dead husband being a very slight man and always sickly, never really managed to satisfy her needs.

It was almost six months after his demise, that Gladys, now desperate to earn some money opened her home to strangers for boarding purposes.

The very first person, who took up the offer of a room, was a Cornishman, an engineer from one of the many tin mines that abounded throughout Cornwall. He was in Portsmouth trying to secure a new life for himself as the mine he worked for was soon to close down having become played out.

The very first night that he took residence he came home from a pub, not completely drunk, but extremely merry, having consumed several pints of ale. Gladys, had stayed up to wait for him, and then helped him up the stairs to his room. She was very angry as she didn't approve of strong liquor, and thus could barely abide men being drunk. After she had settled him into his room she too went to bed. She had just fallen off to sleep when she was awoken by someone crawling into her bed. Before she could utter a word of distress, he was kissing her passionately and forcing himself upon her. The trouble was, that because this was her first time in over a year, she enjoyed the experience very much, demanding that he perform several more times that night.

From then on, Gladys was a changed person, and would like to experiment with the various good looking fitter men that boarded with her. For some reason James Jolly didn't seem interested, which made her even more determined. It wasn't that he didn't feel his loins couldn't be aroused, he knew they could, it wasn't that he didn't find Gladys somewhat appealing, he did, he could imagine what an evening with her might be like.

No, none of these things were interesting to him, at least not right now. His mind had taken control of his body, lust was out and intellect was in. He wanted to read his Jung, nothing, food or sex was going to stop him. Every page threw his mind into turmoil, he didn't agree with all of Jung's theories, but he saw were the philosopher was coming from.

The greatest excitement to James was that as he read this book, he could actually understood and even argue around various points. He now knew he would actually write the book that was on his mind, and then he would send it to Mr. Cluff, for analysis. The excitement was far better than swapping bodily fluids with a middle aged over sexually developed woman.

He read on, right through the night, squinting in the dim gas lighting, as his eyes strained to capture the essence of the printed word, but he was determined, nothing would now upset his very being. He felt almost God like as he absorbed all of what Jung had to expand upon. There was absolutely no tiredness in his mind or body, when a four in the morning, he turned the last page over and came to that magic words – The End -.

He put the book down, looked at the fading wallpaper, stopped chewing and put the pencil down which he had used for writing in the margins and then thought.

'I have become brains itself. What an idiot I was as a child, I couldn't be bothered to learn from those teachers. Though what cretins most of them were, that is other than Cluff. Would any of them even know who Jung is let alone read one of his books. I will try and sleep now, but after getting up I shall start my own book of philosophical thoughts. I still think the title -'God in the real world, is he there for us, or for himself?'- is a very good one. I now know what line I shall start with and where it will all lead too? Ah well! Try and sleep. Now if Gladys what's her name came in I might just manage to slip the dear woman a right crippler, that would make me tired, but as she is not here, I will have to make do with planning my book.'

The next morning, James woke at seven thirty, still extremely tired from his heavy nights work. But he didn't want to offend Gladys, so he made his way down to breakfast. There were two other gentlemen staying at the house at this time, and as soon as James saw them he knew why Gladys had taken a shine to him.

Neither of them were under sixty years of age, both were bald, and very rotund. He smiled in Mrs. Rourke's direction, which didn't go unnoticed by her good self. She then walked briskly into the kitchen and retrieved some porridge, followed by one egg, one rasher of very fatty bacon and two slices of toast, which was most definitely part of the stale bread contingent. A very welcome mug of steaming strong over brewed tea was poured, this helped Jolly recover somewhat from his state of stupor.

Soon the two fat men left to go to work, this left Gladys and James together. Gladys was rather voluptuous and her two big breasts heaved gently under her blouse and pinafore. James could feel himself getting somewhat aroused as he knew she was very interested in him.

"Tell me, er, Mr. Jolly, can I call you James?"

"Yes of course Gladys, call me whatever you want."

"Right James. I suspect that you might be interested in me, am I correct?"

James was thrown, completely taken aback. This was most definitely a curved ball, he wasn't expecting such a route one approach.

"Well Gladys, you do surprise me, I wasn't expecting you to say that. But, it is true, I find you very desirable. You have a fine rounded voluptuous body, one that I would just love to explore."

He put one finger into the air, just as Gladys, started to remove her right breast for him to study.

"One thing though, and you must agree to this. I will give you this entire morning, we can make love until lunchtime, but then I need to work. I am writing a book, but unless I start now, I know it will never happen. So please agree to my demand and let me chase you to my bedroom!"

Gladys lay on the bed completely naked. Her two breast heaving up and down, a slight wobble of her tummy occurred on a regular basis. As James was indeed starting to admire her curvature, he noticed this wobble and realised she was actually shaking in anticipation of what was to come. He let his eyes wonder further down. She had largish hips, always thought to be excellent for having babies, not that Gladys had ever experienced that joy. Her Venus mound protruded downwards looking so large that for a moment James thought she was sporting testicles. Her pubic hair was turning grey and curled in a large mass. As she opened her legs for him to espy even more feminine delights he noticed her clitoris protruding through, even above the hair. His eyes looked at her two legs and admired her shape, for a woman of her age she was very, very voluptuous, and his joy showed at least six inches ahead of him.

James was almost dribbling with excitement, in fact one could say he was leaking gently from both ends. He gently stroked her legs, running his hands up and down, up and down. Gladys sighed heavily and her tummy wobbled even more. He moved between her legs and forced them open enough so that he could get down there and suck at her clitoris. As he got closer he was delighted to smell that she had indeed sprayed rose water in that area, now they could both enjoy the experience. After less than five minutes of James kissing and sucking at her mound of pleasure, Gladys exploded into a frenzy of orgasms. Though James didn't know it, these were the first orgasms that Gladys had ever had, in fact it was such a shock to her system, she screamed thinking that she was about to die. James lifted his head from between her legs, a worried look was upon his face.

"What did you do to me? I thought I was going to explode. Can you do it again please?"

She pushed his head down once again.

James started licking frantically at her clitoris. Once again Gladys exploded, but this time she was half expecting the feeling so didn't scream, just moaned and rolled from side to side. The bed was now wet beneath her body, the combination of sweat, dribble and female ejaculation, made James look at the soaking sheet, he knew that he would have to sleep in the middle of that wet patch.

Finally, having received five orgasms, she asked James quietly to enter her and satisfy his own lustful pleasure. James couldn't say a word as his tongue had more or less dried up and stuck to the top of his pallet, he once again forced her legs apart, carefully inserting his penis, which by now was almost bursting with anticipation.

He just pushed gently in, then pushed further and further until once again Gladys was quivering with pleasure, then turning her on her side he took her from behind. She had never experienced this position before and was eager to experiment with James. After some minutes, now almost completely exhausted James asked her to get on top, this Gladys did without being asked twice. There James was lying on his back with Gladys astride of him rocking backwards and forwards. He pulled her buttocks gently this way and that, so then after just two more minutes James could no longer contain himself. They both let out huge satisfying burst of air from their mouths, and James lurched this way and that as all his semen slipped gently right into Gladys's open virginal areas.

For a whole two minutes they both lay on the bed breathing heavily, then Gladys said,

"James, without doubt this has been the very best love making that I have ever experienced. I never knew I could get feelings like you brought on for me. It was truly wonderful. Let me get dressed, and then I shall go and make us both a pot of tea. How does that sound?"

By the way she spoke, James knew that he had a fat chance of doing any work today. Gladys was going to demand a repeat performance, and very soon.

As soon as she rose from the bed, James fell into a dreamy sleep, all that was on his mind was writing. Writing a book was now his goal, one he had a very limited time to complete.

He dreamed that he was handing the vast manuscript, his crowning achievement to a gowned and boarded Mr. Cluff, his old teacher. But the trouble was that Cluff in all his finery, just kept looking at Jolly with a very disdained expression, it was only when Jolly glanced in a mirror that just happened to be on the stage, that he noticed just how scruffy he looked, and as if to cap that, his penis was hanging out of his trousers still dripping from having been used on Gladys O'Rourke. Cluff never did take hold of the papers, which frustrated James right to the bitter end of the dream, and as he was awakened he immediately wondered what Freud would have made of that sleeping imagery.

He was wakened when Gladys came back carrying a tray bearing his reward for services rendered, a steaming pot of tea. And as previously guessed, after the reward, came the expectations once again. Gladys then demanded much the same as what had already happened.

'So much for the writing for today!'

The next morning, James made sure that he was up at the crack of dawn, washing and shaving, he then decided that he would go for a brisk walk and pick up the local and national newspaper.

The headline of the Portsmouth Post read - 'Killer rapes and strangles a young girl of thirteen, leaving he broken body in a ditch near the dockside. No witnesses saw anything suspicious, nothing out of the ordinary. And the police are looking for strangers, possibly a sailor'. He never got a chance to see the national headlines.

As he turned back into the road that housed him, a policeman came up and asked him some questions.

"Who are you? I have never seen you before. What do you do for a living?"

As James was ambling trying to read the paper at the same time, he jumped like mad when the policeman stopped him. He just hadn't spotted him coming so was startled out of his day dreaming, but this immediately made the constable suspicious.

"I, er, I am a sailor, on leave staying here at Gladys O'Rourke's boarding house. Actually I am a stoker on HMS Westfield. I'm here for possibly just two weeks."

James shifted from one foot to the other, and then continued,

"My name is James Jolly and before you ask I come from Glasgow, that's in Scotland you know."

The young constable was not impressed by this sailor fellow, everyone knows that the Jocks and all thieves and murderers.

"I think you had better come down to the station with me, we need to get a few facts right about you."

"I don't want to spend any more time by coming to your police station. If you want to know anything about me, then ask my landlady. What is all this about anyway?"

"Well, I saw that you were reading the Post, and I just want to know who the hell you are and what you were up to last night. You saw in the paper that a young girl was raped and murdered, it's just a few questions. If your story tallies then we will release you post haste. What's the hurry anyway, you're on leave, your times your own, you can come and go as you please. I don't think this will take too long. Now, are you coming quietly or do I have to force you?"

"I am writing a book on an important matter, I only have eleven days left before I must return to duty, I don't want to spend my precious time down at the local copper's shop."

"What rubbish is this, you writing a book, why the likes of you couldn't even spell your own name, let alone write a book. What's the book supposed to be about anyway?"

"It's about whether God exists or not, and if he does, why is the world so screwed up! It certainly isn't just about free will. I need the time to write, so if you don…"

He was cut off in mid sentence as the young policeman quickly cuffed him and started towards the station dragging James Jolly behind.

As he was not actually charged with anything, officially he should have been allowed to come and go as he wished, but when they arrived at the station, there were dozens of suspects all crowding around, so gradually they were all locked in cells before being processed by a higher officer of the law.

James was hungry and thirsty and extremely angry.

'Why hadn't that stupid young man listened to me. What the hell was he doing locking me up? Someone will pay for this!'

But as the day wore on, no one came to talk to him, there had been no food and no water supplied. As it was hot and sticky in the cell, his tongue had started to swell inside his mouth. To James this was fast becoming a nightmare.

James started to get cold as well as thirsty, he called out for someone to come, but apart from a huge babble going on in the background Jolly got absolutely no response. He knew that morning had now turned into late afternoon, still nobody came. Then through the small glass window, not more than six inches by six inches of toughened opaque glass, he watched as it turned to darkness. A whole day had been wasted and for what? James wondered who he could complain too, and what would he say to that person. He knew about civil liberties, after all he had read a great deal of law, but there was something about the police that still scared him, so maybe he wouldn't make too much fuss. But why didn't someone come to see if he was alright?

It was just short of midnight when the door was finally opened and a burly unfriendly policeman stood there and gave him two slices of bread and a glass of water.

"After this, you can leave. The killer has been caught and confessed. Now hurry up, we will need your cell as there is going to be a lot of traffic tonight, your lot are in Port and the drinking will be furious, which means, fights, troubles galore."

The man rubbed his hands together and concluded with,

"I just love nights like tonight. It gives me a chance to catch up on my greetings to our Scottish cousins. The only people on these green islands that are as bad as the Glaswegians are those fucking shit head Irish. God, they are arseholes to a man and woman. I hate the lot of them, and I hate jocks too."

James looked horrified, drank the water, ate the bread, and then started.

"What the hell do you mean by locking an innocent man up all day? Not once has anyone been to see how I was. If I was ill, I might have died. This is an infringement of my civil liberties. Take me immediately to see the Chief Constable."

"Listen here Jock. Unless you hold your tongue, two of my mates will come in to pay you a visit, then we will say that you tried to rough us up. The very least you would get is two years. Then there would be your navy, how long would they give you on top of our custodial sentence? Just think yourself lucky that I am a very nice person with a very good sense of humour, because I am going to laugh at all your problems, and if by the time I count to ten you haven't left this establishment, then I promise you, you won't be laughing and you certainly won't be leaving in a hurry."

He then leaned up against the cell wall, scratched his nose, clicked his knuckles and started counting.

"One, two, three…"

He didn't have to go any further than that, James had left the building.

When he returned to his boarding house, all the lights were out.

'What shall I do? Which is her bedroom? I will just have to keep knocking until someone finally comes.'

After roughly twenty seconds he witnessed a light in the hall being lit. It was Gladys, and she didn't seem to be in a good mood.

"Well! What do you want? I told you when you came here that I would indulge in tardiness, everyone must be in by midnight, so tell me why I should let you back in?"

"I will be happy to tell you everything once we are warmed up in my bed. How does that sound?"

He pushed gently passed her making sure that her breast rubbed hard against him, he then followed that up with his hand gently gliding across her bottom, which was wearing no underwear.

"I haven't been drinking, I just got caught up in some of your local trouble. Are we going to my bedroom? I told you, I will explain everything after some bodily heat has been exchanged, I am extremely cold and in need of some female company."

Gladys visibly melted at the thought of more of what she already received.

"Ooo, James. I could never resist a smooth talking man."

After washing, drinking a small whisky, then making love, both James and Gladys fell into a deep dreamless sleep. Gladys woke first, roused herself and started to dress to go down stairs and make the breakfast for the other guests. James eventually woke, completely exhausted, but ready and able to finally start on his ambitious book writing expedition.

As he was actually starting to rouse, the entire idea of the first chapter came to him, like a bolt of lightning. He knew that he had the most incredible weaknesses where English language was concerned, plus his grammar might yet let him down, but the years of reading various and varied subjects would stand him in good stead. Anyway, his imagination was alive with ideas and he knew it and knew which way to turn on chapter one. His education might have been suspect while he was at school, but nobody could ever doubt his abilities now. He had travelled a long way, from an ignorant peasant of a scruffy Glaswegian boy, hardly even knowing how to spell his own name, yet now he was well educated, maybe still scruffy, but so well versed in literature that he was quite capable of writing this tome that was floating around in his now developed brain. He knew he could achieve big things. It was all going to be a matter of the first word to write down and then things would surely fall into place easily. 'Please just give me time and peace, I can do this!' He knew he could, if only!

James went down stairs and enjoyed a big breakfast. Now he was ready to start work. All through breakfast Gladys eyed him with expressions of lust, but James choose to ignore them.

"Gladys, I like you very much, but please allow me to work today. I want to get my book well underway without interruptions. Please respect my wishes, there is always tonight, and every night should you so wish, but the days belong to my work, I have such a limited time zone that I really have to crack on. Is that going to be acceptable?"

Her smile said it all.

Once back upstairs, James felt a trembling within his very being, this experience was the height of his life to date. He withdraw the pens and papers that he so carefully had put in the draw supplied, sat down at the table, placed the dictionary and thesaurus by his right hand, picked up his pen and wrote the following.

Does God exist in modern day society? Is he going to control us as his creations, or is it a fact that we are all part of being God, and do we control, not just our own destiny, but everything around us?

I believe in a form of ethereism, which implies that we are all experiencing life on many, many plains or levels......

Yes, this was the way he wanted his tome to go. Within one hour his right arm hurt from all the writing he had achieved. He was amazed at what was oozing from the grey cells within his brain, he knew he would need a lot of help to edit the book, but no one would be allowed to change his written ideas, this was him, James Jolly speaking. Having read so many books, he had thought out many theories concerning life, death and afterlife. Now he was scribing his own thoughts and this even surprised him how quickly all this came to the surface.

By the end of his first day of writing he had already written forty pages which constituted two chapters. This was just what he needed and wanted. Hunger finally drove him to putting the pen down and going down stairs to get some dinner, then maybe he would take Gladys out for a stroll, maybe taking in a drink or two.

When he went downstairs Gladys was somewhat indifferent to him, she made him sit down and wait for the other two guests to appear on the pretence that they could all eat together. It was a good meal of Roast Pork and various vegetables. When Gladys came to allot portions James was most definitely given the least and by a long shot. James said nothing, but every time he looked in her direction, she would look away, deliberately so, making the other two guests very well aware, thus creating the bad atmosphere that was present within the dining room. Eventually James Jolly's patience ran out.

"What the hell have I done to upset you Gladys?"

Gladys in returned looked at him in a very pathetic way, her lower lip trembled, she went red in the face, got up from her chair, then burst into tears and ran out of the room.

All three of the men sat there felt extremely embarrassed by the awkward situation that was hovering there spoiling their dinners. James, coughed and felt terrible awry, he tried to say sorry though he wasn't entirely sure why he should apologise.

"Er, I feel as if I have done something awful, but I am not sure what I have done to upset Gladys so badly. Anyway, I am sorry for possibly spoiling your meals."

The man directly on James left, coughed back and answered back to his fellow guests statement.

"Listen old man, you haven't done much that I am sure. My guess would be that having been intimate with our Gladys, have you probably scorned her advances today. Yes, no, am I right?"

He looked across the table to the other older man, they were both half smiling, then he continued,

"The reason I know this is what probably happened, is because it happened to me, plus Arthur there, just the same. She wanted one hundred percent attention, constant sex, and that is just about enough attention to drive a fellow clean out of his skull."

He coughed again, smiled warmly as he looked James directly in his eyes, and then concluded with,

"Is it the same for you?"

James decided that he would still offer Gladys a walk and a drink, that's if she so wanted, but it was for purely selfish reasons, he hadn't quite over indulged in enough sex yet, and it was true to say that in James's head there was still something quite interesting in her body, he most certainly couldn't take his eyes away from looking at her virginal areas. Gladys made a show of being extremely upset, but when James had more or less given up on the idea of taking her out she said she would give him one more chance.

Once again the sex was quite sensational for both of them. As they lay in his bed trying hard to recover, young Jolly put his plans to her.

"Look Gladys, I don't want to upset you, both during the daylight hours, you must allow me to work. I have just over one week to finish the book that I am writing, if I have to take my work back to the ship, it will never get finished. All I ask is peace and quiet during the day. After dinner I am all yours. How does that sound?"

"Oo, darling, all mine mmm, yes I accept, you are going to be all mine."

James frowned deeply, wondering to himself if he had actually suggested something inappropriate such as a lifetime of togetherness?

'Maybe I should tell her I am already married? Err, maybe not!'

The next morning James was given two boiled eggs to eat, along with plenty of cut bread and real butter, even quince jam to go with the brad. Then up came lashings of hot sweet tea, then the daily newspaper. Gladys was now looking after her man, once again James felt a twinge of worry streaking down his neck and his back right down to his toes.

This day he was left completely alone, so he progressed with his book at a faster rate of knots.

By the end of the second day of writing, James had managed to explain his underlying feeling concerning afterlife, plus peoples near death experiences. The supposed coming of a great white light and a feeling of calm and serenity. But each person whom he quoted was not a personal interview, but a part of other authors books. How could he have ever hoped to meet such people.

He explained his own personal thoughts concerning the human soul and the question about the moment of death when the dying person actually started towards the great light, but managed somehow to be brought back from the brink on many occasions, plus they all seemed to have remembered that incredible moment. James, like so many other authors tried to explain the human spirit at the moment of departing the body. Psychiatrist, psychologist, they all seemed to have managed to come up with their own explanations of the white light and calmness, which in so many cases were remembered by people who had been so close to death.

Though James had his own theories, which he had now written down they were in fact just that, theories, ideas, but never meeting and talking to people that had gone through that moment of death, plus returning from it. James's only experienced these events through other people's books, he could not quote anybody that he knew had been through such happenings. But, somehow he thought that quoting other authors and adding his own personal touches was just fine, after all he wasn't stealing, just adding.

By the end of the first week he had written over one hundred and fifty pages, with many quotations and asides to show how he obtained his information. He had managed to spend many hours down the local library exploring past books he had read for reference, and his time had been spent well. He still wasn't sure if he would manage to finish before having to go back to duty, but he was certainly going to give it his best shot.

But there was a price to pay, after each day, came each night. Gladys expected things, fireworks, flashes of light, new positions, and it had to go on most of the night.

After the eleventh day and the eleventh night, James looked as if he was about to have his own white light experience, but not with serenity.

He was utterly exhausted, not just physically, but mentally too. Long days working over paper and pens, plus hard long nights working over Gladys, it was seriously taking its toll.

On his last full day he finally finished his book, he spent that last day going over it again and again. Making sure that the grammar was correct and that the spelling was right. He rewrote several passages but didn't really change any of his ideas. He now felt that he had put some seriously different ideas forward, that he had managed to fathom out of the depths of his grey matter. The idea of the tome, was to put before the reader the idea that we were all part of being the one God, that when we died we were brought out of our dead shells that being our bodies, shown into the light then moved on to different etheric plain, maybe even some plains being in other galaxies, millions of light years away from the existence that we know here on Earth.

James explained how he thought we had had thousand of past lives, all generating a greater experience that was there to enlighten us to the greater glory of what we can only think of as heaven. He carried on by saying that when we died, we were being taught how to develop from what we had achieved in the last existence. If we had been a Genghis Khan figure, then we would be brought back again, to make sure that the next life would not be devoted to slaughter or degradation. The whole point of life was to move forward, expand our brains and thus learn from our mistakes.

Whether it was a good book or not, he didn't know, but he knew a man who would have a good idea.

Though he had already decided that he would send the manuscript to Mr. Cluff in Glasgow, his old teacher, he was quite sure that he would still be alive. In an accompanying letter he asked him to edit it within the margin areas, and then tell him what he thought of his ideas. Then if he thought it was good enough, help him try to get the book published, and whatever he earned from it would be split with the old teacher.

The strangest part of this need to write the book was that James Jolly didn't have a clue as to whether he believed what he had just written, he just wanted to write something. But things powerful enough to be interesting, things that people dwelt on throughout their adult lives. Believe yes, believe no? That was the one question to be answered within his own head.

The evening before he had to return to HMS Westfield, was spent once more being given a third degree by Gladys. She was quite convinced that the next step in their relationship was marriage, now she was just waiting for James to ask for her hand, she thought that he nearly asked before, but it wasn't something that would stand up in a court of law.

After dinner, Gladys took James by the hand and led him to the bathroom. There she had meticulously filled the copper tub with boiling kettles of water, that was until there was enough for the both of them to clamber into. She started to lather him all over, trying hard to remove the years of grime that came with the territory of being a stoker. Then she started to lather his penis, it took all of three seconds to be rock hard and large. She tickled his testicles, then played around his anus which heightened his feeling even more. Then as his blood pressure rose to bursting point, she slid herself on top of him. She very gently rocked backwards and forwards, mainly so as to not splash water all over the floor. But that feeling was a fine pleasure for James, who always seemed to be the one to working on top, now he lay back and let the world pass him by.

"James!"

Said Gladys, with a certain whiny emotion being allowed to creep into her voice. James became almost rigid with tension, as he thought he knew what was coming next.

"As you are going away tomorrow, and I don't know when I will see you again. Don't you think we should formalise our relationship?"

His erect penis now started on the downward journey, its attention spoilt by that last sentence. Gladys wasn't going to be put off by a limp penis, she started tickling his testicles once more.

"You know that I love you, and you did say that could have you forever, did you mean it?"

Trapped, it wasn't checkmate but it was check.

"Gladys!"

He began in a not too convincing manner which immediately made his landlady prick up her ears.

"My problem is that I have at least fifteen more years in the navy. But I am extremely fond of you, it's true, I would like to spend my days with you."

His lying wasn't very convincing, but it was what Gladys wanted to hear.

"I suggest that we postpone any formal agreement before this coming Christmas. I will be back in Portsmouth by then, and we can pick up again, er, as from where we leave off, er, from now. Er, what do you think about that?"

'Too many er's,' he thought to himself.

But Gladys starting up her moving and tickling once more, obviously happy with what he had just imparted, Gladys now felt that this was indeed some sort of statement of faith in their relationship. When it was finally time for James to depart, Gladys insisted that she would follow him to the port gates to wave him goodbye. James didn't want the fuss, he also didn't want other shipmates to see who he had ended up with. His business was his business, but saying that, he really had no choice.

James had enjoyed the interlude and he did like Gladys, but he knew that very soon she would have yet another Jolly enjoying the warmth of her body, and he too would be exhausted at the end of his stay. So, he decided that he would visit her from time to time, anyway he really wanted to see where the relationship could go, after all, this woman owns her own house, something he could never hope to aspire too.

HMS. Westfield.

'There she is, and she looks grand. God almighty, I am getting emotional about a large lump of metal.'

But that large lump of metal was going to take him away from Portsmouth to the safety of another war zone. But now more than anything else, James wanted to sleep and sleep soundly and long. After Gladys, throwing coal into a furnace would be like sipping wine and watching the world go by, easy!

13

It was the 23rd of February nineteen hundred and thirteen, James had been in the service of his Majesty more years now than he wanted to remember. His life had changed little since joining the navy, he was older, very much wiser, but still a lowly stoker.

His book, -'God in the real world, is he there for us, or for himself?'- was published just before Mr. Cluff died. But Cluff died a happy man, somewhere deep within the recesses of his consciousness he knew that his pupil James Jolly had what it takes to develop his brain power, and on receiving this incredible manuscript, it proved his point.

Mr. Cluff spent the last three months of his life editing this vast work of Jolly's, and though he didn't change his ideas, he did strengthen them somewhat with better phrasing and better use of the English language. Because it was somewhat revolutionary in ideas, it captured the imagination of the publisher Espartos Press. Once making it to the bookshops, it must have sold all of a thousand copies, thus making Mr. James Jolly roughly fifty pounds in money, and that money ended up in the hands of James's wife. In fact James, though signing a contract never saw any money as he had put his home address in Glasgow as the place of contact.

He managed to receive a few copies for his own pleasure, he knew that most libraries had them sticking there on their shelves, other than that he wondered if anyone had ever bothered to read the work? Not that that thought worried him to much, as said before it was actually writing a book that brought its own pleasure, he just wanted to know that now getting older, he had the mental power to achieve that goal in his life. James never worried about the so called monitory rewards that should have come his way from having got the tome published, the reward, and it was a big one for James, was knowing that as a lad he could hardly speak the Kings English let alone write it, and now he was an author and what is better for him, he was a scholar and he knew it.

What James didn't know was that Mr. Cluff was so taken by the work that he became a firm believer, and died expecting to come back as a headmaster and not just a lowly teacher. When his wife found him, he had a broad grin upon his countenance. He had indeed died a happy contented man, he died having achieved what he always wanted to achieve, that was to bring a little enlightenment to at least one pupil in his life, and by God he had done just that.

James rarely went back to Glasgow. Though he missed his mother, the last time he did see her she seemed to be settled with her Polish chef. But he had absolutely no desire to see his wife or children, though he felt terrible pangs of guilt about his behaviour, he had now pretty well taken mistresses in every port around the country. He hoped that by now she had managed to find someone else, someone better suited to married life than he could ever hope to be. But guilt was brought on knowing that with two children in tow that was going to be tough for her.

The world had moved along at a tremendous pace since James had left home to join the navy. There was now a world wide escalation of shipping for so called defence.

Once HMS Dreadnought had been built in nineteen hundred and six, it made everything which had been built before, totally obsolete. What England had, other nations decided they wanted too. First it was the Kaiser, he insisted that his country should now in the twentieth century have its own place in the sun, and anyway, why should England always supposedly rule the waves? It should now be Germanys turn.

Then Russia wanted such ships, having been totally humiliated by the Japanese in the Russo-Japanese War in nineteen hundred and five. The Japanese, by sinking almost all the Russian ships without a loss of a single Japanese vessel, destroyed in one foul swoop the aspirations of the dying Tsarist Empire. So, Russia got her own Dreadnoughts, as this became the name for all these class of vessels. Then Italy and America wanted their own Dreadnoughts, so England now had to design and build Super-Dreadnoughts, thus so it became a world wide arms race.

Conflict was continuous all over the world, so one might be inclined to say – NO CHANGE THERE THEN!

Another hot spot was the Balkans, with the old sick man of Europe that being the Ottoman Empire, now floundering and losing control of its vast colonial conquests. It was gradually being booted out of the Balkans with two wars with Greece, Bulgaria, Macedonia, Serbia and Croatia. But even when the success of kicking Abdul Hamid the second of Turkey, the supreme Sultan, in his garish coloured bloomers, out of the region, did the fighting stop? Of course not! Having pushed Turkey out, the two allies Bulgaria and Greece turned on one another. So the fighting went on.

America was embroiled in troubles in Cuba. Mexico was staging a minor revolution. Central America, was forever on the boil. China was in turmoil, having slightly recovered from the Boxer rebellion, plus Britain's infamous opium trade war, now it was having to face problems with Japan. Africa was still troubled, with the Boers still feeling aggrieved with the aggressive way the British treated them meant that trouble bubbled continuously throughout the entire continent.

It was an almost certainty that the world was plunging precipitately towards global conflict, and Britain and its navy would be drawn into the forefront of this catastrophe.

So on the night of the 23rd February, it came as no surprise that a telegram reached HMS Westfield, stating that,

There is trouble yet again in Mexico, President Francisco Madero and his Vice-President had been shot dead in a local coup. But, sadly there was no secret that the American Ambassador, one Henry Wilson, was heavily involved, he has subsequently fled back to the United States of America.

But this event has creating a terrible diplomatic incident in which all the Western Powers were now being closely scrutinised by the rebel forces, these forces are now in opposition to the newly formed government but have the protection and support of the local indigenous population.

The so called western developed countries all understood that there was going to be a lot of trouble, the implications of other foreign powers being involved could have devastating consequences.

In plain language, this meant that if the situation seriously escalated, it might mean that the Ambassador and all the British staff could be in serious jeopardy, their lives were at stake.

It is Captains Steiner's duty to take the ship to Mexico, dock at the port of Tuxpan, hopefully that simple show of strength will be enough, but if there is no word from the Ambassador by the time you arrive, then an armed escort must proceed with all haste to Mexico City, with the objective of a rescue attempt for the entire Ambassadorial staff.

Fortunately for Captain Steiner and the crew, they had literally just coaled up and were awaiting orders to proceed to the Aegean Sea, to show some force to local bandits that were terrorising the sea ways in the confusion of the ongoing Balkan troubles. So now, instead of Greece, they were racing to restock the ship with supplies, then immediately get underway for Mexico.

Four days later when the cruiser was half way across the Atlantic, something extraordinary happened. Westfield was flat out doing roughly thirteen knots. The weather was appalling with waves reaching between fifteen to twenty feet high, the wind was whistling and icy rain was making the ship gather ice on its superstructure as the wind chill factor took the temperature to well below freezing, and as Westfield always tended to be low in the water, ice was the last thing they needed. The wind was taking the tops off the waves and sending the spray over right into the vessel. Nothing or anyone on the bridge was excused from a thorough freezing soaking. All of a sudden Captain Steiner collapsed, when a spray hit into him hard, he was swept backwards with the force and fell backwards down a small iron flight of steps. Then before anyone could react to the situation another wave broke over the deck and swept the Captain into the sea.

"O my God! That was Captain Steiner wasn't it?"

Petty officer Stewart stood there still holding onto the railings as he then realised that it this weather the Captain would be dead in seconds. But as quickly as he thought that, another wave crashed into the Westfield, delivering a cold stunned Captain right onto the furthermost portside rear six inch gun. By shear chance a gunner was in the booth checking that all the shells were fastened down well and then, lo and behold, there was his Captains face, looking extremely angry and cold staring back at him through the only porthole. The rating rushed outside and pulled the very lucky man into the gun turret booth.

"Thank you, sorry, who are you? Anyway you probably saved my life. Come and join the officers and me for a meal tonight. Now get me downstairs, so that I can change into something dry and warm before I still manage to die of hypothermia."

Everyone was struggling to come to terms with the simple fact that a very lucky Captain Steiner was actually saved from drowning in the freezing Atlantic Ocean. As dinner was being served a huge ration of rum was issued to all the crew, so that they could toast the luck of HMS Westfield, now for the first time thought to be a lucky ship.

The young rating, Gordon Johnson, was now the welcome guest of the Captain and officers on board. He really didn't know what to say or do, he just sat at the table along with those ranks of officers, this might be something for the scrapbook and diary, but Johnson knew that this exulted class of men were way beyond his expectations, he knew his place in the order of things, officer class was well out of his reach, he would never attain any such ennobled rank. Yet here he was the toast of the table, and even Captain Steiner smiled at him, once!

The next day the change in the weather was truly astounding, from icy rain and almost hurricane force winds, to a dead calm and a sun that showed them they were now moving into almost tropical waters.

It had been decided that the ship would stop in Nassau, in the Bahamas, listen for any further news and then coal up once more. And once they stopped they could once again get more provisions and also see to some new bearings within the main shaft to the portside propeller.

It was a huge job for the ship engineers to perform, but they were up to the task and in just a matter of several hours, all that could be done while the vessel coaled up, was completed. Also one of the boilers needed to be cleaned thoroughly, as it was seriously fouling the air with black putrid smoke, and even flames were seen coming from the forward stack. This was one of those jobs that the stokers hated to do. It was dangerous and extremely dodgy to a sailor's health. The task was always done by stokers lucky enough to lose, having draw lots for that awful pleasure. Strangely enough though, James Jolly really didn't mind doing this task. It reminded him of when he had to clean the train engine boilers in the engine shed in Glasgow, only these were easier, why? Simply because they were that much bigger, easier to crawl into.

When they reached Nassau, no leave was allowed as they anticipated only being there a matter of hours. Captain Steiner immediately went to see the High Commissioner, this was for news of what was happening in Mexico, and to ascertain if there were any further orders. There was nothing new, just a telegram to inform Stoker Jolly that his mother had died suddenly having fallen from the tenement window where she had lived. Jolly was informed about his mother's accident, but he wondered what the heck she was doing hanging out of the window. But he soon became upset when the news sank into his consciousness, so at that moment he went into his bunk and wept a torrent, but then it was more or less out of his system.

Having thought long and hard about what had happened, he wrote a long letter to his brother Charles, asking him to look into the affair. They both knew their mother was cohabitating with a Polish chef called Ivan somebody or other? But they knew that their mother wouldn't commit suicide, she was just not the sort. After all she had brought up three boys, with absolutely no money, first husband dying in a mining accident, she had been to hell and back, but survived. Her mental strength was incredible, so as far as James was concerned – suicide – not an option - never!

It took just two more days to reach the port of Tuxpan, though it was a deep water harbour, it was a nothing place with no facilities, the only industry being fishing. As it was a natural harbour, with hills all around sheltering it from the weather, but most space was taken up by the small open fishing boats. As no one was expecting to see an English cruiser man-of-war entering their waters, the appearance of this leviathan of the high seas took some surprising difficult manoeuvring for the small local boats, and there were one or two nasty collisions amongst them.

Captain Steiner was warned not to create bad feelings amongst the locals, so he took it upon himself to quickly pay off the fishermen for their damaged craft. This eased tensions quickly and peacefully. Then once ashore thousands of English cigarettes were distributed among the local people which really only went to make them realise that the British were a pushover for handouts.

Having asked around the locals, who now were seemingly friendly having received numerous gifts, if there had been any British diplomats hanging around, then finding out that there had been nothing to indicate that anyone was going to even appear.

Steiner decided that he would only wait forty-eight hours, then he would send a team to find the British contingent. All the telephone wires had been cut down, so other than going there, there seemed no other way of finding the staff of the Embassy. Captain Steiner knew that who ever went, could possibly come under serious possibilities of running into all sorts of trouble, trouble that could and would involve Britain as a country, the prospect of a successful outcome was indeed slim. There was always the possible danger of being taken for rebels or bandits themselves, that was just about every faction that was warring within the country. If they were captured either by regular troops loyal to the assassinated President, or by the now ruling rebels, their chances of survival would be minimal, they would be lined up against the nearest wall and executed by firing squad. But, orders were orders, they had to try and retrieve Britain's own countrymen whatever the cost. But it did leave a indelible mark in the planning of the operation.

To rescue upwards of twenty Embassy staff then bring them across country to Tuxpan, a journey that even under normal circumstances would be hard, but if then possibly being chased either by government troops or the rebels, didn't go to make easy thinking, let alone planning.

Now he was well and truly planted in Tuxpan, Captain Steiner studied the local maps carefully. There were no trains that he could catch, and the journey consisted of mule's tracks and bad unmade roads, nothing that one could rely on for transport even if there was any to be had. The only way was going to be overland by mules and horses. Steiner had already sent forth negotiators to hire plenty of horse and mules, plus to pay a generous sum in dollars to have three local people showing the way. One as a guide, one a mule packer, and the last as a cook and interpreter.

The forty-eight hours passed all too quickly, in the eyes of Captain Steiner it really hadn't been enough time, and he sweated a great deal, not just from the warm weather but mainly from not really having a clue as to what to do next. Steiner got all the men on deck and asked for volunteers. He wanted around fifteen men to go, most would be marines, but he had also to think of the welfare of the vessel, so if he took eight marines, that would leave plenty in case of attack from the local indigenes population, so that meant the other seven would be ordinary seamen, all would be armed, and all would have to leave off their uniforms and go in mufti. If there were questions, they would have to bluff their way out of the problems, only as a last resort was the use of firearms to be used. That meant this expedition was now a life or death situation.

When he asked for those volunteers, most of the marines stepped forward, all wanting and hoping that some small action might come their way, he chose eight of who he thought might just suit the situation.

Then he asked for seven more to come forward from the ships not so important crew members. Immediately without any thought as to what he was doing James Jolly experienced the sensation of movement, it was a shock to his system as he saw himself moving forward.

As James was the first to take that two steps forward, he was accepted, then another six were chosen. Steiner had his fifteen men. The three locals were vetted carefully, as the chief of the settlement spoke some American English having sold most of his catch to American fishermen over the last twenty years. It wasn't good English, but it was acceptably understandable.

He was told that when they returned to the ship, after a successful operation, they would all receive a bonus of three hundred dollars each. But should there be any problems concerning treachery, then their families would be held responsible. As there was absolutely no disguising what he meant, the Mexicans now felt trapped into serving new masters? Bad enough to kowtow to the Gringo's, but now they were going to have to be extra careful, maybe even the town's future depended on their personal success.

The very next day, just before dawn, the party set off. A stranger assortment of men one would never see. Local Mexicans leading fifteen men wearing anything from three piece suits to overalls and sportswear. They all looked ridiculous, especially as they all sported guns, army issue rifles and officer's sidearms.

As the sun rose low and red over the Mexican hills, finally warming the soil, plus the very souls of all the men trudging across the stony slopes of the tundra, The dry countryside showed itself in all its Central American beauty, with its gagged rocks, occasional lonely looking cacti and the various wind swept trees that all seem to be bent in an easterly direction. It was a lonely place, missing the vast hordes of people that occupied Mexico within its vast cities and towns. But being a vast empty vacuum of a desert region, made the caravan of people feel somewhat safer. Every now and again they passed by some dwellings, most were sheep herders, who did little but sit and chew tobacco leaves, watching over a small herd of bony skinny sheep.

Others may have a field of corn or maize, but it seemed that no one showed the slightest interest in a bunch of strangely dressed foreigners, heavily armed and riding scrawny mules and horses.

They didn't stop for breakfast or even lunch, the going was hard, they all knew that they had a long journey ahead of them. It was estimated that the round trip might be anything up to four hundred miles. As the entire trip was going to be over very rough terrain they knew that they would be lucky just to get there in less than ten days. Hopefully, they might meet the Embassy staff coming from Mexico City as this was pretty well the only way across.

The more Lieutenant Parkinson of the marines thought about they lack of planning, the more stupid the whole idea seemed to him that they were even attempting this crossing.

Parkinson was a career marine, he joined the armed forces when he was just fourteen, and then from bugler to Lieutenant, it took just ten years. This went to prove that being of low rank, one could still rise higher up the chain of command, and but only if you had the right name, background and education, which of course Parkinson did.

But ten hard loyal years that had seen him fighting in two Boer wars. He personally had knowingly killing at least thirteen people in various small battles and skirmishes.

He had also been in trouble in Dublin, it was an undercover operation around the time of the death of Queen Victoria, though nothing to do with the covert operation, he had quietly got involved with a nationalist, they had got into a fight and that melee became a serious affair, under duress Parkinson strangled the man to death, and all the luckless fellow had done was to show nothing but his contempt for the British Royal Family. But Parkinson was having none of it, 'How dare this swine insult the Royal family, which he should be loyal too.'

Though his superiors knew of the event, it had been completely and thoroughly hushed up. The man's body was never found as if was burnt to nothing in a tub of acid, then the slurry washed down the drains. He wasn't really missed, but people did complain about the acrid smell that was seeping from the drains for months to come, plus a surfeit of dying rats appearing seemingly badly burnt from acid burns.

Captain Steiner knew what he was doing when he asked George Parkinson to lead the group. He knew that he could use any amount of force necessary to get the job done, and the man wouldn't blink an eye.

That night was there first night under the stars. As they actually seemed to be miles from absolutely anywhere, Parkinson thought that it would not be a problem to light a fire and have a hot meal. But he did have the sense to put four sentries out just in case, and they would be replaced every two hours. Actually, part of George's thinking was more to keep an eye on the three Mexican so called volunteers, and make sure they didn't try to abscond in the darkness.

James ate a meal of stewed lamb and potatoes, very spiced up with hot chilli's. This meal had a seriously bad effect on him, first it burnt him going down into his stomach, secondly it burnt him on the way out two hours later.

Strangely though, everyone liked this way of cooking, lots of flavour and taste, but those prone to stomach upsets all went down with pretty speedy problems of evacuation of their bowels. The camp area quickly became an unpleasant place with the appalling smells that enveloped the very air around them.

As they were up quite high, and their line of vision was for many miles, Parkinson knew that if there was anyone out there, they too could be seen because of the glow from the fire. But to him it was a risk worth taking.

James finished his watch with nothing to report, he went to the fire and laid some extra wood onto it, then kicked in a scorpion that had ventured close enough into the glow of the flames. It instantly shrivelled up as the fire caught its armoured shell, and that very rapid funeral pyre exploded briefly but brightly. James smiled at the awesome wonder of fire, he then drifted over to the cooking pot and took yet another scoop of the stew, even though he had already lost the first batch.

'Yes, I like the taste very much, and that flat bread which the Mexicans use instead of forks and spoons is so very satisfying. This stew certainly finds the spot, challenging my taste buds, along with sating my hunger pangs. I do hope this sort of food is the norm?'

He spread his bedroll quite close to the fire, even knowing that it was attracting nasty biting insects. But he liked the warmth and the cosy feeling that fire gives. He lay back, feeling quite content with his life, especially as he wasn't throwing coal into an already hot furnace. He looked at the stars, wondering the age old question - Are there planets circling all those suns, if there are, is there intelligent life on those planets, if so are they like us humans?

'Maybe I shall write another book about that ancient question?'

But with his hands tucked between his legs, he soon fell into a dreamless sleep.

They moved steadily for four days, probably covering half the distance. Not once had they passed a town, not even a village, occasionally they passed small individual settlements, even a small cattle ranch was bypassed.

The cattle looked fierce and didn't seem to appreciate these strange people passing close to their personal feeding grounds. No one appeared from the house, so that area was quickly passed. The house was built as they all were, from a mixture of straw and mud walls, and open windows that had wooden shutters which could be closed from the inside. The roofs were all a sort of thatch, but very simply constructed with reeds.

What people they did come across seemed docile, it was if they couldn't see or hear anything about them, and years of rebellion and banditry had been the cause of their quiet acceptance of this servile state.

The old adage still applied to the peasant folk of Mexico.

Hear no evil, see no evil, and definitely speak no evil!

That night they made camp on a hillside that actually overlooked a wonderfully full fast flowing river. As the water would be clean and fresh, it was decided that everyone should take a bath and take the opportunity to cleanse their clothing, which by now smelled worse than the horses.

The water was ice cold, but clean and fresh as first thought. Everyone was enjoying the chance to actually clean away their feelings of soreness and personal filth. As per normal, a guard was left standing on the side of the river watching first for danger from possible bandits or soldiers, and then because they might be in a better position to see if anyone got into difficulties in the fast flowing torrent. It wasn't deep, but it was fast, and if one lost ones footing, it might be half a mile before you got a chance to get to ones feet and scramble on land again.

Everyone was enjoying themselves, it was still light and they had made good time, and now were enjoying a well earned rest.

Crack, a gunshot was heard right from the other side of the valley. The guard looked shocked turned and looked in the direction of the sound, then suddenly started to sink to his knees.

Peter Sparkes clutched at his ribcage, blood was oozing between his fingers and down his jacket, which was an aging sports jacket white with dark stripes, but now streaking with red life juices. He wanted to scream out, but for what reason? He felt as if he had been stung by a wasp, but why the blood, but his chest felt hot and sticky. Then reality set in and he knew he had actually been shot. Still, he couldn't scream, it didn't hurt enough to warrant a burst of temperament. He kept telling himself that if he was dying he would feel tremendous pain and fear, he felt neither, but he was dying. There was another crack, and this time Peter Sparkes fell forward dead, a bullet had passed clean through his temple.

Before private Sparkes hit the ground several cracks could be heard, but this time it was return fire from Parkinson and others that had started making camp. As the firepower increased the men in the water were scrambling to get out and join in the fight. Naked men were now chasing back up the hill to retrieve their weapons.

They now could see who they were returning fire to, there were three soldiers, all dressed in military uniforms firing and scrambling down the hill towards their side of the river, they must have been no more than two hundred yards away when the first dropped his gun and fell forward. The second stopped running and knelt on one knee, first to see how his comrade was, then to take very careful aim and fire towards the Gringo's. He was quickly dispatched too. The third turned and started back up the hill, but was cut down by a lucky shot that skimmed and sizzled off a rock. This was fired by one stoker James Jolly, though he never knew that it was his bullet that caught the poor luckless Mexican soldier.

"Right men, stop firing and bring in the four dead men. We have to bury them carefully, no one must know what, how or when this happened, all our lives depend on the utmost secrecy."

The four men were gradually dragged to the top of the small hill. There Lieutenant Parkinson examined the bodies very carefully. Sadly Peter Sparkles was stripped of any identification and interned in a narrow shallow hole in the hard ground, a few words were said over his unmarked grave.

The three Mexican soldiers looked like renegades, and the reason that was assumed was because all three were extremely filthy and their uniforms were in a very sorry state.

"I think that they might well be deserters. My God, look at the state of them, but we cannot take a chance. Break camp, we will eat on the hoof and make some more miles before we bed down for the night. But if others are around, they would have heard the firing from miles off. Sorry men, but safety first. Who knew Sparkes?"

A lean hungry and now angry man stepped forward.

"You take his gear, if he was married then when we get back to civilisation we will return his personal stuff to his wife. But now he is gone, forget him, we have to proceed and leave the dead to the worms. Dig a shallow scrape and throw these three pigs in it. Make sure that they are completely stripped of any identification and then quickly burn their stuff. If they have any money or jewels, share them out amongst the three guides, which should appease them somewhat, by the way where are they?"

The three frightened Mexican civilians came out behind a large boulder, the one that spoke English was shaking violently.

"These three men were deserters from the Presidents guard, I am sure there will be others. We will help you get rid of the bodies."

There was some money, not much just a few Pesos, which would have amounted to several dollars, but all three had mouths full of gold teeth, and they had gold watches and several other precious items of jewels. It was obvious that they were now bandits roaming the terrain scavenging off anyone and anything. The teeth were knocked out and everything was given to the three Mexicans, who just took what they could without saying a word of thanks. The three bodies were buried in a shallow grave, which was then covered with dusty sand and brushwood. Their clothing was quickly set on fire and burnt to just black ash, this was then kicked into the wind. Once all this was done, which had taken less than one hour from the firing to the spreading of the ash, they once again got underway. That night was a very nervy affair, no fire was lit, and the only food was dried beef jerky and cold water.

The only one who slept well that night was George Parkinson, who now felt as if his life had started once again.

The next day they passed through their first town, nobody troubled to find out what it was called, but everyone was wary about the locals, not least of all the three men from Tuxpan. Some local stared at the strangers, several children ran away when they approached, but nobody tried to talk to them, probably out of fear of their guns. But now civilisation was starting to close in on them, mule tracks became cart tracks, which soon became roads. Then bigger roads with real traffic, and even signposts.

They now knew they were only forty miles from Mexico City. What hit them straight away was that they could even see the smoke and filth that hung over this ancient area of the world. All had gone reasonably smoothly, so far their luck had held.

They camped that night in some woods, now less than thirty miles from their goal, no one was watching when they individually went off the road and into the trees. They found an area slightly below the roadway, and right out of sight or sound of any passing traffic, here they felt comparatively safe, at least safe enough to light a fire and even cook some hot food. This they did, but it was still a very nervy night. No one really slept well even though Parkinson had posted plenty of guards that spent their guarding time individually looking everywhere, just in case.

The next morning they had breakfast, they found some water which was not so clean and had to be boiled before being used for any purpose. Lady luck still shone on them and fortune was still on their side, there literally a couple of roads away was a smaller less conspicuous roadway that ran parallel to the other main road, this they took hoping that it wouldn't attract too much attention to them as they entered the city. They hadn't gone but half a mile when they came to a small village, the locals seemed to be interested in them and kept pointing to them either in their doorways or behind a window or two. It was obvious to Parkinson that this wasn't the indigenous peoples normal behaviour, after all no one up till now had shown the slightest interest in them, so why now? Then he found the reason! As the column turned a corner there was a line of Mexican soldiers all armed to the teeth with their rifles held at a ready, waiting there to greet them.

Before Parkinson could order a withdrawal more soldiers closed in behind.

An officer in his full uniform along with a bright array of medals stepped forward and spoke in almost perfect English.

"Lieutenant Parkinson I presume?"

He was a well read young man with a very young face, though by all his medals he must have fought in several campaigns. He was mimicking the famous meeting between Doctor Livingstone and Henry Morton Stanley in Africa.

Parkinson could see no way out of this predicament, and put his hands up in surrender. But instead of taking his gun, the officer held out his hand to be shaken.

"We guessed you would take this road. We have been here for two days now. I understand your journey has been tedious and long, and I regret to say completely wasted. Your Embassy along with all its staff are working normally in their Embassy building. Since the assassination of President Madero, things have been somewhat chaotic, but I am extremely happy to say, things are back to some sort of normality. I shall personally escort you and your men to the Embassy and then you will get your instructions from your own Ambassador. We will take my car, your men can follow with mine on horseback, does that comply with your own thinking?"

Parkinson was dumbstruck for some seconds, then burst out laughing. He slapped his counterpart on the back and turned to his men.

"Men, it seems we have journeyed for nothing. I shall get to ride in one of those automobiles and the rest of you will follow on by horseback. Everything seems to be all right, so see you all real soon."

Two hours later up drove this car with its four passengers to the gates of the British Embassy. It was well guarded by very heavily armed Mexican police, they even had a Gatling machine gun placed on the roof. The gates were opened and in drove the officer very adept in his driving skills. The entire journey he had averaged a speed of twenty-two miles per hour, it was so fast Parkinson thought that his eyes would be pushed through the back of his head.

The Ambassador greeted all four of them shaking their hands vigorously. He then turned to the officer and said,

"Pedro, it's good to see you again. Come in, come in and have a drink! I've got some wonderful Scotch whisky. What about you Mr. Parkinson, fancy a drink?"

Once again George was completely dumbstruck.

The five men now sat down within the private chambers of the Ambassador and drank their drinks and expanded on the last couple of weeks within the confines of Mexican past history, and the future chronicling of events.

Ambassador Bennett was a wise old diplomat who had lived a life of near things, having been in many countries and many revolutions and troubles, which often were possibly instigated by the British themselves. Many near scrapes with bullets flying had seasoned him to understanding the various factions that may contend for power within any country that he had to be working in.

He had learned never to take sides, his personal charm that unarmed the most dour opposition was that he and his staff knew how to be willow trees, bend with the prevailing wind, even and it was fare to say he might well have been advised by the Home Office back in London more or less the self same attitude, always smile towards the winning side, that is until they get too get toppled. Sir Adrian Bennett was now finally at retirement age being an extremely fit young sixty-five years of age. Having lived and worked in perilous situations all his working life he wasn't about to end his career on a note of death. He knew when the assassination took place to batten down the hatches and wait until the storm blew over.

As all communication had ceased to the outside world because of the bringing down of the telephone system, there was no way of letting London know that things were serious, but not fatal. But since Westfield had sent the men across country to do their level best in a rescue operation, the telephones had been reconnected. Word had got through to the Captain of the cruiser to halt the operation, but it was too late. So Steiner thought it more prudent to allow things to proceed and hope for the best.

They were lucky, but they did lose one good man, private Peter Sparkes, who actually left a wife and two young daughters.

Soon the rest of the motley crew arrived escorted by the Mexican cavalry. It made a grand sight as they all came galloping into the centre of Mexico City, the Mexicans on their wonderful charges of white and mottled Arabian Horses, while the British with their three guides were riding their mules and very scraggy, mangy horses. It did make the Ambassador and Parkinson laugh when the small flotilla of horses not vessels, draw into the compound.

Later Parkinson was taken aside to talk privately to Sir Adrian.

"So what really happened out there, did you get into any serious trouble?"

"Yes sir, we did."

George then went on to relate the entire journey which actually enthralled Bennett immensely.

"One thing though Mr. Parkinson."

He drew heavily on his huge Havana cigar, blew a smoke ring, and then continued,

"Never tell anyone about the loss of your man or the three deserters that you killed. Though it is a great yarn, let sleeping dogs lie, eh? No need to create a bigger hornets nest than has already been, get my meaning?"

Another draw, another smoke ring, and then he picked up his glass of whisky, swirled it around the crystal glass, drank a small sip, he then started on a new tact of conversation.

"I have here some orders for you and your men. It was imprudent for HMS Westfield to be in Tuxpan uninvited, so they were instructed by London to remove themselves post haste. The ship has taken flight to Miami in the United States. I have booked you and your men on a train to Nuevo Laredo. Once there we should cross the border into American territory, then get transport to take us towards Miami where we shall all pick up your ship. Yes, Lieutenant, I shall be coming too. I have finally and gratefully reached retirement and your exploits have made me want to get home for the last time. So young Lieutenant Parkinson I too will be travelling on your iron bucket and it will be taking me back to London along with the rest of your gang of ruffians, that is if that's alright with you?"

He smiled warmly at the officer, then took another sip of his whisky, at that they both stared wistfully into their glasses.

"Though I will see when we get to Nuevo Laredo. You see I do have the chance to visit New York one last time, I might just take that chance."

He paused, blew more smoke, looked wistfully into his fast diminishing glass of malt whisky, then sighed a deep almost sad sigh and continued in a softer tone of voice,

"We will see how things pan out. One of the great things of being an Ambassador is that you can create choices for your self. So, we will see what we will see!"

He smiled and took a deeper draft of his drink.

"I have managed to get visas papers for all of you so there will be no problem with the American government, they owe us deeply anyway, that stupid American diplomat who helped bring off the coup nearly caused a huge civil war, one that would vastly eclipse the problems with Pancho Villa and General Pershing the so called United States Cavalry man. Ah! Pershing, Pershing, Pershing, that man!"

Another last sip on his drink,

"He has been chasing the illusive Villa for over a year now and without any serious chance of capturing the man. All the Yanks have done is create huge antagonism towards all western foreigners."

He sighed deeply and then added,

"We are all Gringos here now. The most annoying aspect of the affair is that Pershing should be fighting elsewhere. Stupid bloody Americans never seem to get enemies and friends right."

Now the Ambassador stood up looked around the palatial room as if for the last time. He walked to the grand fireplace which had never been lit, but still had an incredible presence with its huge Louis the sixteenth French mirror and a wonderful nineteenth century English skeleton clock, standing proud and ticking loud enough to be heard in the next room.

"I'm going to miss Mexico and its people. I loved the food, so many varieties, and all so very tasty."

He really emphasised on the word tasty, drew on his cigar again, then refilled both their glasses with more Scotch, then without a toasting to the new King he took another sip of the hard stuff.

"I never got used to tequila, but when I have had too I could consume even that gut rot, that is until the end of a bottle appears, I could never get myself to consume the remains of the worm that they drop into the bottle. Did you know that the Mexicans eat worms? Strange habit that."

He made as if to shudder at the very thought.

"At least I managed to take some from the top of the bottle. That thought of drinking down some earthworm really didn't set my taste buds alight."

Again the Ambassador shuddered as he reiterated his feelings concerning the earthworms in the tequila.

"But you know, I shall miss this country."

He sighed heavily once again, drew on his cigar for the last time, and then stubbed it into the remains of his whisky.

"Lieutenant, I am going to leave you now, there is someone I must see before we leave tomorrow night. You and your men can be housed very comfortably here in the Embassy, I will come by in the morning and we will prepare for the journey. Please don't allow any of your men to leave the compound, it is still not safe. Oh, one last thing, I understand that the three guides were promised three hundred dollars each, is that correct?"

Parkinson nodded.

"Well we have paid them off, and they have been told that they have safe passage back to their town, and what is more they get to keep the horses as well. I have also sworn them to secrecy concerning the trip with you. They will keep the faith, because they know if anyone finds out their lives, plus the lives of their kin wouldn't be worth a carrot. Anyway, enjoy your night here, have anything you want to eat and drink. It might well be a while before you will get such a good service as here, take advantage of it."

He shook George Parkinson's hand warmly, smiled deeply, but somehow had the look of a man off to his own funeral.

Actually, the Ambassador was off to see his favourite whore for the very last time. Had he been forty years younger, would he have attempted to make an honest woman of her, and who knows? But he did love her very much even though she was still seeing other clients.

The next morning was beautiful, a cold start with slight mist from the cold night's condensation, but that soon passed to show a bright clear sunny blue sky.

Mexico City was a vast metropolis, with incredible ancient ruins, sporting the outskirts and suburbs of the city. Plus those tourist attractions and the colourfully attired indigenous peoples that within themselves, brightened any dull drab area of town with their very presence, the city looked to what it was and that is a metropolis, it was good.

It was a city to match any European capital and maybe more so, as it had a vibrancy that kept it very much alive, it was this self same vibrancy that created problems that often led to coups.

Generally the people were friendly, but because of the United States pursuing the infamous Villa, thus making a bandit into a hero figure, that said though, the locals understood that America had a finger in all of Mexico's pies. This United States interference went a long way to make all foreigners look untrustworthy no matter who they were, or where they came from, all had become Gringo's.

As a rule it was safe for Europeans to live and work in Mexico, but at this particular time it was somewhat dangerous, and that was certainly down to the internal meddling of their northern neighbours across the Rio-Grande.

The next morning Ambassador Bennett was waiting for the men to appear so that they could all eat together, one last hearty breakfast with just about the best food that money could buy. The table that had been laid seated the fifteen people there with consummate ease. It could seat twenty-four if needed, without feeling hemmed in. The table was dressed out with the very best silverware, and even flowers adorned each section. The different foods were waiting in a huge array of silver trays, these lined the side table all the way along. In fact there were twelve different platter serving a dozen different foods, and that was just the main courses, on a side table opposite, there were collections of fruit juices that made the eyes water just to see them. Fruit abounded in its lushness and festooned the table like the day it was all picked, fresh and succulent.

All that was missing were the fourteen guests.

"Andros, ask out guests to get a move on breakfast is waiting and we all have a lot of work to do. Tell them in your politest tones, to move their arses...Please!"

The Mexican servant bowed graciously, smiled knowing that his master was indeed joking in that age old British way, the way that no foreigners ever understood. Smiling to himself Andros left the room and went up stairs, and then started to knock on bedroom doors. Most of the men were actually up and ready for breakfast, but out of politeness waited to be called.

Ten minutes later they were all assembled around that huge dining room table, awaiting the Ambassador to say grace, then start eating.

"Gentlemen, good morning!"

A mumbling reply came back.

"Firstly, allow me to tell you what there is under the platters. There is baked fish, somewhat like herrings, but not really. There is deep fried giant squid. There are devilled kidneys, slices of Argentinean beef that have been cooked very slowly in a succulent sauce made from the guava fruit. There is bacon, sausages, eggs, some poached, some fried. There are goose eggs and duck eggs. I fact there is just about anything your stomach may desire. Over on this table there, is fruit and assorted juices. Now eat heartily as it is going to be a long day. Once we board that train tonight, it will be a very long thirty-two hour journey to the American border. We will have our own section of the train, away from the local peasants, but the food aboard will be somewhat restricted and limited, so, as I have already said eat your fill now and enjoy. Now if you would all bow your heads."

Sir Adrian enjoyed that little speech, so rounded it off with,

"Lord, we thank you for this sparse array of food for our consumption this day. May your bounteous efforts take us through this day without too many problems? May you keep the beasties at bay and deliver us all in the safe hands of our American cousins. God save the King. Amen."

There was an amused chuckle from around those who had actually been listening, and then the attack came in all its fury and violence, war had at once started, fourteen men scrambled for the food.

All the Ambassador ate was two devilled kidneys, with a small helping of scrambled eggs, but he made hay with the coffee, lashings of wonderful freshly ground and freshly made coffee, all served with a hint of fresh thinned cream which had been sweetened.

Sir Adrian looked around with a wistful tear entering into his eyes.

'This is the last breakfast, the last meal, and the very last day that I shall be Ambassador in this wonderfully naïve country, with its simple folk and beautiful women. O Mexico, I'm sure going to miss you. Back to the wind and rain of England, and back to the lousy food, poorly heated houses and its poorly educated people.'

He sighed deeply as he ate his last piece of kidney, then looked towards the fruit juices.

'All I'll be back in Blighty is plain old Sir Adrian, not Ambassador Bennett, or his Excellency. What a way to spend my last days as plain old Sir Adrian, oh well!'

That day was spent packing all the equipment that was to be taken either back to the ship, or in the Ambassador's case special black attaché case along with his special secret papers, back to Britain, and was there plenty of it. Sir Adrian had all the men line up so then he could inform them of procedure.

"Men, while you are under my protection you will have Diplomatic Immunity. But, I hasten to add, that is not a licence to steal and get away with heinous crimes, no sir, but it mean that you can carry your sidearms as long as they are well hidden, but your rifles and bandoleers of ammunition must be packed in cases that I shall supply for you, then they will be numbered and processed through the proper channels, which means they will be properly sealed with wax, which must not be broken, these rules apply whilst going through American immigration. I will allow you to keep those cases in our carriage, just in case of problems. But, and this is a big but, if there are problems along the way, and that would mean bandit trouble, you must and will only act under my supervision. I rule the roost not Lieutenant Parkinson, that must be completely understood. Obviously should something happen to me, then the Lieutenant will have carte-blanche. I suspect it will be a long tedious journey so if there are any readers amongst you please feel free to scrounge some reading matter from the Embassies extensive library."

With that last remark James Jolly's ears pricked up, new reading matter! Things that he might well become interested in?

'Wow, what an opportunity!'

"Lastly, we will leave within the hour, may I suggest that you take that time to smarten yourselves up. You are after all representing our country."

They finally boarded the train at seven in the evening, the sun had gone down and the darkness enveloped everything accept the gas lighting in the station and on the platform, not that much light seeped out as the insects and lizards monopolised most of the lighting, shrouding any excess from escaping to actually light up anything.

There was just a hazy dim glow coming from the fluttering of wings and legs of creatures struggling to get their own space in the light and warmth.

The train had six carriages of which the diplomatic coach was second in line, just behind the goods wagon. Behind the luxurious coach that the Ambassador and marines were occupying was then the first class carriage, then a second class, followed on by two third class very plain carriages, so plain that they didn't even have panes of glass in the windows.

The train did have electric lighting, which was supplied by batteries that kept failing. But of course this light only applied to the Ambassadorial coach and first class, the rest did the best they could and slept the night away in darkness and the returning smoke from the engine.

The engine itself was old rusty and looking as if it would have been better suited to being in a museum than actually still working, it dated back to eighteen seventy-five. It was an American made wood burning beast built in Philadelphia. It came equipped with two front bogies, four drive and four bogies wheels at the rear. It was pulling a huge tender along with a water carrier, as refuelling and obtaining extra water were going to be hard to obtain on most of the journey. It was a journey that would leave the train completely isolated on most of its travels, so if there were any mishaps, not that trouble was anticipated, then the two extra engineers would be expected to manage well enough without calling out non existent rescue squads.

Sir Adrian had done this journey several times over the last years, but though nothing untoward had ever happened he always felt nervous and apprehensive. Actually, truth be known, he was kind of glad to be travelling with some British marines, and all armed to the teeth to boot.

Once everyone had boarded the train, a thin sounding whiny whistle blew, explaining to the moths, bugs and lizards that the light that they so cosseted was about to be extinguished. As early as this was, this happened to be the last locomotive to leave the station that day. The huge smoke stack bellowed out huge plumes of black acrid smoke which got into eyes noses and throats of the third class passengers through the lack of windows to close. The light on the front of the beast was bright and lit the track a long way ahead.

But that light was very important as often cattle and other animals would lay on the tracks at night to gather the warmth that the iron rails exuded. The driver and fireman took control of the locomotive with consummate care, even though to the alert watching eye the outside components never seemed to be cleaned. Unlike their European counterparts, where trains would be so clean one could eat ones dinner from the footplate, and brass work shone so brightly that they could be used as mirrors, in Mexico it was not so important, better not to show the wealth of a train company by overstressing the value in bright paint and shiny brass plates. But the engineers were extremely good at keeping these leviathans running perfectly, even though they couldn't even supply the right sort of wood to burn, usually just quite new pine, which gave off gasses and tar, meaning that the boiler and pipe work had to be cleaned almost daily. To be a train driver meant a job for life and a good job for life, one that brought good money and a good pension, plus the opportunity to advance in the company. This train was no different from any other, the driver and fireman knew their stuff and did it well.

The engine lumbered through the darkness with the driver keeping a very alert eye on the track ahead. Often the train would slow down meaning that some animal was lying prone across the rails, and had to be either shoved off by the long cow catcher welded on the front, or the fireman would take a burning piece of wood and actually chase the animal off. Throughout that dark night period this happened three times, which meant that they were perfectly on time.

When dawn came it sprang forth with a wonderful exuberance that had anyone other than the driver been awake, they would have enjoyed the experience. For the assisting two crewmen, they had seen it a thousand times already and were completely nonchalant about the wondrous nature.

Gradually the marines and Ambassador returned to life. Sir Adrian had a bed in the corner of the coach with a screen that could be pulled around. He had managed to snore his way throughout the entire night, thus making sure that he was probably the only one to get a good nights sleep.

Parkinson and his men slept as best they could either on the seats provided or by being prone on the floor. Lying on a much ornately patterned carpet that had been brought all the way back from Istanbul in Turkey, didn't give them much satisfaction or excess of comfort, it may have been special, it was probably extremely expensive, but it had its own problems as it carried a silk bug. The insect didn't actually bite when on ones body, but it did make the person itch and sweat terribly, a very uncomfortable experience.

As there was a toilet compartment gradually all the men did their ablutions, even managing to beget a shave. Breakfast was a welcome function to receive as every man knew that the food hampers were crammed tight will all sorts of goodies to eat.

After breakfast having now been on the train for more than ten hours, they pulled into a small siding station, which meant that all the other passengers could use toilet facilities, get some sort of fast food, and generally walk around and exercise tired weary feet bringing blood back to vacant parts of the body.

The second driver and engineer now took control of the engine, allowing the first crew to climb back into the goods section to try and eat and sleep. They loaded some more wood onto the tender, and filled the water tank to overflowing. The next stage of the journey was all up hill and would need every reserve of energy that they could muster out of the beast. It was interesting to James Jolly watching the men prepare their charge, he knew about these wonderful dinosaurs and he was hoping that he could be of some use to them, but they too knew their onions. He walked over to the new driver and asked if he spoke any English, the man just smiled and looked blank. James then indicated through sign language that he knew the points of reference that needed oiling on the wheels and their bearing, and he knew where the grease points were, which he indicated by showing the driver with a pointing finger. Now the driver understood and handed him first the oil can which James accepted with a glee in his eye, then started to oil all the relevant places much to the delight of the driver. Now thoroughly dirty, he asked for the grease gun, and proceeded to use it with a certain expertise. The driver called to the fireman and showed him how clever this Gringo was, and then they both laughed.

But for Jolly, this small experience made the entire trip worthwhile, he was back in that engine shed in Glasgow a place he had been most happy in.

Later that morning as the train puffed and panted on the ascent of a ravine, ever so gradually climbing higher and higher, they had to cross many wild flowing rivers, always on what seemed to be rickety wooden bridges. The structure seemed to have been there forever, and now it looked so flimsy that to any discerning eye it would be ready to fall into the bubbling boiling water below. On one bridge they slowed to a crawl, the single track looked extremely precarious, and a dead cow, half eaten by probably a big cat, leopard or cougar, had to be cleared off the track before they could cross. The engine sighed with relief not having to move forward, it hissed and throbbed and held still while the driver and fireman had to try and push the dead animal into the river. Between the two of them they could not budge it, so they asked for volunteers from the marines to see if they would help? Four men jumped down eager to get some life back into the limbs. Jolly also leaped onto the side of the track, mainly to watch, they certainly didn't need his muscle.

Very gradually they pushed the carcass aside and balanced it upon the rail, then with a mighty shove down it went, hitting rocks and finally splashing headlong into the froth below. Instantly it disappeared from view so deep was the river.

Just as everyone was once again climbing back into their various coaches a shot rang out. It must have been a very long way off as the spent bullet fell harmlessly onto some loose shale a little way before them. But that shot made the driver and fireman wary as to what might be around the corner. Once inside the Ambassador asked the men just to get their revolvers ready, forget the rifles, they were to stay where they were unless things became drastic.

The engine moved forward, slowly at first but gradually picking up some speed, it was struggling with the incline, also because somehow the tracks seemed slippery. The track turned a sharp right on the other side of the ravine and headed in the direction that they thought the shot came from. But after two hundred yards there was a small tunnel in which they must pass, this was obviously the worrying spot.

Who would attack them and why?

The train got to the tunnel but the wheels started to slip desperately so much so that the driver thought that they might start slipping backwards. Someone had greased the tracks. The carcass had been a ruse to slow the train down so much that it could get enough speed to ski across the slippery parts. The driver stopped and put the breaks firmly on, fortunately the train held, so it didn't slide back, but it wasn't going forward either. And then another crack was heard, then another, then the firing became continuous, bullets were flying everywhere.

As they were in the tunnel, there wasn't a lot that that they could do, but that also applied to those firing at them. It was a sort of stand off, maybe that phrase associates itself – A Mexican Standoff. The engine was being raked with a withering fire, but that tough hombre of a machine was thick enough to withstand rifle fire, especially as the rifles were probably very old and worn.

One marine stuck his head out of the window, and with his pistol raised, he thought that he might be of some use. But because the angle that the train was stuck in the tunnel, he couldn't possibly see out into daylight.

"What do you suggest we do Lieutenant?"

Sir Adrian was still sitting comfortably on the most comfortable chair in the carriage, seemingly oblivious to the danger that was coming from beyond the tunnel. He was puffing calmly on one of his Havana cigars, plus drinking whisky from his crystal glass. He pushed back his grey hair and awaited the answer.

"I think we have a problem sir. First we cannot stay here, this train must move forward, I really think it would be exceedingly dangerous to reverse over that so called bridge. Yet if we proceed outside into the light we will be sitting ducks. I only hope that these, we will call bandits, are stupid people and don't try and take us from the other end of the tunnel, then we do have problems. But on seeing what was there I cannot imagine how the hell they could easily descend to the rails, there didn't seem to be any way down. Though having said that, someone must have climbed down to grease the rails, so maybe they are already down behind us."

Parkinson couldn't believe that he had been that stupid. Without asking permission he gave the order.

"Men, grab your rifles and plenty of ammunition, we have a serious job to perform."

The fourteen sailors and marines clambered down onto the track, bullets were still whizzing, but at this time they were in no danger.

"Four of you crawl forward, get into the engine and try and make the driver understand that you are there to help him. Don't do anything that might cause you to get injured, let Sparkes be the only casualty on this adventure. The rest of you follow me and quietly and easily. Ambassador, close this door, there is still one rifle take it and wait for us to return, the gun is for just in case. Men, lets go."

Parkinson and his men very carefully made their way to the back of the train, they could see daylight clearly. Everyone on the train was now cowering below window line, so he didn't try and speak to anyone. He indicated that two of his men should go over to the other side of the track and keep close to the darkness of the wall.

The other eight moved stealthily forward on the river side of the wall, again it was all in total darkness. They could easily see out into daylight but outside could not easily see into the tunnel.

"Look Jolly, can you see in the distance ropes being lowered, there, see them? Three men preparing to help the others down. Don't fire, they don't know we are armed, we will give them a huge surprise, but only when there are enough to warrant the use of our bullets. Here they come, crikey, how many are coming down on those three, no four ropes; there must be at least a dozen. Men wait until I give the signal, and then create hell and mayhem. I promise you all, you will enjoy this day. But don't get careless. Like I said, one casualty is enough. I want to take you all home safely. Another batch coming down, that will be at least twenty."

Parkinson was almost rubbing his hands together with glee, this was what he was meant for.

"Wait for it! Sadly, if that is all that climb down we will just have to make do."

There was a small ripple of nervous laughter.

Two more minutes went by, the bandits had now gathered and were preparing to advance on what they thought was an unguarded unarmed train. Parkinson checked his weapon yet again. Made sure that he was sighted onto the men furthest away, after all he wanted them all, then he fired. The man just crumpled forward kicking slightly as his death throws flicked his nervous system, and then all hell broke loose. All Parkinson's men were in good positions to fire without serious problems of being fired back on, only a lucky shot could do any damage as they just couldn't be seen. The bandits just didn't know what to do, they fired wildly, and one even accidentally shot the man in front of him. Within twenty seconds it was all over, every last one of the Mexicans was either serious wounded or dead. Parkinson ordered a cease fire, and then cautiously went forward into daylight. He immediately looked skyward to see if any others there that might be waiting to come down or even fire down from above, but that area was quiet too.

As it was once again impossible to seriously see down onto the tracks, how anyone would know that their raid had been a total catastrophe was somewhat unlikely. Anyone up there was probably thinking that the quiet meant that they had won the day. George went up to the first man lying in a pool of blood. He was quite dead, shot directly through the head. He very carefully went from body to body checking for life. Two were whining with pain, both seriously injured, both probably dying. And the next to last was just coming too, having been knocked unconscious by a rock hitting his head. Here was their captive. This is what he had been hoping for?

"Jolly, come forward! Take this man, bind him tightly and put him in our coach. The rest of you, help me to dispose of these vermin. We will search them for anything worth while, just like they would have done with us, then we will dump them in the river."

The Lieutenant was seriously enjoying himself, and to make his men feel at ease he added,

"A good day for the fish, food a plenty. See, I said you would enjoy this day. But do take care, no one wants to go swimming so a rescue is out of the question, if you fall in you have to swim back to England. Now come on, time is important."

They quickly searched each body even looking for gold teeth which when found were hammered out. And then they dragged the corpses over to the edge and watched them plummet. None of them made much of a splash and none of them complained. The two seriously injured got the same treatment, and the extraction of teeth was the final insult to the youngest man who was about to die anyway, he just moaned once and stopped breathing. The last one cried and begged for mercy but got none, he too found the water cold and deep. All of this was done in less than three minutes.

"Jones, Gordon, stay here out of sight and wait to see if anyone else was foolish enough to clamber down. Wait until they are on the ground, and then if no one else comes, dispatch them like the others, clear?"

"Sir!"

Firing was still continuing, coming from the front of the train, so it was time to organise something there.

"Follow me men."

Parkinson was in his element, he was playing at soldiers, enjoying every blasted moment. He took the men to the very front of the engine but still in a safe area. Bullets were still whizzing here there and everywhere, but not one had done any serious damage to man or machine. But as he looked he knew this was the tricky one, if he tried to attack the perpetrators down here, then he and his men were sitting ducks like the Mexicans that he had already killed had been. What to do, where to go, this was a poser that he couldn't quite fathom out.

Just then, the shooting stopped, Parkinson could clearly hear other shots being fired, but far behind those who had fired down on the train. That firing got louder, but no shots were now coming down onto the tracks. There was a different sound, one of horses being galloped away from the area, and disappearing into the distance. They waited for roughly five minutes then a voice was heard shouting in English,

"Is anyone still alive down there?"

General Pershing and his cavalry had finally very nearly caught up with his aging foe. It seemed that Pancho Villa had sent many of his band to stop and rob this train totally unaware that it contained English marines on board, they thought it would be a pushover, something to tell the kids about, but now sadly many of those kids were now without fathers.

The driver and fireman took the whole affair in their stride, just another day at the office. The driver now went out and placed masses of sand on the tracks and under the wheels. Gradually starting up the steam once again, he got the engine moving, forward, slip, forward, slip, slip back a couple of feet, then forward again. Very gradually they got the machine over the hurdle, so all jumped on board. It was time to meet the Yanks.

Why Villa's men had attacked at this precise place was strange, not a good ambushing place, too exposed for both sides. Had they caught the train in the open, they might have had a better chance of success, as it was they had lost twenty-five dead and one captured.

Soon the cliff evened out so that the train was now on the plateau, and there was a striking element of by gone days, the US cavalry in all its splendour. Wonderful horsemen with incredibly beautiful animals, all the men armed to the teeth with their fast repeating carbines and their strings of bandoleers slung over each shoulder, there light brown khaki uniforms almost shining in the bright sunshine. This time of year was dry and sometimes cold, but in the sun it was a different matter, things shone in the brilliance of sunlight, somehow it always seemed brighter in the winter than in the summer months. It was crisp, clean and wonderful to see.

General Pershing was an interesting man to meet, he knew of Sir Adrian Bennett, and of course he knew of the troop of English marines that were travelling through Mexico to Miami, there to pick up their cruiser HMS Westfield.

General Pershing was a slight man in his early fifties, he wore a characteristic moustache which by now had become his personal trade mark. If it wasn't for the simple fact that he was much older than his men, one would have been hard pressed to know who he was, he wore exactly the same sort of clothing that his fellow horse soldiers wore and sported the same amount of bandoliers, also an automatic ten shot pistol in a holster. On his horse were the normal accoutrements of a horseman, his whip, ropes and a sword. His horse looked as if it had been with him for years as it too looked old with its mane greying ever so slightly. But it was obviously loved, and extremely well groomed. As he dismounted from his charger Pershing showed his age, as after years of riding horses he now had a very distinct bow legged walk.

His career had been phenomenal in the speed that he rose through the ranks. He left West Point after completing his training in eighteen eighty-six, at the not too tender age of twenty-six. He had served as a cavalry officer in the infamous campaign against the Indian Chief Geronimo, and then another terribly destructive campaign against the Sioux Indians tribes in eighteen ninety-one. He then went on to fight in the Spanish American War, right up until this present expedition against the so called bandit Pancho Villa there in Mexico. He was at this time supposed to be in the Philippines, but had made it his own business to break the destructive back of the Mexican so called revolutionaries. But for once he wasn't having much real success.

He walked over to Bennett as if he was greeting an old and dear friend.

"Sir Adrian I suspect, am I right?"

As Bennett was the oldest and the one that stood out amongst the rest, there was no real challenge for Pershing. He held out his hand. He then turned to Parkinson.

"Lieutenant Parkinson, nice to meet you."

Again he held out his hand to be shaken. This was all very cosy, but it didn't get the train back on route.

"Can I count on both your discretion as I am not supposed to be here."

He laughed at his own joke, the whole world knew he was now in Mexico even though he should have been in the Philippines stopping, or ending the war there. But both George and Sir Adrian laughed as if the entire thing was one big joke.

Parkinson looked agitated as he realised that time was of the essence.

"General Pershing, we managed to capture one man for you. The nasty little blighter is slightly wounded but nothing serious, just a bump on the head. Would you like him? Otherwise I might have to dump him in the river along with the others that we dispatched. Maybe you can get him to tell where Villa's hideout is?"

"Well bless your heart, a captive! Yes he might be useful, we will take him off your hands. Did you say you killed some of Villa's men?"

"Yes general, we killed twenty-four I think. We checked if they had anything of interest, none of them did. They will all be at least two or three miles down river by now. We were lucky, they obviously had no idea that the train would have us on board and that gave us a clear advantage, plus their idea of an ambush was ludicrous, they stopped the train in a tunnel back yonder and then tried to storm from behind by climbing down ropes, they were easy pickings."

Before Parkinson or Pershing could say any more, the train whistle blew, and so Bennett said the last words.

"General Pershing, you are a legend in your own time, it has been our pleasure to bump into you, you probably came at the moment that things might have got sticky for us, and so I and my band of merry men thank you for that. But it seems we must go, a train schedule waits for no man."

The whistle blew again, it was time to board. They handed over the prisoner who at once started to cry for mercy, it would have been unlikely that he survived the night.

It was another twelve hours before they reached the outskirts of Nuevo Laredo and the end of the line. The station was no more than two hundred yards from the American border post, and thus sported a huge railway station, all made from imported European red bricks. The grandeur of the edifice was equally matched by the beauty of the interior, marble columns held up a roof that was made from a wonderful worked iron framework, with glass showing the world what delightful weather Mexico had to offer.

Sadly over the years since the completion, the glass had become filthy from the smoke of hundreds of trains that had thrown soot and grit onto the panes, but that dirt didn't hide the obvious exquisite workmanship that had been lovingly expanded into the making of a station erected to match any of its European counterparts. This station had been constructed to show those damn Yankees that they weren't the only ones that could illuminate to the world a thing or two.

The sadness was that behind and all around this wonderful station was a complete slum of a town, with housing that was erected from any piece of scrap that the builder found lying around, plus to make matter worse a couple of thousand people lived in these dwellings, most with the hope that they might be lucky enough to get over the border and make their way north to wealth and happiness. That very rarely happened, those that did cross over became known as wet backs, working as cheap labourers for farms, or industry, but earning a fraction of what their American neighbours would. They had been given that title because of the amount of Mexicans that drowned trying to cross the Rio Grande.

The rest of the towns folk, scraped a living and were resigned to their personal fate of misery and poverty, knowing that they were now stuck in a void, never making it across, mainly because they were now just to old and sickly, and too poor to ever manage to pay for the many rogues that set up so called escape to wealth routes.

Apart from coffee and beer shops, the only real trade was in whores. There were many whore houses catering for the American cowboys that came down to relieve their frustrations on one or two luckless Mexican women. And as there were so many of those Mexican women plying for trade, the competition drove the price right down, which meant that the American male could buy a female for the price of a beer.

By the time the engine stopped and hissed and spluttered its last chord from the boiler, Bennett and Parkinson had got off the carriage and made their way forward to find some porters to carry the huge amount of luggage that they all carried.

There stood this simple train, dwarfed in this vast chasm of a building. A couple of dozen people milled around some trying hard to sell things, mainly water melons, but there was a cigarette vendor that sold the most amazing array of cigarettes and cigars, he had one of the only shops within the station that was occupied, the rest being closed, possibly having never really opened. But this man obviously did a roaring trade, and to Parkinson it all seemed so bizarre.

"Sir Adrian, how does this place survive? What was the government thinking about building such a place?"

"Aaa, my boy! The wisdom that goes into governing a country!"

He choked back a little cackle of laughter.

"I love Mexico, and what's more I adore Mexicans. And mainly because of the huge joke that is here two hundred yards away, that being the United States. Generally speaking the Mexicans hate and detest their neighbours, partly because the Europeans that make up America were and probably are unscrupulous scoundrels that never gave a hoot to the countries or peoples bordering them. Think how over the last hundred years they have treated the Indian population. As you know the original indigenous peoples of North America was made up by many tribes of Indians, fine healthy uncomplicated peoples that fought no one and lived in harmony with the abounding countryside and nature. Along comes the so called white man, and heh-ho, kick those black devils into touch. The same applies and applied to the Mexicans! The white man cometh, and being white and unscrupulous he wants more, so he takes more in the name of freedom and liberty and fraternity, which of course most couldn't even spell. What then you ask! Once they attain enough land for now, they make sure that the local peoples don't receive any of the wealth that the land now stolen has to offer. Keep them out either by the simple expedient of the terrain, desert and rivers, or place huge fencing and barbed wire across vast stretches of land, and then place border posts just to tantalise those that would like to cross over. Oh, don't get me started on the bloody Yankee doodle dandies."

They had now reached the engine. Bennett stopped dead in his tracks, he went up to the driver and firemen that were cleaning out the firebox and making the footplate almost fit for humans again.

"Pedro, I wish to thank you and your crew for getting us here safely. This will be the last time you ever see me, I am now going back to

England. But you have always managed to get me here safely and almost comfortably, so I would like to give you this token of my gratitude."

Sir Adrian spoke perfect Spanish, so George Parkinson could only guess at what was being said. But he guessed right when he thought that Bennett had handed over an envelope full of money. the Ambassador had given the four crewmen a total of two hundred dollars, more than a years money for each of them. The driver almost broke down in tears and thanked the old Ambassador profusely. This made Parkinson smile inwardly.

'That sentimental bugger! How could he have ever become an Ambassador? He actually cares about people, and if he thinks the Americans are troublesome peoples. O dear, what about the British and their so called colonisation of the countries that gave Great Britain the very title it holds. Britain never gave a beggar a moment's chance in life, especially if there was money to be made. My bewildered friend, it's not just the Americans, its people in general. Oh no, it's greed that rules everything in life! For most of the western world, there is never enough!'

Everything had been stowed away again, and was now ready for the porters to carry across to the border post. The Ambassador gave the instructions and with four porters and handcarts, they all walked that short distance to the bridge that spanned the Rio Grande into the conquered territories of the United States. It took two handshakes and some smiles and laughing before the Ambassador signalled the marines to pass through. No one even looked at the trunks or cases, it was all done on the nod.

Now they were in the United States of America, the land of the free and the oppressed. A country of complete contrasts, extremely rich go ahead young men, incredibly poor no hop[ers, beautiful scenery with rich growing potential, rough desert like areas, the most luxurious cities, cities that are complete slum areas What now, what else could happen?

Sir Adrian came up and thanked each man individually for his efforts in the last weeks, he was very sincere in his appreciation, and when each man shook his hand he would take their one hand in both his hands. His expression was of pain at their loss of private Sparkes, and the emotion showed in his voice and there were genuine tears in his eyes.

Then he produced a sealed envelope for Lieutenant Parkinson.

"Mr. Parkinson, I cannot tell you how touched and grateful I am for all the efforts that you and your men have gone to, firstly to try and rescue me from possible danger in the coup, but also your show of courage and leadership while fending off those Mexican bandits. I shall always be grateful to you all and to that end I shall recommend that you and your men are decorated when you get back to England, and though how, I do not know yet as this whole affair must be kept in the dark."

He became very thoughtful, rubbed his chin, lowed his eyes and sniffed the air.

"But leave that with me, I have friends and will find a way. Anyway, have a safe journey back to your ship, and who knows maybe we will meet again?"

Then he was whisked off to his life of retirement, he had decided to see an old girlfriend in New York, who knows, with luck he may never reach the rain and wind of Blighty. George turned away, and more than a little pensive opened his sealed envelope.

You and your crew will proceed directly to the port at Corpus Christi, which is a journey that will take no more than one day by train. It is just less than two hundred miles from where you are now in Nuevo Laredo. Once at the port, present yourselves to Captain Furlong and he will direct you to one of the American navy's war ships, where you will be the guests of the United States navy. They will then set sail and take you to Miami, where you will pick up HMS Westfield once again. I know I don't have to remind you that anything you may have done or experienced is now top secret. Swear your men to an oath, making sure that they all keep their mouths firmly and permanently shut at all times. That responsibility is entirely down to you.

It was signed by the first Sea Lord.

'Well, it seems our mission in Mexico is well and truly over. Where do we get the train from?'

Just three miles outside of town was a small station, and a train with just the one carriage waiting there just for them. This all seemed very strange to Lieutenant Parkinson, all very cloak and dagger stuff, he just couldn't imagine what they had done or knew that constituted a special train. 'Normally the navy would have even made them walk all the way to Miami, just to find their ship had left, with a message saying – now swim home!' One thing about Parkinson, he had developed a vivid imagination and a good sense of homour.

George made all his men line up as smartly as possible considering they were dressed like something out of a hobo's fancy dress party.

"Men before we board this special train for us, I need you all to take an oath of secrecy for the last couple of weeks, and that my fellow comrades is orders from on high. So, swear after me - I swear that everything I have seen, heard or done, since leaving HMS Westfield will be kept completely under wraps until told otherwise by a superior. So help me God!"

The men all looked extremely startled by the news of having to do this, but each raised his right hand and took the oath.

The train journey didn't take a day, it took very nearly twenty-four hours. Every few miles their train would pull into a siding while another locomotive ran the rails as priority. But the men managed to sleep most of the way there, and whom ever had supplied the transport had left food and drink for the use of.

But boredom and lethargy were soon dispelled when they reached their final destination. This locomotive actually took them right into the dockyard, right down onto the mole that had their particular warship awaiting.

It was almost new, dating back to nineteen hundred and seven. It was one of the new breed of American taskforce ships that they had been gradually building up since the launch of HMS Dreadnought in Britain, in nineteen hundred and four. Her name was painted clearly on her starboard side close to the aft, it was the US Chester, a very fast cruiser whose top speed was around twenty-four knots. The marines looked on admiringly at the clean, freshly painted grey ironwork. She was four hundred and thirty feet long and forty-seven feet wide. She only had small armaments, being just two five inch and six three inch guns, but her speed would make up for what she lacked in firepower. Her sleek appearance and her four straight funnels gave her some sort of elegant beauty, one that was noticed by all fourteen of the British. What they were to find out later was that she was equipped with the latest Parsons Propulsion Unit that gave the cruiser a head start of most of the other ships in the United States fleet. They were piped on board, and there waiting on deck was the second officer, who greeted each one as if they were long lost relatives.

"Welcome on board the US Chester gentlemen. I hope your journey here hasn't been too arduous? We will endeavour to make the trip round to Miami as comfortable as possible, so many people want to talk to you all, you have almost become a legend with your exploits. I have a rating here who will show you to your cabins, which I am sorry to say you will have to double up on. When you have cleaned up and got out of those clothes and into something more appropriate, I will take you to the wardroom and will toast your King and our President."

"Err, before we go, thank you for your welcome. As to changing, we don't have any other clothes, everything was lost, what you see, is what you get. But the thought of a hot shower and a shave sounds wonderful."

"Lieutenant, we have enough clothes to dress a city, let us equip you with some US navy issues?"

There were three rooms for their use. Two housed eight marine each and the other was for the officer. The showers were just down the corridor and awaiting their pleasure.

Soon a familiar throbbing sound was heard indicating that US Chester was gathering steam ready to depart.

Once again Parkinson reminded the men of their oath. It did seem obvious that they were all about to be pumped with questions, but what secrets could they possibly divulge that would harm Britain's interests in world affairs?

One more hour and the fourteen clean marines later, having showered and shaved they went up onto the deck dressed in their new grey coloured smart overalls.

The lines were being cast off and US Chester was now getting underway. They met an array of officers, all enquiring as to their adventures in Mexico, all kept quiet thinking that hardly speaking was better suited to outright lying. That was except for one man, James Jolly couldn't keep his mouth shut for one minutes, but instead of telling the American sailors anything, he was pumping them for information concerning the Parsons Propulsion Unit. Because of Jolly's persistence a young lieutenant decided to show him around the engine room and give him a detailed account of the working of the unit. It seemed that this steam turbine was invented in eighteen eighty-four by an Englishman, one Sir Charles Parsons.

So how come it was not being used in the British navy, and why hadn't James even heard of it before this moment. His knowledge of all things steam was astounding yet he hadn't come across Parsons before, that annoyed him greatly. It seemed that Parson used the devise to generate electricity from a steam driven dynamo, but now the theory was put to practicicle use in helping to turn the screws of this American cruiser quicker and more productively than any other propulsion. James was shown everything even the manual that their engineers used to service the machine. He asked if he could study the book and was indeed surprisingly given permission. James Jolly was in his element, those American engineers had everything to hand in the engine room, the best tools and equipment, even electric lathes and drills, so that when anything went wrong, they hopefully could replace or mend the offending item. He was green with envy and he told them so.

As James's knowledge was in fact far superior to the chief engineer on the Chester they assumed that he must be a senior officer even though they could barely understand the way he spoke. James knew that at most they would be on board no more than three days, so he was determined that he would glean every ounce of knowledge from this young engineer, then write a paper and present it to Captain Steiner. This should be his way out of those bloody awful engine rooms and into something a bit more salubrious, James knew he wasn't cut out to keep shovelling coal.

James spent the entire three days that it took to reach Miami reading and studying the Parson Propulsion Unit thoroughly, he was allowed untold access to anywhere within the confines of the engine room, what is more he didn't lift a single shovel of coal. At night he had already started write out his proposals to the Admiralty, he might even have the first draft complete before the ship docked in Florida's Miami port.

Parkinson and the other men hardly even noticed that Jolly wasn't amongst them, they were too busy eating, drinking and generally sunning themselves taking advantage of the warmish weather. There could be serious storms at this time of year, even hurricanes, but the sea was like a mill pond the entire way. On the third morning Captain Hastings the rather allusive master of US Chester, appeared before Lieutenant Parkinson knowing that he wouldn't see him anymore.

"Lieutenant Parkinson, tell me all about Mexico, what did you do there and what was the outcome of your venture?"

"Captain, I am quite sure you realise that I cannot actually tell you anything, I have been sworn, as have my men to secrecy. What I can say is we came because of the assassination of the President and his number two, we were led to believe that the coup may bring serious troubles to foreign diplomats. That turned out to be entirely wrong, so there is really nothing to report, even if I could."

"Yes, I see that. But we heard that you had problems coming to Nuevo Laredo. What happened on your train?"

"Sir, that was nothing. Just a few bandits letting off steam. Nothing to worry about at all."

"But I heard that you got involved with some of our troops, isn't that so?"

"Like I said before, I am not at liberty to divulge anything that occurred on any part of our trip. Best not keep asking me sir! I shall only say the same thing over again to you."

"Mmm! Well, I guess you win. I am sorry that tried to wheedle information out of you Lieutenant. Good man for keeping the faith. In a couple of hours we will dock right next to your ship. I am happy you have had a peaceful journey and that you and your men have felt comfortable enough to relax and catch your collective breath. I shall endeavour to make an acquaintance with your Captain Steiner, he is lucky to have such men as yourselves. Now, I suggest that you go gather your men together and get ready for off loading. It's been a pleasure."

With that Hastings turned and left the bridge with Parkinson now wondering if he had in some way offended the old gentleman, but as they started the procedure to dock he quickly forgot all about the possibility of offending Captain Hastings.

As they came into port, there in all its rusting glory was HMS Westfield. It was bedecked with hundred of bunting flags, and there were crowds of friendly looking people wondering all over it.

'So, that's how they managed to swing our passage on the Chester, Westfield has created an open day for the people of Miami and invited the Chester to partner her. Great idea, I wonder if that directive came from the US diplomatic corp., or the Admiralty in London, or if old Steiner had swung this one himself?'

Parkinson chuckle at the thought of Steiner informing the First Sea Lord that he wanted to create an open and show time in Miami, it seemed hardly likely! This was going to be one of those mysteries that wouldn't get solved, not unless Steiner was going to divulge the information to his Lieutenant, and how likely was that, not at all!

That afternoon the Westfield threw a feast for all the officer and crew of US Chester. To say it was an extraordinary affair would be a huge understatement. The ships chefs and cooks came up with the most luxurious foods that the English pounds could buy. That in itself did cement a good relationship between the two crews and the two Captains. There was a great deal of toasting, which of course included the King and the US President.

All in all this had been a fine good will visit. Even the local people of Miami came out in their droves to see HMS Westfield depart to return to British shores once more.

When the cruiser was well out to sea, Captain Steiner ordered his Lieutenant Parkinson to report and debrief the entire experience.

"Lieutenant, I have heard extraordinary good reports about you and your men's conduct, and I believe there will be a medal coming your way when we reach Portsmouth. So well done. Now tell me about the men? And about the one you lost, something most be done for his family."

Everything was relayed as if it was just happening, and Steiner was enthralled by the story. He even remembered to say how well the stoker had done, and how on the Chester he seemed to have done some sort of thesis on their turbo propulsion system, which he was actually going to submit to Captain Steiner. At this point Steiner had somewhat lost interest but nodded in the appropriate places.

Then he asked about the train journey and those Mexican bandits. Once again the entire rail journey was related to Steiner almost sleeper by sleeper. He of course told the Captain how he had met General Pershing and the part they played in running the bandits off.

"Lieutenant Parkinson, thank you and your men for all their splendid efforts. But, as previously stated, from now on none of these things happened. The American are hopefully our allies they don't want the world to know what is going on in Mexico, so annoyingly, it's become totally top secret. Sorry, because it would all make a good penny thriller."

One week later they had docked in Portsmouth and James Jolly, now resigned to shovelling coal once again, Left the ship for a four day leave, he was going to visit his Gladys. He almost ran to the house where she had her boarding business, he then knocked on the door and a short while later the door was opened by a very surprised plumper Gladys.

"Oh, it's you back again. I am afraid I am completely full up, there is nothing for you here."

"Gladys, what do you mean? You wanted me to settle down here with you, and that's exactly what I was going to do. What went wrong?"

"You were what went wrong. You leave and I never get so much as a postcard from you, I am only flesh and blood, sadly for you there is someone else now."

For a moment Gladys looked wistful as she was obviously remembering their times together, times of fantastic unselfish sex, with many, many orgasms.

But now she had met a cotton reel salesman who actually did want to marry her. He wasn't James in the bed department, but he was there for her twenty-four hours in every day.

For a brief minute James felt crestfallen, but on reflection he knew it would never have worked, he thought he knew he was destined for a life of celibacy, at least that was between affairs with other women.

14

Life quickly got back to normal on the Westfield, but there was no surprise when the old bucket sprang leaks and developed some more serious problems.

Captain Steiner had accepted his paper of the Parsons Propulsion Unit, but as Jolly was a scruffy lowly stoker, it got placed on a shelf, and then eventually filed under unit systems, never to be read. When Parkinson and his marines were awarded medals, Jolly was completely overlooked. He hated them all for just bypassing him, especially when he knew he was more intelligent than them all put together. He felt yet again destroyed and alone, no one really liked him, they used his knowledge, but other than a single word – 'Thanks', no other recognition was ever forthcoming. No one would know who he was, or what he was capable of, they most certainly didn't know his name. It was as always, stoker James Jolly the scruffy, smelly, unkempt nondescript.

HMS Westfield was forever breaking down, always springing leaks, engine troubles, electrical faults were in abundance, there were even shaft problems. But somehow she was patched up and kept going, mainly because of those four enormous guns.

Everyone could see that war was going to rear its ugly head any day now, though the navy was ready, there was a huge worry about those accursed submarines, or in Germanys case U-boats.

Sir Winston Churchill had been the first to give a sailors warning of the potential danger that they imposed. In fact he had quite seriously suggested that any U-boat Captain and crew that would be caught, should be hung high on the yardarm as a warning to others.

"They are nothing but pirates, all of them. It is not a fair war with those accursed iron coffins, it is piracy, hang 'em all, hang 'em high!"

All German U-boat Captains should be designated as pirates, well that is until it was realised that what is good for the goose might just come back on us, and end up good for the gander. After all, it was well known that Churchill was thought to be a fair man himself, and would never go beyond the rules laid down for war.

Then finally within the House of Commons, it was pointed out to him that in that case what would happen to our own submariners if caught by the Germans, or come to that any enemy soldiers? One could visualise a situation that when any enemy soldiers on either side were caught they could be summarily executed! Of course that became the end of thoughts of instant retribution.

Then it happened, two shots were fired in Sarajevo.

On the first of August nineteen hundred and fourteen, first Austria declared war on Serbia, then Germany declared war on Russia. Because of the entente cordiale between France and England, and which was signed in nineteen hundred and three, England was tied into an alliance with France, who in turn had an alliance with Russia, who in turn had and alliance with Serbia, which had been attacked by the Austrians over the assassination of Archduke Ferdinand and his wife Sophia.

Once the ball started rolling, there was absolutely nothing that could stop it. Once Germany entered neutral Belgium, England was obliged to declare war on the central powers, as Britain had a neutrality pact with Belgium promising to defend their country in case of invasion. So once Germany broke the neutrality by marching into little Belgium, it was Britain's duty to declare war of Germany and the central powers, and that infamous date was the fourth of August. Anyway, the entente cordiale created a no way out situation. Those dominoes just kept falling down!

Immediately war was declared, German cruisers such as the Emden which was already serving in Asiatic waters, started immediately to sink British merchant shipping. Emden made her way into the Indian Ocean where very quickly she sank sixteen British vessels.

It was the task of the British cruisers, and that included Westfield, to find and intercept those marauding German hunter killers, and despatch them forthwith. Easier said than done, especially when the cruiser in question is always breaking down. In everyone's eyes except the Admiralty, the Westfield was a jinxed ship. But jinxed only in the way of faults mark you, not in, as always stressed, firepower!

It seemed that this particular cruiser might be best suited for coastal duties as apposed to chasing around the world after ghost ships.

The year passed quickly with very little action, except when a German U-boat surfaced by chance, and was spotted before going down again, this was off the Dover Straits.

As Westfield just happened to be in the vicinity at the time she gave chase. The idea that Captain Steiner came up with, was with a view to ramming the submarine. The cruiser did get somewhat close, even managed to drop some depth charges, one of which exploded prematurely and created yet another leak that had to be repaired. Nobody knew what happened to the submarine, but it was exceedingly unlikely that it was damaged by any of the explosions that occurred.

Once again Westfield went in for repair, and once again in dry dock they found yet more work that needed to be done. The faults were so numerous that the Admiralty thought to convene a board of enquiry thinking that just maybe some of the damage was deliberate sabotage.

In nineteen fifteen, HMS Westfield was on a routine patrol up the east coast of Scotland when yet more problems occurred.

The cruiser had located yet another U-boat not far from Aberdeen, this time the submarine had surfaced during the night to take on a clean air supply and rid themselves of the carbon monoxide that had built up within the confines of the vessel, but as the cruiser was down wind of the submarine, firstly it heard the throbbing of her engines and then the low outline was spotted against the glare of the moon. Steiner immediately ordered the gunners to take careful aim and sink the beast before she could blow her ballast tanks and sink beneath the waves and be illusive once again.

The first gun fired and the shell landed two hundred yards aft of the German craft, the next gun was much closer, but by the time the third gun had brought the submarine into its sights, it was already rushing forward and starting to go down. The huge gun fired and obviously hit the U-boat in the conning tower, completely destroying it. This was the only fatal blow that the cruiser had against a submarine. U-56 popped back up to the surface for one last time, then started to settle. At this time Westfield was closing the gap between them fast, and as the guns prepared to fire once more the crew of the cruiser could see all her hatches were open and men were spilling out into the icy North Sea.

Captain Steiner knew that he had acquired his first kill of the war, this was a special day for him. He decided that he would be magnanimous and pick up the German survivors. He had a net thrown over the side and would allow the German crew to ascend. This he did, and he saved the entire crew of the vessel, but as all the men were plucked from the brine the sub actually was not sinking, her stern was now sticking almost ninety degrees in the air, but she just wasn't going down. Obviously there was enough air within the ship to keep her afloat.

Now she was a menace to shipping in another way. So it was deduced that one last shell at one hundred yards would do the job. Number four gun was ready for that task, took careful aim and fired, there was a tremendous explosion, and then a second and even bigger report occurred as the shell had started an avalanche of explosions as torpedoes and shells started to erupt. Had the cruiser been another hundred yards away, it would have enjoyed the fireworks, but as it was so close the last explosion was like being hit by a huge underwater shock wave. And yet once again the ship started a very large leak within her keel, the leak was much more serious than first thought, it meant an immediate rush to the nearest port, that being Aberdeen itself.

Her prisoners were given over to the authorities and poor old Westfield was once again being patched up.

It was while in dry dock that the yard workers discovered the appalling state of the keel ironwork. This was going to take time and effort, plus the Admiralty were once again perplexed by yet more trouble from that accursed cruiser. This time she was saved by the simple expedient of having just sunk one of the Kaiser's steel coffins.

Jolly was now forty years of age. He was the single most read man in the Kings navy, yet still a simple stoker. He was now resigned to the fact that his life had just literally passed him by, the old adage applied, once a stoker always a stoker, the same old adage repeated constantly throughout his working life. He had become overweight balding, getting into all sorts of scrapes, most of which had cost him black eyes and broken teeth.

Yet James just kept reading more and more books on any subject that took his fancy. Had he kept all the tomes that he had read, he would have had a good thousand or more volumes. But over the years he had decided that he would only keep the books on psychiatry and philosophy and of course psychology, the rest, unless something really special came along, would be swapped for other subject matter.

Having been given leave to visit his wife which he had already decided against, knowing that by now she would have divorced him and met someone else, and his philosophy was one of, good for her. He didn't want to disturb her life any more. But he might take a trip back to Glasgow to satisfy himself that his mother's death was indeed an accident. But that was after a couple of days hard drinking with his dockyard mates.

In many ways drinking for James was just a huge waste of money, he never got drunk, sometimes a little merry, except it wasn't always merry more just a little tipsy. But it seemed that the dockers were the only people on the planet that were prepared to listen to what he had to say.

Plus pontificating was after all a somewhat pleasurable experience for James to relax in.

Two days after his fortieth birthday he made up his mind to take the plunge and get a train to Glasgow. After all he hadn't heard from either of his brothers so it was finally time to sort things out himself.

Next morning James took the train to Glasgow, he was reticent about the journey and not sure who he would meet and what sort of reception he would receive by anyone he did meet.

It was midday when he arrived at his mother old tenement building. It was a dull day with overcast drizzly weather, it was the sort of rain that you could barely see or feel, but it managed to permeate into every pore of ones body making one decidedly wet through. It wasn't just the wet that depressed James, it was that awful smell of sulphur from the cheap coal that was burning in every hearth. Plus that aroma, there was the grit that one ate with every breath one took. Smog was a terrible side affect that came with the industrial revolution, it was killing old people and young children all over the industrial world in their droves, yet nobody in any sort of authority was prepared to do anything about changing the situation, let well enough alone was the order of the day. So when Jolly saw an old lady coming out of the block that he knew, he wasn't at all surprised to see how much she had aged. The bent old lady was Sarah McKinnon who actually had the apartment next door to James's mother, she was in her early fifties but so weather beaten as to look at least eighty years of age, she was even bent through years of toil. Of course smoking twenty cigarettes a day hadn't helped her cause.

"Sarah, how are you? Long time no see."

Then realisation hit Jolly between the eyes, she hadn't a clue who he was.

"It's me James Jolly. I have just come down from Aberdeen to find out about mum. Can you spare me a few minutes to talk?"

"Aye, little Jamie, is that really you? Your mother, aye, I can give you some time. Take me for a gin at the Nags Head and we can talk about Mary Stuart. But you had better prepare yourself laddie."

James looked furtively at the upper window that Mary fell from, and then he looked at more or less the spot she must have hit on the pavement. It must have been awful, those heavy pavement slabs wouldn't have gone to make a smooth landing, it would have been very messy.

At the Nags Head James ordered a large glass of gin for Sarah and a small dark beer for himself.

"So what the heck happened on the day that mother fell? Did she throw herself out of the window as suggested?"

"I will tell you what I heard that day but you cannot use it in any way. If you try, I shall deny any knowledge of whatever you say. Is that entirely understood?"

"What the heck are you inferring, but yes I agree, but it all sounds strange already. What happened to her?"

"I was woken quite early the morning of your mothers death. There was a terrible row going on between your Mary and that awful toffee nosed posh Polish chef that she had fallen in love with. Mary had told me that she was putting the flat back to the landlord, as she was about to move into a new apartment around Govan area. But from the row that was proceeding within the apartment, yon Pole had other ideas. It was obvious that your mother had been led to believe that she would live with yon Pole, but it was obvious to all that knew them both that he didn't want her any more. I even heard him say that there was no room for your mother as he now had another woman who he wanted to join him. Someone half your mothers age. The shouting went on for several minutes, and then I heard the window being thrown open, a scream from your mother and what sounded like dragging across the floor, then it went silent, until I heard the scream of a passer by, someone had found the lifeless body of Mary Stuart. It is my belief that that scoundrel threw her out of the window but I couldn't prove it, anyway, you know what the bobbies are like round these parts, they wouldn't believe an oldie like me, then where would I be agin' yon Pole? I just don't wish to be involved. But much later I heard that your mother's lover had denied even being there, and I do know that it was him there, I recognised his voice and I could hear the occasional word here and there. I think that man is dangerous, and I am not going to be approached by him or the police."

James bought her several drinks, all doubles. But he couldn't get anything more out of her concerning his mother and the chef. By the time lunch was called, both Sarah and James were feeling hunger pangs, even though Sarah was almost legless with alcohol.

'I think I had better get us both some food, something to soak up the booze.' Thought James as he looked at the old women who was now quite obviously teetering on passing out.

After a fish and chip lunch James managed to take Sarah back to the tenement block and deposit her within her small flat. The place was a complete mess, things spewed everywhere, it had the appearance of a room that had been ransacked by thieves. The smell that oozed from everything was one of human urine, sweat and damp. Not the most salubrious of aromas, in fact it was a very unpleasant combination of smells.

'God Sarah, I remember when you were quite a handsome girl, whatever happened to you?'

It was now time for James to approach one Ivan Kolinsky the Polish chef who cohabitated with Mary Stuart. It wouldn't take much detective work to find out which restaurant he worked in, that is if he still worked in Glasgow, he should have been interned in a camp as an undesirable alien. After all the Poles were mostly fighting with the Kaiser's army. If nothing else James would make sure that the authorities got to hear of this possible enemy of the country. But secretly he hoped he was still available to be talked too. If it was true that he had killed Mary Stuart he must pay the price.

Just as James walked down the road towards the centre he passed on the opposite side of the road a very recognisable woman, it was his wife Lucy. She didn't notice him even though shock made him stop in his tracks and stare directly at her. Lucy was showing serious aging problems. Almost completely white she had also put on a great deal of weight. But once again she too looked worn out like most of the women he came across within the Gorbals area. His heart sank, and remorse and guilt whelmed up inside of him. Should he approach her, should he see what he could do for her, could he see his children, who would be working or in the army by now, his mind raced and he trembled with a heavy heart, should he do any of these things? But as he thought about it Lucy disappeared into another tenement and was gone.

Tears came to James eyes, tears of years of regrets, tears of remorse, tears of a wasted love life and lives.

He looked at the tenement noting that it was just the same as all the others, grey, drab and unrelenting in the depressing squalor that exuded from the very fabric of the edifice. James turned and walked away sunk in a deep depression. From that feeling of misery there started a feeling of resentment. James was not stupid, he knew that he couldn't blame anyone or anything on the simple fact that he was a virtual nothing of a human being. All the intelligence in the world won't make up for the huge disappointment of being nothing.

But now he was beginning to feel like someone at least should be punished for the death of Mary Stuart, and that person was definitely going to be Ivan Kolinsky. With each step that he took his feelings of frustration and resentment whelmed higher and higher in his gizzard, his face was developing a rosy purplish hue to the skin, his blood pressure was almost at explosion proportions. His teeth, what ones he had left, were well and truly clenched and his breathing was hard and shallow. Walking towards Glasgow centre was an exceedingly angry man and woe betides anyone who came within his sphere of anger.

James remembered that Ivan had worked at the Queen Anne Hotel, somehow he would find out what has happened to him if anything at all?

He finally saw the imposing edifice of the Victorian red bricked building that stood so proudly in the centre of Alexander Park Way. It stood eight stories high with four towers rounding off each corner of the building. It oozed luxury and opulence. Even in these hard times of war when every other male on the streets was in some sort of uniform, it smelt and exhaled money, probably very corrupt money, but however, it was producing plenty of it however, one way or another.

While most of Glasgow and Scotland in general was having problems with just feeding itself, with there being so many shortages, yet here at Queen Anne's you could acquire any sort of food you wanted, as long as you had enough money to pay for it.

James casually went up to the doorman a hard brutish fellow sporting a huge muscular arms, chest and all his frame, but showing proudly the flattest broken nose that James had ever seen before. It was obvious that this man had been through the mills more than once, probably being a boxer.

"Excuse me my friend, I would like to know if the famous chef Ivan Kolinsky is still working here?"

The bruiser looked disdainfully in the direction of Jolly, and then answered with,

"Who wants' to know?"

As he spoke he breathed heavily through his two nostrils almost snorting and snoring at each word, what made it worse for James Jolly was the fact the man was an East End Londoner, with an extremely broad cockney accent.

"No, no! I write articles about cooking and the chefs who are gradually becoming famous. I need to have an interview with Mr. Kolinsky, that's all, quite simple really."

He was excited and truly amazed how he gave such a quick and convincing retort to the doorman.

"Well, he'll be in tonight, shall I say who asked?"

"No, no; I'll call back later and see if I can get that interview?"

"'Ere, you look familiar to me, don't I knows you? Do you write for the Glasgow 'Erald?"

"Yes, I do, well, well! I'll see you later, many thanks."

"'Ere wait up! Tell me your name again?"

But he was too late James had walked away in the direction of the post office.

'Ivan is famous now, he must have his own telephone, that's how I will get his address.'

A little while later James was once again walking purposefully in the direction of Govan, to number thirty-five Cromwell Street.

James just hoped that he lived in a tall tenement like his mother did.

It took the best part of an hour to walk there, it was a better part of Glasgow, and the tenements weren't really anything like the Gorbals tenements. For a start each one was painted in clean black or brown paint, the windows were all clean and curtained, something practically unheard of in the Gorbals. Some of the buildings had small front gardens and the rest had fine window boxes, all once holding seasonal flowers.

It was most definitely a step in the right direction concerning living conditions. There was number thirty-five on his left hand side. He looked up to see just how high it went, four stories, five if you count the basement. This particular building had spiked railings all around the bottom onto the pavement. Now James stood still for a moment, looked around to see if anyone was watching, then casually bent down to tie up a shoe lace that wasn't undone, but it gave him time to think.

Jolly went up to the door and looked at the name plates.

'Oh joy of joys! He lives at the top. Right in I go.'

He quietly went up the stairwell making as little noise as possible, he noted that there was a back exit for him to use if necessary. No one was about just silence. He got to the top and there bold as brass, on a large brass plate was the name Ivan Kolinsky. Knock, knock; but not loudly, hoping it would be loud enough to be heard inside. Silence was his answer. Knock, knock, this time a touch louder. After several seconds he heard above the beating of his own heart, the steps of another human within the flat. The door opened and there stood Ivan, older and much larger than James ever remembered, he had put on at least thirty more pounds in weight. He stood there in his pyjamas, obviously just woken with the knocking. He was red in the face and was already puffing from just the walk from the bedroom.

"Yes, what do you want? You have got me out of bed, so it had better be good?"

"Don't you recognise me? I am James, James Jolly. You lived with my mother, or have you already forgotten her?"

Ivan almost fell over himself as his breath was completely taken away.

"James, is that you? Christ almighty I would never have known you. Come in lad, come in."

So far so good, James had managed to get entry, now what?

They both walked into a beautifully furnished front room, one that overlooked the pavement.

"So what brings you here? Are you still in the navy? What about this awful war, so many dead, its frightening isn't it?"

"I've come to Glasgow just to see you. I want to know what happened to my mother Mary Stuart. Why did she jump or did she get pushed?"

James was looking directly into the eyes of Ivan who in return couldn't bring himself to look back at James. He noted that as he asked the questions his face turned even redder than before, the man was practically glowing.

"I really don't know what happened to your mother, I had moved out some weeks before her death, and I hadn't seen her from then on. The police did come to see me, and they said that she jumped or fell, maybe trying to clean the windows, though there was absolutely no evidence of those window cleaning clothes and things. I am as baffled as you are James, what's more I miss her very much."

James knew he was lying, his whole demeanour spelt out liar, liar, liar. Ivan's face was almost crimson, sweat was streaming down his face and soaking his pyjama top. It didn't go unnoticed to James that the man was trembling rather badly and not just from the legs.

James was now almost matching Ivan with blood pressure and agitation. But Jolly knew what he had to do. He went over to the nearest window, opened it wide and looked out. There was absolutely no one around. While he was doing this Ivan was backing off towards the door. He wasn't a stupid man, he knew that this was a problem and he wasn't quite the man he once was. He was far too fat and indolent for any confrontational problems. James made some waving gestures as if calling someone to come. He then turned to Ivan once again who was now shaking uncontrollably.

"I have conclusive evidence that you killed my mother. You were heard rowing, you were heard hitting the poor woman, and then while she screamed you threw her out of the window, you were actually seen. The police are outside here just awaiting my call, so why don't you make a clean breast of it and call them yourself?"

He offered up the window for Ivan to look at the supposed policemen. Ivan almost crying went to the window and stuck his head out.

"There are no policemen, you were bluffing….Aaaaaaa!"

James even before he knew what he was doing bent down and pulled at Ivan pyjama trousers around his ankles, over he went leaving his trousers behind him.

Phwappp! Ivan hit the steel railing at the bottom and they pierced through his back killing him instantly.

James felt cool and collected, his shaking had stopped and his redness subsided. He didn't need to look down, the scream may well have produced some interest, though he heard nothing.

He dropped the trousers onto the window ledge, and then he decided to quickly see what was in the apartment. He entered the bedroom and there in the double bed still sound asleep, was a young woman.

James quickly and quietly retraced his steps and left the flat. He quickly made his way down the stairs and out through the back door. He didn't stop for anything or anyone, but purposefully made his way back to the city centre. No one would ever know he had even been to Glasgow, only Sarah McKinnon and she wasn't about to say anything to anyone.

James boarded the next train to Aberdeen, and then went back to the pub that he knew his old dockyard cronies would be supping. It was time for that well earned drink.

"Heh, Jamie boy, where have you been?"

"Oh, just for a walk."

"So James, what's all this existentialist stuff about? You said yesterday that you would explain it too me?"

James Jolly smiled broadly, now completely relaxed he started,

"Existentialism, right where do I start?"

Two weeks passed quickly and the ships keel was being replaced in many places. Finally, the Admiralty in the infinite wisdom had also decided to convert the engine with turbines, thus allowing another four knots on the overall speed, but that might be the difference between being hit by torpedoes or outrunning one of them.

Finally at the end of July nineteen fifteen, HMS Westfield was once again ready for duty. Only the older members of the crew had been retained, the rest had been placed in other vessels to fair as well as they could. At last for Jolly this was heaven, new stokers along with him. Maybe, hopefully, no more fights and a chance to make a friend or two.

Sea trials were made all around the coast. The engines worked well, and Eureka, there were no more leaks. They went out into the vast expanse of North Sea, towing a target platform, small enough to be hard to spot and even harder to hit. Land had long disappeared, and the raft was finally let loose, the cruiser went around in a large arc being a good three miles away from the platform, in fact it was very hard to see even with a telescope. The big guns were brought round to bear, and as soon as they were ready they fired a single shot, one after the other. The shooting was really rather good, and by the fifth round the platform was seen to lift into the air, then disappear under the waves. A very successful practice.

Stoker Jolly was finally rewarded for years of loyal service. His dream was finally coming into fruition, he was made an engineer, completely in charge of the turbine units. He was standing by those turbines almost day and night, the slightest squeak and he would be fussing over his beauties in some way or another.

Nineteen sixteen came like thunder in the night. Everywhere the allies were doing badly, but the saving grace was that so were the Central Powers. Already more than five million men had paid the ultimate sacrifice world wide, and that was just turning out to be the tip of the iceberg.

But for once within the career of HMS Westfield, this year had been one of continuous success. They had very successfully branded the iron fist at several German raiders sinking two, and even sunk another U-boat, though the lookout suspected that it might have been an American one. Never mind, it was yet another steel coffin for the fish to use as home sweet home. Things had been going well, possibly for the superstitious too well. They were now called to go the Scapa Flow. This was something special for Captain Steiner as now he could meet some of his contemporaries, as most of the Royal Navy was anchored there awaiting orders.

Westfield re-coaled and took on provisions. The cruiser was now ready and eager and chaffing at the bit. She literally shone with pride and that manifested itself down the chain of command all the way down to the lowest ratings. They were doing well, and Steiner was going to make the rest of the fleet know that a humble Jew could instruct a crew of raw ratings, and turn them very quickly into fighting machines.

15

Early in the morning of thirty-first of May nineteen hundred and sixteen, a signal was radioed to the combined fleet -

Proceed at all speed to intercept the German High Seas Fleet of the Kaiserliche Marine, which has now left Kiel, Hamburg and other ports. They are trying to break the British blockade deadlock that is starving Germany.

God save the King.

The combined fleet which included, Admiral Jellicoe at Scapa Flow, Admiral Jerram at Cromarty, and Admiral Beatty from the Firth of Fourth. They were to gather and chase and destroy the Kaiser's vessels, that meant try and sink as many ships as possible, drowning thousands of men.

But first they had to actually find them.

This could be the very blow that could wipe out Germany as a force to be reckoned with. Sink their fleet and what happens to the population? They starve! The blockade is working and will continue to work.

On the side of the King were twenty-eight battleships, nine battle-cruisers, of which Westfield was the biggest and most powerful yet still possibly the slowest, eight armoured cruisers, twenty-six light cruisers, seventy-eight destroyers, one minelayer, plus one seaplane carrier.

On the Kaiser's fleet were sixteen battleships, five battle-cruisers, six pre-dreadnoughts, eleven light cruisers, also sixty-one torpedo boats.

As the British out gunned and completely out manned the German fleet, the battle should have been just a matter of course, but things never go quite to plan.

Germany had leaked the exiting of the fleet deliberately hoping that they could split the three sections of the British High Fleet and turn the confusion into something useful for Germany. More than anything they wanted to break that blockade.

It is true to say that Jellicoe fell for the ruse, but if Germany thought that they could actually break the force of Britain's High Fleet surely they were in cuckoo land, and after all everyone knew that Britain ruled the waves and that wasn't about to change.

One of the first ships to fire up and leave port was Westfield, but then as she was still one of the slowest vessels she needed that head start.

By the afternoon of that first day Admiral Beatty encountered Admiral Franz Hipper's force of battle-cruisers. He gave chase and was successfully lured into the clever German trap. Finally realising his mistake Beatty witnessed coming towards him the larger German force. Beatty turned back towards the British main fleet, but to a degree it was too late the damage had started to be done. Two of his battle-cruisers were quickly sunk and that was half his battle-cruiser force. There were battleships being commanded by Rear-Admiral Sir Hugh Evan-Thomas, and they were the last to turn, but they made a good rearguard to protect the rest of Beatty's ships.

Between six-thirty that evening when the sun was lowering in the west, it outlined the German fleet beautifully and two more huge clashes of ships occurred. A total of two hundred and fifty vessels clashed on the seas off of Jutland, of which fourteen British and eleven German ships were sunk. There was huge loss of life on both sides.

Yet both sides claimed a sort of victory. The difference being that what was left of the German fleet once entering their harbour, they were never to leave it again as threatening agents of the high seas. So in many ways, Britain claimed a moral high ground victory.

HMS Westfield was nearly up to Jellicoe's fleet at Jutland when the first salvos were exchanged. Steiner ordered his guns to come to bear hoping to claim a victory over a German battleship which now loomed within the sights of all her four big guns. The command was given to fire in the normal single rotating way. The first gun blasted a shell toward her opponent which splashed harmlessly nearly half a mile from its target.

The second shell thrust forth from the barrel and burst very close to the German ship, the third even closer, Steiner was smiling thinking that the next shot might hit the ship. There was a huge report and the fourth shell flew to find its mark, and it hit the German battle-cruiser square amidships. Though the ship was too far away to hear the blast as the shell tore into the metal and burst within the ship causing tremendous damage and loss of life, but the ship was not sinking and was still dangerous. The next shell that came from the German ship hit the open bridge of Westfield, it killed instantly and Captain and two of his officers, plus it totally destroyed any chance of communicating with either the rest of the fleet, or below decks.

HMS Westfield was now completely out of control and was now veering quite hard to portside. As no one could now communicate with the big guns, the rule was that each gunner should select targets themselves, which they did, more or less together. The sea was getting quite rough and the ship was lifting and dropping with each consecutive swell. As the ship it was still at full speed, turning hard to port was pushing the ship over portside considerably.

Another German pre-Dreadnought was only five thousand yards away when the gunners spotted it together at the same moment. All four gun turrets turned towards the oncoming early battleship, and as if their brains were now interlocked they fired all eight guns together. The sound of eight guns blasting was incredible, but the worst aspect was that the ship already leaning badly, now was pushed over at an alarming angle. And then the pre-Dreadnought's mighty guns came into play, the very first round hit Westfield in amidships, entering right into the engine room and blasting everything. Almost everyone within that area was vaporised, yet by a strange quirk of fate, the very shell that hit the engine room blasted not more than ten feet away from Engineer stoker James Jolly, but instead of vaporising him along with his comrades, he was thrown with tremendous force back straight out the entry point of the shell. James landed in the sea some fifty yards from the ship, which now had completely broken it back and the two halves of that vessel were quickly disappearing under the waves through their own turbo charged momentum.

James was unconscious and was actually drowning when his head hit against a wooden platform, the thud brought him to some sort of awareness, then with his last ounce of strength he managed to climb up and lay out of the water on this wooden life raft. His life and work was instantly over, he was going to either die of exposure or drown when a large wave swept him off his raft. He managed to raise his head and look around, all he could see were huge waves crashing here and there, and there were definitely no ships anywhere to be seen, though he could still hear the devastating report of explosions, but soon they too were in the distance. James lay back and awaited his fate.

Death by exposure was preferable to drowning, so he made sure that he was more or less tied to the raft with the aid of his trousers belt. He then lay back listening to the wind and the waves, he gently fell into a cold numbing sleep which he never expected to awaken from.

The loss of life on the world's biggest sea battle was staggering. On the British side, they had lost six thousand and ninety-four men, either drowned or blown to pieces, they had a further five hundred and ten men seriously wounded, also lastly one hundred and seventy-seven men were picked up by the German torpedo boats and taken back as prisoners.

The German losses were not quite so bad. They had lost two thousand, five hundred and fifty-one dead, five hundred and seven badly wounded.

The British had the loss of three battle-cruisers, three armoured cruisers and eight destroyers, which constituted one hundred and thirteen thousand three hundred tons of shipping, a very heavy blow for the Admiralty to bear.

The Germans lost sixty-two thousand and three hundred tons of shipping. For the Kaiser they were entirely irreplaceable. There was no more good steel left for building yet more ships, this was definitely the end of his expansion of shipping. But the Kaiser had one more punch to give the allies, he had the biggest and deadliest fleet of U-boats, from now on it was unrestricted warfare as far as the submariners were concerned.

By the second of June Beatty and Jellicoe's remaining battle scarred fleet were back in port licking their wounds, all that time a raft had been floating in the sea edging its way closer and closer to Iceland.

It was the evening of the second that a small whaling vessel flying the Icelandic flag and prominently having NEUTRAL painted with bright white lettering on both sides, spotted a raft floating with what looked like a body strapped on board. At first the crew thought that they wouldn't touch a dead sailor obviously killed in the huge sea battle that they heard going on the night and day before. Let the dead rest in peace, don't disturb him just watch him pass by. But then one of the Icelanders thought that they saw movement from the chest as breath was inhaled and exhaled. So maybe the man is still alive.

They took Jolly on board but he was actually more dead than alive, and all the Icelandic crew thought that his chances of survival were slim. But they covered him well in Eider duck duvets, and the youngest member of the crew was allotted the chance to take care of the sailor, hoping that he might just come too before passing into the Viking Valhalla.

But James Jolly refused to die and after another ten hours passed, his eyes opened and he murmured something undecipherable under his breath.

"Quick, he has said something, his chapped cracked lips parted and he mumbled something."

The Icelandanders knew he was English because the raft stated HMS Westfield, which they knew to be British. The Captain whose name was Aynor Wogger, touched Jolly's face gently, trying to get him to say something. But then he realised that the man would probably be extremely thirsty, so offered him some piping hot coffee which the ship always had on brew twenty-four hours in each day. 'That should revive him a little'. It did and James lifted the cup further to his lips scalding his mouth in the process. But he now knew that he hadn't died he had been captured by the Germans instead.

Aynor's English was very, very limited. But to be fair, he tried hard to make some sort of understanding.

"You who? Ship come you?"

But though James more or less understood he couldn't remember what ship he had come from, or what his name actually was? His memory had left him completely. He couldn't remember what had happened to him or anything about his life. All he could say was,

"Parsons Turbine Propulsion Units must give in my papers on the idea."

He then fell back into a deep sleep, but this time not anything life threatening. He was most certainly going to live, but who was he, that was the burning question on the Icelandic whalers minds?

Four days later they landed their catch in Reykjavik, and handed James Jolly to the local doctor. All the time in the whaler James had drifted in and out of sleep, but towards the end, just before landing he managed to eat a hearty meal, thus reviving all his faculties except his memory.

'Who am I, why can't I remember? Was I some sort of officer of HMS Westfield? I cannot even remember what the ship looked like.'

He was taken to a small hospital rest house, which was used mainly for trauma patients that had suffered some appalling depression, usually the sort that came in the winter and ended in suicide, after heavy drinking bouts.

But this was summer so the few rooms that were there were empty, yet there was always staff on hand. They would take care of James Jolly while he recovered. Sadly, there was no embassy staff left in Iceland that could have helped repatriate James, all the British Embassy staff had left for England at the very beginning of the war. So who would pay the bill for looking after Jolly? As he was rescued by a whaler that belonged to Peterson Fishing Cooperative, it was suggested that they might feel they have some sort of responsibility.

The partner and manager was one Jon Johnson and he had already heard of the rescue, and was pleased and excited that it had been one of the companies whaling fleet to actually have found the man. So he then decided the good name of the company was at stake, if having saved the fellow, they now couldn't possibly abandon him. So quickly before the board of directors, it was unanimously agreed that PFC, would take it upon themselves as a charitable company to sponsor the sailors recharging health. The company would pay all food, medical and hotel bills as long as the man needed assistance, but when he was considered better he could work off his debt within the company in some way or another.

Over the next few weeks James's health got almost back to normal. His strength was up to speed so was his metabolism. This meant all his parts were now working perfectly, but he still had no memory concerning himself or the ship. Everything was still a blank. But James was now walking halfway around Reykjavik almost every day, partly to keep his strength going in the right direction, but also because the constant daylight meant he was having problems sleeping, so he would rise early and do his walking.

On the twenty-eighth of June, Jon Johnson once again came to visit him. Jon spoke pretty well perfect English so conversations with James were easy. Having visited Scotland on numerous occasions, Jon quickly ascertained that Jolly was from Glasgow, though his command of the Kings English was so good, he really thought that he hadn't lived there for many, many years, as there was a touch of fine old Oxford English scattered amongst the Scots broad accent. And it was also obvious that the man was an educated man, probably an officer. Again this was deduced more from observation than anything else. For a start James was almost too old to be anything other than an officer, and his rough features would be down to the trauma of being alone on a raft and quite obviously for some considerable time. Then there was the fact that when asked a question about himself, the only response would be quotations from Shakespeare, Dickens, Fraud, Jung and many other scholars. He would babble on about engines, machinery, engineering in general and just about anything one could imagine. But he still couldn't remember his own name.

Jon got talking to his fellow directors about Jolly.

"I am amazed how knowledgeable this man is."

He paused took a breath and looked around at his fellow directors, he then added with some feeling,

"His brain seems to hold the secrets of the entire world, he pontificates on any and every subject, and once started, it's hard to stop him. I think that we have here in our midst, the Captain of HMS Westfield and to that end we ought to treat him with more respect. I offered to take him to the whaling station tomorrow and he has accepted the offer, but now we had better think up a name for him at least until he remembers his own again. I think we couldn't do better than calling him Olav, in fact Olav Peterson after the founder of the company, what do you all think?"

There was a stunned silence followed by a small chuckle of laughter from one nervous individual.

"Do the think Elsa would like a Scots seaman to be called after her dead husband? Don't you think it is somewhat irreverent? After all, what do we really know about this man, only that he is from Britain, he could a worthless bum for all we know."

"No, no, Sven, not a chance, you just wait until you start talking to him. For sure there is something special about this fellow, oh yes!"

Another pause while Jon contemplated what he had just said.

"Yes, something special. Actually, I am looking forward to showing him around tomorrow, why don't some of you come with us?"

The next morning Jon drove the buggy around to pick James up, they were off to the whaling factory.

"Mister Scotsman, at least we think you are Scottish. The board of directors have decided that we have to call you by a name so unless you can think up a name, we would like to call you Olav, Olav Peterson after our founder who is sadly dead and gone. How do you feel about having the name of a dead man?"

"Jon I am honoured, so I am Olav Peterson eh! Sounds strong and good, I like it."

They reached the station after one hour, as it was warm and sunny Jon got the horse to stroll leisurely giving Olav time to look around and enjoy the scenery. The sea was milky smooth and the reflection of the mountain on the other side of the bay was so brilliant as it showed itself in the sea, one could have been forgiven for wondering if they were indeed upside down, and watching everything in some strange perspective.

"What is the name of that mountain?"

"It is called mount Esja. It's a Viking word."

"It's beautiful, and look at that mirror image in the sea, this city and countryside looks so beautiful. I envy you these views."

Olav was mesmerised by the staggering beauty of the panorama, everywhere he looked took his breath away.

They reached the whaling station just in time to hear a huge bang, along with a flash of light. It made both men jump visibly, Jon had his work cut out to control the Icelandic pony that wad pulling their buggy. Both men alighted and ran into the building to find out what had gone awry. A dynamo along with the main winch for pulling up the carcasses had blown up, obviously fusing badly and grinding to a halt.

Jon was mortified as this was a major catastrophe as far as he was concerned. They didn't have engineers that could mend these sorts of problems, it would mean ordering an entire new unit, and that would be costly, and there was no chance of doing that, not while this dangerous war was commencing. So they would be stuck and forced to return to the old days before electricity when everything would be done by hand. That meant slow and arduous work.

Olav looked at the machine, traced the wires back to the main steam generator, one of the first thermal steam generators of its kind. It was large and quite complicated. Olav looked at this monster, smiled to himself, scratched his left ear and then said to Jon,

"Jon I can mend this, in fact this generator might be a good idea, but I could design something better and more reliable. I want you to stop the monster from generating any more electricity, thus making it safe to scrutinise the winch and dynamo. Do I have your permission?"

Jon looked at Olav with a new wondrous admiration.

Olav then got to work.

Three hours later. He had stripped both the winch and the dynamo. The winch had a broken rod, which had jammed making the dynamo overheat and explode.

"Do you have a forge and do you have steel rods anywhere?"

"We have a forge just in the next section over there."

Jon was pointing along the main left-hand side wall to where a small door was closed and looking very inconspicuous. Olav went over and opened the door. There to his surprise was this beautifully equipped room with a forge against the wall, and just about every conceivable tool hanging on the wall. Everything looked dusty and totally unused.

"Where's your forge worker?"

Jon looked puzzled than answered in a mildly subdued voice.

"We don't actually have anyone that can work the forge. We had a Danish worker here when it was first installed, by he moved back to Copenhagen roughly one month after the initial installation, he came with a view to teaching someone to work the forge but it just never happened."

Jon shuffled his feet a little and looked quite embarrassed.

"Now when something goes wrong, we have to replace the component with a newly ordered part, we don't have the ability to remake or repair something that has gone wrong."

All the time Jon was talking Olav was fingering the part that had broken and thinking almost aloud.

"Can I have someone to help me? Someone on the younger side, and who knows some little thing about engineering."

Olav once again scratched at his ear.

"Then I might be able to teach him something. I want to get this furnace working, if it hasn't been used for a long time there may well be rust in the flue. We will have to burn that out, but we need to see if the smoke reaches the outside, I don't want to burn your buildings down."

He smiled at Jon.

"How do you know these things?"

"I can't say, I really haven't a clue, but back within the darkest reaches of my brain I do know about things, and I really think you need my help. It would please me to repay your kindness in saving my life with some hard toil from me. Now, where is the coke kept?"

Between them and the young man that had been seconded to help, they got the fire blazing and found some robs good enough for the purpose that Olav had in mind. Then over the next few hours, Olav managed to turn out two of the broken components, one to be placed on the shelf in case it breaks again, the other to be used immediately. Then he turned his attention to the dynamo. That proved easy to fix, the copper wire had fused together whilst the broken winch had jammed the dynamo from working. All he had to do now under the watchful eye of several Icelanders, was strip the entire thing down to its individual components, clean them all, separate the fused wire, rewind and put everything back together again. It started first time and worked better than before.

"Good God man! You are some sort of genius. This is fantastic, wonderful, great. What about coming back tomorrow and tackling some of the other engineering problems that we have accrued?"

From that moment onward the now called Olav Peterson had become a valuable member of the PFC team.

Jon took him for a meal that night in Hotel Gullfoss, then he proposed two things to the unflappable Scotsman. Firstly, that for the duration of the war he should stay in Iceland and make himself useful concerning restoration of machine parts, not just at the Whaling factory but everywhere. Secondly, he should try and learn to speak Icelandic, to that end he handed him a book of English to Icelandic. It was an old book but it covered most things pretty well.

As the months passed Olav learned to speak quite good Icelandic, his memory had not returned, but his helpful ways increased his popularity to the extent that he became an adviser on the board of directors with the company of Peterson Fishing Cooperative. His words went a long way in the decisions that the company made.

Exports and imports had dried to a minimum as shipping was totally unsafe since the Kaiser allowed unrestricted torpedoing of any vessel on the high seas that wasn't intended for Germany. The best that happened was that certain goods were brought into Iceland via Canada, when the whaling ships landed special catches in various

Canadian ports, the money from the sale of the whales was used to bring necessities back to Iceland. As all the Icelandic fleet where known to the U-boat Captains with their big white Neutral painted on each side, they were always left to proceed on their merry way, anyway, some or most submarine skippers, would surface close to a fishing boat and negotiate and barter items for fish, thus keeping everything friendly and above board. There had been one occasion when the Captain of a whaler helped an injured U-boat crewman, by performing a small operation on the man. That made them friends for life.

But no cargo vessels other than fishing boats were given the same sanctuary.

One very old Icelandic single mast sloop was caught by an irate U-boat Captain and crew that had been previously shelled upon by a sailing vessel, not actually damaging the U-boat, but given it one heck of a fright. The vessel in question had been made into one of the British Q-boats, they looked like cargo vessels but were in fact submarine hunter killers, extremely heavily armed. So the Captain of the U-boat decided to take active revenge on any sailing ships, big or small. Thus the sloop was shelled until she sunk with a loss of all hands. Of course there had been nothing on board that could have compromised the vessel, it was on its way to Denmark with the hope of getting some supplies. No one in Iceland ever found out what happened to the craft, assuming that it probably hit a rogue mine. Nobody wanted the think that it had been deliberately sunk by submariners, after all there had been women and children on board.

Olav had now lost all the scarring that had been on his face and body through the explosion, he had regained the complete use of his limbs which had also been badly seared, and though he felt completely normal he was still without any memory of the accident and he still didn't know who or what he was, or anything about his past life. He knew that he probably had been a sailor, maybe an officer or even the Captain, after all, he was perfectly aware of his own intelligence, he was fully aware that he knew a great deal about almost any subject. He would often be approached by complete strangers and quizzed about some subject or another, and once started he would talk for hours.

He had quickly become, probably the most celebrated foreigner in Reykjavik, if not the whole of the couintry.

He seemed to know about all electrical things, all mechanical machinery, or anything that had meant one had to think and process ideas about the said item. But most of all he was completely in his element in Iceland and with Icelanders.

The company had given him a small wooden house close to Lake Tchurnin. It was kept clean by a widow woman whose husband had worked for the company as a fisherman and just disappeared at sea, presumed to have drowned. Her name was Lilli Selsdondottier, and her age would have been around the same as Olav's if anyone actually knew his age. She was forty-nine, but she had been a great beauty in her younger days, and those clean features still resembled good looks. Her figure was of a teenager and she sported a full head of blond hair with just a hint of grey creeping in here and there.

Olav took a liking to Lilli immediately and when he was sitting reading which is how he spent all his free time, he would occasionally look up and admire her elegant beauty. Lilli in return hadn't really noticed Olav, at least certainly not in any romantic way. But she admired his learning ability, something she had always wished for herself. She had no children, and because of that misfortune, she threw herself into any activity that presented itself with incredible enthusiasm.

One day right in the middle of a hard bleak January Monday morning after Olav had awakened himself and risen. He washed and dressed wondering what book he would read today, when the door opened and in scrambled a wet windswept Lilli, looking more like a half drowned rat than a beautiful middle aged woman.

"Lilli let me make you some tea, you look frozen. Get in front of hot water tank and dry yourself off, if you are not careful you will catch a chill?"

For the first time she noticed his caring way, that thought made her smile inwardly. She took the towel that was offered and started as best she could to dry herself. The tea came and Olav insisted that she sit down on the chair and they would talk. They talked for an hour, eventually Lilli saying how much she missed her dead husband, but he also had been a serious drinker and at times been known to beat her for no apparent reason just because he had been out of his head with strong alcohol.

Olav comforted her showing real sympathy, he stroked her arm and smiled at her.

"Lilli, I have a good idea. No work today for either of us, but I would like to cook you a meal. I think I can. I have a leg of lamb and some potatoes, and there is the dough for making a loaf. I'll make the meal, you make the bread. What do you say?"

Lilli smiled, she was warm dry and feeling very comfortable in this small cottage, and this man was friendly and pleasant. He wasn't good looking in any way whatsoever, but there was no question he was caring and nice, far better than her husband had ever been.

That evening as the weather worsened they both sat in the small lounge that the cottage had in front of the water boiler which constituted for central heating. The pipes came directly from the ground and ran through every room giving plenty of heat, this happened in all of Iceland's houses, free permanent hot boiling water coming directly from the thermal springs within the ground.

"Lilli, don't go home! Stay here for the night. I have two bedrooms, I promise I won't try any funny business."

He was smiling broadly and held his right hand high in the air and repeated what he had already stated.

"No funny business I promise. Look at that weather out there, you will be frozen to death before you get outside the gate."

They both laughed at that thought, it was cold and it was wet, but not that cold or wet as to be able freeze anyone to death.

"Olav, thank you. I will stay on one condition."

"Anything, what is it?"

"That I can sleep with you."

The next morning came slowly but almost too fast for the sleepy pair, it had already been decided that Lilli would move in with Olav. But the weather had got even worse, and the rain had now turned to snow. She would have to stay until it subsided and calmed down. Then he would go back with her and help collect all her belongings.

For the first time in James's life he was totally happy. Olav late of James just wanted to jump up and down with elation, this was ecstasy, life at its very best. He had acquired a new name, he had his own property, a job that brought satisfaction, plus the respect of others, a chance to love and cherish the woman of his dreams.

All this was a dream which he loved, except for that nagging doubt that was always scratching at his grey matter.

'Who am I?'

It was July nineteen eighteen, the weather in Reykjavik was warm and pleasant. It was never hot, but sunshine brought its own reward. Olav and Lilli had decided that they would take a buggy, one of the companies and go for a day trip around the bay to mount Esja and enjoy the scenic beauty together. Lilli had made a loaf and they had several types of jam made from the very small red berries that grew in the lava fields, plus some quince that grew in and around Reykjavik. So a picnic, that was the idea, a wonderful idea that could only get better as the sunny day progressed.

They were very much in love with one another, and though Olav worked hard for the company, and enjoyed the work. But he only felt complete and really content when Lilli was there beside him.

They had gone several miles towards the end of the fjord and the start of the mountain when suddenly, Olav spotted a thin line of smoke coming from across the horizon out at sea. He knew that this would be a ship, he hoped it would be a ship hoping to trade fish. Reykjavik was in bad need of coal and coke, which had long run out, they also needed petrol for the whalers which after all this time in isolation, had now run down to a dangerous low level.

But most of all Olav craved for news of the outside world. Was the war still raging? He knew it must be as U-boats were still being spotted by fishing boats. But who was winning? Maybe he could hear some news concerning the sinking of HMS Westfield? He knew that he had probably been a sailor on the vessel as that name was painted on the life raft that he had been found on.

"Lilli, I think we must turn back. I am so sorry, but look out there, it's a ship coming towards Iceland, and at least I hope so. Maybe we can trade with it?"

"Does this mean you will leave Reykjavik?"

There was alarm in her voice and tears were quickly welling in her eyes. She looked helpless and vulnerable and was on the verge of serious crying. Olav smiled sweetly took her left hand in his and kissed it gently and then answered her query,

"My darling woman, the only time I shall leave you is when they carry me off in a wooden box. I love you so much, you are my life. I love this country and I love this way of life. Nothing, and I repeat, nothing could drag me away from all of this."

They arrived back in Reykjavik before the ship actually had gained sight over the horizon which now made Olav wonder if it was actually coming to Iceland. But within the hour a small shape blowing a large black cloud of smoke could be seen heading the way of Reykjavik. Within another two hours she was large and everything could be made out about here. She was an American battleship and she was most definitely making for the countries capital port.

Late that afternoon she was lined up against the harbour wall, with her gangway down and officers and men coming and going at will.

It was called USS Michigan, a huge beast of a vessel which to the surprise of all that stood looking at her, sported two vast aerial towers for something that Iceland were oblivious too, that something was radio. It had eight huge guns, two doubles aligned at each end of the vessel, these were twelve inch weapons with devastating firepower. It also had twenty-two, three inch guns all amidships. The armour plating was formidable and would be capable of taking huge punishment before suffering any major problems.

Olav went to the gangway and asked to speak to an officer, after a few minutes a Lieutenant came to the top of the gangway.

"Yes, can I help you?"

"Firstly, I would like to know what you are doing here, what do you want with us?"

"Are you Icelandic? You sound like a Scotsman to me. We have come here on a goodwill visit. America is now in this little melee of Europe's, so we need a base, and it was suggested that Iceland might be a good place so that we can keep an eye on the comings and goings of the Hun."

He squinted at Olav, and then added,

"Are you a Scotsman? You certainly sound like one."

Olav refused to be drawn into who he was or wasn't. His name was Olav Peterson and that's all they would need to know.

"So who's winning the war?"

"Well that's a good question. I would say that it was a close call, but now we have at least six million men to put into the arena you can guess for yourself. It shouldn't last more than four or five more years."

And then the American remembered his manners.

"Hey, buddy, why don't you come on board and I will give you a drink or two."

"That's kind, but I ought to get back to my office, you will need to talk to the President of Iceland, and or at least your senior officer should. His name is Sveinn Björnsson, and as he isn't actually here, I can only guess that he is probably at the parliament building which you can see from here. I would further guess that the fact that he is not already here, would probably indicate that he is dead drunk, which he is prone to be."

"One last thing, when did the US down tools and join the army to fight the Hun?"

"That's easy, it was on my birthday the sixth of April nineteen seventeen. Come back for that drink, bye!"

Olav walked back to the main office he wanted to find Jon. It was time to do some hard bargaining with those damn Yankees.

"Jon, they want a base and we want fuel! Surely we can do some sort of trade off. I suspect that they are going to get their base one way or another. We can hardly fight them off with our shotguns. But I think with some persuasion we might all get what we want. You see that they have radio, that we should have here too. So there is your first part of negotiation, get us a radio station. We desperately need coal and coke. I doubt very much that a battleship will part with any fuel, but they can get it for us. We need petrol and other fuels, we need food stuffs. In fact we should present them with a list a mile long. Once agreed give them somewhere like Keflavik, a deep water area that is open to the sea, easy for them to get out and sink German ships and submarines."

As Olav spoke, Jon was writing furiously at a list, he then started to add extras himself.

"Olav, come with me, we must go to see Sveinn Björnsson. We will demand that he squares everything off in our favour. After all America is rich, we are poor, and they can afford to lose a few luxuries."

The next morning there was a general meeting between a negotiator from the US diplomatic corp. and the Captain of USS Michigan, not to forget the so called President Sveinn Björnsson, Jon Johnson, Olav Peterson and four men from the parliament, two of which were also board members of PFC. Now the bargaining started in earnest.

Three hours and five bottles of bourbon later, a deal was concluded. The United States got Keflavik as its deep water base in perpetuity, and Iceland got a ship full of coke and coal, enough food stuff to last at least two years, and a crew of builders to assemble a new fangled radio station.

After the Americans had returned to their ship, Sveinn Björnsson turned to Olav and said loud enough for all the Icelanders assembled could hear.

"Olav Peterson, or whatever your name is. We thank you, this was your triumph and it has really saved the day. There were plenty of folk out there close to starving, now we can help the outlying towns and villages with grain and certain food stuffs. This is entirely down to your good offices, well done. When you decide to make an honest woman out of Lilli Selsdondottier, call me and I will marry you both."

There was a huge smile appearing on all the faces, then laughter coming from those fellows still attending. His shoulder became sore from all the patting it took. Olav went bright red in the face, he answered the only way he could.

"You have all made me welcome here in this country of Vikings, and believe me you are all heroic Vikings, and though I still don't know who I am, I really don't care. You gave me the honour of calling me after someone you all revered, so forever and a day I shall be known as Olav Peterson."

He paused for a second thought, a broad smile came across his face.

"Mr. President, me marry Lilli. Wow, that sounds like a fine idea."

Olav now felt ten feet tall as he walked slowly to his home.

"Lilli, can you spare a moment darling?"

The date for the wedding was set for July the twenty-first, the drizzle that was in the air didn't for a moment mar the proceedings. The President was on fine form and conducted the ceremony in a wonderfully formal but relaxed way.

It seemed as if the population of Reykjavik had turned out to cheer the happy couple, and flowers were thrown onto the carriage as they slowly moved back to Lake Tchurnin where the couple would now spend their days as man and wife.

Finally the eleventh of November came, and as the radio was heard to hear the scratchy sound of President Woodrow Wilson tell his country that the Great War was now concluded. Guns had been lowered and all firing had ceased. Things would quickly get back to some sort of normality, but not really until the hundreds of thousand of mines that lay around the various parts of the sea had been cleared.

Spring came in nineteen-nineteen in a wet cold way. Things had got steadily better, the fish could be caught once more, whaling was harder, but there were still enough of the animals to make it worthwhile for the whaling fleet to operate.

Life in Reykjavik soon forgot the war, after all, other than being kept from trading they had suffered little by the battling events. The Great War was more of a nuisance than a shattering happening event for the Icelandic populace. It's true to say that some people did go hungry, but not one person died of starvation throughout the entire conflict, that couldn't be said about many other countries.

On May the tenth, it was to become a very special day, bunting and flags were flying high once more, this was a special day, one to savour. the Danish ferry was going to arrive, the first since the hostilities began. Jon had received a garbled radio message stating that he should be ready to receive…? The signal died at that point, so there he was down on the seafront waiting for the new Danish ferry to tie up at the quayside. And then he saw someone waving towards him from on board, it was Elsa.

When she finally alighted, he threw his arms around her and kissed both her cheeks, after all she was a sort of family member.

"My goodness, have I some stories to tell you. I guess you have missed your monthly money? Since the war started all our banks stopped any overseas transactions, there was no way the money could be got to you. But it is all here awaiting your pleasure, though at this moment it is in Icelandic Kroner, and I must warn you that the banks have absolutely no foreign currencies to exchange it for. Now come back to the office, you will see a lot of changes."

Elsa hadn't actually managed to say one single word.

The next day, after Elsa had washed and dressed in the hotel, she went down to breakfast to meet Jon with their latest recruit.

"Aaa! You must be the one they called after my husband, and Olav Peterson I presume?"

"Yes madam, I am extraordinarily pleased to meet you. And may I introduce you to my wife Lilli, now Lilli Peterson."

"Jon has told me so much about you, how fantastic you are in mechanics and electronics, and how all your ideas that have been incorporated into the business have been tremendously successful. Well sir, what are we to do with you?"

She smiled warmly scratched her chin and then added,

"I think that we either send you back to Britain or we make you a director. Err, what do you think?"

Olav laughed, he had remembered one vital thing and felt he should impart that information, after all it might concern Elsa, and he certainly didn't want to start his new life with certain possibly unpleasant truth hanging over him.

"You know madam, I believe I came from Glasgow, and though most things are a foggy puzzle to me I sort of remember a Polish chef who escaped to Glasgow having got a young woman into trouble. From what Jon has told me, and by the look of shocked horror that is now written on your face, I think that person is you. Am I right?"

"God man, is it possible? His name was Ivan kolinsky, you know him? I bore his son who is now growing up to be a fine man. How could this coincidence be happening?"

Elsa looked extremely distressed at hearing that name again, even if it was her that said it.

"One thing I have learned madam, or may I call you Elsa? One thing I have learned is that all things tend to go in a circle, what goes around, comes around. I believe in destiny, and it was my destiny to find Iceland and be involved with your company. I believe I was in the past and am still an honest man, someone that craves learning just about above everything else. Oh, that is except for my wife Lilli."

He took her hand and squeezed it gently.

"I must tell the truth, I feel that strongly. So when I heard all your story, things started gently coming back to me."

Olav stumbled a little and reddened as he knew he must impart memories that are just returning to him,

"I just had to tell you, I would have felt it was wrong not too. I don't know if you loved him, or if you still do. But I have to tell you that he actually killed a woman by pushing her out of a window he then threw himself out, these things I do remember."

He looked at Jon and then looked back at Elsa, both had their mouths drooping, both were in a state of shock.

"Maybe I have brought you nothing but grief, in which case I will leave your employ and leave the country."

He looked at Lilli, who now looked horrified.

'Shit, maybe I have gone too far, maybe I should have kept my big mouth shut?'

"My God! I had almost forgotten the man. This is by far the weirdest experience of my entire life. You here! Knowing Ivan! What are the chances?"

She sat down hard on the nearest chair. Elsa was silent for one whole minute, just stared at the threadbare carpet. And then she looked towards Jon, who on seeing her shocked countenance shrugged his shoulders towards her. And then after another minute against all the odds, she burst out laughing.

"Well, well! You have been honest with me, knocked me for six but been honest. The man was a complete oaf, and I sort of despised him and myself, I became unpleasantly infatuated with him. I was entangled with him in a very strange way. I am sorry he is dead but in another way that lets me completely off the hook."

She laughed again.

"Well make up your mind Mr. Peterson, director or nothing?"

"I love this country, and I love the people. If I can spend my days here productively, so then I accept thankfully and graciously."

He bowed deeply, and then offered his hand to seal the deal.

"Anyway, I like being Olav Peterson, I never did like that awful waster James Jolly. He was going absolutely no where."

Olav Peterson turned to his wife, kissed her sweetly and smiled, and then turned to Jon and winked.

Epitaph

HMS Westfield sank on the 1st of June 1916. She had been hit by two twelve inch shells. The first completely took out her bridge killing many officers and men, including Captain Steiner. The second shell entered directly into the engine room and then exploded. The shock wave that erupted from the engine room blast, plus the unfortunate salvo of all eight big guns which nearly tipped Westfield over onto her portside, the combination of all those factors coinciding at more or less the same moment causing a catastrophic reaction that then started a chain reaction, the end was obviously doom, nothing could save the ship from destruction.

When that first shell exploded, it made the boilers explode and then the armoury. Those explosions broke the back of the vessel, which is why she sank in under one minute.

Three survivors were picked out of the sea by a passing destroyer. One was a gunner and two were marines, everyone else was either blown to pieces or drowned.

In later life Olav became a tutor in English, mathematics, history and geography to children that needed a helping hand. He refused any form of payment for his service. And when sitting in the local café he would talk on philosophy and psychiatry to anyone brave enough to listen to him.

In the early nineteen twenties, he made contact with his two brothers; he paid for them and their families to come to Iceland for a holiday. It was a wonderful time for all the Jolly contingents. After they left, they never ever saw James again, though they did keep in touch via letters.

The people of Reykjavik always revered the new Olav Peterson, as they did the original.

Elsa was a very frequent visitor to the land of snow and ice, but never stayed very long. Though she was to marry another Icelander, this time a man who was working for the radio station, not in Reykjavik, but in Hilversum. There were of course no more children, but there was a sort of happiness for them both and they lived out their lives in contentment.

James Jolly alias Olav Peterson lived a full and contented life. He died just one month before a small minded Austrian who had risen to power in Germany, got the Axis to invade Poland. His wife Lilli outlived him by only four days, she had decided a long time before that when her Olav passed away, she wanted to be in the afterlife with him, so deep was their love for one another.

FICTION FROM APS BOOKS
(www.andrewsparke.com)

Davey J Ashfield: Footsteps On The Teign
Davey J Ashfield Contracting With The Devil
Davey J Ashfield: A Turkey And One More Easter Egg
Des Tong: Whatever It Takes Babe
Des Tong: In Flames
Fenella Bass: Hornbeams
Fenella Bass:: Shadows
Fenella Bass: Darkness
HR Beasley: Nothing Left To Hide
Lee Benson: So You Want To Own An Art Gallery
Lee Benson: Where's Your Art gallery Now?
Lee Benson: Now You're The Artist…Deal With It
Lee Benson: No Naked Walls
TF Byrne Damage Limitation
Nargis Darby: A Different Shade Of Love
J.W.Darcy Looking For Luca
J.W.Darcy: Ladybird Ladybird
J.W.Darcy: Legacy Of Lies
J.W.Darcy: Love Lust & Needful Things
Paul Dickinson: Franzi The Hero
Jane Evans: The Third Bridge
Simon Falshaw: The Stone
Peter Georgiadis: The Mute Swan's Song
Peter Georgiadis: Not Cast In Stone
Peter Georgiadis:The Murderous Journey
Peter Georgiadis: Stoker Jolly
Milton Godfrey: The Danger Lies In Fear
Felix Gomez: The Tunnel Killer
Chris Grayling: A Week Is…A Long Time
Jean Harvey: Pandemic
Michel Henri: Mister Penny Whistle
Michel Henri: The Death Of The Duchess Of Grasmere
Michel Henri: Abducted By Faerie
Laurie Hornsby: Postcards From The Seaside
Hugh Lupus An Extra Knot (Parts I-VI)
Alison Manning: World Without Endless Sheep
Colin Mardell: Keep Her Safe
Colin Mardell: Bring Them Home
Ian Meacheam: An Inspector Called
Ian Meacheam: Time And The Consequences

Printed in Great Britain
by Amazon

24687539R00159